dizzying array of voices and places that allows the reader to luxuriate in Hosseini's rich, textured language' *Literary Review*

'Heartbreaking' *Grazia*

'A multi-generational saga of familial love, honour, sacrifice and betrayal, that not only meets all expectations but surpasses them . . . A breathtaking achievement . . . Mr Hosseini's best and most ambitious work yet' *Irish Examiner*

'Hosseini skilfully unpicks the ties that bind' *Vogue*

'Hosseini is a master storyteller' *Spectator*

'A moving saga about sacrifice, betrayal, and the power of family' ★ ★ ★ ★ *People*

'While it hits all the Hosseini sweet spots – nostalgia, devastating details, triumph over the odds – *And the Mountains Echoed* covers more ground, both geographically and emotionally, than his previous works. It's not until Hosseini makes the novel small again, for the poignant conclusion, that you fully appreciate what he's accomplished' *Entertainment Weekly*

'An exquisite novel, a must-read for anyone with an interest in what it means to be alive, anywhere and everywhere' *USA Today*

'Had tears dripping from my eyes by page 45 . . . It's hard to do justice to a novel this rich' *Washington Post*

'Instantly relatable. Reading this novel feels like watching a time-lapse video of a flower blossoming' *Marie Claire*

'Beautifully written, masterfully crafted . . . *And the Mountains Echoed* is painfully sad but also radiant with love' *Los Angeles Times*

'Mesmeric . . . Breaks hearts yet again with this sacrificial tale . . . It's an emotional roller-coaster of a journey' *The Australian*

A NOTE ON THE AUTHOR

KHALED HOSSEINI is one of the most widely read and beloved novelists in the world, with over 38 million copies of his books sold in more than seventy countries. *The Kite Runner* was a major film and a Book of the Decade, chosen by *The Times*, the *Daily Telegraph* and the *Guardian*. *A Thousand Splendid Suns* was the Richard & Judy Best Read of the Year in 2008. Hosseini is also a Goodwill Envoy to the United Nations High Commissioner for Refugees, the UN Refugee Agency and the founder of The Khaled Hosseini Foundation, a not-for-profit organisation which provides humanitarian assistance to the people of Afghanistan. He was born in Kabul, Afghanistan, and lives in northern California.

Also by Khaled Hosseini

The Kite Runner

A Thousand Splendid Suns

And the
Mountains
Echoed

KHALED

HOSSEINI

BLOOMSBURY
LONDON · NEW DELHI · NEW YORK · SYDNEY

First published in Great Britain 2013
First published in India 2013
This paperback edition published 2014

Epigraph copyright Coleman Barks

This edition published with permission from
Bloomsbury Publishing Plc, 50 Bedford Square, London, WC1B 3DP

Bloomsbury Publishing is a trademark of Bloomsbury Plc

Bloomsbury Publishing, London, New Delhi, New York and Sydney

A CIP catalogue record for this book is available from the British Library

For sale in the Indian subcontinent only

ISBN 978 9 3848 9808 3

10 9 8 7 6 5 4 3 2 1

Bloomsbury Publishing India
Vishrut Building, DDA Complex, Building No. 3
Ground Floor, Pocket C – 6 & 7, Vasant Kunj
New Delhi 110070
www.bloomsbury.com

Book design by Amanda Dewey and Claire Vaccaro
Printed and bound in India by Thomson Press India Ltd.

This book is dedicated to Haris and Farah,
both the noor of my eyes, and to my father,
who would have been proud

For Elaine

Out beyond ideas
of wrongdoing and rightdoing,
there is a field.
I'll meet you there.

—JELALUDDIN RUMI, 13th century

One

Fall 1952

S o, then. You want a story and I will tell you one. But just the one. Don't either of you ask me for more. It's late, and we have a long day of travel ahead of us, Pari, you and I. You will need your sleep tonight. And you too, Abdullah. I am counting on you, boy, while your sister and I are away. So is your mother. Now. One story, then. Listen, both of you, listen well. And don't interrupt.

Once upon a time, in the days when *div*s and *jinn*s and giants roamed the land, there lived a farmer named Baba Ayub. He lived with his family in a little village by the name of Maidan Sabz. Because he had a large family to feed, Baba Ayub saw his days consumed by hard work. Every day, he labored from dawn to sundown, plowing his field and turning the soil and tending to his meager pistachio trees. At any given moment you could spot him in his field, bent at the waist, back as curved as the scythe he swung all day. His hands were always callused, and they often bled, and every night sleep stole him away no sooner than his cheek met the pillow.

I will say that, in this regard, he was hardly alone. Life in Maidan Sabz was hard for all its inhabitants. There were other, more fortunate villages to the north, in the valleys, with fruit trees and flowers and pleasant air, and streams that ran with cold, clear water. But Maidan Sabz was a desolate place, and it didn't resemble in the slightest the image that its name, Field of Green, would have you picture. It sat in a flat, dusty plain ringed by a chain of craggy mountains. The wind was hot, and blew dust in the eyes. Finding water was a daily struggle because the village wells, even the deep ones, often ran low. Yes, there was a river, but the villagers had to endure a half-day walk to reach it, and even then its waters flowed muddy all year round. Now, after ten years of drought, the river too ran shallow. Let's just say that people in Maidan Sabz worked twice as hard to eke out half the living.

Still, Baba Ayub counted himself among the fortunate because he had a family that he cherished above all things. He loved his wife and never raised his voice to her, much less his hand. He valued her counsel and found genuine pleasure in her companionship. As for children, he was blessed with as many as a hand has fingers, three sons and two daughters, each of whom he loved dearly. His daughters were dutiful and kind and of good character and repute. To his sons he had taught already the value of honesty, courage, friendship, and hard work without complaint. They obeyed him, as good sons must, and helped their father with his crops.

Though he loved all of his children, Baba Ayub privately had a unique fondness for one among them, his youngest, Qais, who was three years old. Qais was a little boy with dark blue eyes. He charmed anyone who met him with his devilish laughter. He was also one of those boys so bursting with energy that he drained others of theirs. When he learned to walk, he took such delight in it that he did it all day while he was awake, and then, troublingly, even at night in his sleep. He would sleepwalk out of the family's mud house and wander off into the moonlit darkness. Naturally, his parents worried. What if he fell into a well, or got lost, or, worst of all, was attacked by one of the creatures lurking the plains at night? They took stabs at many remedies, none of which worked. In the end, the solution Baba Ayub found was a simple one, as the best solutions often are: He removed a tiny bell from around the neck of one of his goats and hung it instead around Qais's neck. This way, the bell would wake someone if Qais were to rise in the middle of the night. The sleepwalking stopped after a time, but Qais grew attached to the bell and refused to part with it. And so, even though it didn't serve its original use, the bell remained fastened to the string around the boy's neck. When Baba Ayub came home after a long day's work, Qais would run from the house face-first into his father's belly, the bell jingling with each of his tiny steps. Baba Ayub would lift him up and take him into the house, and Qais would watch with great attention as his father washed up, and then he would sit beside Baba Ayub at suppertime. After they had eaten, Baba Ayub would sip his tea, watching his family, picturing a day when all of his children married and gave him children of their own, when he would be proud patriarch to an even greater brood.

Alas, Abdullah and Pari, Baba Ayub's days of happiness came to an end.

It happened one day that a *div* came to Maidan Sabz. As it approached the village from the direction of the mountains, the earth shook with each of its footfalls. The villagers dropped their shovels and hoes and axes and scattered. They locked themselves in their homes and huddled with one another. When the deafening sounds of the *div*'s footsteps stopped, the skies over Maidan Sabz darkened with its shadow. It was said that curved horns sprouted from its head and that coarse black hair covered its shoulders and powerful tail. They said its eyes shone red. No one knew for sure, you understand, at least no one living: The *div* ate on the spot those who dared steal so much as a single glance. Knowing this, the villagers wisely kept their eyes glued to the ground.

Everyone at the village knew why the *div* had come. They had heard the tales of its visits to other villages and they could only marvel at how Maidan Sabz had managed to escape its attention for so long. Perhaps, they reasoned, the poor, stringent lives they led in Maidan Sabz had worked in their favor, as their children weren't as well fed and didn't have as much meat on their bones. Even so, their luck had run out at last.

Maidan Sabz trembled and held its breath. Families prayed that the *div* would bypass their home for they knew that if the *div* tapped on their roof, they would have to give it one child. The *div* would then toss the child into a sack, sling the sack over its shoulder, and go back the way it had come. No one would ever see the poor child again. And if a household refused, the *div* would take all of its children.

So where did the *div* take the children to? To its fort, which sat atop a steep mountain. The *div*'s fort was very far from Maidan Sabz. Valleys, several deserts, and two mountain chains had to be cleared before you could reach it. And what sane person would, only to meet death? They said the fort was full of dungeons where cleavers hung from walls. Meat hooks dangled from ceilings. They said there were giant skewers and fire pits. They said that if it caught a trespasser, the *div* was known to overcome its aversion to adult meat.

I guess you know which rooftop received the *div*'s dreaded tap. Upon hearing it, Baba Ayub let an agonized cry escape from his lips, and his wife fainted cold. The children wept with terror, and also sorrow, because they knew that the loss of one among them was now assured. The family had until the next dawn to make its offering.

What can I say to you of the anguish that Baba Ayub and his wife suffered that night? No parent should have to make a choice such as this. Out of the children's earshot, Baba Ayub and his wife debated what they should do. They talked and wept and talked and wept. All night, they went back and forth, and, as dawn neared, they had yet to reach a decision—which was perhaps what the *div* wanted, as their indecision would allow it to take five children instead of one.

In the end, Baba Ayub collected from just outside the house five rocks of identical size and shape. On the face of each he scribbled the name of one child, and when he was done he tossed the rocks into a burlap sack. When he offered the bag to his wife, she recoiled as though it held a venomous snake.

"I can't do it," she said to her husband, shaking her head. "I cannot be the one to choose. I couldn't bear it."

"Neither could I," Baba Ayub began to say, but he saw through the window that the sun was only moments away from peeking over the eastern hills. Time was running short. He gazed miserably at his five children. A finger had to be cut, to save the hand. He shut his eyes and withdrew a rock from the sack.

I suppose you also know which rock Baba Ayub happened to pick. When he saw the name on it, he turned his face heavenward and let out a scream. With a broken heart, he lifted his youngest son into his arms, and Qais, who had blind trust in his father, happily wrapped his arms around Baba Ayub's neck. It wasn't until Baba Ayub deposited him outside the house and shut the door that the boy realized what was amiss, and there stood Baba Ayub, eyes squeezed shut, tears leaking from both, back against the door, as his beloved Qais pounded his small fists on it, crying for Baba to let him back in, and Baba Ayub stood there, muttering, "Forgive me, forgive me," as the ground shook with the *div*'s footsteps, and his son screeched, and the earth trembled again and again as the *div* took its leave from Maidan Sabz, until at last it was gone, and the earth was still, and all was silence but for Baba Ayub, still weeping and asking Qais for forgiveness.

Abdullah. Your sister has fallen asleep. Cover her feet with the blanket. There. Good. Maybe I should stop now. No? You want me to go on? Are you sure, boy? All right.

Where was I? Ah yes. There followed a forty-day mourning period. Every day, neighbors cooked meals for the family and kept vigil with them. People brought over what offerings they could—tea, candy, bread, almonds—and they brought as well their condolences and sympathies. Baba Ayub could hardly bring himself to say so much as a word of thanks. He sat in a corner, weeping, streams of tears pouring from both eyes as though he meant to end the village's streak of droughts with them. You wouldn't wish his torment and suffering on the vilest of men.

Several years passed. The droughts continued, and Maidan Sabz fell into even worse poverty. Several babies died of thirst in their cribs. The wells ran even lower and the river dried, unlike Baba Ayub's anguish, a river that swelled and swelled with each passing day. He was of no use to his family any longer. He didn't work, didn't pray, hardly ate. His wife and children pleaded with him, but it was no good. His remaining sons had to take over his work, for every day Baba Ayub did nothing but sit at the edge of his field, a lone, wretched figure gazing toward the mountains. He stopped speaking to the villagers, for he believed they muttered things behind his back. They said he was a coward for willingly giving away his son. That he was an unfit father. A real father would have fought the *div*. He would have died defending his family.

He mentioned this to his wife one night.

"They say no such things," his wife replied. "No one thinks you are a coward."

"I can hear them," he said.

"It is your own voice you are hearing, husband," she said. She, however, did not tell him that the villagers *did* whisper behind his back. And what they whispered was that he'd perhaps gone mad.

And then one day, he gave them proof. He rose at dawn. Without waking his wife and children, he stowed a few scraps of bread into a burlap sack, put on his shoes, tied his scythe around his waist, and set off.

He walked for many, many days. He walked until the sun was a faint red glow in the distance. Nights, he slept in caves as the wind whistled outside. Or else he slept beside rivers and beneath trees and among the cover of boulders. He ate his bread, and then he ate what he could find—wild berries, mushrooms, fish that he caught with his bare hands from streams—and some days he didn't eat at all. But still he walked. When passersby asked where he was going, he told them, and some laughed, some hurried past for fear he was a madman, and some prayed for him, as they too had lost a child to the *div*. Baba Ayub kept his head down and walked. When his shoes fell apart, he fastened them to his feet with strings, and when the strings tore he pushed forward on bare feet. In this way, he traveled across deserts and valleys and mountains.

At last he reached the mountain atop which sat the *div*'s fort. So eager he was to fulfill his quest that he didn't rest and immediately began his climb, his clothes shredded, his feet bloodied, his hair caked with dust, but his resolve unshaken. The jagged rocks ripped his soles. Hawks pecked at his cheeks when he climbed past their nest. Violent gusts of wind nearly tore him from the side of the mountain. And still he climbed, from one rock to the next, until at last he stood before the massive gates of the *div*'s fort.

Who dares? the *div*'s voice boomed when Baba Ayub threw a stone at the gates.

Baba Ayub stated his name. "I come from the village of Maidan Sabz," he said.

Do you have a wish to die? Surely you must, disturbing me in my home! What is your business?

"I have come here to kill you."

There came a pause from the other side of the gates. And then the gates creaked open, and there stood the *div*, looming over Baba Ayub in all of its nightmarish glory.

Have you? it said in a voice thick as thunder.

"Indeed," Baba Ayub said. "One way or another, one of us dies today."

It appeared for a moment that the *div* would swipe Baba Ayub off the ground and finish him with a single bite of its dagger-sharp teeth. But something made the creature hesitate. It narrowed its eyes. Perhaps it was the craziness of the old man's words. Perhaps it was the man's appearance, the shredded garb, the bloodied face, the dust that coated him head to toe, the open sores on his skin. Or perhaps it was that, in the old man's eyes, the *div* found not even a tinge of fear.

Where did you say you came from?

"Maidan Sabz," said Baba Ayub.

It must be far away, by the look of you, this Maidan Sabz.

"I did not come here to palaver. I came here to—"

The *div* raised one clawed hand. Yes. Yes. You've come to kill me. I know. But surely I can be granted a few last words before I am slain.

"Very well," said Baba Ayub. "But only a few."

I thank you. The *div* grinned. May I ask what evil I have committed against you so as to warrant death?

"You took from me my youngest son," Baba Ayub replied. "He was in the world the dearest thing to me."

The *div* grunted and tapped its chin. I have taken many children from many fathers, it said.

Baba Ayub angrily drew his scythe. "Then I shall exact revenge on their behalf as well."

I must say your courage rouses in me a surge of admiration.

"You know nothing of courage," said Baba Ayub. "For courage, there must be something at stake. I come here with nothing to lose."

You have your life to lose, said the *div*.

"You already took that from me."

The *div* grunted again and studied Baba Ayub thoughtfully. After a time, it said, Very well, then. I will grant you your duel. But first I ask that you follow me.

"Be quick," Baba Ayub said, "I am out of patience." But the *div* was already walking toward a giant hallway, and Baba Ayub had no choice but to follow it. He trailed the *div* through a labyrinth of hallways, the ceiling of each nearly scraped the clouds, each supported by enormous columns. They passed many stairwells, and chambers big enough to contain all of Maidan Sabz. They walked this way until at last the *div* led Baba Ayub into an enormous room, at the far end of which was a curtain.

Come closer, the *div* motioned.

Baba Ayub stood next to the *div*.

The *div* pulled the curtains open. Behind it was a glass window. Through the window, Baba Ayub looked down on an enormous garden. Lines of cypress trees bordered the garden, the ground at their base filled with flowers of all colors. There were pools made of blue tiles, and marble terraces, and lush green lawns. Baba Ayub saw beautifully sculpted hedges and water fountains gurgling in the shade of pomegranate trees. In three lifetimes he could not have imagined a place so beautiful.

But what truly brought Baba Ayub to his knees was the sight of children running and playing happily in the garden. They chased one another through the walkways and around trees. They played games of hide-and-seek behind the hedges. Baba Ayub's eyes searched among the children and at last found what he was looking for. There he was! His son Qais, alive, and more than well. He had grown in height, and his hair was longer than Baba Ayub remembered. He wore a beautiful white shirt over handsome trousers. He laughed happily as he ran after a pair of comrades.

"Qais," Baba Ayub whispered, his breath fogging the glass. And then he screamed his son's name.

He cannot hear you, the *div* said. Nor see you.

Baba Ayub jumped up and down, waving his arms and pounding on the glass, until the *div* pulled the curtains shut once more.

"I don't understand," Baba Ayub said. "I thought . . ."

This is your reward, the *div* said.

"Explain yourself," Baba Ayub exclaimed.

I forced upon you a test.

"A test."

A test of your love. It was a harsh challenge, I recognize, and its heavy toll upon you does not escape me. But you passed. This is your reward. And his.

"What if I hadn't chosen," cried Baba Ayub. "What if I had refused you your test?"

Then all your children would have perished, the *div* said, for they would have been cursed anyway, fathered as they were by a weak man. A coward who would see them all die rather than burden his own conscience. You say you have no courage, but I see it in you. What you did, the burden you agreed to shoulder, took courage. For that, I honor you.

Baba Ayub weakly drew his scythe, but it slipped from his hand and struck the marble floor with a loud clang. His knees buckled, and he had to sit.

Your son does not remember you, the *div* continued. This is his life now, and you saw for yourself his happiness. He is provided here with the finest food and clothes, with friendship and affection. He receives tutoring in the arts and languages and in the sciences, and in the ways of wisdom and charity. He wants for nothing. Someday, when he is a man, he may choose to leave, and he shall be free to do so. I suspect he will touch many lives with his kindness and bring happiness to those trapped in sorrow.

"I want to see him," Baba Ayub said. "I want to take him home."

Do you?

Baba Ayub looked up at the *div*.

The creature moved to a cabinet that sat near the curtains and removed from one of its drawers an hourglass. Do you know what that is, Abdullah, an hourglass? You do. Good. Well, the *div* took the hourglass, flipped it over, and placed it at Baba Ayub's feet.

I will allow you to take him home with you, the *div* said. If you choose to, he can never return here. If you choose not to, *you* can never return here. When all the sand has poured, I will ask for your decision.

And with that, the *div* exited the chamber, leaving Baba Ayub with yet another painful choice to make.

I will take him home, Baba Ayub thought immediately. This was what he desired the most, with every fiber of his being. Hadn't he pictured this in a thousand dreams? To hold little Qais again, to kiss his cheek and feel the softness of his small hands in his own? And yet . . . If he took him home, what sort of life awaited Qais in Maidan Sabz? The hard life of a peasant at best, like his own, and little more. That is, if Qais didn't die from the droughts like so many of the village's children had. Could you forgive yourself, then, Baba Ayub asked himself, knowing that you plucked him, for your own selfish reasons, from a life of luxury and opportunity? On the other hand, if he left Qais behind, how could he bear it, knowing that his boy was alive, to know his where-abouts and yet be forbidden to see him? How could he bear it? Baba Ayub wept. He grew so despondent that he lifted the hourglass and hurled it at the wall, where it crashed into a thousand pieces and its fine sand spilled all over the floor.

The *div* reentered the room and found Baba Ayub stand-ing over the broken glass, his shoulders slumped.

"You are a cruel beast," Baba Ayub said.

When you have lived as long as I have, the *div* replied, you find that cruelty and benevolence are but shades of the same color. Have you made your choice?

Baba Ayub dried his tears, picked up his scythe, and tied it around his waist. He slowly walked toward the door, his head hung low.

You are a good father, the *div* said, as Baba Ayub passed him by.

"Would that you roast in the fires of Hell for what you have done to me," Baba Ayub said wearily.

He exited the room and was heading down the hallway when the *div* called after him.

Take this, the *div* said. The creature handed Baba Ayub a small glass flask containing a dark liquid. Drink this upon your journey home. Farewell.

Baba Ayub took the flask and left without saying another word.

Many days later, his wife was sitting at the edge of the family's field, looking out for him much as Baba Ayub had sat there hoping to see Qais. With each passing day, her hopes for his return diminished. Already people in the village were speaking of Baba Ayub in the past tense. One day she was sitting on the dirt yet again, a prayer playing upon her lips, when she saw a thin figure approaching Maidan Sabz from the direction of the mountains. At first she took him for a lost dervish, a thin man with threadbare rags for clothing, hollow eyes and sunken temples, and it wasn't until he came closer yet that she recognized her husband. Her heart leapt with joy and she cried out with relief.

After he had washed, and after he had been given water to drink and food to eat, Baba Ayub lay in his house as villagers circled around him and asked him question after question.

Where did you go, Baba Ayub?

What did you see?

What happened to you?

Baba Ayub couldn't answer them, because he didn't recall what had happened to him. He remembered nothing of his voyage, of climbing the *div*'s mountain, of speaking to the *div*, of the great palace, or the big room with the curtains. It was as though he had woken from an already forgotten dream. He didn't remember the secret garden, the children, and, most of all, he didn't remember seeing his son Qais playing among the trees with his friends. In fact, when someone mentioned Qais's name, Baba Ayub blinked with puzzlement. Who? he said. He didn't recall that he had ever had a son named Qais.

Do you understand, Abdullah, how this was an act of mercy? The potion that erased these memories? It was Baba Ayub's reward for passing the *div*'s second test.

That spring, the skies at last broke open over Maidan Sabz. What came down was not the soft drizzle of years past but a great, great rainfall. Fat rain fell from the sky, and the village rose thirstily to meet it. All day, water drummed upon the roofs of Maidan Sabz and drowned all other sound from the world. Heavy, swollen raindrops rolled from the tips of leaves. The wells filled and the river rose. The hills to the east turned green. Wildflowers bloomed, and for the first time in many years children played on grass and cows grazed. Everyone rejoiced.

When the rains stopped, the village had some work to do. Several mud walls had melted, and a few of the roofs sagged, and entire sections of farmland had turned into swamps. But after the misery of the devastating drought, the people of Maidan Sabz weren't about to complain. Walls were reerected, roofs repaired, and irrigation canals drained. That fall, Baba Ayub produced the most plentiful crop of pistachios of his life, and, indeed, the year after that, and the one following, his crops increased in both size and quality. In the great cities where he sold his goods, Baba Ayub sat proudly behind pyramids of his pistachios and beamed like the happiest man who walked the earth. No drought ever came to Maidan Sabz again.

There is little more to say, Abdullah. You may ask, though, did a young handsome man riding a horse ever pass through the village on his way to great adventures? Did he perhaps stop for a drink of water, of which the village had plenty now, and did he sit to break bread with the villagers, perhaps with Baba Ayub himself? I can't tell you, boy. What I *can* say is that Baba Ayub grew to be a very old man indeed. I can tell you that he saw his children married, as he had always wished, and I can say that his children bore him many children of their own, every one of whom brought Baba Ayub great happiness.

And I can also tell you that some nights, for no particular reason, Baba Ayub couldn't sleep. Though he was a very old man now, he still had the use of his legs so long as he held a cane. And so on those sleepless nights he slipped from bed without waking his wife, fetched his cane, and left the house. He walked in the dark, his cane tapping before him, the night breeze stroking his face. There was a flat rock at the edge of his field and he lowered himself upon it. He often sat there for an hour or more, gazing up at the stars, the clouds floating past the moon. He thought about his long life and gave thanks for all the bounty and joy that he had been given. To want more, to wish for yet more, he knew, would be petty. He sighed happily, and listened to the wind sweeping down from the mountains, to the chirping of night birds.

But every once in a while, he thought he heard another noise among these. It was always the same, the high-pitched jingle of a bell. He didn't understand why he should hear such a noise, alone in the dark, all the sheep and goats sleeping. Sometimes he told himself he had heard no such thing, and sometimes he was so convinced to the contrary that he called out into the darkness, "Is someone out there? Who is there? Show yourself." But no reply ever came. Baba Ayub didn't understand. Just as he didn't understand why a wave of something, something like the tail end of a sad dream, always swept through him whenever he heard the jingling, surprising him each time like an unexpected gust of wind. But then it passed, as all things do. It passed.

So there it is, boy. That's the end of it. I have nothing more to say. And now it really is late and I am tired, and your sister and I have to wake at dawn. So blow out your candle. Lay your head down and close your eyes. Sleep well, boy. We'll say our good-byes in the morning.

Two

Fall 1952

Father had never before hit Abdullah. So when he did, when he whacked the side of his head, just above the ear—hard, suddenly, and with an open palm—tears of surprise sprung to Abdullah's eyes. He quickly blinked them back.

"Go home," Father said through gritted teeth.

From up ahead, Abdullah heard Pari burst into sobs.

Then Father hit him again, harder, and this time across the left cheek. Abdullah's head snapped sideways. His face burned, and more tears leaked. His left ear rang. Father stooped down, leaning in so close his dark creased face eclipsed the desert and the mountains and the sky altogether.

"I told you to go home, boy," he said with a pained look.

Abdullah didn't make a sound. He swallowed hard and squinted at his father, blinking into the face shading his eyes from the sun.

From the small red wagon up ahead, Pari cried out his name, her voice high, shaking with apprehension. "Abollah!"

Father held him with a cutting look, and trudged back to the wagon. From its bed, Pari reached for Abdullah with outstretched hands. Abdullah allowed them a head start. Then he wiped his eyes with the heels of his hands, and followed.

A little while later, Father threw a rock at him, the way children in Shadbagh would do to Pari's dog, Shuja—except they meant to hit Shuja, to hurt him. Father's rock fell harmlessly a few feet from Abdullah. He waited, and when Father and Pari got moving again Abdullah tailed them once more.

Finally, with the sun just past its peak, Father pulled up again. He turned back in Abdullah's direction, seemed to consider, and motioned with his hand.

"You won't give up," he said.

From the bed of the wagon, Pari's hand quickly slipped into Abdullah's. She was looking up at him, her eyes liquid, and she was smiling her gap-toothed smile like no bad thing would ever befall her so long as he stood at her side. He closed his fingers around her hand, the way he did each night when he and his little sister slept in their cot, their skulls touching, their legs tangled.

"You were supposed to stay home," Father said. "With your mother and Iqbal. Like I told you to."

Abdullah thought, *She's your wife. My mother, we buried.* But he knew to stifle those words before they came up and out.

"All right, then. Come," Father said. "But there won't be any crying. You hear me?"

"Yes."

"I'm warning you. I won't have it."

Pari grinned up at Abdullah, and he looked down at her pale eyes and pink round cheeks and grinned back.

From then on, he walked beside the wagon as it jostled along on the pitted desert floor, holding Pari's hand. They traded furtive happy glances, brother and sister, but said little for fear of souring Father's mood and spoiling their good fortune. For long stretches they were alone, the three of them, nothing and no one in sight but the deep copper gorges and vast sandstone cliffs. The desert unrolled ahead of them, open and wide, as though it had been created for them and them alone, the air still, blazing hot, the sky high and blue. Rocks shimmered on the cracked floor. The only sounds Abdullah heard were his own breathing and the rhythmic creaking of the wheels as Father pulled the red wagon north.

A while later, they stopped to rest in the shadow of a boulder. With a groan, Father dropped the handle to the ground. He winced as he arched his back, his face raised to the sun.

"How much longer to Kabul?" Abdullah asked.

Father looked down at them. His name was Saboor. He was dark-skinned and had a hard face, angular and bony, nose curved like a desert hawk's beak, eyes set deep in his skull. Father was thin as a reed, but a lifetime of work had made his muscles powerful, tightly wound like rattan strips around the arm of a wicker chair. "Tomorrow afternoon," he said, lifting the cowhide water bag to his lips. "If we make good time." He took a long swallow, his Adam's apple rising and dropping.

"Why didn't Uncle Nabi drive us?" Abdullah said. "He has a car."

Father rolled his eyes toward him.

"Then we wouldn't have had to walk all this way."

Father didn't say anything. He took off his soot-stained skullcap and wiped sweat from his brow with the sleeve of his shirt.

Pari's finger shot from the wagon. "Look, Abollah!" she cried excitedly. "Another one."

Abdullah followed her finger, traced it to a spot in the shadow of the boulder where a feather lay, long, gray, like charcoal after it has burned. Abdullah walked over to it and picked it by the stem. He blew the flecks of dust off it. A falcon, he thought, turning it over. Maybe a dove, or a desert lark. He'd seen a number of those already that day. No, a falcon. He blew on it again and handed it to Pari, who happily snatched it from him.

Back home, in Shadbagh, Pari kept underneath her pillow an old tin tea box Abdullah had given her. It had a rusty latch, and on the lid was a bearded Indian man, wearing a turban and a long red tunic, holding up a steaming cup of tea with both hands. Inside the box were all of the feathers that Pari collected. They were her most cherished belongings. Deep green and dense burgundy rooster feathers; a white tail feather from a dove; a sparrow feather, dust brown, dotted with dark blotches; and the one of which Pari was proudest, an iridescent green peacock feather with a beautiful large eye at the tip.

This last was a gift Abdullah had given her two months earlier. He had heard of a boy from another village whose family owned a peacock. One day when Father was away digging ditches in a town south of Shadbagh, Abdullah walked to this other village, found the boy, and asked him for a feather from the bird. Negotiation ensued, at the end of which Abdullah agreed to trade his shoes for the feather. By the time he returned to Shadbagh, peacock feather tucked in the waist of his trousers beneath his shirt, his heels had split open and left bloody smudges on the ground. Thorns and splinters had burrowed into the skin of his soles. Every step sent barbs of pain shooting through his feet.

When he arrived home, he found his stepmother, Parwana, outside the hut, hunched before the *tandoor*, making the daily *naan*. He quickly ducked behind the giant oak tree near their home and waited for her to finish. Peeking around the trunk, he watched her work, a thick-shouldered woman with long arms, rough-skinned hands, and stubby fingers; a woman with a puffed, rounded face who possessed none of the grace of the butterfly she'd been named after.

Abdullah wished he could love her as he had his own mother. Mother, who had bled to death giving birth to Pari three and a half years earlier when Abdullah was seven. Mother, whose face was all but lost to him now. Mother, who cupped his head in both palms and held it to her chest and stroked his cheek every night before sleep and sang him a lullaby:

I found a sad little fairy
Beneath the shade of a paper tree.
I know a sad little fairy
Who was blown away by the wind one night.

He wished he could love his new mother in the same way. And perhaps Parwana, he thought, secretly wished the same, that she could love *him.* The way she did Iqbal, her one-year-old son, whose face she always kissed, whose every cough and sneeze she fretted over. Or the way she had loved her first baby, Omar. She had adored him. But he had died of the cold the winter before last. He was two weeks old. Parwana and Father had barely named him. He was one of three babies that brutal winter had taken in Shadbagh. Abdullah remembered Parwana clutching Omar's swaddled little corpse, her fits of grief. He remembered the day they buried him up on the hill, a tiny mound on frozen ground, beneath a pewter sky, Mullah Shekib saying the prayers, the wind spraying grits of snow and ice into everyone's eyes.

Abdullah suspected Parwana would be furious later to learn that he had traded his only pair of shoes for a peacock feather. Father had labored hard under the sun to pay for them. She would let him have it when she found out. She might even hit him, Abdullah thought. She had struck him a few times before. She had strong, heavy hands—from all those years of lifting her invalid sister, Abdullah imagined—and they knew how to swing a broomstick or land a well-aimed slap.

But to her credit, Parwana did not seem to derive any

satisfaction from hitting him. Nor was she incapable of tenderness toward her stepchildren. There was the time she had sewn Pari a silver-and-green dress from a roll of fabric Father had brought from Kabul. The time she had taught Abdullah, with surprising patience, how to crack two eggs simultaneously without breaking the yolks. And the time she had shown them how to twist and turn husks of corn into little dolls, the way she had with her own sister when they were little. She showed them how to fashion dresses for the dolls out of little torn strips of cloth.

But these were gestures, Abdullah knew, acts of duty, drawn from a well far shallower than the one she reached into for Iqbal. If one night their house caught fire, Abdullah knew without doubt which child Parwana would grab rushing out. She would not think twice. In the end, it came down to a simple thing: They weren't her children, he and Pari. Most people loved their own. It couldn't be helped that he and his sister didn't belong to her. They were another woman's leftovers.

He waited for Parwana to take the bread inside, then watched as she reemerged from the hut, carrying Iqbal on one arm and a load of laundry under the other. He watched her amble in the direction of the stream and waited until she was out of sight before he sneaked into the house, his soles throbbing each time they met the ground. Inside, he sat down and slipped on his old plastic sandals, the only other footwear he owned. Abdullah knew it wasn't a sensible thing he had done. But when he knelt beside Pari, gently shook her awake from a nap, and produced the feather from behind his back like a magician, it was all worth it—worth it for the way her face broke open with surprise first, then delight; for the way she stamped his cheeks with kisses; for how she cackled when he tickled her chin with the soft end of the feather—and suddenly his feet didn't hurt at all.

Father wiped his face with his sleeve once more. They took turns drinking from the water bag. When they were done, Father said, "You're tired, boy."

"No," Abdullah said, though he was. He was exhausted. And his feet hurt. It wasn't easy crossing a desert in sandals.

Father said, "Climb in."

In the wagon, Abdullah sat behind Pari, his back against the wooden slat sides, the little knobs of his sister's spine pressing against his belly and chest bone. As Father dragged them forward, Abdullah stared at the sky, the mountains, the rows upon rows of closely packed, rounded hills, soft in the distance. He watched his father's back as he pulled them, his head low, his feet kicking up little puffs of red-brown sand. A caravan of Kuchi nomads passed them by, a dusty procession of jingling bells and groaning camels, and a woman with kohl-rimmed eyes and hair the color of wheat smiled at Abdullah.

Her hair reminded Abdullah of his mother's, and he ached for her all over again, for her gentleness, her inborn happiness, her bewilderment at people's cruelty. He remembered her hiccuping laughter, and the timid way she sometimes tilted her head. His mother had been delicate, both in stature and nature, a wispy, slim-waisted woman with a puff of hair always spilling from under her scarf. He used to wonder how such a frail little body could house so much joy, so much goodness. It couldn't. It spilled out of her, came pouring out her eyes. Father was different. Father had hardness in him. His eyes looked out on the same world as Mother's had, and saw only indifference. Endless toil. Father's world was unsparing. Nothing good came free. Even love. You paid for all things. And if you were poor, suffering was your currency. Abdullah looked down at the scabby parting in his little sister's hair, at her narrow wrist hanging over the side of the wagon, and he knew that in their mother's dying, something of her had passed to Pari. Something of her cheerful devotion, her guilelessness, her unabashed hopefulness. Pari was the only person in the world who would never, could never, hurt him. Some days, Abdullah felt she was the only true family he had.

The day's colors slowly dissolved into gray, and the distant mountain peaks became opaque silhouettes of crouching giants. Earlier in the day, they had passed by several villages, most of them far-flung and dusty just like Shadbagh. Small square-shaped homes made of baked mud, sometimes raised into the side of a mountain and sometimes not, ribbons of smoke rising from their roofs. Wash lines, women squatting by cooking fires. A few poplar trees, a few chickens, a handful of cows and goats, and always a mosque. The last village they passed sat adjacent to a poppy field, where an old man working the pods waved at them. He shouted something Abdullah couldn't hear. Father waved back.

Pari said, "Abollah?"

"Yes."

"Do you think Shuja is sad?"

"I think he's fine."

"No one will hurt him?"

"He's a big dog, Pari. He can defend himself."

Shuja *was* a big dog. Father said he must have been a fighting dog at one point because someone had severed his ears and his tail. Whether he could, or would, defend himself was another matter. When the stray first turned up in Shadbagh, kids had hurled rocks at him, poked him with tree branches or rusted bicycle-wheel spokes. Shuja never fought back. With time, the village's kids grew tired of tormenting him and left him alone, though Shuja's demeanor was still cautious, suspicious, as if he'd not forgotten their past unkindness toward him.

He avoided everyone in Shadbagh but Pari. It was for Pari that Shuja lost all composure. His love for her was vast and unclouded. She was his universe. In the mornings, when he saw Pari stepping out of the house, Shuja sprang up, and his entire body shivered. The stump of his mutilated tail wagged wildly, and he tap-danced like he was treading on hot coal. He pranced happy circles around her. All day the dog shadowed Pari, sniffing at her heels, and at night, when they parted ways, he lay outside the door, forlorn, waiting for morning.

"Abollah?"

"Yes."

"When I grow up, will I live with you?"

Abdullah watched the orange sun dropping low, nudging the horizon. "If you want. But you won't want to."

"Yes I will!"

"You'll want a house of your own."

"But we can be neighbors."

"Maybe."

"You won't live far."

"What if you get sick of me?"

She jabbed his side with her elbow. "I wouldn't!"

Abdullah grinned to himself. "All right, fine."

"You'll be close by."

"Yes."

"Until we're old."

"Very old."

"For always."

"Yes, for always."

From the front of the wagon, she turned to look at him. "Do you promise, Abollah?"

"For always and always."

Later, Father hoisted Pari up on his back, and Abdullah was in the rear, pulling the empty wagon. As they walked, he fell into a thoughtless trance. He was aware only of the rise and fall of his own knees, of the sweat beads trickling down from the edge of his skullcap. Pari's small feet bouncing against Father's hips. Aware only of the shadow of his father and sister lengthening on the gray desert floor, pulling away from him if he slowed down.

It was Uncle Nabi who had found this latest job for Father—Uncle Nabi was Parwana's older brother and so he was really Abdullah's stepuncle. Uncle Nabi was a cook and a chauffeur in Kabul. Once a month, he drove from Kabul to visit them in Shadbagh, his arrival announced by a staccato of honks and the hollering of a horde of village kids who chased the big blue car with the tan top and shiny rims. They slapped the fender and windows until he killed the engine and emerged grinning from the car, handsome Uncle Nabi with the long sideburns and wavy black hair combed back from his forehead, dressed in his oversize olive-colored suit with white dress shirt and brown loafers. Everyone came out to see him because he drove a car, though it belonged to his employer, and because he wore a suit and worked in the big city, Kabul.

It was on his last visit that Uncle Nabi had told Father about the job. The wealthy people he worked for were building an addition to their home—a small guesthouse in the backyard, complete with a bathroom, separate from the main building—and Uncle Nabi had suggested they hire Father, who knew his way around a construction site. He said the job would pay well and take a month to complete, give or take.

Father did know his way around a construction site. He'd worked in enough of them. As long as Abdullah could remember, Father was out searching for work, knocking on doors for a day's labor. He had overheard Father one time tell the village elder, Mullah Shekib, *If I had been born an animal, Mullah Sahib, I swear I would have come out a mule.*

Sometimes Father took Abdullah along on his jobs. They had picked apples once in a town that was a full day's walk away from Shadbagh. Abdullah remembered his father mounted on the ladder until sundown, his hunched shoulders, the creased back of his neck burning in the sun, the raw skin of his forearms, his thick fingers twisting and turning apples one at a time. They had made bricks for a mosque in another town. Father had shown Abdullah how to collect the good soil, the deep lighter-colored stuff. They had sifted the dirt together, added straw, and Father had patiently taught him to titrate the water so the mixture didn't turn runny. Over the last year, Father had lugged stones. He had shoveled dirt, tried his hand at plowing fields. He had worked on a road crew laying down asphalt.

Abdullah knew that Father blamed himself for Omar. If he had found more work, or better work, he could have bought the baby better winter clothes, heavier blankets, maybe even a proper stove to warm the house. This was what Father thought. He hadn't said a word to Abdullah about Omar since the burial, but Abdullah knew.

He remembered seeing Father once, some days after Omar died, standing alone beneath the giant oak tree. The oak towered over everything in Shadbagh and was the oldest living thing in the village. Father said it wouldn't surprise him if it had witnessed the emperor Babur marching his army to capture Kabul. He said he had spent half his childhood in the shade of its massive crown or climbing its sweeping boughs. His own father, Abdullah's grandfather, had tied long ropes to one of the thick boughs and suspended a swing, a contraption that had survived countless harsh seasons and the old man himself. Father said he used to take turns with Parwana and her sister, Masooma, on this swing when they were all children.

But, these days, Father was always too exhausted from work when Pari pulled on his sleeve and asked him to make her fly on the swing.

Maybe tomorrow, Pari.

Just for a while, Baba. Please get up.

Not now. Another time.

She would give up in the end, release his sleeve, and walk away resigned. Sometimes Father's narrow face collapsed in on itself as he watched her go. He would roll over in his cot, then pull up the quilt and shut his weary eyes.

Abdullah could not picture that Father had once swung on a swing. He could not imagine that Father had once been a boy, like him. A boy. Carefree, light on his feet. Running headlong into the open fields with his playmates. Father, whose hands were scarred, whose face was crosshatched with deep lines of weariness. Father, who might as well have been born with shovel in hand and mud under his nails.

They had to sleep in the desert that night. They ate bread and the last of the boiled potatoes Parwana had packed for them. Father made a fire and set a kettle on the flames for tea.

Abdullah lay beside the fire, curled beneath the wool blanket behind Pari, the soles of her cold feet pressed against him.

Father bent over the flames and lit a cigarette.

Abdullah rolled to his back, and Pari adjusted, fitting her cheek into the familiar nook beneath his collarbone. He breathed in the coppery smell of desert dust and looked up at a sky thick with stars like ice crystals, flashing and flickering. A delicate crescent moon cradled the dim ghostly outline of its full self.

Abdullah thought back to the winter before last, everything plunged into darkness, the wind coming in around the door, whistling slow and long and loud, and whistling from every little crack in the ceiling. Outside, the village's features obliterated by snow. The nights long and starless, daytime brief, gloomy, the sun rarely out, and then only to make a cameo appearance before it vanished. He remembered Omar's labored cries, then his silence, then Father grimly carving a wooden board with a sickle moon, just like the one above them now, pounding the board into the hard ground burnt with frost at the head of the small grave.

And now autumn's end was in sight once more. Winter was already lurking around the corner, though neither Father nor Parwana spoke about it, as though saying the word might hasten its arrival.

"Father?" he said.

From the other side of the fire, Father gave a soft grunt.

"Will you allow me to help you? Build the guesthouse, I mean."

Smoke spiraled up from Father's cigarette. He was staring off into the darkness.

"Father?"

Father shifted on the rock where he was seated. "I suppose you could help mix mortar," he said.

"I don't know how."

"I'll show you. You'll learn."

"What about me?" Pari said.

"You?" Father said slowly. He took a drag of his cigarette and poked at the fire with a stick. Scattered little sparks went dancing up into the blackness. "You'll be in charge of the water. Make sure we never go thirsty. Because a man can't work if he's thirsty."

Pari was quiet.

"Father's right," Abdullah said. He sensed Pari wanted to get her hands dirty, climb down into the mud, and that she was disappointed with the task Father had assigned her. "Without you fetching us water, we'll never get the guesthouse built."

Father slid the stick beneath the handle of the teakettle and lifted it from the fire. He set it aside to cool.

"I'll tell you what," he said. "You show me you can handle the water job and I'll find you something else to do."

Pari tilted up her chin and looked at Abdullah, her face lit up with a gapped smile.

He remembered when she was a baby, when she would sleep atop his chest, and he would open his eyes sometimes in the middle of the night and find her grinning silently at him with this same expression.

He was the one raising her. It was true. Even though he was still a child himself. Ten years old. When Pari was an infant, it was he she had awakened at night with her squeaks and mutters, he who had walked and bounced her in the dark. He had changed her soiled diapers. He had been the one to give Pari her baths. It wasn't Father's job to do—he was a man—and, besides, he was always too exhausted from work. And Parwana, already pregnant with Omar, was slow to rouse herself to Pari's needs. She never had the patience or the energy. Thus the care had fallen on Abdullah, but he didn't mind at all. He did it gladly. He loved the fact that he was the one to help with her first step, to gasp at her first uttered word. This was his purpose, he believed, the reason God had made him, so he would be there to take care of Pari when He took away their mother.

"Baba," Pari said. "Tell a story."

"It's getting late," Father said.

"Please."

Father was a closed-off man by nature. He rarely uttered more than two consecutive sentences at any time. But on occasion, for reasons unknown to Abdullah, something in Father unlocked and stories suddenly came spilling out. Sometimes he had Abdullah and Pari sit raptly before him, as Parwana banged pots in the kitchen, and told them stories his grandmother had passed on to him when he had been a boy, sending them off to lands populated by sultans and *jinn*s and malevolent *div*s and wise dervishes. Other times, he made up stories. He made them up on the spot, his tales unmasking a capacity for imagination and dream that always surprised Abdullah. Father never felt more present to Abdullah, more vibrant, revealed, more truthful, than when he told his stories, as though the tales were pinholes into his opaque, inscrutable world.

But Abdullah could tell from the expression on Father's face that there would be no story tonight.

"It's late," Father said again. He lifted the kettle with the edge of the shawl draping his shoulders and poured himself a cup of tea. He blew the steam and took a sip, his face glowing orange in the flames. "Time to sleep. Long day tomorrow."

Abdullah pulled the blanket over their heads. Underneath, he sang into the nape of Pari's neck:

I found a sad little fairy
Beneath the shade of a paper tree.

Pari, already sleepy, sluggishly sang her verse.

I know a sad little fairy
Who was blown away by the wind one night.

Almost instantly, she was snoring.

Abdullah awoke later and found Father gone. He sat up in a fright. The fire was all but dead, nothing left of it now but a few crimson speckles of ember. Abdullah's gaze darted left, then right, but his eyes could penetrate nothing in the dark, at once vast and smothering. He felt his face going white. Heart sprinting, he cocked his ear, held his breath.

"Father?" he whispered.

Silence.

Panic began to mushroom deep in his chest. He sat perfectly still, his body erect and tense, and listened for a long time. He heard nothing. They were alone, he and Pari, the dark closing in around them. They had been abandoned. Father had abandoned them. Abdullah felt the true vastness of the desert, and the world, for the first time. How easily a person could lose his way in it. No one to help, no one to show the way. Then a worse thought wormed its way into his head. Father was dead. Someone had slit his throat. Bandits. They had killed him, and now they were closing in on him and Pari, taking their time, relishing it, making a game of it.

"Father?" he called out again, his voice shrill this time.

No reply came.

"Father?"

He called for his father again and again, a claw tightening itself around his windpipe. He lost track of how many times and for how long he called for his father but no answer came forth from the dark. He pictured faces, hidden in the mountains bulging from the earth, watching, grinning down at him and Pari with malice. Panic seized him, shriveled up his innards. He began to shiver, and mewl under his breath. He felt himself on the cusp of screaming.

Then, footsteps. A shape materialized from the dark.

"I thought you'd gone," Abdullah said shakily.

Father sat down by the remains of the fire.

"Where did you go?"

"Go to sleep, boy."

"You wouldn't leave us. You wouldn't do that, Father."

Father looked at him, but in the dark his face dissolved into an expression Abdullah couldn't make out. "You're going to wake your sister."

"Don't leave us."

"That's enough of that now."

Abdullah lay down again, his sister clutched tightly in his arms, his heart battering in his throat.

Abdullah had never been to Kabul. What he knew about Kabul came from stories Uncle Nabi had told him. He had visited a few smaller towns on jobs with Father, but never a real city, and certainly nothing Uncle Nabi had said could have prepared him for the hustle and bustle of the biggest and busiest city of them all. Everywhere, he saw traffic lights, and teahouses, and restaurants, and glass-fronted shops with bright multicolored signs. Cars rattling noisily down the crowded streets, hooting, darting narrowly among buses, pedestrians, and bicycles. Horse-drawn *garis* jingled up and down boulevards, their iron-rimmed wheels bouncing on the road. The sidewalks he walked with Pari and Father were crowded with cigarette and chewing-gum sellers, magazine stands, blacksmiths pounding horseshoes. At intersections, traffic policemen in ill-fitting uniforms blew their whistles and made authoritative gestures that no one seemed to heed.

Pari on his lap, Abdullah sat on a sidewalk bench near a butcher's shop, sharing a tin plate of baked beans and cilantro chutney that Father had bought them from a street stall.

"Look, Abollah," Pari said, pointing to a shop across the street. In its window stood a young woman dressed in a beautifully embroidered green dress with small mirrors and beads. She wore a long matching scarf, with silver jewelry and deep red trousers. She stood perfectly still, gazing indifferently at passersby without once blinking. She didn't move so much as a finger as Abdullah and Pari finished their beans, and remained motionless after that too. Up the block, Abdullah saw a huge poster hanging from the façade of a tall building. It showed a young, pretty Indian woman in a tulip field, standing in a downpour of rain, ducking playfully behind some kind of bungalow. She was grinning shyly, a wet sari hugging her curves. Abdullah wondered if this was what Uncle Nabi had called a cinema, where people went to watch films, and hoped that in the coming month Uncle Nabi would take him and Pari to see a film. He grinned at the thought.

It was just after the call to prayer blared from a blue-tiled mosque up the street that Abdullah saw Uncle Nabi pull up to the curb. Uncle Nabi swung out of the driver's side, dressed in his olive suit, his door narrowly missing a young bicycle rider in a *chapan*, who swerved just in time.

Uncle Nabi hurried around the front of the car and embraced Father. When he saw Abdullah and Pari, his face erupted in a big grin. He stooped to be on the same level as them.

"How do you like Kabul, kids?"

"It's very loud," Pari said, and Uncle Nabi laughed.

"That it is. Come on, climb in. You'll see a lot more of it from the car. Wipe your feet before you get in. Saboor, you take the front."

The backseat was cool, hard, and light blue to match the exterior. Abdullah slid across it to the window behind the driver's seat and helped Pari onto his lap. He noticed the envious way bystanders looked at the car. Pari swiveled her head toward him, and they exchanged a grin.

They watched the city stream by as Uncle Nabi drove. He said he would take a longer route so they could see a little of Kabul. He pointed to a ridge called Tapa Maranjan and to the dome-shaped mausoleum atop it overlooking the city. He said Nāder Shah, father to King Zahir Shah, was buried there. He showed them the Bala Hissar fort atop the Koh-e-Shirdawaza mountain, which he said the British had used during their second war against Afghanistan.

"What's that, Uncle Nabi?" Abdullah tapped on the window, pointing to a big rectangular yellow building.

"That's Silo. It's the new bread factory." Uncle Nabi drove with one hand and craned back to wink at him. "Compliments of our friends the Russians."

A factory that makes bread, Abdullah marveled, picturing Parwana back in Shadbagh slapping slabs of dough against the sides of their mud *tandoor*.

Eventually, Uncle Nabi turned onto a clean, wide street lined with regularly spaced cypress trees. The homes here were elegant, and bigger than any Abdullah had ever seen.

They were white, yellow, light blue. Most had a couple stories, were surrounded by high walls and closed off by double metal gates. Abdullah spotted several cars like Uncle Nabi's parked along the street.

Uncle Nabi pulled up to a driveway decked by a row of neatly trimmed bushes. Beyond the driveway, the white-walled, two-story home loomed impossibly large.

"Your house is so big," Pari breathed, eyes rolling wide with wonderment.

Uncle Nabi's head rolled back on his shoulders as he laughed. "That would be something. No, this is my employers' home. You're about to meet them. Be on your best manners, now."

The house proved even more impressive once Uncle Nabi led Abdullah, Pari, and Father inside. Abdullah estimated its size big enough to contain at least half the homes in Shadbagh. He felt as though he had stepped into the *div*'s palace. The garden, at the far back, was beautifully landscaped, with rows of flowers in all colors, neatly trimmed, with knee-high bushes and peppered with fruit trees—Abdullah recognized cherry, apple, apricot, and pomegranate. A roofed porch led into the garden from the house—Uncle Nabi said it was called a veranda—and was enclosed by a low railing covered with webs of green vines. On their way to the room where Mr. and Mrs. Wahdati awaited their arrival, Abdullah spied a bathroom with the porcelain toilet Uncle Nabi had told them about, as well as a glittering sink with bronze-colored faucets. Abdullah, who spent hours every week lugging buckets of water from Shadbagh's communal well, marveled at a life where water was just a twist of the hand away.

Now they sat on a bulky couch with gold tassels, Abdullah, Pari, and Father. The soft cushions at their backs were dotted with tiny octagonal mirrors. Across from the couch, a single painting took up most of the wall. It showed an elderly stone carver, bent over his workbench, pounding a block of stone with a mallet. Pleated burgundy drapes dressed the wide windows that opened onto a balcony with a waist-high iron railing. Everything in the room was polished, free of dust.

Abdullah had never in his life been so conscious of his own dirtiness.

Uncle Nabi's boss, Mr. Wahdati, sat on a leather chair, arms crossed over his chest. He was looking at them with an expression that was not quite unfriendly but remote, impenetrable. He was taller than Father; Abdullah had seen that as soon as he had stood to greet them. He had narrow shoulders, thin lips, and a high shiny forehead. He was wearing a white suit, tapered at the waist, with an open-collared green shirt whose cuffs were held together by oval-shaped lapis stones. The whole time, he hadn't said more than a dozen words.

Pari was looking down at the plate of cookies on the glass table before them. Abdullah had never imagined such a variety of them existed. Finger-shaped chocolate cookies with swirls of cream, small round ones with orange filling in the center, green cookies shaped like leaves, and more.

"Would you like one?" Mrs. Wahdati said. She was the one doing all the talking. "Go ahead. Both of you. I put them out for you."

Abdullah turned to Father for permission, and Pari followed suit. This seemed to charm Mrs. Wahdati, who tented her eyebrows, tilted her head, and smiled.

Father nodded lightly. "One each," he said in a low voice.

"Oh, that won't do," Mrs. Wahdati said. "I had Nabi go to a bakery halfway across Kabul for these."

Father flushed, averted his eyes. He was sitting on the edge of the couch, holding his battered skullcap with both hands. He had angled his knees away from Mrs. Wahdati and kept his eyes on her husband.

Abdullah plucked two cookies and gave one to Pari.

"Oh, take another. We don't want Nabi's troubles to go to waste," Mrs. Wahdati said with cheerful reproach. She smiled at Uncle Nabi.

"It was no trouble at all," Uncle Nabi said, blushing.

Uncle Nabi was standing near the door, beside a tall wooden cabinet with thick glass doors. On the shelves inside, Abdullah saw silver-framed photos of Mr. and Mrs. Wahdati. There they were, alongside another couple, dressed in thick scarves and heavy coats, a river flowing foamily behind them. In another picture, Mrs. Wahdati, holding a glass, laughing, her bare arm around the waist of a man who, unthinkably to Abdullah, was not Mr. Wahdati. There was a wedding photo as well, he tall and trim in a black suit, she in a flowing white dress, both of them smiling with their mouths closed.

Abdullah stole a glance at her, at her thin waist, her small, pretty mouth and perfectly arched eyebrows, her pink toenails and matching lipstick. He remembered her now from a couple of years earlier, when Pari was almost two. Uncle Nabi had brought her to Shadbagh because she had said she wanted to meet his family. She had worn a peach dress without sleeves—he remembered the look of astonishment on Father's face—and dark sunglasses with thick white rims. She smiled the whole time, asking questions about the village, their lives, asking after the children's names and ages. She acted like she belonged there in their low-ceilinged mud house, her back against a wall black with soot, sitting next to the flyspecked window and the cloudy plastic sheet that separated the main room from the kitchen, where Abdullah and Pari also slept. She had made a show of the visit, insisting on taking off her high-heeled shoes at the door, choosing the floor when Father had sensibly offered her a chair. Like she was one of them. He was only eight then, but Abdullah had seen through it.

What Abdullah remembered most about the visit was how Parwana—who had been pregnant with Iqbal then—had remained a shrouded figure, sitting in a corner in stiff silence, shriveled up into a ball. She had sat with her shoulders gathered, feet tucked beneath her swollen belly, like she was trying to disappear into the wall. Her face was shielded from view with a soiled veil. She held a knotted clump of it under her chin. Abdullah could almost see the shame rising from her, like steam, the embarrassment, how small she felt, and he had felt a surprising swell of sympathy for his stepmother.

Mrs. Wahdati reached for the pack next to the cookie plate and lit herself a cigarette.

"We took a long detour on the way, and I showed them a little of the city," Uncle Nabi said.

"Good! Good," Mrs. Wahdati said. "Have you been to Kabul before, Saboor?"

Father said, "Once or twice, Bibi Sahib."

"And, may I ask, what is your impression?"

Father shrugged. "It's very crowded."

"Yes."

Mr. Wahdati picked at a speck of lint on the sleeve of his jacket and looked down at the carpet.

"Crowded, yes, and at times tiresome as well," his wife said.

Father nodded as if he understood.

"Kabul is an island, really. Some say it's progressive, and that may be true. It's true enough, I suppose, but it's also out of touch with the rest of this country."

Father looked down at the skullcap in his hands and blinked.

"Don't misunderstand me," she said. "I would whole-heartedly support any progressive agenda coming out of the city. God knows this country could use it. Still, the city is sometimes a little too pleased with itself for my taste. I swear, the pomposity in this place." She sighed. "It does grow tire-some. I've always admired the countryside myself. I have a great fondness for it. The distant provinces, the *qaria*s, the small villages. The *real* Afghanistan, so to speak."

Father nodded uncertainly.

"I may not agree with all or even most of the tribal traditions, but it seems to me that, out there, people live more authentic lives. They have a sturdiness about them. A refreshing humility. Hospitality too. And resilience. A sense of pride. Is that the right word, Suleiman? *Pride?*"

"Stop it, Nila," her husband said quietly.

A dense silence followed. Abdullah watched Mr. Wahdati drumming his fingers on the arm of his chair, and his wife, smiling tightly, the pink smudge on the butt end of her cigarette, her feet crossed at the ankles, her elbow resting on the arm of the chair.

"Probably not the right word," she said, breaking the silence. "*Dignity*, perhaps." She smiled, revealing teeth that were straight and white. Abdullah had never seen teeth like these. "That's it. Much better. People in the countryside carry a sense of dignity. They wear it, don't they? Like a badge? I'm being genuine. I see it in you, Saboor."

"Thank you, Bibi Sahib," Father muttered, shifting on the couch, still looking down at his skullcap.

Mrs. Wahdati nodded. She turned her gaze to Pari. "And, may I say, you are so lovely." Pari nudged closer to Abdullah.

Slowly, Mrs. Wahdati recited, "Today I have seen the charm, the beauty, the unfathomable grace of the face that I was looking for." She smiled. "Rumi. Have you heard of him? You'd think he'd composed it just for you, my dear."

"Mrs. Wahdati is an accomplished poet," Uncle Nabi said.

Across the room, Mr. Wahdati reached for a cookie, split it in half, and took a small bite.

"Nabi is being kind," Mrs. Wahdati said, casting him a warm glance. Abdullah again caught a flush creeping up Uncle Nabi's cheeks.

Mrs. Wahdati crushed her cigarette, giving the butt a series of sharp taps against the ashtray. "Maybe I could take the children somewhere?" she said.

Mr. Wahdati let out a breath huffily, slapped both palms against the arms of his chair, and made as if to get up, though he didn't.

"I'll take them to the bazaar," Mrs. Wahdati said to Father now. "If that's all right with you, Saboor. Nabi will drive us. Suleiman can show you to the work site out back. So you can see it for yourself."

Father nodded.

Mr. Wahdati's eyes slowly fell shut.

They got up to go.

Suddenly, Abdullah wished Father would thank these people for their cookies and tea, take his hand and Pari's, and leave this house and its paintings and drapes and overstuffed luxury and comfort. They could refill their water bag, buy bread and a few boiled eggs, and go back the way they had come. Back through the desert, the boulders, the hills, Father telling them stories. They would take turns pulling Pari in the wagon. And in two, maybe three, days' time, though there would be dust in their lungs and tiredness in their limbs, they would be back in Shadbagh again. Shuja would see them coming and he would hurry over, prance circles around Pari. They would be home.

Father said, "Go on, children."

Abdullah took a step forward, meaning to say something, but then Uncle Nabi's thick hand was on his shoulder, turning him around, Uncle Nabi leading him down the hallway, saying, "Wait 'til you see the bazaars in this place. You've not seen the likes of it, you two."

Mrs. Wahdati sat in the backseat with them, the air filled with the thick weight of her perfume and something Abdullah didn't recognize, something sweet, a little pungent. She peppered them with questions as Uncle Nabi drove. Who were their friends? Did they go to school? Questions about their chores, their neighbors, games they played. The sun fell on the right half of her face. Abdullah could see the fuzzy little hairs on her cheek and the faint line below her jaw where the makeup ended.

"I have a dog," Pari said.

"Do you?"

"He's quite the specimen," Uncle Nabi said from the front seat.

"His name is Shuja. He knows when I'm sad."

"Dogs are like that," Mrs. Wahdati said. "They're better at it than some people I've come across."

They drove past a trio of schoolgirls skipping down the sidewalk. They wore black uniforms with white scarves tied under their chins.

"I know what I said earlier, but Kabul isn't that bad." Mrs. Wahdati toyed with her necklace absently. She was looking out the window, a heaviness set on her features. "I like it best here at the end of spring, after the rains. The air so clean. That first burst of summer. The way the sun hits the mountains." She smiled wanly. "It will be good to have a child around the house. A little noise, for a change. A little life."

Abdullah looked at her and sensed something alarming in the woman, beneath the makeup and the perfume and the appeals for sympathy, something deeply splintered. He found himself thinking of the smoke of Parwana's cooking, the kitchen shelf cluttered with her jars and mismatched plates and smudged pots. He missed the mattress he shared with Pari, though it was dirty, and the jumbles of springs forever threatened to poke through. He missed all of it. He had never before ached so badly for home.

Mrs. Wahdati slumped back into the seat with a sigh, hugging her purse the way a pregnant woman might hold her swollen belly.

Uncle Nabi pulled up to a crowded curbside. Across the street, next to a mosque with soaring minarets, was the bazaar, composed of congested labyrinths of both vaulted and open alleyways. They strolled through corridors of stalls that sold leather coats, rings with colored jewels and stones, spices of all kinds, Uncle Nabi in the rear, Mrs. Wahdati and the two of them in the lead. Now that they were outside, Mrs. Wahdati wore a pair of dark glasses that made her face look oddly catlike.

Hagglers' calls echoed everywhere. Music blared from virtually every stall. They walked past open-fronted shops selling books, radios, lamps, and silver-colored cooking pots. Abdullah saw a pair of soldiers in dusty boots and dark brown greatcoats, sharing a cigarette, eyeing everyone with bored indifference.

They stopped by a shoe stall. Mrs. Wahdati rummaged through the rows of shoes displayed on boxes. Uncle Nabi wandered over to the next stall, hands clasped behind his back, and gave a down-the-nose look at some old coins.

"How about these?" Mrs. Wahdati said to Pari. She was holding up a new pair of yellow sneakers.

"They're so pretty," Pari said, looking at the shoes with disbelief.

"Let's try them on."

Mrs. Wahdati helped Pari slip on the shoes, working the strap and buckle for her. She peered up at Abdullah over her glasses. "You could use a pair too, I think. I can't believe you walked all the way from your village in those sandals."

Abdullah shook his head and looked away. Down the alleyway, an old man with a ragged beard and two clubfeet begged passersby.

"Look, Abollah!" Pari raised one foot, then the other. She stomped her feet on the ground, hopped. Mrs. Wahdati called Uncle Nabi over and told him to walk Pari down the alley, see how the shoes felt. Uncle Nabi took Pari's hand and led her up the lane.

Mrs. Wahdati looked down at Abdullah.

"You think I'm a bad person," she said. "The way I spoke earlier."

Abdullah watched Pari and Uncle Nabi pass by the old

beggar with the clubfeet. The old man said something to Pari, Pari turned her face up to Uncle Nabi and said something, and Uncle Nabi tossed the old man a coin.

Abdullah began to cry soundlessly.

"Oh, you sweet boy," Mrs. Wahdati said, startled. "You poor darling." She fetched a handkerchief from her purse and offered it.

Abdullah swiped it away. "Please don't do it," he said, his voice cracking.

She hunkered down beside him now, her glasses pushed up on her hair. There was wetness in her eyes too, and when she dabbed at them with the handkerchief, it came away with black smudges. "I don't blame you if you hate me. It's your right. But—and I don't expect you to understand, not now—this is for the best. It really is, Abdullah. It's for the best. One day you'll see."

Abdullah turned his face up to the sky and wailed just as Pari came skipping back to him, her eyes dripping with gratitude, her face shining with happiness.

One morning that winter, Father fetched his ax and cut down the giant oak tree. He had Mullah Shekib's son, Baitullah, and a few other men help him. No one tried to intervene. Abdullah stood alongside other boys and watched the men. The very first thing Father did was take down the swing. He climbed the tree and cut the ropes with a knife. Then he and the other men hacked away at the thick trunk until late afternoon, when the old tree finally toppled with a massive groan. Father told Abdullah they needed the firewood for winter. But he had swung his ax at the old tree with violence, with his jaw firmly set and a cloud over his face like he couldn't bear to look at it any longer.

Now, beneath a stone-colored sky, men were striking at the felled trunk, their noses and cheeks flushed in the cold, their blades echoing hollowly when they hit the wood. Farther up the tree, Abdullah snapped small branches off the big ones. The first of the winter snow had fallen two days before. Not heavy, not yet, only a promise of things to come. Soon, winter would descend on Shadbagh, winter and its icicles and weeklong snowdrifts and winds that cracked the skin on the back of hands in a minute flat. For now, the white on the ground was scant, pocked from here to the steep hillsides with pale brown blotches of earth.

Abdullah gathered an armful of slim branches and carried them to a growing communal pile nearby. He was wearing his new snow boots, gloves, and winter coat. It was secondhand, but other than the broken zipper, which Father had fixed, it was as good as new—padded, dark blue, with orange fur lining inside. It had four deep pockets that snapped open and shut and a quilted hood that tightened around Abdullah's face when he drew its cords. He pushed back the hood from his head now and let out a long foggy breath.

The sun was dropping into the horizon. Abdullah could still make out the old windmill, looming stark and gray over the village's mud walls. Its blades gave a creaky groan whenever a nippy gust blew in from the hills. The windmill was home mainly to blue herons in the summer, but now that winter was here the herons had gone and the crows had moved in. Every morning, Abdullah awoke to their squawks and harsh croaks.

Something caught his eye, off to his right, on the ground. He walked over to it and knelt down.

A feather. Small. Yellow.

He took off one glove and picked it up.

Tonight they were going to a party, he, his father, and his little half brother Iqbal. Baitullah had a new infant boy. A *motreb* would sing for the men, and someone would tap on a tambourine. There would be tea and warm, freshly baked bread, and *shorwa* soup with potatoes. Afterward, Mullah Shekib would dip his finger in a bowl of sweetened water and let the baby suckle it. He would produce his shiny black stone and his double-edged razor, lift the cloth from the boy's midriff. An ordinary ritual. Life rolling on in Shadbagh.

Abdullah turned the feather over in his hand.

I won't have any crying, Father had said. *No crying. I won't have it.*

And there hadn't been any. No one in the village asked after Pari. No one even spoke her name. It astonished Abdullah how thoroughly she had vanished from their lives.

Only in Shuja did Abdullah find a reflection of his own grief. The dog turned up at their door every day. Parwana threw rocks at him. Father went at him with a stick. But he kept returning. Every night he could be heard whimpering mournfully and every morning they found him lying by the door, chin on his front paws, blinking up at his assailants with melancholy, unaccusing eyes. This went on for weeks until one morning Abdullah saw him hobbling toward the hills, head hung low. No one in Shadbagh had seen him since.

Abdullah pocketed the yellow feather and began walking toward the windmill.

Sometimes, in unguarded moments, he caught Father's face clouding over, drawn into confusing shades of emotion. Father looked diminished to him now, stripped of something essential. He loped sluggishly about the house or else sat in the heat of their big new cast-iron stove, little Iqbal on his lap, and stared unseeingly into the flames. His voice dragged now in a way that Abdullah did not remember, as though something weighed on each word he spoke. He shrank into long silences, his face closed off. He didn't tell stories anymore, had not told one since he and Abdullah had returned from Kabul. Maybe, Abdullah thought, Father had sold the Wahdatis his muse as well.

Gone.

Vanished.

Nothing left.

Nothing said.

Other than these words from Parwana: *It had to be her. I am sorry, Abdullah. She had to be the one.*

The finger cut, to save the hand.

He knelt on the ground behind the windmill, at the base of the decaying stone tower. He took off his gloves and dug at the ground. He thought of her heavy eyebrows and her wide rounded forehead, her gap-toothed smile. He heard in his head the tinkle of her laughter rolling around the house like it used to. He thought of the scuffle that had broken out when they had come back from the bazaar. Pari panicking. Shrieking. Uncle Nabi quickly whisking her away. Abdullah dug until his fingers struck metal. Then he maneuvered his hands underneath and lifted the tin tea box from the hole. He swiped cold dirt off the lid.

Lately, he thought a lot about the story Father had told them the night before the trip to Kabul, the old peasant Baba Ayub and the *div*. Abdullah would find himself on a spot where Pari had once stood, her absence like a smell pushing up from the earth beneath his feet, and his legs would buckle, and his heart would collapse in on itself, and he would long for a swig of the magic potion the *div* had given Baba Ayub so he too could forget.

But there was no forgetting. Pari hovered, unbidden, at the edge of Abdullah's vision everywhere he went. She was like the dust that clung to his shirt. She was in the silences that had become so frequent at the house, silences that welled up between their words, sometimes cold and hollow, sometimes pregnant with things that went unsaid, like a cloud filled with rain that never fell. Some nights he dreamed that he was in the desert again, alone, surrounded by the mountains, and in the distance a single tiny glint of light flickering on, off, on, off, like a message.

He opened the tea box. They were all there, Pari's feathers, shed from roosters, ducks, pigeons; the peacock feather too. He tossed the yellow feather into the box. One day, he thought.

Hoped.

His days in Shadbagh were numbered, like Shuja's. He knew this now. There was nothing left for him here. He had no home here. He would wait until winter passed and the spring thaw set in, and he would rise one morning before dawn and he would step out the door. He would choose a direction and he would begin to walk. He would walk as far from Shadbagh as his feet would take him. And if one day, trekking across some vast open field, despair should take hold of him, he would stop in his tracks and shut his eyes and he would think of the falcon feather Pari had found in the desert. He would picture the feather coming loose from the bird, up in the clouds, half a mile above the world, twirling and spinning in violent currents, hurled by gusts of blustering wind across miles and miles of desert and mountains, to finally land, of all places and against all odds, at the foot of that one boulder for his sister to find. It would strike him with wonder, then, and hope too, that such things happened. And though he would know better, he would take heart, and he would open his eyes, and walk.

Three

Spring 1949

Parwana smells it before she pulls back the quilt and sees it. It has smeared all over Masooma's buttocks, down her thighs, against the sheets and the mattress and the quilt too. Masooma looks up at her over her shoulder with a timid plea for forgiveness, and shame—still the shame after all this time, all these years.

"I'm sorry," Masooma whispers.

Parwana wants to howl but she forces herself into a weak smile. It takes strenuous effort at times like this to remember, to not lose sight of, one unshakable truth: This is her own handiwork, this mess. Nothing that has befallen her is unjust or undue. This is what she deserves. She sighs, surveying the soiled linens, dreading the work that awaits her. "I'll get you cleaned up," she says.

Masooma starts to weep without a sound, without even a shift in her expression. Only tears, welling, trickling down.

Outside, in the early-morning chill, Parwana starts a fire

in the cooking pit. When the flames take hold, she fills a pail with water from Shadbagh's communal well and sets it to heat. She holds her palms to the fire. She can see the windmill from here, and the village mosque where Mullah Shekib had taught her and Masooma to read when they were little, and Mullah Shekib's house too, set at the foot at a mild slope. Later, when the sun is up, its roof will be a perfect, strikingly red square against the dust because of the tomatoes his wife has set out to dry in the sun. Parwana gazes up at the morning stars, fading, pale, blinking at her indifferently. She gathers herself.

Inside, she turns Masooma onto her stomach. She soaks a washcloth in the water and rubs clean Masooma's buttocks, wiping the waste off her back and the flaccid flesh of her legs.

"Why the warm water?" Masooma says into the pillow. "Why the trouble? You don't have to. I won't know the difference."

"Maybe. But I will," Parwana says, grimacing against the stench. "Now, quit your talking and let me finish this."

From there, Parwana's day unfolds as it always does, as it has for the four years since their parents' deaths. She feeds the chickens. She chops wood and lugs buckets back and forth from the well. She makes dough and bakes the bread in the *tandoor* outside their mud house. She sweeps the floor. In the afternoon, she squats by the stream, alongside other village women, washing laundry against the rocks. Afterward, because it is a Friday, she visits her parents' graves in the cemetery and says a brief prayer for each. And all day, in between these chores, she makes time to move Masooma, from side to side, tucking a pillow under one buttock, then the other.

Twice that day, she spots Saboor.

She finds him squatting outside his small mud house, fanning a fire in the cooking pit, eyes squeezed against the smoke, with his boy, Abdullah, beside him. She finds him later, talking to other men, men who, like Saboor, have families of their own now but were once the village boys with whom Saboor feuded, flew kites, chased dogs, played hide-and-seek. There is a weight over Saboor these days, a pall of tragedy, a dead wife and two motherless children, one an infant. He speaks now in a tired, barely audible voice. He lumbers around the village a worn, shrunken version of himself.

Parwana watches him from afar and with a longing that is nearly crippling. She tries to avert her eyes when she passes by him. And if by accident their gazes do meet, he simply nods at her, and the blood rushes to her face.

That night, by the time Parwana lies down to sleep, she can barely lift her arms. Her head swims with exhaustion. She lies in her cot, waiting for sleep.

Then, in the darkness:

"Parwana?"

"Yes."

"Do you remember that time, us riding the bicycle together?"

"Hmm."

"How fast we went! Riding down the hill. The dogs chasing us."

"I remember."

"Both of us screaming. And when we hit that rock . . ." Parwana can almost hear her sister smiling in the dark. "Mother was so angry with us. And Nabi too. We ruined his bicycle."

Parwana shuts her eyes.

"Parwana?"

"Yes."

"Can you sleep by me tonight?"

Parwana kicks off her quilt, makes her way across the hut to Masooma, and slips under the blanket beside her. Masooma rests her cheek on Parwana's shoulder, one arm draped across her sister's chest.

Masooma whispers, "You deserve better than me."

"Don't start that again," Parwana whispers back. She plays with Masooma's hair in long, patient strokes, the way Masooma likes it.

They chat idly for a while in hushed voices of small, inconsequential things, one's breath warming the other's face. These are relatively happy minutes for Parwana. They remind her of when they were little girls, curled up nose to nose beneath the blanket, whispering secrets and gossip, giggling soundlessly. Soon, Masooma is asleep, her tongue rolling noisily around some dream, and Parwana is staring out the window at a sky burnt black. Her mind bounces from one fragmented thought to another and eventually swims to a picture she saw in an old magazine once of a pair of grim-faced brothers from Siam joined at the torso by a thick band of flesh. Two creatures inextricably bound, blood formed in the marrow of one running in the veins of the other, their union permanent. Parwana feels a constriction, despair, like a hand tightening inside her chest. She takes a breath. She tries to direct her thoughts to Saboor once more and instead finds her mind drifting to the rumor she has heard around the village: that he is looking for a new wife. She forces his face from her head. She nips the foolish thought.

Parwana was a surprise.

Masooma was already out, wriggling quietly in the midwife's arms, when their mother cried out and the crown of another head parted her a second time. Masooma's arrival was uneventful. *She delivered herself, the angel,* the midwife would say later. Parwana's birth was prolonged, agonizing for the mother, treacherous for the baby. The midwife had to free her from the cord that had wrapped itself around Parwana's neck, as if in a murderous fit of separation anxiety. In her worst moments, when she cannot help being swallowed up by a torrent of self-loathing, Parwana thinks that perhaps the cord knew best. Maybe it knew which was the better half.

Masooma fed on schedule, slept on time. She cried only if in need of food or cleaning. When awake, she was playful, good-humored, easily delighted, a swaddled bundle of giggles and happy squeaks. She liked to suck on her rattle.

What a sensible baby, people said.

Parwana was a tyrant. She exerted upon their mother

the full force of her authority. Their father, bewildered by the infant's histrionics, took the babies' older brother, Nabi, and escaped to sleep at his own brother's house. Nighttime was a misery of epic proportion for the girls' mother, punctuated by only a few moments of fitful rest. She bounced Parwana and walked her all night every night. She rocked her and sang to her. She winced as Parwana ripped into her chafed, swollen breast and gummed her nipple as though she was after the milk in her very bones. But nursing was no antidote: Even with a full belly, Parwana was flailing and shrieking, immune to her mother's supplications.

Masooma watched from her corner of the room with a pensive, helpless expression, as though she pitied her mother this predicament.

Nabi was nothing like this, their mother said one day to their father.

Every baby is different.

She's killing me, that one.

It will pass, he said. *The way bad weather does.*

And it did pass. Colic, perhaps, or some other innocuous ailment. But it was too late. Parwana had already made her mark.

One late-summer afternoon when the twins were ten months old, the villagers gathered in Shadbagh after a wedding. Women worked with fevered focus to pile onto platters pyramids of fluffy white rice speckled with bits of saffron. They cut bread, scraped crusty rice from the bottom of pots, passed around dishes of fried eggplant topped with yogurt and dried mint. Nabi was out playing with some boys. The girls' mother sat with neighbors on a rug spread beneath the village's giant oak tree. Every now and then, she glanced down at her daughters as they slept side by side in the shade.

After the meal, over tea, the babies woke from their nap, and almost immediately, someone snatched up Masooma. She was merrily passed around, from cousin to aunt to uncle. Bounced on this lap, balanced on that knee. Many hands tickled her soft belly. Many noses rubbed against hers. They rocked with laughter when she playfully grabbed Mullah Shekib's beard. They marveled at her easy, sociable demeanor. They lifted her up and admired the pink flush of her cheeks, her sapphire blue eyes, the graceful curve of her brow, harbingers of the startling beauty that would mark her in a few years' time.

Parwana was left in her mother's lap. As Masooma performed, Parwana watched quietly as though slightly bewildered, the one member of an otherwise adoring audience who didn't understand what all the fuss was about. Every now and then, her mother looked down at her, and reached to squeeze her tiny foot softly, almost apologetically. When someone remarked that Masooma had two new teeth coming in, Parwana's mother said, feebly, that Parwana had three. But no one took notice.

When the girls were nine years old, the family gathered at Saboor's family home for an early-evening *iftar* to break the fast after Ramadan. The adults sat on cushions around the perimeter of the room, and the chatter was noisy. Tea, good wishes, and gossip were passed around in equal measure. Old men fingered their prayer beads. Parwana sat quietly, happy to be breathing the same air as Saboor, to be in the vicinity of his owlish dark eyes. In the course of the evening, she chanced glances his way. She caught him in the midst of biting into a sugar cube, or rubbing the smooth slope of his forehead, or laughing spiritedly at something an elderly uncle had said. And if he caught her looking at him, as he did once or twice, she quickly looked away, rigid with embarrassment. Her knees began to shake. Her mouth went so dry she could hardly speak.

Parwana thought then of the notebook hidden under a pile of her things at home. Saboor was always coming up with stories, tales packed with *jinn*s and fairies and demons and *div*s; often, village kids gathered around him and listened in absolute quiet as he made up fables for them. And about six months earlier, Parwana had overheard Saboor telling Nabi that one day he hoped to write his stories down. It was shortly after that that Parwana, with her mother, had found herself at a bazaar in another town, and there, at a stall that sold used books, she had spotted a beautiful note-book with crisp lined pages and a thick dark brown leather binding embossed along the edges. Holding it in her hand, she knew her mother couldn't afford to buy it for her. So Parwana had picked a moment when the shopkeeper was not looking and quickly slipped the notebook under her sweater.

But in the six months that had since passed, Parwana still hadn't found the courage to give the notebook to Saboor. She was terrified that he might laugh or that he would see it for what it was and give it back. Instead, every night she lay in her cot, the notebook secretly clutched in her hands under the blanket, fingertips brushing the engravings on the leather. *Tomorrow,* she promised herself every night. *Tomorrow I will walk up to him with it.*

Later that evening, after *iftar* dinner, all the kids rushed outside to play. Parwana, Masooma, and Saboor took turns on the swing that Saboor's father had suspended from a sturdy branch of the giant oak tree. Parwana took her turn, but Saboor kept forgetting to push her because he was busy telling another story. This time it was about the giant oak tree, which he said had magic powers. If you had a wish, he said, you had to kneel before the tree and whisper it. And if the tree agreed to grant it, it would shed exactly ten leaves upon your head.

When the swing slowed to a near stop, Parwana turned to tell Saboor to keep pushing but the words died in her throat. Saboor and Masooma were smiling at each other, and in Saboor's hand Parwana saw the notebook. *Her* notebook.

I found it in the house, Masooma said later. *Was it yours? I'll pay you back for it somehow, I promise. You don't mind, do you? I just thought it was perfect for him. For his stories. Did you see the look on him? Did you, Parwana?*

Parwana said no, she didn't mind, but inside she was crumpling. Over and over she pictured how her sister and Saboor had smiled at each other, the look they shared between them. Parwana might as well have winked out into thin air like a genie from one of Saboor's stories, so unaware had they been of her presence. It cut her to the bone. That night, on her cot, she cried very quietly.

By the time she and her sister were eleven, Parwana had developed a precocious understanding of the strange behavior of boys around girls they privately liked. She saw this especially as she and Masooma walked home from school. School was really the back room of the village mosque where, in addition to teaching Koran recitation, Mullah Shekib had taught every child in the village to read and write, to memorize poetry. Shadbagh was fortunate to have such a wise man for a *malik*, the girls' father told them. On the way home from these lessons, the twins often came across a group of boys sitting on a wall. As the girls passed, the boys sometimes heckled, sometimes threw pebbles. Parwana usually shouted back and answered their pebbles with rocks, while Masooma always pulled her elbow and told her in a sensible voice to walk faster, to not let them anger her. But she misunderstood. Parwana was angry not because they threw pebbles but because they threw them only at Masooma. Parwana knew: They made a show of the ribbing, and the bigger the show, the deeper their desire. She noticed the way their eyes ricocheted off her and trained themselves on Masooma, forlorn with wonder, helpless to pull away. She knew that behind their crass jokes and lascivious grins, they were terrified of Masooma.

Then, one day, one of them hurled not a pebble but a rock. It rolled to the sisters' feet. When Masooma picked it up, the boys snickered and elbowed one another. An elastic band held a sheet of paper wrapped around the rock. When they were at a safe distance, Masooma unrolled it. They both read the note.

I swear, since seeing Your face,
*   the whole world is fraud and fantasy.*
The garden is bewildered as to what is leaf or blossom.
The distracted birds can't distinguish the birdseed from the
*   snare.*

A Rumi poem, one from Mullah Shekib's teachings.

They're getting more sophisticated, Masooma said with a chuckle.

Below the poem, the boy had written *I want to marry you.* And, below that, he had scribbled this addendum: *I've got a cousin for your sister. He's a perfect match. They can graze my uncle's field together.*

Masooma tore the note in half. *Don't mind them, Parwana,* she said. *They're imbeciles.*

Cretins, Parwana agreed.

Such effort it took to plaster a grin on her face. The note was bad enough, but what really stung was Masooma's response. The boy hadn't explicitly addressed his note to either one of them, but Masooma had casually assumed that he'd intended the poem for her and the cousin for Parwana. For the first time, Parwana saw herself through her sister's eyes. She saw how her sister viewed her. Which was the same as how the rest of them did. It left her gutted, what Masooma said. It flattened her.

Besides, Masooma added with a shrug and a grin, *I'm already taken.*

Nabi has come for his monthly visit. He is the family's success story, perhaps the entire village's too, on account of his working in Kabul, his driving into Shadbagh in his employer's big shiny blue car with the gleaming eagle's-head hood ornament, everyone gathering to watch his arrival, the village kids hollering and running alongside the car.

"How are things?" he asks.

The three of them are inside the hut having tea and almonds. Nabi is very handsome, Parwana thinks, with his fine chiseled cheekbones, his hazel eyes, his sideburns, and the thick wall of black hair swept back from his forehead. He is dressed in his customary olive-colored suit that looks a size or so too big on him. Nabi is proud of the suit, Parwana knows, always tugging at the sleeves, straightening the lapel, pinching the crease of his pants, though he has never quite managed to eradicate its lingering whiff of burnt onions.

"Well, we had Queen Homaira over for tea and cookies yesterday," Masooma says. "She complimented our exquisite choice of décor." She smiles amiably at her brother, revealing her yellowing teeth, and Nabi laughs, looking down at his cup. Before he found work in Kabul, Nabi had helped Parwana care for their sister. Or he had tried for a while. But he couldn't do it. It was too much for him. Kabul was Nabi's escape. Parwana envies her brother, but she does not entirely begrudge him even if he does—she knows that there is more than an element of penance in the monthly cash that he brings her.

Masooma has brushed her hair and rimmed her eyes

with a dash of kohl as she always does when Nabi visits. Parwana knows that she does it only partially for his benefit and more for the fact that he is her tie to Kabul. In Masooma's mind, he connects her to glamour and luxury, to a city of cars and lights and fancy restaurants and royal palaces, regardless of how remote this link might be. Parwana remembers how, long ago, Masooma used to say to her that she was a city girl trapped in a village.

"What about you? Have you found yourself a wife yet?" Masooma asks playfully.

Nabi waves a hand and laughs her off, as he used to when their parents asked him the same question.

"So when are you going to show me around Kabul again, brother?" Masooma says.

Nabi had taken them to Kabul once, the year before. He had picked them up from Shadbagh and driven them to Kabul, up and down the streets of the city. He had shown them all the mosques, the shopping districts, the cinemas, the restaurants. He had pointed out to Masooma the domed Bagh-e-Bala Palace sitting on a hill overlooking the city. At the gardens of Babur, he had lifted Masooma from the front seat of the car and carried her in his arms to the site of the Mughal emperor's tomb. They had prayed there, the three of them, at the Shah Jahan Mosque, and then, at the edge of a blue-tiled pool, they had eaten the meal Nabi had packed for them. It had been perhaps the happiest day of Masooma's life since the accident, and for that Parwana was grateful to her older brother.

"Soon, *Inshallah*," Nabi says, tapping a finger against the cup.

"Would you mind adjusting this cushion under my knees, Nabi? Ah, that's much better. Thank you." Masooma sighs. "I loved Kabul. If I could, I'd march all the way there first thing tomorrow."

"Maybe one day," Nabi says.

"What, me walking?"

"No," he stammers, "I meant . . ." and then he grins when Masooma bursts out laughing.

Outside, Nabi passes Parwana the cash. He leans one shoulder against the wall and lights a cigarette. Masooma is inside, taking her afternoon nap.

"I saw Saboor earlier," he says, picking at his finger. "Terrible thing. He told me the baby's name. I forget now."

"Pari," Parwana says.

He nods. "I didn't ask, but he told me he's looking to marry again."

Parwana looks away, trying to pretend she doesn't care, but her heart is thumping in her ears. She feels a film of sweat blooming on her skin.

"Like I said, I didn't ask. Saboor was the one who brought it up. He pulled me aside. He pulled me aside and told me."

Parwana suspects that Nabi knows what she has carried with her for Saboor all these years. Masooma is her twin, but it is Nabi who has always understood her. But Parwana doesn't see why her brother is telling her this news. What good does it do? What Saboor needs is a woman unanchored, a woman who won't be held down, who is free to devote herself to him, to his boy, his newborn daughter.

Parwana's time is already consumed. Accounted for. Her whole life is.

"I'm sure he'll find someone," Parwana says.

Nabi nods. "I'll be by again next month." He crushes his cigarette underfoot and takes his leave.

When Parwana enters the hut, she is surprised to see Masooma awake. "I thought you were napping."

Masooma drags her gaze to the window, blinking slowly, tiredly.

When the girls were thirteen, they sometimes went to the crowded bazaars of nearby towns for their mother. The smell of freshly sprayed water rose from the unpaved street. The two of them strolled down the lanes, past stalls that sold hookahs, silk shawls, copper pots, old watches. Slaughtered chickens hung by their feet, tracing slow circles over hunks of lamb and beef.

In every corridor Parwana would see men's eyes snapping to attention when Masooma passed by. She saw their efforts to behave matter-of-factly, but their gazes lingered, helpless to tear away. If Masooma glanced in their direction, they looked idiotically privileged. They imagined they had shared a moment with her. She interrupted conversations midsentence, smokers mid-drag. She was the trembler of knees, the spiller of teacups.

Some days it was all too much for Masooma, as if she was almost ashamed, and she told Parwana she wanted to stay inside all day, wanted not to be looked at. On those days, Parwana thought it was as though, somewhere deep inside, her sister understood dimly that her beauty was a weapon. A loaded gun, with the barrel pointed at her own head. Most days, however, the attention seemed to please her. Most days, she relished her power to derail a man's thoughts with a single fleeting but strategic smile, to make tongues falter over words.

It blistered the eyes, beauty like hers.

And then there was Parwana, shuffling next to her, with her flat chest and sallow complexion. Her frizzy hair, her heavy, mournful face, and her thick wrists and masculine shoulders. A pathetic shadow, torn between her envy and the thrill of being seen with Masooma, sharing in the attention as a weed would, lapping up water meant for the lily upstream.

All her life, Parwana had made sure to avoid standing in front of a mirror with her sister. It robbed her of hope to see her face beside Masooma's, to see so plainly what she had been denied. But in public, every stranger's eye was a mirror. There was no escape.

She carries Masooma outside. The two of them sit on the charpoy Parwana has set up. She makes sure to stack cushions so Masooma can comfortably lean her back against the wall. The night is quiet but for the chirping crickets, and dark too, lit only by a few lanterns still shimmering in windows and by the papery white light of the three-quarter moon.

Parwana fills the hookah's vase with water. She takes two matchhead-sized portions of opium flakes with a pinch of tobacco and drops the mix into the hookah's bowl. She lights the coal on the metal screen and hands the hookah to her sister. Masooma takes a deep puff from the hose, reclines against the cushions, and asks if she can rest her legs on Parwana's lap. Parwana reaches down and lifts the limp legs to rest across her own.

When she smokes, Masooma's face slackens. Her lids droop. Her head tilts unsteadily to the side and her voice takes on a sluggish, distant quality. A whisper of a smile forms on the corners of her mouth, whimsical, indolent, complacent rather than content. They say little to each other when Masooma is like this. Parwana listens to the breeze, to the water gurgling in the hookah. She watches the stars and the smoke drifting over her. The silence is pleasant, and neither she nor Masooma feel an urge to fill it with needless words.

Until Masooma says, "Will you do something for me?"

Parwana looks at her.

"I want you to take me to Kabul." Masooma exhales slowly, the smoke twirling, curling, morphing into shapes with each blink of the eye.

"Are you serious?"

"I want to see Darulaman Palace. We didn't get a chance to last time. Maybe go visit Babur's tomb again."

Parwana leans forward to decipher Masooma's expression.

She searches for a hint of playfulness, but in the moonlight she catches only the calm, unblinking glitter of her sister's eyes.

"It's a two-day walk at least. Probably three."

"Imagine Nabi's face when we surprise him at his door."

"We don't even know where he lives."

Masooma listlessly sweeps her hand. "He already told us which neighborhood. We'll knock on some doors and ask. It's not that difficult."

"How would we get there, Masooma, in your condition?"

Masooma pulls the hookah hose from her lips. "When you were out working today, Mullah Shekib came by, and I spoke to him a long time. I told him we were going to Kabul for a few days. Just you and I. He gave me his blessing in the end. Also his mule. So you see, it's all arranged."

"You are insane," Parwana says.

"Well, it's what I want. It's my wish."

Parwana sits back against the wall, shaking her head. Her gaze drifts upward into the cloud-mottled darkness.

"I'm so bored I'm dying, Parwana."

Parwana empties her chest of a sigh and looks at her sister.

Masooma brings the hose to her lips. "Please. Don't deny me."

One early morning, when the sisters were seventeen, they sat on a branch high up the oak tree, their feet dangling.

Saboor's going to ask me! Masooma had said this in a high-pitched whisper.

Ask you? Parwana said, not understanding, at least not immediately.

Well, not him, of course. Masooma laughed into her palm. *Of course not. His father will be doing the asking.*

Now Parwana understood. Her heart sank to her feet. *How do you know?* she said through numb lips.

Masooma began to speak, words pouring from her mouth at a frenzied pace, but Parwana hardly heard any of it. She was picturing instead her sister's wedding to Saboor. Children in new clothes, carrying henna baskets overflowing with flowers, trailed by *shahnai* and *dohol* players. Saboor, opening Masooma's fist, placing the henna in her palm, tying it with a white ribbon. The saying of prayers, the blessing of the union. The offering of gifts. The two of them gazing at each other beneath a veil embroidered with gold thread, feeding each other a spoonful of sweet sherbet and *malida.*

And she, Parwana, would be there among the guests to watch this unfold. She would be expected to smile, to clap, to be happy, even as her heart splintered and cracked.

A wind swept through the tree, made the branches around them shake and the leaves rattle. Parwana had to steady herself.

Masooma had stopped talking. She was grinning, biting her lower lip. *You asked how I know that he's going to ask. I'll tell you. No. I'll show you.*

She turned from Parwana and reached into her pocket.

And then the part that Masooma knew nothing about. While her sister was facing away, searching her pocket, Parwana planted the heels of her hands on the branch, lifted her bottom, and let it drop. The branch shook. Masooma gasped and lost her balance. Her arms flailed wildly. She tipped forward. Parwana watched her own hands move. What they did was not really *push*, but there *was* contact between Masooma's back and the pads of Parwana's fingertips and there was a brief moment of subtle shoving. But it lasted barely an instant before Parwana was reaching for her sister, for the hem of her shirt, before Masooma was calling her name in panic and Parwana hers. Parwana grabbed the shirt, and it looked for just a moment as though she might have saved Masooma. But then the cloth ripped as it slipped from her grip.

Masooma fell from the tree. It seemed to take forever, the fall. Her torso slamming into branches on the way down, startling birds and shaking leaves free, her body spinning, bouncing, snapping smaller branches, until a low, thick branch, the one from which the swing was suspended, caught her lower back with a sick, audible crunch. She folded backward, nearly in half.

A few minutes later, a circle had formed around her. Nabi and the girls' father crying over Masooma, trying to shake her awake. Faces peering down. Someone took her hand. It was still closed into a tight fist. When they uncurled the fingers, they found exactly ten crumbled little leaves in her palm.

Masooma says, her voice shaking a bit, "You have to do it now. If you wait until morning, you'll lose heart."

All around them, beyond the dim glow of the fire Parwana has stoked from shrubs and brittle-looking weeds, is the desolate, endless expanse of sand and mountains swallowed up by the dark. For nearly two days they have traveled through the scrubby terrain, heading toward Kabul, Parwana walking alongside the mule, Masooma strapped to the saddle, Parwana holding her hand. They have trudged along steep paths that curved and dipped and wound back and forth across rocky ridges, the ground at their feet dotted with ocher- and rust-colored weeds, etched with long spidery cracks creeping every which way.

Parwana stands near the fire now, looking at Masooma, who is a horizontal blanketed mound on the other side of the flames.

"What about Kabul?" Parwana says.

"Oh, you're supposed to be the smart one."

Parwana says, "You can't ask me to do this."

"I'm tired, Parwana. It's not a life, what I have. My existence is a punishment to us both."

"Let's just go back," Parwana says, her throat beginning to close. "I can't do this. I can't let you go."

"You're not." Masooma is crying now. "I'm letting *you* go. I am releasing you."

Parwana thinks of a long-ago night, Masooma up on the swing, she pushing her. She had watched as Masooma had straightened her legs and tipped her head all the way

77

back at the peak of each upward swing, the long trails of her hair flapping like sheets on a clothesline. She remembers all the little dolls they had coaxed out of corn husks together, dressing them in wedding gowns made of shreds of old cloth.

"Tell me something, sister."

Parwana blinks back the tears that are blurring her vision now and wipes her nose with the back of her hand.

"His boy, Abdullah. And the baby girl. Pari. You think you could love them as your own?"

"Masooma."

"Could you?"

"I could try," Parwana says.

"Good. Then marry Saboor. Look after his children. Have your own."

"He loved you. He doesn't love me."

"He will, given time."

"This is all my doing," Parwana says. "My fault. All of it."

"I don't know what that means and I don't want to. At this point, this is the only thing I want. People will understand, Parwana. Mullah Shekib will have told them. He'll tell them that he gave me his blessing for this."

Parwana raises her face to the darkened sky.

"Be happy, Parwana, please be happy. Do it for me."

Parwana feels herself standing on the brink of telling her everything, telling Masooma how wrong she is, how little she knows the sister with whom she shared the womb, how for years now Parwana's life has been one long unspoken apology. But to what end? Her own relief once again at

Masooma's expense? She bites down the words. She has inflicted enough pain on her sister.

"I want to smoke now," Masooma says.

Parwana begins to protest, but Masooma cuts her off. "It's time," she says, harder now, with finality.

From the bag slung around the saddle's tip, Parwana fetches the hookah. With trembling hands, she begins to prepare the usual mixture in the hookah's bowl.

"More," Masooma says. "Put in a lot more."

Sniffling, her cheeks wet, Parwana adds another pinch, then another, and yet more again. She lights the coal and places the hookah next to her sister.

"Now," Masooma says, the orange glow of the flames shimmering on her cheeks, in her eyes, "if you ever loved me, Parwana, if you were ever my true sister, then leave. No kisses. No good-byes. Don't make me beg."

Parwana begins to say something, but Masooma makes a pained, choking sound and rolls her head away.

Parwana slowly rises to her feet. She walks to the mule and tightens the saddle. She grabs the reins to the animal. She suddenly realizes that she may not know how to live without Masooma. She doesn't know if she can. How will she bear the days when Masooma's absence feels like a far heavier burden than her presence ever had? How will she learn to tread around the edges of the big gaping hole where Masooma had once been?

Have heart, she almost hears Masooma saying.

Parwana pulls the reins, turns the mule around, and begins to walk.

She walks, slicing the dark, as a cool night wind rips across her face. She keeps her head down. She turns around once only, later. Through the moisture in her eyes, the campfire is a distant, dim, tiny blur of yellow. She pictures her twin sister lying by the fire, alone in the dark. Soon, the fire will die, and Masooma will be cold. Her instinct is to go back, to cover her sister with a blanket and slip in next to her.

Parwana makes herself wheel around and resume walking once more.

And that is when she hears something. A faraway, muffled sound, like wailing. Parwana stops in her tracks. She tilts her head and hears it again. Her heart begins to ram in her chest. She wonders, with dread, if it's Masooma calling her back, having had a change of heart. Or maybe it is nothing but a jackal or a desert fox howling somewhere in the dark. Parwana can't be sure. She thinks it might be the wind.

Don't leave me, sister. Come back.

The only way to know for sure is to go back the way she had come and Parwana begins to do just that; she turns around and takes a few steps in Masooma's direction. Then she stops. Masooma was right. If she goes back now, she will not have the courage to do it when the sun rises. She will lose heart and end up staying. She will stay forever. This is her only chance.

Parwana shuts her eyes. The wind makes the scarf flap against her face.

No one has to know. No one would. It would be her secret, one she would share with the mountains only. The question is whether it is a secret she can live with, and Parwana thinks she knows the answer. She has lived with secrets all her life.

She hears the wailing again in the distance.

Everyone loved you, Masooma.

No one me.

And why, sister? What had I done?

Parwana stands motionless in the dark for a long time.

At last, she makes her choice. She turns around, drops her head, and walks toward a horizon she cannot see. After that, she does not look back anymore. She knows that if she does, she will weaken. She will lose what resolve she has because she will see an old bicycle speeding down a hill, bouncing on rocks and gravel, the metal pounding both their rears, clouds of dust kicked up with each sudden skid. She sits on the frame, and Masooma is the one on the saddle, she is the one who takes the hairpin turns at full speed, dropping the bike into a deep lean. But Parwana is not afraid. She knows that her sister will not send her flying over the handlebars, that she will not hurt her. The world melts into a whirligig blur of excitement, and the wind whooshes in their ears, and Parwana looks over her shoulder at her sister and her sister looks back, and they laugh together as stray dogs give chase.

Parwana keeps marching toward her new life. She keeps walking, the darkness around her like a mother's womb, and when it lifts, when she looks up in the dawn haze and catches a band of pale light from the east striking the side of a boulder, it feels like being born.

Four

In the Name of Allah the Most Beneficent, the Most
Merciful,

I know that I will be gone when you read this letter,
Mr. Markos, for when I gave it to you I requested that you
not open it until after my death. Let me state now what a
pleasure it has been to know you over the last seven years,
Mr. Markos. As I write this, I think fondly of our yearly
ritual of planting tomatoes in the garden, your morning
visits to my small quarters for tea and pleasantry, our
impromptu trading of Farsi and English lessons. I thank
you for your friendship, your thoughtfulness, and for the
work that you have undertaken in this country, and I trust
that you will extend my gratitude to your kindhearted
colleagues as well, especially to my friend Ms. Amra
Ademovic, who has such capacity for compassion, and to
her brave and lovely daughter, Roshi.

I should say that I intend this letter not just for you, Mr.

Markos, but for another as well, to whom I hope you will pass it on, as I shall explain later. Forgive me, then, if I repeat a few things you may already know. I include them out of necessity, for her benefit. As you will see, this letter contains more than an element of confession, Mr. Markos, but there are also pragmatic matters that prompt this writing. For those, I fear I will call upon your assistance, my friend.

I have thought long on where to begin this story. No easy task, this, for a man who must be in his mid-eighties. My exact age is a mystery to me, as it is to many Afghans of my generation, but I am confident in my approximation because I recall quite vividly a fistfight with my friend, and later to be brother-in-law, Saboor, on the day we heard that Nāder Shah had been shot and killed, and that Nāder Shah's son, young Zahir, had ascended to the throne. That was 1933. I could begin there, I suppose. Or somewhere else. A story is like a moving train: no matter where you hop onboard, you are bound to reach your destination sooner or later. But I suppose I ought to begin this tale with the same thing that ends it. Yes, I think it stands to reason that I bookend this account with Nila Wahdati.

I met her in 1949, the year she married Mr. Wahdati. At the time, I had already been working for Mr. Suleiman Wahdati for two years, having moved to Kabul from Shadbagh, the village where I was born, back in 1946—I had worked for a year in another household in the same neighborhood. The circumstances of my departure from Shadbagh are not something I am proud of, Mr. Markos. Consider it the first of my confessions, then, when I say that I felt stifled by the life I had in the village with my sisters, one of whom was an invalid. Not that it absolves me, but I was a young man, Mr. Markos, eager to take on the world, full of dreams, modest and vague as they may have been, and I pictured my youth ebbing away, my prospects increasingly truncated. So I left. To help provide for my sisters, yes, that is true. But also to escape.

Since I was a full-time worker for Mr. Wahdati, I lived at his residence full-time as well. In those days, the house bore little resemblance to the lamentable state in which you found it when you arrived in Kabul in 2002, Mr. Markos. It was a beautiful, glorious place. The house shone sparkling white in those days, as if sheathed with diamonds. The front gates opened onto a wide asphalt driveway. One entered into a high-ceilinged foyer decorated with tall ceramic vases and a circular mirror framed in carved walnut, precisely the spot where you for a while hung the old homemade-camera photo of your childhood friend at the beach. The marble floor of the living room glistened and was partly covered by a dark red Turkoman carpet. The carpet is gone now, as are the leather sofas, the hand-crafted coffee table, the lapis chess set, the tall mahogany cabinet. Little of the grand furniture has survived, and I am afraid it is not in the shape it once was.

The first time I entered the stone-tiled kitchen, my mouth fell wide open. I thought it had been built large enough to feed all of my home village of Shadbagh. I had a six-burner stove, a refrigerator, a toaster, and an abundance of pots, pans, knives, and appliances at my disposal. The bathrooms, all four of them, had intricately carved marble tiles and porcelain sinks. And those square holes in your bathroom counter upstairs, Mr. Markos? They were once filled with lapis.

Then there was the backyard. You must one day sit in your office upstairs, Mr. Markos, look down on the garden, and try to picture it as it was. One entered it through a semilunar veranda bordered by a railing sheathed with green vines. The lawn in those days was lush and green, dotted with beds of flowers—jasmine, sweetbriar, geraniums, tulips—and bordered by two rows of fruit trees. A man could lie beneath one of the cherry trees, Mr. Markos, close his eyes and listen to the breeze squeezing through the leaves and think that there wasn't on earth a finer place to live.

My own living space was a shack in the back of the yard. It had a window, clean walls with white paint, and provided enough space to accommodate an unmarried young man his meager needs. I had a bed, a desk and a chair, and enough room to unroll my prayer rug five times a day. It suited me just fine then and it suits me fine now.

I cooked for Mr. Wahdati, a skill I had picked up first from observing my late mother and later from an elderly Uzbek cook who worked at a household in Kabul where I had served for a year as his help. I was also, and quite happily, Mr. Wahdati's chauffeur. He owned a mid-1940s model

Chevrolet, blue with a tan top, matching blue vinyl seats, and chrome wheels, a handsome car that drew lingering looks wherever we went. He allowed me to drive because I had proven myself to be a prudent and skilled driver, and, besides, he was the rare breed of man who did not enjoy the act of operating a car.

Please do not think I am boasting, Mr. Markos, when I say I was a good servant. Through careful observation, I had familiarized myself with Mr. Wahdati's likes and dislikes, his quirks, his peeves. I had come to know his habits and rituals well. For instance, every morning after breakfast he liked to go for a stroll. He disliked walking alone, however, and thus I was expected to accompany him. I abided by this wish, of course, though I did not see the point of my presence. He hardly said a word to me in the course of these walks and seemed forever lost in his own thoughts. He walked briskly, hands clamped behind his back, nodding at passersby, the heels of his well-polished leather loafers clicking against the pavement. And because his long legs made strides I could not match, I was always falling behind and forced to catch up. The rest of the day, he mostly retreated to his study upstairs, reading or playing a game of chess against himself. He loved to draw—though I could not attest to his skills, at least not then, because he never shared his artwork with me—and I would often catch him up in the study, by the window, or on the veranda, his brow furrowed in concentration, his charcoal pencil looping and circling over the sketch pad.

I drove him around the city every few days. He went to

see his mother once a week. There were also family gatherings. And though Mr. Wahdati avoided most of them, he did attend on occasion, and so I would drive him there, to funerals, birthday parties, weddings. I drove him monthly to an art supply store, where he restocked his pastel pencils, his charcoal, and his erasers and sharpeners and sketchbooks. Sometimes, he liked to sit in the backseat and just go for a drive. I would say, *Where to, Sahib?* and he would shrug, and I would say, *Very well, Sahib,* and I would shift into gear and off we would go. I would drive us around the city, for hours, without aim or purpose, from one neighborhood to another, alongside the Kabul River, up to Bala Hissar, sometimes out to the Darulaman Palace. Some days, I drove us out of Kabul and up to Ghargha Lake, where I would park near the banks of the water. I would turn off the engine, and Mr. Wahdati would sit perfectly still in the backseat, not saying a word to me, seemingly content enough to just roll down the window and look at the birds darting from tree to tree, and the streaks of sunlight that struck the lake and scattered into a thousand tiny bobbing specks on the water. I would gaze at him in the rearview mirror and he looked to me like the most lonesome person on earth.

Once a month, Mr. Wahdati, quite generously, let me borrow his car, and I would drive down to Shadbagh, my native village, to visit my sister Parwana and her husband, Saboor. Whenever I drove into the village, I would be greeted by hordes of hollering children, who would scamper alongside the car, slapping the fender, tapping at the window. Some of the little runts would even try to climb atop the roof, and I would have to shoo them away for fear that they would scratch the paint or cause a dent in the fender.

Look at you, Nabi, Saboor said to me. *You are a celebrity.*

Because his children, Abdullah and Pari, had lost their natural mother (Parwana was their stepmother), I always tried to be attentive to them, especially to the older boy, who most seemed to need it. I offered to take him alone for rides in the car, though he always insisted on bringing his baby sister, holding her tightly in his lap, as we circled the road around Shadbagh. I let him work the wipers, honk the horn. I showed him how to switch the headlights from dim to full.

After all the fuss about the car died down, I would sit for tea with my sister and Saboor and I would tell them about my life in Kabul. I took care not to say too much about Mr. Wahdati. I was, in truth, quite fond of him, for he treated me well, and speaking of him behind his back seemed to me like a betrayal. If I had been a less discreet employee, I would have told them that Suleiman Wahdati was a mystifying creature to me, a man seemingly satisfied with living the rest of his days off the wealth of his inheritance, a man with no profession, no apparent passion, and apparently no impulse to leave behind something of himself in this world. I would have told them that he lived a life lacking in purpose or direction. Like those aimless rides I took him on. A life lived from the backseat, observed as it blurred by. An indifferent life.

This is what I would have said, but I did not. And a good thing I did not. For how wrong I would have been.

One day, Mr. Wahdati came into the yard wearing a handsome pin-striped suit, one I had never seen on him before, and requested that I drive him to an affluent neighborhood of the city. When we arrived, he instructed me to park on the street outside a beautiful high-walled house, and I watched him ring the bell at the gates and enter when a servant answered. The house was huge, bigger than Mr. Wahdati's, and even more beautiful. Tall, slender cypresses adorned the driveway, along with a densely packed array of bushes of a flower I did not recognize. The backyard was at least twice the size of Mr. Wahdati's, and the walls stood tall enough that if a man climbed on the shoulders of another, he still could hardly steal a peek. This was wealth of another magnitude, I recognized.

It was a bright early-summer day, and the sky was brilliant with sunshine. Warm air wafted in through the windows, which I had rolled down. Though a chauffeur's job is to drive, he actually spends most of his time waiting. Waiting outside stores, engine idling; waiting outside a wedding hall, listening to the muffled sound of the music. To pass the time that day, I played a few games of cards. When I tired of cards, I stepped out of the car and took a few steps in one direction, then the other. I sat inside once more, thinking I might steal a nap before Mr. Wahdati returned.

It was then that the front gates opened and a black-haired young woman emerged. She wore sunglasses and a short-sleeved tangerine-colored dress that fell short of the knees. Her legs were bare, and so were her feet. I did not know whether she had noticed me sitting in the car, and, if she had, she offered no indication. She rested the heel of one foot against the wall behind her and, when she did, the hem of the dress pulled up slightly and thus revealed a bit of the thigh beneath. I felt a burning spread down from my cheeks to my neck.

Allow me to make another confession here, Mr. Markos, one of a somewhat distasteful nature, leaving little room for elegant handling. At the time, I must have been in my late twenties, a young man at the prime of his desires for a woman's company. Unlike many of the men I grew up with in my village—young men who had never seen the bare thigh of a grown woman and married, in part, for the license to at last cast their gaze upon such a sight—I did have some experience. I had found in Kabul, and on occasion visited, establishments where a young man's needs could be addressed with both discretion and convenience. I mention this only to make the point that no whore I had ever lain with could compare with the beautiful, graceful creature who had just stepped out of the big house.

Leaning against the wall, she lit a cigarette and smoked without hurry and with bewitching grace, holding it at the very tip of two fingers and cupping her hand before her mouth each time she raised it to her lips. I watched with rapt attention. The way her hand bent at its slender wrist reminded me of an illustration I had once seen in a glossy book of poems of a long-lashed woman with flowing dark hair lying with her lover in a garden, offering him a cup of wine with her pale delicate fingers. At one point, something seemed to catch the woman's attention up the street in the opposite direction, and I used the brief chance to quickly finger-brush my hair, which was beginning to mat down in the heat. When she turned back, I froze once more. She took a few more puffs, crushed the cigarette against the wall, and sauntered back inside.

At last, I could breathe.

That night, Mr. Wahdati called me into the living room and said, "I have news, Nabi. I am getting married."

It seemed I had overestimated his fondness for solitude after all.

News of the engagement spread swiftly. And so did rumors. I heard them from the other workers who came and went through Mr. Wahdati's house. The most vocal of these was Zahid, a gardener who came in three days a week to maintain the lawn and trim the trees and bushes, an unpleasant fellow with the repulsive habit of flicking his tongue after each sentence, a tongue with which he cast rumors as offhandedly as he tossed fistfuls of fertilizer. He was part of a group of lifelong laborers who, like me, worked in the neighborhood as cooks, gardeners, and errand men. One or two nights a week, after the workday was over, they squeezed into my shack for after-dinner tea. I do not recall how this ritual started, but, once it did, I was powerless to stop it, wary of seeming rude and inhospitable, or, worse, of appearing to think myself superior to my own kind.

Over tea one night, Zahid told the other men that Mr. Wahdati's family did not approve of the marriage because of his bride-to-be's poor character. He said it was well known in Kabul that she had no *nang* and *namoos*, no honor, and that though she was only twenty she had already been "ridden all over town" like Mr. Wahdati's car. Worst of all, he said, not only had she made no attempt to deny these allegations, she wrote poems about them. A murmur of disapproval spread through the room when he said this. One of the men remarked that in his village they would have slit her throat by now.

That was when I rose and told them that I had heard enough. I berated them for gossiping like a sewing circle of old women and reminded them that without people like Mr. Wahdati the likes of us would be back in our villages collecting cow dung. *Where is your loyalty, your respect?* I demanded.

A brief moment of quiet passed during which I thought I had made an impression on the dullards and then laughter broke out. Zahid said I was an ass-licker, and perhaps the soon-to-be mistress of the house would ink a poem and call it "Ode to Nabi, the Licker of Many Asses." I stomped indignantly out of the shack to an uproar of cackles.

But I did not stray too far. Their gossip, by turns, revolted and fascinated me. And despite my show of righteousness, for all my talk of propriety and discretion, I stayed within earshot. I did not want to miss a single lurid detail.

The engagement lasted only days and culminated not in a big ceremony with live singers and dancers and merriment all around but with a brief visit by a mullah, a witness, and the scribbling of two signatures across a sheet of paper. And with that, less than two weeks after I had laid eyes on her for the first time, Mrs. Wahdati moved into the house.

Allow me a brief pause here, Mr. Markos, to say that I will from here on refer to Mr. Wahdati's wife as Nila. Needless to say, this is a liberty I was not allowed back then and one I would not have accepted even if it had been offered to me. I referred to her always as Bibi Sahib, with the deference expected of me. But for the purposes of this letter, I will dispense with etiquette and refer to her the way I always *thought* of her.

Now, I knew from the start that the marriage was an unhappy one. Rarely did I see a tender look pass between the couple or hear an affectionate word uttered. They were two people occupying the same house whose paths rarely seemed to intersect at all.

In the mornings, I served Mr. Wahdati his customary breakfast—a piece of toasted *naan*, half a cup of walnuts, green tea with a sprinkle of cardamom and no sugar, and a single boiled egg. He liked the yolk to run just so when he punctured the egg, and my initial failures to master this particular consistency had proved a source of considerable anxiety on my part. While I accompanied Mr. Wahdati on his daily morning walk, Nila slept in, often until noon or even later. By the time she rose, I was all but ready to serve Mr. Wahdati his lunch.

All morning, as I tended to my chores, I ached for the moment when Nila would push the screen door that opened from the living room out onto the veranda. I would play games in my head, guessing at her appearance that particular day. Would her hair be up, I wondered, tied in a bun at the back of her neck, or would I see it loose, tumbling down over her shoulders? Would she wear sunglasses? Would she opt for sandals? Would she choose the blue silk robe with the belt or the magenta one with the big round buttons?

When she made her entrance at last, I would busy myself in the yard, pretending the hood of the car needed wiping, or else I would find a sweetbriar bush to water, but the whole time I watched. I watched when she pushed up her sunglasses to rub her eyes, or when she removed the elastic band from her hair and threw back her head to let the dark lustrous curls fall loose, and I watched when she sat with her chin resting on her knees, staring into the yard, taking languid drags of her cigarette, or when she crossed her legs and bobbed one foot up and down, a gesture that suggested to me boredom or restlessness or perhaps heedless mischief barely held in check.

Mr. Wahdati was, on occasion, at her side, but often not. He spent most of his days as he had before, reading in his upstairs study, doing his sketches, his daily routines more or less unaltered by the fact of marriage. Nila wrote most days, either in the living room or else on the veranda, pencil in hand, sheets of paper spilling from her lap, and always the cigarettes. At night, I served them dinner, and they each received the meal in pointed silence, gaze lowered to the platter of rice, the quiet broken only by a muttered *Thank you* and the tinkling of spoon and fork against china.

Once or twice a week, I had to drive Nila when she needed a pack of cigarettes or a fresh set of pens, a new notepad, makeup. If I knew ahead of time that I would be driving her, I always made sure to comb my hair and brush my teeth. I washed my face, rubbed a sliced lemon against my fingers to rid them of the scent of onions, patted the dust off my suit, and polished my shoes. The suit, which was olive colored, was in fact a hand-me-down from Mr. Wahdati, and I hoped that he hadn't told this to Nila—though I suspected he may have. Not out of malice, but because people in Mr. Wahdati's position often cannot appreciate how small, trivial things like this could bring shame to a man like me. Sometimes, I even wore the lambskin cap that had belonged to my late father. I would stand there before the mirror, tilting the cap this way and that on my head, so absorbed in the act of rendering myself presentable to Nila that if a wasp had landed on my nose it would have had to sting me to make its presence known.

Once we were on the road, I looked for minor detours to our destination, if possible, detours designed to prolong the trip by a minute—or maybe two, but no more lest she grow suspicious—and thereby extend my time with her. I drove with both hands clenching the wheel, and my eyes firmly on the road. I exercised rigid self-control and did not look at her in the rearview mirror, doing so only if she addressed me. I contented myself with the mere fact of her presence in the backseat, with breathing in her many scents—expensive soap, lotion, perfume, chewing gum, cigarette smoke. That, most days, was sufficient to lend wings to my spirits.

It was in the car that we had our first conversation. Our first *real* conversation, that is, discounting myriad times she had asked me to fetch this or carry that. I was taking her to a pharmacy to pick up medicine, and she said, "What is it like, Nabi, your village? What is it called again?"

"Shadbagh, Bibi Sahib."

"Shadbagh, yes. What is it like? Tell me."

"There isn't much to say, Bibi Sahib. It is a village like any other."

"Oh, surely there is some distinguishing thing."

I stayed calm in my appearance, but I was frantic inside, desperate to retrieve something, some clever oddity, that might be of interest to her, that might amuse her. It was no use. What could a man like me, a villager, a small man with a small life, possibly have to say that would capture the fancy of a woman like her?

"The grapes are excellent," I said, and no sooner had I uttered the words than I wished to slap my own face. *Grapes?*

"Are they," she said flatly.

"Very sweet indeed."

"Ah."

I was dying a thousand deaths inside. I felt moisture beginning to form under my arms.

"There is one particular grape," I said from a suddenly dry mouth. "They say it grows only in Shadbagh. It is very brittle, you see, very fragile. If you try to grow it in any other place, even the next village over, it will wither and die. It will perish. It dies of sadness, people in Shadbagh say, but, of course, that is not true. It's a matter of soil and water. But that is what they say, Bibi Sahib. Sadness."

"That's really lovely, Nabi."

I chanced a quick glance at the rearview mirror and saw

that she was looking out her window, but I also found, to my great relief, the corners of her mouth curled up just so, in a shadow of a smile. Heartened now, I heard myself say, "May I tell you another story, Bibi Sahib?"

"By all means." The lighter clicked, and smoke drifted toward me from the backseat.

"Well, we have a mullah in Shadbagh. All villages have a mullah, of course. Ours is named Mullah Shekib, and he is full of stories. How many he knows, I could not tell you. But one thing he always told us was this: that if you look at any Muslim's palms, no matter where in the world, you will see something quite astonishing. They all have the same lines. Meaning what? Meaning that the lines on a Muslim's left hand make the Arabic number eighty-one, and the ones on the right the number eighteen. Subtract eighteen from eighty-one and what do you get? You get sixty-three. The Prophet's age when he died, peace be upon him."

I heard a low chuckle from the backseat.

"Now, one day a traveler was passing through, and, of course, he sat with Mullah Shekib for a meal that evening, as is custom. The traveler heard this story and he thought about it, and then he said, 'But, Mullah Sahib, with all due respect, I met a Jew once and I swear his palms bore the very same lines. How do you explain it?' And Mullah said, 'Then the Jew was a Muslim at heart.'"

Her sudden outburst of laughter bewitched me for the rest of the day. It was as though it—God forgive me for this blasphemy—had descended down on me from Heaven itself, the garden of the righteous, as the book says, where rivers flow beneath, and perpetual are the fruits and the shade therein.

Understand that it wasn't merely her beauty, Mr. Markos, that had me so spellbound, though that alone might have been enough. I had never in my life encountered a young woman like Nila. Everything she did—the way she spoke, the way she walked, dressed, smiled—was a novelty to me. Nila pushed against every single notion I had ever had of how a woman was to behave, a trait that I knew met with the stout disapproval of people like Zahid—and surely Saboor too, and every man in my village, and all the women—but to me it only added to her already enormous allure and mystery.

And so her laughter still rang in my ears as I went about my work that day, and later, when the other workers came over for tea, I grinned and muted their cackles with the sweet tinkle of her laughter, and I prided myself on knowing that my clever story had given her a bit of reprieve from the discontent of her marriage. She was an extraordinary woman, and I went to bed that night feeling like I was perhaps more than ordinary myself. This was the effect she had on me.

Soon, we were conversing daily, Nila and I, usually in the late morning when she sat sipping coffee on the veranda. I would saunter over under the pretense of some task or other and there I was, leaning against a shovel, or tending to a cup of green tea, speaking to her. I felt privileged that she had chosen me. I was not the only servant, after all; I have already mentioned that unscrupulous toad Zahid, and there was a jowly-faced Hazara woman who came twice a week to wash laundry. But it was me she turned to. I was the only one, I believed, including her own husband, with whom her loneliness lifted. She usually did most of the talking, which suited me well; I was happy enough to be the vessel into which she poured her stories. She told me, for instance, of a hunting trip to Jalalabad she had taken with her father and how she had been haunted for weeks by nightmares of dead deer with glassy eyes. She said she had gone with her mother to France when she was a child, before the Second World War. To get there, she had taken both a train and a ship. She described to me how she had felt the jostling of the train wheels in her ribs. And she remembered well the curtains that hung from hooks and the separated compartments, and the rhythmic puff and hiss of the steam engine. She told me of the six weeks she had spent the year before in India with her father when she had been very ill.

Now and then, when she turned to tap ash into a saucer, I stole a quick glance at the red polish on her toenails, at the gold-tinged sheen of her shaved calves, the high arch of her foot, and always at her full, perfectly shaped breasts. There were men walking this earth, I marveled, who had touched those breasts and kissed them as they had made love to her. What was left to do in life once you had done that? Where did a man go next once he'd stood at the world's summit? It was only with a great act of will that I would snap my eyes back to a safe spot when she turned to face me.

As she grew more comfortable, she registered with me, during these morning chats, complaints about Mr. Wahdati. She said, one day, that she found him aloof and often arrogant.

"He has been most generous to me," I said.

She flapped one hand dismissively. "Please, Nabi. You don't have to do that."

Politely, I turned my gaze downward. What she said was not entirely untrue. Mr. Wahdati did have, for instance, a habit of correcting my manner of speech with an air of superiority that could be interpreted, perhaps not wrongly, as arrogance. Sometimes I entered the room, placed a platter of sweets before him, refreshed his tea, wiped his crumbs off the table, and he would no more acknowledge me than he would a fly crawling up the screen door, shrinking me into insignificance without even lifting his eyes. In the end, though, this made for a minor quibble, given that I knew people living in the same neighborhood—people I had worked for—who beat their servants with sticks and belts.

"He has no sense of fun or adventure," she said, listlessly stirring her coffee. "Suleiman is a brooding old man trapped in a younger man's body."

I was a little startled by her offhand candor. "It is true that Mr. Wahdati is uniquely comfortable with solitude," I said, opting for cautious diplomacy.

"Maybe he should live with his mother. What do you think, Nabi? They make a good match, I tell you."

Mr. Wahdati's mother was a heavy, rather pompous woman who lived in another part of town, with the obligatory team of servants and her two beloved dogs. These dogs she doted on and treated not as equals to her servants but as superiors, and by several ranks at that. They were small, hairless, hideous creatures, easily startled, full of anxiety, and prone to a most grating high-pitched bark. I despised them, for no sooner would I enter the house than they would hop on my legs and foolishly try to climb them.

It *was* clear to me that every time I took Nila and Mr. Wahdati to the old woman's house, the air in the backseat would be heavy with tension, and I would know from the pained furrow on Nila's brow that they had quarreled. I remember that when my parents fought, they did not stop until a clear victor had been declared. It was their way of sealing off unpleasantness, to caulk it with a verdict, keep it from leaking into the normalcy of the next day. Not so with the Wahdatis. Their fights didn't so much end as dissipate, like a drop of ink in a bowl of water, with a residual taint that lingered.

It did not take an act of intellectual acrobatics to surmise that the old woman had not approved of the union and that Nila knew it.

As we carried on with these conversations, Nila and I, one question about her bubbled up again and again in my head. Why had she married Mr. Wahdati? I lacked the courage to ask. Such trespass of propriety was beyond me by nature. I could only infer that for some people, particularly women, marriage—even an unhappy one such as this—is an escape from even greater unhappiness.

One day, in the fall of 1950, Nila summoned me.

"I want you to take me to Shadbagh," she said. She said she wanted to meet my family, see where I came from. She said I had served her meals and chauffeured her around Kabul for a year now and she knew scarcely a thing about me. Her request confounded me, to say the least, as it was unusual for someone of her standing to ask to be taken some distance to meet the family of a servant. I was also, in equal measure, buoyed that Nila had taken such keen interest in me and apprehensive, for I anticipated my discomfort—and, yes, my shame—when I showed her the poverty into which I had been born.

We set off on an overcast morning. She wore high heels and a peach sleeveless dress, but I didn't deem it my place to advise her otherwise. On the way, she asked questions about the village, the people I knew, my sister and Saboor, their children.

"Tell me their names."

"Well," I said, "there is Abdullah, who is nearly nine. His birth mother died last year, so he is my sister Parwana's stepson. His sister, Pari, is almost two. Parwana gave birth to a baby boy this past winter—Omar, his name was—but he died when he was two weeks old."

"What happened?"

"Winter, Bibi Sahib. It descends on these villages and takes a random child or two every year. You can only hope it will bypass your home."

"God," she muttered.

"On a happier note," I said, "my sister is expecting again."

At the village, we were greeted by the usual throng of barefoot children rushing the car, though once Nila emerged from the backseat the children grew quiet and pulled back, perhaps out of fear that she may chide them. But Nila displayed great patience and kindness. She knelt down and smiled, spoke to each of them, shook their hands, stroked their grubby cheeks, tousled their unwashed hair. To my embarrassment, people were gathering for a view of her. There was Baitullah, a childhood friend of mine, looking on from the edge of a roof, squatting with his brothers like a line of crows, all of them chewing *naswar* tobacco. And there was his father, Mullah Shekib himself, and three white-bearded men sitting in the shade of a wall, listlessly fingering their prayer beads, their ageless eyes fixed on Nila and her bare arms with a look of displeasure.

I introduced Nila to Saboor, and we made our way to his and Parwana's small mud house trailed by a mob of onlookers. At the door, Nila insisted on taking off her shoes, though Saboor told her it was not necessary. When we entered the room, I saw Parwana sitting in a corner in silence, shriveled up into a stiff ball. She greeted Nila in a voice hardly above a whisper.

Saboor flicked his eyebrows at Abdullah. "Bring some tea, boy."

"Oh no, please," Nila said, taking a seat on the floor beside Parwana. "It's not necessary." But Abdullah had already disappeared into the adjoining room, which I knew served both as kitchen and sleeping quarters for him and Pari. A cloudy plastic sheet nailed to the threshold separated it from the room where we had all gathered. I sat, toying with the car keys, wishing I had had the chance to warn my sister of the visit, give her time to clean up a bit. The cracked mud walls were black with soot, the ripped mattress beneath Nila layered with dust, the lone window in the room flyspecked.

"This is a lovely carpet," Nila said cheerfully, running her fingers over the rug. It was bright red with elephant-footprint patterns. It was the only object of any value that Saboor and Parwana owned—to be sold, as it turned out, that same winter.

"It belonged to my father," Saboor said.

"Is it a Turkoman rug?"

"Yes."

"I do love the sheep fleece they use. The craftsmanship is incredible."

Saboor nodded his head. He didn't look her way once even as he spoke to her.

The plastic sheeting flapped when Abdullah returned with a tray of teacups and lowered it to the ground before Nila. He poured her a cup and sat cross-legged opposite her. Nila tried speaking to him, lobbing him a few simple questions, but Abdullah only nodded his shaved head, muttered a one- or two-word answer, and stared back at her guardedly. I made a mental note to speak to the boy, gently chide him about his manners. I would do it in a friendly way for I liked the boy, who was serious and competent by nature.

"How far along are you?" Nila asked Parwana.

Her head down, my sister said the baby was due in the winter.

"You are blessed," Nila said. "To be awaiting a baby. And to have such a polite young stepson." She smiled at Abdullah, who remained expressionless.

Parwana muttered something that might have been *Thank you*.

"And there is a little girl too, if I recall?" Nila said. "Pari?"

"She's asleep," Abdullah said tersely.

"Ah. I hear she is lovely."

"Go fetch your sister," Saboor said.

Abdullah lingered, looking from his father to Nila, then rose with visible reluctance to bring his sister.

If I had any wish, even at this late hour, to somehow acquit myself, I would say that the bond between Abdullah and his little sister was an ordinary one. But it was not so. No one but God knows why those two had chosen each other. It was a mystery. I have never seen such affinity between two beings. In truth, Abdullah was as much father to Pari as sibling. When she was an infant, when she cried at night, it was he who sprung from the sleeping cot to walk her. It was he who took it upon himself to change her soiled linens, to bundle her up, to soothe her back to sleep. His patience with her was boundless. He carried her around the village, showing her off as though she were the world's most coveted trophy.

When he carried a still-groggy Pari into the room, Nila asked to hold her. Abdullah handed her over with a cutting look of suspicion, as though some instinctive alarm inside him had been set off.

"Oh, she is darling," Nila exclaimed, her awkward

bounces betraying her inexperience with small children. Pari gazed with confusion at Nila, looked toward Abdullah, and began to cry. Quickly, he retrieved her from Nila's hands.

"Look at those eyes!" Nila said. "Oh, and these cheeks! Isn't she darling, Nabi?"

"That she is, Bibi Sahib," I said.

"And she's been given the perfect name: Pari. She is indeed as beautiful as a fairy."

Abdullah watched Nila, rocking Pari in his arms, his face growing cloudy.

On the way back to Kabul, Nila slumped in the backseat with her head resting on the glass. For a long while, she didn't say a word. And then, suddenly, she started to cry.

I pulled the car over to the side of the road.

She didn't speak for a long time. Her shoulders shook as she sobbed into her hands. Finally, she blew her nose into a handkerchief. "Thank you, Nabi," she said.

"For what, Bibi Sahib?"

"For taking me there. It was a privilege to meet your family."

"The privilege was all theirs. And mine. We were honored."

"Your sister's children are beautiful." She removed her sunglasses and dabbed at her eyes.

I considered for a moment what to do, at first opting to remain quiet. But she had wept in my presence, and the intimacy of the moment called for kind words. Softly I said, "You will have your own soon, Bibi Sahib. *Inshallah*, God will see to it. You wait."

"I don't think He will. Even He can't see to this."

"Of course He can, Bibi Sahib. You're so very young. If He wishes it, it will happen."

"You don't understand," she said tiredly. I had never seen her look so exhausted, so drained. "It's gone. They scooped it all out of me in India. I'm hollow inside."

To this I could think of nothing to say. I longed to climb into the backseat beside her and pull her into my arms, to soothe her with kisses. Before I knew what I was doing, I had reached behind me and taken her hand into mine. I thought she would withdraw, but her fingers squeezed my hand gratefully, and we sat there in the car, not looking at each other but at the plains around us, yellow and withering from horizon to horizon, furrowed with dried-up irrigation ditches, pocked with shrubs and rocks and stirrings of life here and there. Nila's hand in mine, I looked at the hills and the power poles. My eyes traced a cargo truck lumbering along in the distance, trailed by a puff of dust, and I would have happily sat there until dark.

"Take me home," she said at last, releasing my hand. "I'm going to turn in early tonight."

"Yes, Bibi Sahib." I cleared my throat and dropped the shift into first gear with a slightly unsteady hand.

She went into her bedroom and didn't leave it for days. This was not the first time. On occasion, she would pull up a chair to the window of her upstairs bedroom and plant herself there, smoking cigarettes, shaking one foot, staring out the window with a blank expression. She would not speak. She would not change out of her sleeping gown. She would not bathe or brush her teeth or hair. This time, she would not eat either, and this particular development caused Mr. Wahdati uncharacteristic alarm.

On the fourth day, there was a knock at the front gates. I opened them to a tall, elderly man in a crisply pressed suit and shiny loafers. There was something imposing and rather forbidding about him in the way he did not so much stand as loom, the way he looked right through me, the way he held his polished cane with both hands like it was a scepter. He had not said a word as yet, but I already sensed he was a man accustomed to being obeyed.

"I understand my daughter is not well," he said.

So he was the father. I had never met him before. "Yes, Sahib. I'm afraid that is true," I said.

"Then move aside, young man." He pushed past me.

In the garden, I busied myself, chopping a block of wood for the stove. From where I worked, I had a good clear view of Nila's bedroom window. Framed in it was the father, bent at the waist, leaning into Nila, one hand pressing on her shoulder. On Nila's face was the expression people have when they have been startled by an abrupt loud noise, like a firecracker, or a door slammed by a sudden draft of wind.

That night, she ate.

A few days later, Nila summoned me into the house and said she was going to throw a party. We rarely, if ever, had parties at the house back when Mr. Wahdati was single. After

Nila moved in, she arranged them two or three times a month. The day prior to the party, Nila would give me detailed instructions on what appetizers and meals I was to prepare, and I would drive to the market to purchase the necessary items. Chief among these necessary items was alcohol, which I had never procured before, as Mr. Wahdati did not drink—though his reasons had nothing to do with religion, he merely disliked its effects. Nila, however, was well acquainted with certain establishments—*pharmacies*, as she called them jokingly—where for the equivalent of double my monthly salary a bottle of *medicine* could be purchased subversively. I had mixed feelings about running this particular errand, playing the part of sin enabler, but, as always, pleasing Nila superseded everything else.

You must understand, Mr. Markos, that when we had parties in Shadbagh, be it for a wedding or to celebrate a circumcision, the proceedings took place at two separate houses, one for women, the other for us men. At Nila's parties, men and women mingled with one another. Most of the women dressed as Nila did, in dresses that showed the entire lengths of their arms and a good deal of their legs as well. They smoked, and they drank too, their glasses half filled with colorless or red- or copper-colored liquor, and they told jokes and laughed and freely touched the arms of men I knew to be married to someone else in the room. I carried small platters of *bolani* and *lola kabob* from one end of the smoke-filled room to the other, from one cluster of guests to another, as a record played on the turntable. The music was not Afghan but something Nila called *jazz*, a kind of music that, I learned decades later, you appreciate as well, Mr. Markos. To my ears, the random tinkling of piano and the strange wailing of horns sounded an inharmonious mess. But Nila loved it, and I kept overhearing her telling guests how they simply had to hear this recording or that. All night, she held a glass and tended to it far more than the food I served.

Mr. Wahdati made limited effort to engage his guests. He made a token show of mingling, but mostly he occupied a corner, with a remote expression on his face, swirling a glass of soda, smiling a courteous, closemouthed smile when someone talked to him. And, as was his habit, he excused himself when the guests began asking Nila to recite her poetry.

This was my favorite part, by far, of the evening. When she started, I always found some task that would keep me nearby. There I would be, frozen in place, towel in hand, straining to hear. Nila's poems did not resemble any I had grown up with. As you well know, we Afghans love our poetry; even the most uneducated among us can recite verses of Hafez or Khayyám or Saadi. Do you recall, Mr. Markos, telling me last year how much you loved Afghans? And I asked you why, and you laughed and said, *Because even your graffiti artists spray Rumi on the walls.*

But Nila's poems defied tradition. They followed no preset meter or rhyming pattern. Nor did they deal with the usual things, trees and spring flowers and bulbul birds. Nila wrote about love, and by love I do not mean the Sufi yearnings of Rumi or Hafez but instead physical love. She wrote about lovers whispering across pillows, touching each other. She wrote about pleasure. I had never heard language such as this spoken by a woman. I would stand there, listening to Nila's smoky voice drift down the hallway, my eyes closed and my ears burning red, imagining she was reading to me, that *we* were the lovers in the poem, until someone's call for tea or fried eggs would break the spell, and then Nila would call my name and I would run.

That night, the poem she chose to read caught me off guard. It was about a man and his wife, in a village, mourning the death of the infant they had lost to the winter cold. The guests seemed to love the poem, judging by the nods and the murmurs of approval around the room, and by their hearty applause when Nila looked up from the page. Still, I felt some surprise, and disappointment, that my sister's misfortune had been used to entertain guests, and I could not shake the sense that some vague betrayal had been committed.

A couple of days after the party, Nila said she needed a new purse. Mr. Wahdati was reading the newspaper at the table, where I had served him a lunch of lentil soup and *naan*.

"Do you need anything, Suleiman?" Nila asked.

"No, *aziz*. Thank you," he said. I rarely heard him address her by anything other than *aziz*, which means "beloved," "darling," and yet never did the couple seem more distant from each other than when he said it, and never did this term of endearment sound so starched as when it came from Mr. Wahdati's lips.

On the way to the store, Nila said she wanted to pick up a friend and gave me directions to the home. I parked on the street and watched her walk up the block to a two-story house with bright pink walls. At first, I left the engine running, but when five minutes passed and Nila hadn't returned I shut it off. It was a good thing I did for it was not until two hours later that I saw her slim figure gliding down the sidewalk toward the car. I opened the rear passenger door and, as she slid in, I smelled on her, underneath her own familiar perfume, a second scent, something faintly like cedarwood and perhaps a trace of ginger, an aroma I recognized from having breathed it at the party two nights before.

"I didn't find one I liked," Nila said from the backseat as she applied a fresh coat of lipstick.

She caught my puzzled face in the rearview mirror. She lowered the lipstick and gazed at me from under her lashes. "You took me to two different stores but I couldn't find a purse to my liking."

Her eyes locked onto mine in the mirror and lingered there awhile, waiting, and I understood that I had been made privy to a secret. She was putting my allegiance to the test. She was asking me to choose.

"I think maybe you visited three stores," I said weakly.

She grinned. *"Parfois je pense que tu es mon seul ami, Nabi."*

I blinked.

"It means 'Sometimes I think you are my only friend.'"

She smiled radiantly at me, but it could not lift my sagging spirits.

The rest of that day, I set about my chores at half my normal speed and with a fraction of my customary enthusiasm. When the men came over for tea that night, one of them sang for us, but his song failed to cheer me. I felt as though I had been the one cuckolded. And I was sure that the hold she had on me had loosened at last.

But in the morning I rose and there it was, filling my living quarters once more, from floor to ceiling, seeping into the walls, saturating the air I breathed, like vapor. It was no use, Mr. Markos.

I cannot tell you when, precisely, the idea took hold. Perhaps it was the windy autumn morning I was serving tea to Nila, when I had stooped and was cutting for her a slice of *roat* cake, that from the radio sitting on her windowsill came a report that the coming winter of 1952 might prove even more brutal than the previous one. Perhaps it was earlier, the day I took her to the house with the bright pink walls, or perhaps earlier still, the time I held her hand in the car as she sobbed.

Whatever the timing, once the idea entered my head there was no purging it.

Let me say, Mr. Markos, that I proceeded with a mostly clean conscience, and with the conviction that my proposal was born of goodwill and honest intentions. Something that, though painful in the short term, would lead to a greater long-term good for all involved. But I had less honorable, self-serving motives as well. Chief among them this: that I would give Nila something no other man—not her husband, not the owner of that big pink house—could.

I spoke to Saboor first. In my defense, I will say that if I had thought Saboor would accept money from me, I gladly would have given it to him in lieu of this proposal. I knew he needed the money for he had told me of his struggles finding work. I would have borrowed an advance against my salary from Mr. Wahdati for Saboor to see his family through the winter. But Saboor, like many of my countrymen, had the affliction of pride, an affliction both misbegotten and unshakable. He would never take money from me. When he married Parwana, he even put an end to the small remittances I had been giving her. He was a man and he would provide for his own family. And he died doing just that, when he was not yet forty, collapsing one day while he was out harvesting a field of sugar beets somewhere near Baghlan. I heard he died with the beet hook still in his blistered, bleeding hands.

I was not a father and thus will make no pretense at understanding the anguished deliberations that led to Saboor's decision. Nor was I privy to the discussions between the Wahdatis. Once I revealed the idea to Nila, I only asked that in her discussions with Mr. Wahdati she put forth the idea as her own and not mine. I knew that Mr. Wahdati would resist. I had never glimpsed in him a sliver of paternal instinct. In fact, I had wondered if Nila's inability to bear children may have swayed his decision to marry her. Regardless, I steered clear of the tense atmosphere between the two. When I lay down to sleep at night, I saw only the sudden tears that had leaked from Nila's eyes when I told her and how she had taken both my hands and gazed into me with gratitude and—I was sure of it—something quite like love. I thought only of the fact that I was offering her a gift that men with far greater prospects could not. I thought only of how thoroughly I had given myself over to her, and how happily. And I thought, hoped—foolishly, of course—that she may begin to see me as something more than the loyal servant.

When Mr. Wahdati eventually buckled—which didn't surprise me, Nila was a woman of formidable will—I informed Saboor and offered to drive him and Pari to Kabul. I will never fully understand why he chose to instead walk his daughter from Shadbagh. Or why he allowed Abdullah to come along. Perhaps he was clinging to what little time he had left with his daughter. Perhaps he sought a measure of penance in the hardship of the journey. Or perhaps it was Saboor's pride, and he would not ride in the car of the man who was buying his daughter. But, in the end, there they were, the three of them, coated in dust, waiting, as agreed, near the mosque. As I drove them to the Wahdati home, I did my best to seem cheerful for the children's benefit, the children who were oblivious to their fate—and to the terrible scene that would soon unfold.

There is little point in recounting it in detail, Mr. Markos, the scene that *did* unfold precisely as I had feared. But all these years later, I still feel my heart clench when the memory of it forces its way to the fore. How could it not? I took those two helpless children, in whom love of the simplest and purest kind had found expression, and I tore one from the other. I will never forget the sudden emotional mayhem. Pari slung over my shoulder, panic-stricken, kicking her legs, shrieking, *Abollah! Abollah!* as I whisked her away. Abdullah, screaming his sister's name, trying to fight past his father. Nila, wide-eyed, her mouth covered with both hands, perhaps to silence her own scream. It weighs on me. All this time has passed, Mr. Markos, and it still weighs on me.

Pari was nearly four years old at the time, but, despite her young age, there were forces in her life that needed to be reshaped. She was instructed not to call me Kaka Nabi any longer, for instance, but simply Nabi. And her mistakes were gently corrected, by me included, over and over until she came to believe that we bore no relation to each other. I became for her Nabi the cook and Nabi the driver. Nila became "Maman," and Mr. Wahdati "Papa." Nila set about teaching her French, which had been her own mother's tongue.

Mr. Wahdati's chilly reception of Pari lasted only a brief time before, perhaps to his own surprise, little Pari's tearful anxiety and homesickness disarmed him. Soon, Pari joined us on our morning strolls. Mr. Wahdati lowered her into a stroller and pushed her around the neighborhood as we walked. Or else he sat her up on his lap behind the wheel of the car and smiled patiently while she pushed the horn. He hired a carpenter and had him build a three-drawer trundle bed for Pari, a maple chest for toys, and a small, short armoire. He had all the furniture in Pari's room painted yellow since he had discovered this was her favorite color. And I found him one day sitting cross-legged before the armoire, Pari at his side, as he painted, with rather remarkable skill, giraffes and long-tailed monkeys over its doors. It should speak volumes about his private nature, Mr. Markos, when I tell you that in all the years I had watched him sketch, this was the first time I had actually laid eyes on his artwork.

One of the effects of Pari's entrance was that for the first time the Wahdati household resembled a proper family. Bound now by their affection for Pari, Nila and her husband took all their meals together. They walked Pari to a nearby park and sat contentedly beside each other on a bench to watch her play. When I served them tea at night after I had cleared the table, I often found one or the other reading a children's book to Pari as she reclined on their laps, she, with each passing day, more forgetful of her past life in Shadbagh and of the people in it.

The other consequence of Pari's arrival was one I had not anticipated: I receded into the background. Judge me charitably, Mr. Markos, and remember that I was a young man, but I admit I had hopes, foolish as they might have been. I was the instrument of Nila's becoming a mother, after all. I had uncovered the source of her unhappiness and delivered an antidote. Did I think we would become lovers now? I want to say I was not so foolish as that, Mr. Markos, but that wouldn't be entirely truthful. I suspect the truth is that we are waiting, all of us, against insurmountable odds, for something extraordinary to happen to us.

What I did not foresee was that I would fade away. Pari consumed Nila's time now. Lessons, games, naps, walks, more games. Our daily chats went by the wayside. If the two of them were playing with building blocks or working on a puzzle, Nila would hardly notice that I had brought her coffee, that I was still in the room standing back on my heels. When we did speak, she seemed distracted, always eager to cut the conversation short. In the car, her expression was distant. For this, though it shames me, I will admit to feeling a shade of resentment toward my niece.

As part of the agreement with the Wahdatis, Pari's family was not allowed to visit. They were not allowed any contact at all with her. I drove to Shadbagh one day soon after Pari moved in with the Wahdatis. I went there bearing a small present each for Abdullah and for my sister's little boy, Iqbal, who was a toddler by then.

Saboor said pointedly, "You've given your gifts. Now it's time to go."

I told him I didn't understand the reason for his cold reception, his gruff manner with me.

"You do understand," he said. "And don't feel like you have to come out and see us anymore."

He was right, I did understand. A chill had grown between us. My visit had been awkward, tense, even contentious. It felt unnatural to sit together now, to sip tea and chat about the weather or that year's grape harvest. We were feigning a normalcy, Saboor and I, that no longer was.

Whatever the reason, I was, in the end, the instrument of his family's rupture. Saboor did not want to set eyes on me again and I understood. I stopped my monthly visits. I never saw any of them again.

It was one day early in the spring of 1955, Mr. Markos, that the lives of all of us in the household changed forever. I remember it was raining. Not the galling kind that draws frogs out to croak, but an indecisive drizzle that had come and gone all morning. I remember because the gardener, Zahid, was there, being his habitual lazy self, leaning on a rake and saying how he might call it a day on account of the nasty weather. I was about to retreat to my shack, if only to get away from his drivel, when I heard Nila screaming my name from inside the main house.

I rushed across the yard to the house. Her voice was coming from upstairs, from the direction of the master bedroom.

I found Nila in a corner, back to the wall, palm clasped over her mouth. "Something's wrong with him," she said, not removing her hand.

Mr. Wahdati was sitting up in bed, dressed in a white undershirt. He was making strange guttural sounds. His face was pale and drawn, his hair disheveled. He was repeatedly trying, and failing, to perform some task with his right arm, and I noticed with horror that a line of spittle was streaking down from the corner of his mouth.

"Nabi! Do something!"

Pari, who was six by then, had come into the room, and now she scampered over to Mr. Wahdati's bedside and pulled on his undershirt. "Papa? Papa?" He looked down at her, wide-eyed, his mouth opening and closing. She screamed.

I picked her up quickly and took her to Nila. I told Nila to take the child to another room because she must not see her father in this condition. Nila blinked, as if breaking a trance, looked from me to Pari before she reached for her. She kept asking me what was wrong with her husband. She kept saying that I must do something.

I summoned Zahid from the window and for once the good-for-nothing fool proved of some use. He helped me put a pair of pajama pants on Mr. Wahdati. We lifted him off the bed, carried him down the stairs, and lowered him into the backseat of the car. Nila climbed in next to him. I told Zahid to stay at the house and look after Pari. He started to protest, and I struck him, open-palmed, across the temple as hard as I could. I told him he was a donkey and that he must do as he was told.

And, with that, I backed out of the driveway and peeled out.

It was two full weeks before we brought Mr. Wahdati home. Chaos ensued. Family descended upon the house in hordes. I was brewing tea and cooking food almost around the clock to feed this uncle, that cousin, an elderly aunt. All day the front gates' bell rang and heels clicked on the marble floor of the living room and murmurs rippled in the hallway as people spilled into the house. Most of them I had rarely seen at the house, and I understood that they were clocking in an appearance more to pay respect to Mr. Wahdati's matronly mother than to see the reclusive sick man with whom they had but a tenuous connection. She came too, of course, the mother—minus the dogs, thank goodness. She burst into the house bearing a handkerchief in each hand to blot at her reddened eyes and dripping nose. She planted herself at his bedside and wept. Also, she wore black, which appalled me, as though her son were already dead.

And, in a way, he was. At least the old version of him. Half of his face was now a frozen mask. His legs were almost of no service. He had movement of the left arm, but the right was only bone and flaccid meat. He spoke with hoarse grunts and moans that no one could decipher.

The doctor told us that Mr. Wahdati felt emotions as he had before the stroke and he understood things well, but what he could not do, at least for the time being, was to act on what he felt and understood.

This was not entirely true, however. Indeed, after the first week or so he made his feelings quite clear about the visitors, his mother included. He was, even in such extreme sickness, a fundamentally solitary creature. And he had no use for their pity, their woebegone looks, all the forlorn headshaking at the wretched spectacle he had become. When they entered his room, he waved his functional left hand in an angry shooing motion. When they spoke to him, he turned his cheek. If they sat at his side, he clutched a handful of bedsheet and grunted and pounded the fist against his hip until they left. With Pari, his dismissal was no less insistent, if far gentler. She came to play with her dolls at his bedside, and he looked up at me pleadingly, his eyes watering, his chin quivering, until I led her out of the room—he did not try to speak with her for he knew his speech upset her.

The great visitor exodus came as a relief to Nila. When people were packing the house wall to wall, Nila retreated upstairs into Pari's bedroom with her, much to the disgust of the mother-in-law, who doubtless expected—and, really, who could blame her?—Nila to remain at her son's side, at least for the sake of appearances if nothing else. Of course Nila cared nothing about appearances or what might be said about her. And plenty was. "What sort of wife is this?" I heard the mother-in-law exclaim more than once. She complained to anyone who would listen that Nila was heartless, that she had a gaping hole in her soul. Where was she now that her husband needed her? What sort of wife abandoned her loyal, loving husband?

Some of what the old woman said, of course, was accurate. Indeed, it was I who could be found most reliably at Mr. Wahdati's bedside, I who gave him his pills and greeted those who entered the room. It was me to whom the doctor spoke most often, and therefore it was me, and not Nila, whom people asked about Mr. Wahdati's condition.

Mr. Wahdati's dismissal of visitors relieved Nila of one discomfort but presented her with another. By holing up in Pari's room and closing the door, she had kept herself at a remove not only from the disagreeable mother-in-law but also from the mess that her husband had become. Now the house was vacant, and she faced spousal duties for which she was uniquely ill suited.

She couldn't do it.

And she didn't.

I am not saying she was cruel or callous. I have lived a long time, Mr. Markos, and one thing I have come to see is that one is well served by a degree of both humility and charity when judging the inner workings of another person's heart. What I *am* saying is that I walked into Mr. Wahdati's room one day and found Nila sobbing into his belly, a spoon still in her hand, as pureed lentil *daal* dripped from his chin onto the bib tied around his neck.

"Let me, Bibi Sahib," I said gently. I took the spoon from her, wiped his mouth clean, and went to feed him, but he moaned, squeezed his eyes shut, and turned his face.

It was not long after that I was lugging a pair of suitcases down the stairs and handing them to a driver, who stowed them in the trunk of his idling car. I helped Pari, who was wearing her favorite yellow coat, climb into the backseat.

"Nabi, will you bring Papa and visit us in Paris like Maman said?" she asked, giving me her gap-toothed smile.

I told her I certainly would when her father felt better. I kissed the back of each of her little hands. "Bibi Pari, I wish you luck and I wish you happiness," I said.

I met Nila as she came down the front steps with puffy eyes and smudged eyeliner. She had been in Mr. Wahdati's room saying her good-byes.

I asked her how he was.

"Relieved, I think," she said, then added, "although that may be my wishful thinking." She closed the zipper to her purse and slung the strap over her shoulder.

"Don't tell anyone where I'm going. It would be for the best."

I promised her I would not.

She told me she would write soon. She then looked me long in the eyes, and I believe I saw genuine affection there. She touched my face with the palm of her hand.

"I'm happy, Nabi, that you're with him."

Then she pulled close and embraced me, her cheek against mine. My nose filled with the scent of her hair, her perfume.

"It was you, Nabi," she said in my ear. "It was always you. Didn't you know?"

I didn't understand. And she broke from me before I could ask. Head lowered, boot heels clicking against the asphalt, she hurried down the driveway. She slid into the backseat of the taxi next to Pari, looked my way once, and pressed her palm against the glass. Her palm, white against the window, was the last I saw of her as the car pulled away from the driveway.

I watched her go, and waited for the car to turn at the end of the street before I pulled the gates shut. Then I leaned against them and wept like a child.

Despite Mr. Wahdati's wishes, a few visitors still trickled in, at least for a short while longer. Eventually, it was only his mother who turned up to see him. She came once a week or so. She would snap her fingers at me and I would pull up a chair for her, and no sooner had she plopped down next to her son's bed than she would launch into a soliloquy of assaults on the character of his now departed wife. She was a harlot. A liar. A drunk. A coward who had run to God knows where when her husband needed her most. This, Mr. Wahdati would bear in silence, looking impassively past her shoulder at the window. Then came an interminable stream of news and updates, much of it almost physically painful in its banality. A cousin who had argued with her sister because her sister had had the gall to buy the same exact coffee table as she. Who had got a flat tire on the way home from Paghman last Friday. Who had got a new haircut. On and on. Sometimes Mr. Wahdati would grunt something, and his mother would turn to me.

"You. What did he say?" She always addressed me in this manner, her words sharp and angular.

Because I was at his side more or less all day, I had slowly come to unlock the enigma of his speech. I would lean in close, and what sounded to others like unintelligible groans and mumbles I would recognize as a request for water, for the bedpan, an appeal to be turned over. I had become his de facto interpreter.

"Your son says he would like to sleep."

The old woman would sigh and say that it was just as well, she ought to be going anyway. She would lean down and kiss his brow and promise to come back soon. Once I had walked her out to the front gates, where her own chauffeur awaited her, I would return to Mr. Wahdati's room and sit on a stool next to his bed and we would relish the silence together. Sometimes his eyes caught mine, and he would shake his head and grin crookedly.

Because the work I had been hired for was so limited now—I drove only to get groceries once or twice a week, and I had to cook for only two people—I saw little sense in paying the other servants for work that I could perform. I expressed this to Mr. Wahdati, and he motioned with his hand. I leaned in.

"You'll wear yourself out."

"No, Sahib. I'm happy to do it."

He asked me if I was sure, and I told him I was.

His eyes watered and his fingers closed weakly around my wrist. He had been the most stoic man I had ever known, but since the stroke the most trivial things made him agitated, anxious, tearful.

"Nabi, listen to me."

"Yes, Sahib."

"Pay yourself any salary you like."

I told him we had no need to talk about that.

"You know where I keep the money."

"Get your rest, Sahib."

"I don't care how much."

I said I was thinking of making *shorwa* soup for lunch. "How does that sound, *shorwa*? I would like some myself, come to think of it."

I put an end to the evening gatherings with the other workers. I no longer cared what they thought of me; I would not have them come to Mr. Wahdati's house and amuse themselves at his expense. I had the considerable pleasure of firing Zahid. I also let go of the Hazara woman who came in to wash clothes. Thereafter, I washed the laundry and hung it on a clothesline to dry. I tended to the trees, trimmed the shrubs, mowed the grass, planted new flowers and vegetables. I maintained the house, sweeping the rugs, polishing the floors, beating the dust from the curtains, washing the windows, fixing leaky faucets, replacing rusty pipes.

One day, I was up in Mr. Wahdati's room dusting cobwebs from the moldings while he slept. It was summer, and the heat was fierce and dry. I had taken all the blankets and sheets off Mr. Wahdati and rolled up the legs of his pajama pants. I had opened the windows, the fan overhead wheeled creakily, but it was little use, the heat pushed in from every direction.

There was a rather large closet in the room I had been meaning to clean for some time and I decided to finally get to it that day. I slid the doors open and started in on the suits, dusting each one individually, though I recognized that, in all probability, Mr. Wahdati would never don any of them again. There were stacks of books on which dust had collected, and I wiped those as well. I cleaned his shoes with a cloth and lined them all up in a neat row. I found a large cardboard box, nearly shielded from view by the hems of several long winter coats draping over it. I pulled it toward me and opened it. It was full of Mr. Wahdati's old sketchbooks, one stacked atop another, each a sad relic of his past life.

I lifted the top sketchbook from the box and randomly opened it to a page. My knees nearly buckled. I went through the whole book. I put it down and picked up another, then another, and another, and another after that. The pages flipped before my eyes, each fanning my face with a little sigh, each bearing the same subject drawn in charcoal. Here I was wiping the front fender of the car as seen from the perch of the upstairs bedroom. Here I was leaning on a shovel by the veranda. I could be found on these pages tying my shoelaces, chopping wood, watering bushes, pouring tea from kettles, praying, napping. Here was the car parked along the banks of Ghargha Lake, me behind the wheel, the window rolled down, my arm hanging over the side of the door, a dimly drawn figure in the backseat, birds circling overhead.

It was you, Nabi.

It was always you.

Didn't you know?

I looked over to Mr. Wahdati. He was sleeping soundly on his side. I carefully placed the sketchbooks back in the cardboard box, closed the top, and pushed the box back in the corner beneath the winter coats. Then I left the room, shutting the door softly so as not to wake him. I walked down the dim hallway and down the stairs. I saw myself walk on. Step out into the heat of that summer day, make my way down the driveway, push out the front gates, stride down the street, turn the corner, and keep walking, without looking over my shoulder.

How was I to stay on now? I wondered. I was neither disgusted nor flattered by the discovery I had made, Mr. Markos, but I *was* discomfited. I tried to picture how I could stay, knowing what I knew now. It cast a pall over everything, what I had found in the box. A thing like this could not be escaped, pushed aside. Yet how could I leave while he was in such a helpless state? I could not, not without first finding someone suitable to take over my duties. I owed Mr. Wahdati at least that much because he had always been good to me, while I, on the other hand, had maneuvered behind his back to gain his wife's favors.

I went to the dining room and sat at the glass table with my eyes closed. I cannot tell you how long I sat there without moving, Mr. Markos, only that at some point I heard stirrings from upstairs and I blinked my eyes open and saw that the light had changed, and then I got up and set a pot of water to boil for tea.

One day, I went up to his room and told him that I had a surprise for him. This was sometime in the late 1950s, long before television had made its way to Kabul. He and I passed our time those days playing cards, and, of late, chess, which he had taught me and for which I was showing a bit of a knack. We also spent considerable time with reading lessons. He proved a patient teacher. He would close his eyes as he listened to me read and shake his head gently when I erred. *Again,* he would say. By then, his speech had improved quite dramatically over time. *Read that again, Nabi.* I had been more or less literate when he had hired me back in 1947, thanks to Mullah Shekib, but it was through Suleiman's tutoring that my reading truly advanced, as did my writing by consequence. He did it to help me, of course, but there was also a self-serving element to the lessons for I now could read to him books that he liked. He could read them on his own, naturally, but only for short bursts, as he tired easily.

If I was in the midst of a chore and could not be with him, he didn't have much to occupy himself with. He listened to records. Often, he had to make do with looking out the window, at the birds perched on the trees, the sky, the clouds, and listen to the children playing on the street, the fruit vendors pulling their donkeys, chanting, *Cherries! Fresh cherries!*

When I told him about this surprise, he asked me what it was. I slid my arm under his neck and told him we were going downstairs first. In those days, I had little trouble carrying him for I was still young and able. I lifted him with ease and carried him to the living room, where I gently reclined him on the sofa.

"Well?" he said.

I pushed in the wheelchair from the foyer. For over a year, I had lobbied for it, and he had obstinately refused. Now I had taken the initiative and bought one anyway. Immediately, he was shaking his head.

"Is it the neighbors?" I said. "Are you embarrassed by what people will say?"

He told me to take him back upstairs.

"Well, I don't give one damn what the neighbors think or say," I said. "So, what we are going to do today is go for a walk. It's a lovely day and we are going for a walk, you and I, and that is that. Because if we don't get out of this house, I am going to lose my mind, and where would that leave you if I went insane? And honestly, Suleiman, quit your crying. You're like an old woman."

Now he was crying *and* laughing, and still saying, "No! No!" even as I lifted him and lowered him into the wheelchair, and as I covered him with a blanket and wheeled him through the front door.

It would merit mentioning here that I *did* at first search for a replacement for myself. I did not tell Suleiman I was doing so; I thought it best to find the right person and then bring the news to him. A number of people came to inquire about the work. I met with them outside the house so as to not rouse suspicion in Suleiman. But the search proved far more problematic than I had anticipated. Some of the candidates were clearly made of the same cloth as Zahid, and those—whom I sniffed out easily due to my lifelong dealings with their sort—I dismissed swiftly. Others didn't have the necessary cooking skills, for, as I mentioned earlier, Suleiman was a rather fussy eater. Or they could not drive. Many could not read, which was a serious impediment now that I habitually read to Suleiman late in the afternoons. Some I found to be impatient, another grave shortcoming when it came to caring for Suleiman, who could be exasperating and at times childishly petulant.

Others I intuitively judged to lack the necessary temperament for the arduous task at hand.

And so three years on, I was still at the house, still telling myself I intended to leave once I felt assured Suleiman's fate was in hands I could trust. Three years on, I was still the one washing his body every other day with a wet cloth, shaving his face, clipping his nails, cutting his hair. I fed him his food and helped him on the bedpan, and I wiped him clean, the way you do an infant, and I washed the soiled diapers I pinned on him. In that time, we had developed between us an unspoken language born of familiarity and routine, and, inevitably, a degree of previously unthinkable informality had seeped into our relationship.

Once I got him to agree to the wheelchair, the old ritual of morning strolls was restored. I wheeled him out of the house, and we would go down the street and say hello to the neighbors as we passed by. One of them was Mr. Bashiri, a young, recent graduate of Kabul University who worked for the Ministry of Foreign Affairs. He, his brother, and their respective wives had moved into a big two-story home three houses down across the street from us. Sometimes we ran into him as he was warming up his car in the morning to go to work, and I always stopped for a few pleasantries. I often wheeled Suleiman over to Shar-e-Nau Park, where we sat in the shade of the elms and watched the traffic—the taxi drivers pounding palms against horns, the ding-a-ding of bicycles, donkeys braying, pedestrians suicidally stepping into the path of buses. We became a familiar sight, Suleiman and I, in and around the park. On the way home, we paused often for good-humored exchanges with magazine vendors and butchers, a few cheerful words with the young police-men directing traffic. We chatted up drivers leaning against their fenders, waiting for pickups.

Sometimes I lowered him into the backseat of the old Chevrolet, stowed the wheelchair in the trunk, and drove out to Paghman, where I could always find a pretty green field and a bubbling little stream shaded by trees. He tried his hand at sketching after we ate lunch, but it was a struggle, for the stroke had affected his dominant right hand. Still, using his left hand, he managed to re-create trees and hills and bundles of wildflowers with far greater artistry than I could with my intact faculties. Eventually, Suleiman would tire and doze off, the pencil slipping from his hand. I would cover his legs with a blanket and lie on the grass beside his chair. I would listen to the breeze catching the trees, gaze up at the sky, the strips of clouds gliding overhead.

Sooner or later, I would find my thoughts drifting to Nila, who was an entire continent away from me now. I would picture the soft sheen of her hair, the way she bounced her foot, the sandal slapping her heel to the crackle of a burn-ing cigarette. I thought of the curve of her back and the swell of her chest. I longed to be near her again, to be engulfed in her smell, to feel the old familiar flutter of the heart when she touched my hand. She had promised to write me, and though years had passed and in all likelihood she had forgotten me, I cannot lie now and claim I did not still feel an upsurge of anticipation each time we received correspondence at the house.

One day, in Paghman, I was sitting on the grass, studying the chessboard. This was years later, in 1968, the year after Suleiman's mother died, and also the year both Mr. Bashiri and his brother became fathers, boys they had named, respectively, Idris and Timur. I often spotted the little baby cousins in their strollers as their mothers took them for leisurely walks around the neighborhood. That day, Suleiman and I had started a chess game, before he had dozed off, and I was trying now to find a way to equalize my position after his aggressive opening gambit, when he said, "Tell me, how old are you, Nabi?"

"Well, I'm past forty," I said. "I know that much."

"I was thinking, you should marry," he said. "Before you lose your looks. You're already graying."

We smiled at each other. I told him my sister Masooma used to say the same to me.

He asked if I remembered the day he had hired me, back in 1947, twenty-one years earlier.

Naturally, I did. I had been working, rather unhappily, as an assistant cook at a house a few blocks from the Wahdati residence. When I had heard that he needed a cook—his own had married and moved away—I had walked straight to his house one afternoon and rung the bell at the front gates.

"You were a spectacularly bad cook," Suleiman said. "You work wonders now, Nabi, but that first meal? My God. And the first time you drove me in my car I thought I would have a stroke." Here he paused, then chuckled, surprised at his own unintended joke.

This came as a complete surprise to me, Mr. Markos, a

shock, really, for Suleiman had never submitted to me in all these years a single complaint about either my cooking or my driving. "Why did you hire me, then?" I asked.

He turned his face to me. "Because you walked in, and I thought to myself that I had never seen anyone as beautiful."

I lowered my eyes to the chessboard.

"I knew when I met you that we weren't the same, you and I, that it was an impossible thing what I wanted. Still, we had our morning walks, and our drives, and I won't say that was enough for me but it was better than not being with you. I learned to make do with your proximity." He paused, then said, "And I think you understand something of what I am describing, Nabi. I know you do."

I could not lift my eyes to meet his.

"I need to tell you, if only this once, that I have loved you a long, long time, Nabi. Please don't be angry."

I shook my head no. For minutes, neither of us spoke a word. It breathed between us, what he had said, the pain of a life suppressed, of happiness never to be.

"And I am telling you this now," he said, "so you understand why I want you to go. Go and find yourself a wife. Start your own family, Nabi, like everyone else. There is still time for you."

"Well," I said at last, aiming to ease the tension with flippancy, "one of these days I just might. And then you'll be sorry. And so will the miserable bastard who has to wash your diapers."

"You always joke."

I watched a beetle crawl lightly across a green-gray leaf.

"Don't stay for me. This is what I'm saying, Nabi. Don't stay for me."

"You flatter yourself."

"Again the joking," he said tiredly.

I said nothing even though he had it wrong. I was not joking that time. My staying was no longer for him. It had been at first. I had stayed initially because Suleiman needed me, because he was wholly dependent on me. I had run once before from someone who needed me, and the remorse I still feel I will take with me to the grave. I could not do it again. But slowly, imperceptibly, my reasons for staying changed. I cannot tell you when or how the change occurred, Mr. Markos, only that I was staying for me now. Suleiman said I should marry. But the fact is, I looked at my life and realized I already had what people sought in marriage. I had comfort, and companionship, and a home where I was always welcomed, loved, and needed. The physical urges I had as a man—and I still had them, of course, though less frequent and less pressing now that I was older—could still be managed, as I explained earlier. As for children, though I had always liked them I had never felt a tug of paternal impulse in myself.

"If you mean to be a mule and not marry," Suleiman said, "then I have a request of you. But on the condition that you accept before I ask."

I told him he could not demand that of me.

"And yet I am."

I looked up at him.

"You can say no," he said.

He knew me well. He smiled crookedly. I made my promise, and he made his request.

What shall I tell you, Mr. Markos, of the years that ensued? You know well the recent history of this beleaguered country. I need not rehash for you those dark days. I tire at the mere thought of writing it, and, besides, the suffering of this country has already been sufficiently chronicled, and by pens far more learned and eloquent than mine.

I can sum it up in one word: *war*. Or, rather, wars. Not one, not two, but many wars, both big and small, just and unjust, wars with shifting casts of supposed heroes and villains, each new hero making one increasingly nostalgic for the old villain. The names changed, as did the faces, and I spit on them equally for all the petty feuds, the snipers, the land mines, bombing raids, the rockets, the looting and raping and killing. Ah, enough! The task is both too great and too unpleasant. I lived those days already, and I intend to relive them on these pages as briefly as possible. The only good I took from that time was a measure of vindication about little Pari, who by now must have grown into a young woman. It eased my conscience that she was safe, far from all this killing.

The 1980s, as you know, Mr. Markos, were actually not so terrible in Kabul since most of the fighting took place in the countryside. Still, it was a time of exodus, and many families from our neighborhood packed their things and left the country for either Pakistan or Iran, with hopes of resettling somewhere in the West. I remember vividly the day Mr. Bashiri came to say good-bye. I shook his hand and wished him well. I said my farewells also to his son, Idris, who had grown into a tall, lanky fourteen-year-old with long hair and peach fuzz above his lip. I told Idris I would miss very much the sight of him and his cousin Timur flying kites and playing soccer on the street. You may recall that we met the cousins many years later, you and I, Mr. Markos, when they were grown men, at a party you threw at the house in the spring of 2003.

It was in the 1990s that fighting at last broke out within the city limits. Kabul fell prey to men who looked like they had tumbled out of their mothers with Kalashnikov in hand, Mr. Markos, vandals all of them, gun-toting thieves with grandiose, self-given titles. When the rockets began to fly, Suleiman stayed in the house and refused to leave. He stoutly declined information about what was going on outside the walls of his house. He unplugged the television. He cast aside the radio. He had no use for newspapers. He asked that I not bring home any news of the fighting. He scarcely knew who was battling whom, who was winning, who was losing, as though he hoped that by doggedly ignoring the war it would return the favor.

Of course it did not. The street where we lived, once so quiet and pristine and gleaming, turned into a war zone. Bullets hit every house. Rockets whistled overhead. RPGs landed up and down the street and blasted craters in the asphalt. At night, red-and-white tracers flew every which way until dawn. Some days, we would have a bit of reprieve, a few hours of quiet, and then sudden bursts of fire would break it, rounds cracking off from every direction, people on the street screaming.

It was during those years, Mr. Markos, that the house absorbed most of the damage that you witnessed when you first saw it in 2002. Granted, some of it was due to the passage of time and neglect—I had aged into an old man by then and no longer had the wherewithal to tend to the house as I once had. The trees were dead by then—they had not borne fruit in years—the lawn had yellowed, the flowers perished. But war was ruthless on the once beautiful house. Windows shattered by nearby RPG blasts. A rocket pulverized the wall on the eastern face of the garden as well as half of the veranda, where Nila and I had held so many conversations. A grenade damaged the roof. Bullets scarred the walls.

And then the looting, Mr. Markos. Militiamen would walk in at will and make off with whatever struck their fancy. They whisked away most of the furniture, the paintings, the Turkoman rugs, the statues, the silver candlesticks, the crystal vases. They chiseled loose lapis tiles from the bathroom counters. I woke one morning to the sound of men in the foyer. I found a band of Uzbek militiamen ripping the rug from the stairwell with a set of curved knives. I stood by and watched them. What could I do? What was another old man with a bullet in the head to them?

Like the house, Suleiman and I too were wearing down. My eyesight dimmed, and my knees took to aching most days. Forgive me this vulgarity, Mr. Markos, but the mere act of urinating turned into a test of endurance. Predictably, the aging hit Suleiman harder than it did me. He shrank and became thin and startlingly frail. Twice, he nearly died, once during the worst days of the fighting between Ahmad Shah Massoud's group and Gulbuddin Hekmatyar's, when bodies lay unclaimed for days on the streets. Suleiman had pneumonia that time, which the doctor said he got from aspirating his own saliva. Though both doctors and the medicines they prescribed were in short supply, I managed to nurse Suleiman back from what was surely the brink of death.

Perhaps because of the daily confinement and the close proximity to each other, we argued often in those days, Suleiman and I. We argued the way married couples do, stubbornly, heatedly, and over trivial things.

You already cooked beans this week.

No I didn't.

But you did. On Monday you did!

Disagreements on how many games of chess we had played the day before. Why did I always set his water on the windowsill, knowing the sun would warm it?

Why didn't you call for the bedpan, Suleiman?

I did, a hundred times I did!

Which are you calling me, deaf or lazy?

No need to pick, I'm calling you both!

You have some gall calling me lazy for someone who lies in bed all day.

On and on.

He would snap his head side to side when I tried to feed him. I would leave him and give the door a good slam on my way out. Sometimes, I admit, I willfully made him worry. I left the house. He would cry, *Where are you going?* and I would not answer. I pretended I was leaving for good. Of course I would merely go down the street somewhere and smoke—a new habit, the smoking, acquired late in life—though I did it only when I was angry. Sometimes I stayed out for hours. And if he had really roiled me up, I would stay out until dark. But I always came back. I would enter his room without saying a word and I would turn him over and fluff his pillow, both of us averting our eyes, both of us tight-lipped, waiting for a peace offering from the other.

Eventually, the fighting ended with the arrival of the Taliban, those sharp-faced young men with dark beards, kohl-rimmed eyes, and whips. Their cruelty and excesses have also been well documented, and once again I see little reason to enumerate them for you, Mr. Markos. I should say that their years in Kabul were, ironically enough, a time of personal reprieve for me. They saved the bulk of their contempt and zealotry for the young, especially the poor women. Me, I was an old man. My main concession to their regime was to grow a beard, which, frankly, spared me the meticulous task of a daily shave.

"It's official, Nabi," Suleiman breathed from the bed, "you've lost your looks. You look like a prophet."

On the streets, the Taliban walked past me as though I were a grazing cow. I helped them in this by willfully taking on a muted bovine expression so as to avoid any undue attention. I shudder to think what they would have made of—and done to—Nila. Sometimes when I summoned her in my mind, laughing at a party with a glass of champagne in hand, her bare arms, her long, slender legs, it was as though I had made her up. As though she had never truly existed. As though none of it had ever been real—not only she but I too, and Pari, and a young, healthy Suleiman, and even the time and the house we had all occupied together.

Then one morning in the summer of 2000 I walked into Suleiman's room carrying tea and freshly baked bread on a platter. Immediately, I knew something had happened. His breathing was ragged. His facial droop had suddenly become far more pronounced, and when he tried to speak he produced croaking noises that barely rose above a whisper. I put down the platter and rushed to his side.

"I'll fetch a doctor, Suleiman," I said. "You just wait. We'll get you better, like always."

I turned to go, but he was shaking his head violently. He motioned with the fingers of his left hand.

I leaned in, my ear close to his mouth.

He made a series of attempts at saying something but I could not make out any of it.

"I'm sorry, Suleiman," I said, "you must let me go and find the doctor. I won't be long."

He shook his head again, slowly this time, and tears leaked from his cataract-laden eyes. His mouth opened and closed. He motioned toward the nightstand with his head. I asked him if there was something there he needed. He shut his eyes and nodded.

I opened the top drawer. I saw nothing there but pills, his reading glasses, an old bottle of cologne, a notepad, charcoal pencils he had stopped using years before. I was about to ask him what I was supposed to find when I did find it, tucked underneath the notepad. An envelope with my name scribbled on the back in Suleiman's clumsy penmanship. Inside was a sheet of paper on which he had written a single paragraph. I read it.

I looked down at him, his caved-in temples, his craggy cheeks, his hollow eyes.

He motioned again, and I leaned in. I felt his cold, rough, uneven breaths on my cheek. I heard the sound of his tongue struggling in his dry mouth as he collected himself. Somehow, perhaps through sheer force of will—his last—he managed to whisper in my ear.

The air whooshed out of me. I forced the words around the lump that had lodged itself in my throat.

"No. Please, Suleiman."

You promised.

"Not yet. I'm going to nurse you back. You'll see. We'll get through it like we always have."

You promised.

How long did I sit there by him? How long did I try to negotiate? I cannot tell you, Mr. Markos. I do remember that I finally rose, walked around the side of the bed, and lay down next to him. I rolled him over so he faced me. He felt light as a dream. I placed a kiss on his dry, cracked lips. I put a pillow between his face and my chest and reached for the back of his head. I held him against me in a long, tight embrace.

All I remember after was the way the pupils of his eyes had spread out.

I walked over to the window and sat, Suleiman's cup of tea still on the platter at my feet. It was a sunny morning, I remember. Shops would open soon, if they hadn't already. Little boys heading off to school. The dust rising already. A dog loped lazily up the street escorted by a dark cloud of mosquitoes swirling around its head. I watched two young men ride past on a motorcycle. The passenger, straddling the rear carrier pack, had hoisted a computer monitor on one shoulder, a watermelon on the other.

I rested my forehead against the warm glass.

The note in Suleiman's drawer was a will in which he had left me everything. The house, his money, his personal belongings, even the car, though it had long decayed. Its carcass still sat in the backyard on flat tires, a sagging hulk of rusted-over metal.

For a time, I was quite literally at a loss as to what to do with myself. For more than half a century I had looked after Suleiman. My daily existence had been shaped by his needs, his companionship. Now I was free to do as I wished, but I found the freedom illusory, for what I wished for the most had been taken from me. They say, Find a purpose in your life and live it. But, sometimes, it is only after you have lived that you recognize your life had a purpose, and likely one you never had in mind. And now that I had fulfilled mine, I felt aimless and adrift.

I found I could not sleep in the house any longer; I could hardly stay in it. With Suleiman gone, it felt far too big. And every corner, every nook and cranny, evoked ripe memories. So I moved back into my old shack at the far end of the yard. I paid some workers to install electricity in the shack so that I would have a light to read by and a fan to keep me cool in the summer. As for space, I did not need much. My possessions amounted to little more than a bed, some clothes, and the box containing Suleiman's drawings. I know this may strike you as odd, Mr. Markos. Yes, legally the house and everything in it belonged to me now, but I felt no true sense of ownership over any of it, and I knew I never really would.

I read quite a bit, books I took from Suleiman's old study. I returned each when I had finished. I planted some tomatoes, a few sprigs of mint. I went for walks around the neighborhood, but my knees often ached before I had covered even two blocks, forcing me to return. Sometimes I pulled up a chair in the garden and just sat idly. I was not like Suleiman: Solitude did not suit me well.

Then one day in 2002 you rang the bell at the front gates.

By then, the Taliban had been driven out by the Northern Alliance, and the Americans had come to Afghanistan. Thousands of aid workers were flocking to Kabul from all over the world to build clinics and schools, to repair roads and irrigation canals, to bring food and shelter and jobs.

The translator who accompanied you was a young local Afghan who wore a bright purple jacket and sunglasses. He asked for the owner of the house. There was a quick exchange of glances between the two of you when I told the translator he was speaking to the owner. He smirked and said, "No, Kaka, the owner." I invited you both in for tea.

The conversation that ensued, on the surviving section of the veranda over cups of green tea, was in Farsi—I have, as you know, Mr. Markos, learned some English in the seven years since, largely thanks to your guidance and generosity. Through the translator, you said you were from Tinos, which was an island in Greece. You were a surgeon, part of a medical group that had come to Kabul to operate on children who had suffered injuries to their face. You said you and your colleagues needed a residence, a *guesthouse*, as it is called these days.

You asked how much I would charge you for rent.

I said, "Nothing."

I recall still how you blinked after the young man in the purple jacket translated. You repeated your question, perhaps thinking I had misunderstood.

The translator drew himself forward to the edge of his chair and leaned toward me. He spoke in a confidential tone. He asked if my mind had gone to rot, whether I had any idea what your group was willing to pay, did I have any notion of what rentals were going for now in Kabul? He said I was sitting on gold.

I told him to remove his sunglasses when he spoke to an elder. Then I instructed him to do his job, which was to translate, not give advice, and I turned to you and offered, among my many reasons, the one that was not private. "You have left behind your country," I said, "your friends, your family, and you have come here to this godforsaken city to help my homeland and my countrymen. How could I profit off you?"

The young translator, whom I never saw with you again, tossed his hands up and chuckled with dismay. This country has changed. It was not always like this, Mr. Markos.

Sometimes at night, I lie in the dark privacy of my quarters and I see the lights burning in the main house. I watch you and your friends—especially the brave Miss Amra Ademovic, whose enormous heart I admire to no end—on the veranda or in the yard, eating food from plates, smoking cigarettes, drinking your wine. I can hear the music too, and at times it is jazz, which reminds me of Nila.

She is dead now, this I know. I learned it from Miss Amra. I had told her about the Wahdatis and shared with her that Nila had been a poet. She found a French publication on the computer. They had published online an anthology of their best pieces of the last forty years. There was one about Nila. The piece said she had died in 1974. I thought of the futility of all those years, hoping for a letter from a woman who was already long dead. I was not altogether surprised to learn that she had taken her own life. I know now that some people feel unhappiness the way others love: privately, intensely, and without recourse.

Let me finish with this, Mr. Markos.

My time is near now. I weaken by the day. It will not be much longer. And thank God for that. Thank you as well, Mr. Markos, not only for your friendship, for taking the time to visit me daily and sit down for tea and for sharing with me news of your mother on Tinos and your childhood friend Thalia, but also for your compassion for my people and the invaluable service you are providing children here.

Thank you as well for the repair work that you are doing around the house. I have spent now the bulk of my life in it, it is home to me, and I am certain that I will soon take my last breath under its roof. I have borne witness to its decline with dismay and heartbreak. But it has brought me great joy to see it repainted, to see the garden wall repaired, the windows replaced, and the veranda, where I spent countless happy hours, rebuilt. Thank you, my friend, for the trees you have planted, and for the flowers blooming once more in the garden. If I have in some way aided in the services you render the people of this city, then what you have graciously done for this house is more than enough payment for me.

But, at the risk of appearing greedy, I will take the liberty of asking you for two things, one for me, one for another. First is that you have me buried in the Ashuqan-Arefan cemetery, here in Kabul. I am sure you know it. Walk to the north end from the main entrance and if you look for a short while you will find Suleiman Wahdati's grave. Find me a plot nearby and bury me there. This is all I ask for myself.

The second is that you try to find my niece Pari after I am gone. If she is still alive, it may not prove too difficult—this Internet is a wondrous tool. As you can see enclosed in the envelope along with this letter is my will, in which I leave the house, the money, and my few belongings to her. I ask that you give her both this letter and the will. And please tell her, tell her that I cannot know the myriad consequences of what I set into motion. Tell her I took solace only in hope. Hope that perhaps, wherever she is now, she has found as much peace, grace, love, and happiness as this world allows.

I thank you, Mr. Markos. May God protect you.

Your friend always,

Nabi

Five

Spring 2003

The nurse, whose name is Amra Ademovic, had warned Idris and Timur. She had pulled them aside and said, "If you show reaction, even little, she going to be upset, and I kick you out."

They are standing at the end of a long, poorly lit hallway in the men's wing of Wazir Akbar Khan Hospital. Amra said the only relative the girl had left—or the only one who visited—was her uncle, and if she'd been placed in the women's wing he would not be permitted to visit her. So the staff had placed her in the men's wing, not in a room—it would be indecent for the girl to room with men who were not relatives—but here, at the end of the hallway, a no-man's- and no-woman's-land.

"And here I thought the Taliban had left town," Timur says.

"It's crazy, no?" Amra says, then lets out a bewildered chuckle. In the week that Idris has been back in Kabul, he has found this tone of lighthearted exasperation common among the foreign-aid workers, who've had to navigate the inconveniences and idiosyncrasies of Afghan culture. He is vaguely offended by this entitlement to cheerful mocking, this license to condescend, though the locals don't seem to take notice, or take it as an insult if they do, and so he thinks he probably shouldn't either.

"But they let *you* here. You come and go," Timur says.

Amra arches an eyebrow. "I don't count. I am not Afghan. So I am not real woman. You don't know this?"

Timur, unchastised, grins. "Amra. Is that Polish?"

"Bosnian. No reaction. This is hospital, not zoo. You make promise."

Timur says, "I make promise."

Idris glances at the nurse, worried that this tease, a little reckless and unnecessary, might have offended her, but it appears Timur has gotten away with it. Idris both resents and envies his cousin for this ability. He has always found Timur coarse, lacking in imagination and nuance. He knows that Timur cheats on both his wife and his taxes. Back in the States, Timur owns a real-estate mortgage company, and Idris is all but certain that he is waist-deep in some kind of mortgage fraud. But Timur is wildly sociable, his faults forever absolved by good humor, a determined friendliness, and a beguiling air of innocence that endears him to people he meets. The good looks don't hurt, either—the muscular body, the green eyes, the dimpled grin. Timur, Idris thinks, is a grown man enjoying the privileges of a child.

"Good," Amra says. "All right." She pulls the bedsheet

that has been nailed to the ceiling as a makeshift curtain and lets them in.

The girl—Roshi, as Amra had called her, short for "Roshana"—looks to be nine, maybe ten. She is sitting up on a steel-frame bed, back to the wall, knees bent up against her chest. Idris immediately drops his gaze. He swallows down a gasp before it can escape him. Predictably, such restraint proves beyond Timur. He tsks his tongue, and says, "Oh! Oh! Oh!" over and over in a loud, pained whisper. Idris glances over to Timur and is not surprised to find swollen tears shivering theatrically in his eyes.

The girl twitches and makes a grunting sound.

"Okay, finished, we go now," Amra says sharply.

Outside, on the crumbling front steps, the nurse pulls a pack of Marlboro Reds from the breast pocket of her pale blue scrubs. Timur, whose tears have vanished as swiftly as they'd materialized, takes a cigarette and lights both hers and his. Idris feels queasy, light-headed. His mouth has gone dry. He worries he's going to vomit and disgrace himself, confirm Amra's view of him, of them—the wealthy, wide-eyed exiles—come home to gawk at the carnage now that the boogeymen have left.

Idris expected Amra to reprimand them, at least Timur, but her manner is more flirtatious than scolding. This is the effect Timur has on women.

"So," she says, coquettishly, "what do you say for yourself, Timur?"

In the States, Timur goes by "Tim." He changed his name after 9/11 and claims that he has nearly doubled his business since. Losing those two letters, he has said to Idris, has already done more for his career than a college degree would have—if he'd gone to college, which he hadn't; Idris is the Bashiri family academic. But now since their arrival in Kabul, Idris has heard him introduce himself only as Timur. It is a harmless enough duplicity, even a necessary one. But it rankles.

"Sorry about what happened in there," Timur says.

"Maybe I punish you."

"Easy, pussycat."

Amra turns her gaze to Idris. "So. He's cowboy. And you, you are quiet, sensitive one. You are—what do they call it?—*introvert*."

"He's a doctor," Timur says.

"Ah? It must be shocking for you, then. This hospital."

"What happened to her?" Idris says. "To Roshi. Who did that to her?"

Amra's face closes. When she speaks, it is with the pitch of maternal determination. "I fight for her. I fight government, hospital bureaucracy, bastard neurosurgeon. Every step, I fight for her. And I don't stop. She has nobody."

Idris says, "I thought there was an uncle."

"He's bastard too." She flicks her cigarette ash. "So. Why you come here, boys?"

Timur launches into it. The outline of what he says is more or less true. That they are cousins, that their families fled after the Soviets rolled in, that they spent a year in Pakistan before settling in California in the early eighties. That this is the first time back for them both in twenty years. But then he adds that they have come back to "reconnect," to "educate" themselves, "bear witness" to the aftermath of all these years of war and destruction. They want to go back to the States, he says, to raise awareness, and funds, to "give back."

"We want to give back," he says, uttering the tired phrase so earnestly it embarrasses Idris.

Of course Timur does not share the real reason they have come back to Kabul: to reclaim the property that had belonged to their fathers, the house where both he and Idris had lived for the first fourteen years of their lives. The property's worth is skyrocketing now that thousands of foreign-aid workers have descended on Kabul and need a place to live. They were there earlier in the day, at the house, which is currently home to a ragtag group of weary-looking Northern Alliance soldiers. As they were leaving, they had met a middle-aged man who lived three houses down and across the street, a Greek plastic surgeon named Markos Varvaris. He had invited them to lunch and offered to give them a tour of Wazir Akbar Khan Hospital, where the NGO he worked for had an office. He also invited them to a party that night. They had learned about the girl only upon their arrival at the hospital—overhearing two orderlies talking about her on the front steps—after which Timur had elbowed Idris and said, *We should check it out, bro.*

Amra seems bored with Timur's story. She flings her cigarette away and tightens the rubber band that holds her curly blond hair in a bun. "So. I see you boys at party tonight?"

It was Timur's father, Idris's uncle, who had sent them to Kabul. The Bashiri family home had changed hands a number of times over the last two decades of war. Reestablishing ownership would take time and money. Thousands of cases of property disputes already clogged the country's courts. Timur's father had told them that they would have to "maneuver" through the infamously sluggish, ponderous Afghan bureaucracy—a euphemism for "find the right palms to grease."

"That would be my department," Timur had said as if it needed saying.

Idris's own father had died nine years before after a long bout with cancer. He had died at his home, with his wife, two daughters, and Idris at his bedside. The day he died, a mob descended on the house—uncles, aunts, cousins, friends, and acquaintances—sitting on the couches, the dining chairs, and, when those were taken, on the floor, the stairs. Women gathered in the dining room and kitchen. They brewed thermos after thermos of tea. Idris, as the only son, had to sign all the papers—papers for the medical examiner, who arrived to pronounce his father dead; papers for the polite young men from the funeral home, who came with a stretcher to take his father's body.

Timur never left his side. He helped Idris answer phone calls. He greeted the waves of people who came to pay respects. He ordered rice and lamb from Abe's Kabob House, a local Afghan restaurant run by Timur's friend Abdullah, whom Timur teasingly called *Uncle Abe*. Timur parked cars for elderly guests when it started to rain. He called a buddy of his at one of the local Afghan TV stations. Unlike Idris, Timur was well connected in the Afghan community; he once told Idris that he had over three hundred contact names and numbers on his cell phone. He made arrangements for an announcement to run on Afghan TV that same night.

Early that afternoon, Timur drove Idris to the funeral home in Hayward. It was pouring by then, and traffic was slow on the northbound lanes of the 680.

"Your dad, he was all class, bro. He was old-school," Timur croaked as he took the Mission off-ramp. He kept wiping tears with the palm of his free hand.

Idris nodded somberly. His whole life he'd not been able to cry in the presence of other people, at events where it was called for such as funerals. He saw this as a minor handicap, like color blindness. Still, he felt vaguely—and, he knew, irrationally—resentful toward Timur for upstaging him back at the house with all the running around and dramatic sobbing. As if it was *his* father who had died.

They were escorted to a sparely lit, quiet room with heavy dark-toned furniture. A man in a black jacket and hair parted in the middle greeted them. He smelled like expensive coffee. In a professional tone, he offered Idris his condolences, and had him sign the Interment Order and Authorization form. He asked how many copies of the death certificate the family would desire. When all the forms were signed, he tactfully placed before Idris a pamphlet titled "General Price List."

The funeral home director cleared his throat. "Of

course these prices don't apply if your father had membership with the Afghan mosque over on Mission. We have a partnership with them. They'll pay for the lot, the services. You'd be covered."

"I have no idea if he did or not," Idris said, scanning the pamphlet. His father had been a religious man, he knew, but privately so. He'd rarely gone to Friday prayer.

"Shall I give you a minute? You could call the mosque."

"No, man. No need," Timur said. "He wasn't a member."

"You're sure?"

"Yeah. I remember a conversation."

"I see," the funeral director said.

Outside, they shared a cigarette by the SUV. It had stopped raining.

"Highway robbery," Idris said.

Timur spat into a puddle of dark rainwater. "Solid business, though—death—you have to admit. Always a need for it. Shit, it beats selling cars."

At the time, Timur co-owned a used-car lot. It had been failing, quite badly, until Timur had gone in on it with a friend of his. In less than two years, he had turned it around into a profitable enterprise. *A self-made man,* Idris's father had liked to say of his nephew. Idris, meanwhile, was earning slave wages finishing up his second year of internal medicine residency at UC Davis. His wife of one year, Nahil, was putting in thirty hours a week as a secretary at a law firm while she studied for her LSATs.

"This is a loan," Idris said. "You understand that, Timur. I'm paying you back."

"No worries, bro. Whatever you say."

That wasn't the first or the last time that Timur had come through for Idris. When Idris got married, Timur had given him a new Ford Explorer for a wedding present. Timur had cosigned the loan when Idris and Nahil bought a small condo up in Davis. In the family, he was by far every kid's favorite uncle. If Idris ever had to make *one phone call*, he'd almost surely call Timur.

And yet.

Idris found out, for instance, that everyone in the family knew about the loan cosigning. Timur had told them. And at the wedding, Timur had the singer stop the music, make an announcement, and the key to the Explorer had been offered to Idris and Nahil with great ceremony—on a tray, no less—before an attentive audience. Cameras had flashed. This was what Idris had misgivings about, the fanfare, the flaunting, the unabashed showmanship, the bravado. He didn't like thinking this of his cousin, who was the closest thing Idris had to a brother, but it seemed to him that Timur was a man who wrote his own press kit, and his generosity, Idris suspected, was a calculated piece of an intricately constructed character.

Idris and Nahil had a minor spat about him one night as they were putting fresh sheets on their bed.

Everyone wants to be liked, she said. *Don't you?*

Okay, but I won't pay for the privilege.

She told him he was being unfair, and ungrateful as well, after everything Timur had done for them.

You're missing the point, Nahil. All I'm saying is that it's crass to plaster your good deeds up on a billboard. Something to be said for doing it quietly, with dignity. There's more to kindness than signing checks in public.

Well, Nahil said, snapping the bedsheet, *it does go a long way, honey.*

"Man, I remember this place," Timur says, looking up at the house. "What was the owner's name again?"

"Something Wahdati, I think," Idris says. "I forget the first name." He thinks of the countless times they had played here as kids on this street outside of these front gates and only now, decades later, are they passing through them for the first time.

"The Lord and His ways," Timur mutters.

It's an ordinary two-story house that in Idris's neighborhood in San Jose would draw the ire of the HOA folks. But by Kabul standards, it's a lavish property, with high walls, metal gates, and a wide driveway. As he and Timur are led inside by an armed guard, Idris sees that, like many things he has seen in Kabul, the house has a whiff of past splendor beneath the ruin that has been visited upon it—of which there is ample evidence: bullet holes and zigzagging cracks in the sooty walls, exposed bricks beneath wide missing patches of plaster, dead bushes in the driveway, leafless trees in the garden, yellowed lawn. More than half of the veranda that overlooks the backyard is missing. But also like many things in Kabul, there is evidence of slow, hesitant rebirth. Someone has begun to repaint the house, planted rosebushes in the garden, a missing chunk of the garden's east-facing wall has been replaced, albeit a little clumsily. A ladder is propped against the side of the house facing the street, leading Idris to think that roof repair is under way. Repair on the missing half of the veranda has apparently begun.

They meet Markos in the foyer. He has thinning gray hair and pale blue eyes. He wears gray Afghan garments and a black-and-white-checkered *kaffiyeh* elegantly wrapped around his neck. He shows them into a noisy room thick with smoke.

"I have tea, wine, and beer. Or maybe you prefer something heavier?"

"You point and I pour," Timur said.

"Oh, I like you. There, by the stereo. Ice is safe, by the way. Made from bottled water."

"God bless."

Timur is in his element at gatherings like this, and Idris cannot help but admire him for the ease of his manners, the effortless wisecracking, the self-possessed charm. He follows Timur to the bar, where Timur pours them drinks from a ruby bottle.

The twenty or so guests sit on cushions around the room. The floor is covered with a burgundy red Afghan rug. The décor is understated, tasteful, what Idris has come to think of as "expat chic." A Nina Simone CD plays softly. Everyone is drinking, nearly everyone smoking, talking about the new war in Iraq, what it will mean for Afghanistan. The television in the corner is tuned to CNN International, the volume muted. Nighttime Baghdad, in the throes of *Shock and Awe*, keeps lighting up in flashes of green.

Vodka on ice in hand, they are joined by Markos and a pair of serious-looking young Germans who work for the World Food Program. Like many of the aid workers he has met in Kabul, Idris finds them slightly intimidating, world savvy, impossible to impress.

He says to Markos, "This is a nice house."

"Tell the owner, then." Markos goes across the room and returns with a thin, elderly man. The man has a thick wall of salt-and-pepper hair combed back from the brow. He has a closely cropped beard, and the sunken cheeks of the nearly toothless. He is wearing a shabby, oversize olive-colored suit that may have been in style back in the 1940s. Markos smiles at the old man with open affection.

"Nabi jan?" Timur exclaims, and suddenly Idris remembers too.

The old man grins back shyly. "Forgive me, have we met before?"

"I'm Timur Bashiri," Timur says in Farsi. "My family used to live down the street from you!"

"Oh great God," the old man breathes. "Timur jan? And you must be Idris jan?"

Idris nods, smiling back.

Nabi embraces them both. He kisses their cheeks, still grinning, and eyes them with disbelief. Idris remembers Nabi pushing his employer, Mr. Wahdati, in a wheelchair up and down the street. Sometimes he would park the chair on the sidewalk, and the two men would watch him and Timur play soccer with the neighborhood kids.

"Nabi jan has lived in this house since 1947," Markos says, his arm around Nabi's shoulder.

"So you *own* this place now?" Timur says.

Nabi smiles at the look of surprise on Timur's face. "I served Mr. Wahdati here from 1947 until 2000, when he passed away. He was kind enough to will the house to me, yes."

"He *gave* it to you," Timur says incredulously.

Nabi nods. "Yes."

"You must have been one hell of a cook!"

"And you, if I may say, were a bit of a troublemaker, as I recall."

Timur cackles. "Never did care for the straight and narrow, Nabi jan. I leave that to my cousin here."

Markos, swirling his glass of wine, says to Idris, "Nila Wahdati, the wife of the previous owner, she was a poet. Of some small renown, as it turns out. Have you heard of her?"

Idris shakes his head. "All I know is that she'd already left the country by the time I was born."

"She lived in Paris with her daughter," one of the Germans, Thomas, says. "She died in 1974. Suicide, I think. She had problems with alcohol, or, at least, that is what I read. Someone gave me a German translation of one of her early volumes a year or two ago and I thought it was quite good, actually. Surprisingly sexual, as I recall."

Idris nods, again feeling a little inadequate, this time

because a foreigner has schooled him on an Afghan artist. A couple of feet away, he can hear Timur engaged in an animated discussion with Nabi over rent prices. In Farsi, of course.

"Do you have any idea what you could charge for a place like this, Nabi jan?" he is saying to the old man.

"Yes," Nabi says, nodding, laughing. "I am aware of rental prices in the city."

"You could fleece these guys!"

"Well . . ."

"And you're letting them stay for free."

"They've come to help our country, Timur jan. They left their homes and came here. It doesn't seem right that I should, as you say, 'fleece them.'"

Timur issues a groan, downs the rest of his drink. "Well, either you hate money, old friend, or you are a far better man than I am."

Amra walks into the room, wearing a sapphire Afghan tunic over faded jeans. "Nabi jan!" she exclaims. Nabi seems a little startled when she kisses his cheek and coils an arm around his. "I love this man," she says to the group. "And I love to embarrass him." Then she says it in Farsi to Nabi. He tilts his head back and forth and laughs, blushing a little.

"How about you embarrass me too," Timur says.

Amra taps him on the chest. "This one is big trouble." She and Markos kiss Afghan-style, three times on the cheek, same with the Germans.

Markos slings an arm around her waist. "Amra Ademovic.

The hardest-working woman in Kabul. You do not want to cross this girl. Also, she will drink you under the table."

"Let's put that to the test," Timur says, reaching for a glass on the bar behind him.

The old man, Nabi, excuses himself.

For the next hour or so, Idris mingles, or tries to. As liquor levels in the bottles drop, conversations rise in pitch. Idris hears German, French, what must be Greek. He has another vodka, follows it up with a lukewarm beer. In one group, he musters the courage to slip in a Mullah Omar joke that he had learned in Farsi back in California. But the joke doesn't translate well into English, and his delivery is harried. It falls flat. He moves on, and listens in on a conversation about an Irish pub that is set to open in Kabul. There is general agreement that it will not last.

He walks around the room, warm beer can in hand. He has never been at ease in gatherings like this. He tries to busy himself inspecting the décor. There are posters of the Bamiyan Buddhas, of a Buzkashi game, one of a harbor in a Greek island named Tinos. He has never heard of Tinos. He spots a framed photograph in the foyer, black-and-white, a little blurry, as though it had been shot with a homemade camera. It's of a young girl with long black hair, her back to the lens. She is at a beach, sitting on a rock, facing the ocean. The lower left-hand corner of the photo looks like it had burned.

Dinner is leg of lamb with rosemary and imbedded little cloves of garlic. There is goat cheese salad and pasta topped with pesto sauce. Idris helps himself to some of the salad, and ends up toying with it in a corner of the room. He spots Timur sitting with two young, attractive Dutch women. Holding court, Idris thinks. Laughter erupts, and one of the women touches Timur's knee.

Idris carries his wine outside to the veranda and sits on a wooden bench. It's dark now, and the veranda is lit only by a pair of lightbulbs dangling from the ceiling. From here, he can see the general shape of some sort of living quarters at the far end of the garden, and, off to the right side of the garden, the silhouette of a car—big, long, old—likely American, by the curves of it. Forties model, maybe early fifties—Idris can't quite see—and, besides, he has never been a car guy. He is sure Timur would know. He would rattle off the model, year, engine size, all the options. It looks like the car is sitting on four flats. A neighborhood dog breaks into a staccato of barks. Inside, someone has put on a Leonard Cohen CD.

"Quiet and Sensitive."

Amra sits beside him, ice tinkling in her glass. Her feet are bare.

"Your cousin Cowboy, he is life of party."

"I'm not surprised."

"He is very good-looking. He is married?"

"With three kids."

"Too bad. I behave, then."

"I'm sure he'd be disappointed to hear that."

"I have rules," she says. "You don't likc him very much."

Idris tells her, quite truthfully, that Timur is the closest thing he has to a brother.

"But he make you embarrassed."

It's true. Timur *has* embarrassed him. He has behaved like the quintessential ugly Afghan-American, Idris thinks. Tearing through the war-torn city like he belongs here, backslapping locals with great bonhomie and calling them *brother, sister, uncle,* making a show of handing money to beggars from what he calls the *Bakhsheesh bundle,* joking with old women he calls *mother* and talking them into telling their story into his camcorder as he strikes a woebegone expression, pretending he is one of them, like he's been here all along, like he wasn't lifting at Gold's in San Jose, working on his pecs and abs, when these people were getting shelled, murdered, raped. It is hypocritical, and distasteful. And it astonishes Idris that no one seems to see through this act.

"It isn't true what he told you," Idris says. "We came here to reclaim the house that belonged to our fathers. That's all. Nothing else."

Amra snorts a chuckle. "Of course I know. You think I was fooled? I have done business with warlords and Taliban in this country. I have seen everything. Nothing can give me shock. Nothing, nobody, can fool me."

"I imagine that's true."

"You are honest," she says. "At least you are honest."

"I just think these people, everything they've been through, we should respect them. By 'we,' I mean people like Timur and me. The lucky ones, the ones who weren't here when the place was getting bombed to hell. We're not like these people. We shouldn't pretend we are. The

stories these people have to tell, we're not *entitled* to
them . . . I'm rambling."

"Rambling?"

"I'm not making sense."

"No, I understand," she says. "You say their stories, it is
gift they give you."

"A gift. Yes."

They sip some more wine. They talk for some time, for
Idris the first genuine conversation he has had since arriving in Kabul, free of the subtle mocking, the vague reproach
he has sensed from the locals, the government officials,
those in the aid agencies. He asks about her work, and she
tells him that she has served in Kosovo with the UN, in
Rwanda after the genocide, Colombia, Burundi too. She has
worked with child prostitutes in Cambodia. She has been in
Kabul for a year now, her third stint, this time with a small
NGO, working at the hospital and running a mobile clinic
on Mondays. Married twice, divorced twice, no kids. Idris
finds it hard to guess at Amra's age, though likely she's
younger than she looks. There is a fading shimmer of beauty,
a roughshod sexuality, behind the yellowing teeth, the
fatigue pouches under the eyes. In four, maybe five years,
Idris thinks, that too will be gone.

Then she says, "You want to know what happen to
Roshi?"

"You don't have to tell," he says.

"You think I am drunk?"

"Are you?"

"Little bit," she says. "But you are honest guy." She taps

him on the shoulder gently, and a little playfully. "You ask to know for right reasons. For other Afghans like you, Afghans coming from West, it is like—how do you say?—stretching the neck."

"Rubbernecking."

"Yes."

"Like pornography."

"But maybe you are good guy."

"If you tell me," he says, "I will take it as a gift."

So she tells him.

Roshi lived with her parents, two sisters, and her baby brother in a village a third of the way between Kabul and Bagram. One Friday last month, her uncle, her father's older brother, came to visit. For almost a year, Roshi's father and the uncle had had a feud over the property where Roshi lived with her family, property which the uncle felt belonged rightfully to him, being the older brother, but which his father had passed to the younger, and more favored, brother. The day he came, though, all was well.

"He say he want to end their fight."

In preparation, Roshi's mother had slaughtered two chickens, made a big pot of rice with raisins, bought fresh pomegranates from the market. When the uncle arrived, he and Roshi's father kissed and embraced. Roshi's father hugged his brother so hard, his feet lifted off the carpet. Roshi's mother wept with relief. The family sat down to eat. Everyone had seconds, and thirds. They helped themselves to the pomegranates. After that, there was green tea and small toffee candies. The uncle then excused himself to use the outhouse.

When he came back, he had an ax in his hand.

"The kind for chopping tree," Amra says.

The first one to go was Roshi's father. "Roshi told me her father never even know what happened. He didn't see anything."

A single strike to the neck, from behind. It nearly decapitated him. Roshi's mother was next. Roshi saw her mother try to fight, but several swings to the face and chest and she was silenced. By now the children were screaming and running. The uncle chased after them. Roshi saw one of her sisters make a run for the hallway, but the uncle grabbed her by the hair and wrestled her to the ground. The other sister did make it out to the hallway. The uncle gave chase, and Roshi could hear him kicking down the door to the bedroom, the screams, then the quiet.

"So Roshi, she decide to escape with the little brother. They run out of the house, they run for front door but it is locked. The uncle, he did it, of course."

They ran for the yard, out of panic and desperation, perhaps forgetting that there was no gate in the yard, no way out, the walls too tall to climb. When the uncle burst out of the house and came for them, Roshi saw her little brother, who was five, throw himself into the *tandoor*, where, only an hour before, his mother had baked bread. Roshi could hear him screaming in the flames, when she tripped and fell. She turned onto her back in time to see blue sky and the ax whooshing down. And then nothing.

Amra stops. Inside, Leonard Cohen sings a live version of "Who By Fire."

Even if he could talk, which he cannot at the moment, Idris wouldn't know the proper thing to say. He might have said something, some offering of impotent outrage, if this had been the work of the Taliban, or al-Qaeda, or some megalomaniacal Mujahideen commander. But this cannot be blamed on Hekmatyar, or Mullah Omar, or Bin Laden, or Bush and his War on Terror. The ordinary, utterly mundane reason behind the massacre makes it somehow more terrible, and far more depressing. The word *senseless* springs to mind, and Idris thwarts it. It's what people always say. *A senseless act of violence. A senseless murder.* As if you could commit sensible murder.

He thinks of the girl, Roshi, back at the hospital, curled up against the wall, her toes knotted, the infantile look on her face. The crack in the crown of her shaved head, the fist-sized mass of glistening brain tissue leaking from it, sitting on her head like the knot of a sikh's turban.

"She told you this story herself?" he finally asks.

Amra nods heavily. "She remember very clearly. Every detail. She can tell to you every detail. I wish she can forget because of the bad dreams."

"The brother, what happened to him?"

"Too many burns."

"And the uncle?"

Amra shrugs.

"They say be careful," she says. "In my job, they say be careful, be professional. It's not good idea to get attached. But Roshi and me . . ."

The music suddenly dies. Another power outage. For a

few moments all is dark, save for the moonlight. Idris hears people groaning inside the house. Halogen torches promptly come to life.

"I fight for her," Amra says. She never looks up. "I don't stop."

The next day, Timur rides with the Germans to the town of Istalif, known for its clay pottery. "You should come."

"I'm going to stay in and read," Idris says.

"You can read in San Jose, bro."

"I need the rest. I might have had too much to drink last night."

After the Germans pick up Timur, Idris lies in bed for a while, staring at a faded sixties-era advertising poster hanging on the wall, a quartet of smiling blond tourists hiking along Band-e-Amir Lake, a relic from his own childhood here in Kabul before the wars, before the unraveling. Early afternoon, he goes for a walk. At a small restaurant, he eats kabob for lunch. It's hard to enjoy the meal with all the grimy young faces peering through the glass, watching him eat. It's overwhelming. Idris admits to himself that Timur is better at this than he is. Timur makes a game of it. Like a drill sergeant, he whistles and makes the beggar kids queue up, whips out a few bills from the *Bakhsheesh* bundle. As he hands out the bills, one by one, he clicks his heels and salutes. The kids love it.

They salute back. They call him Kaka. Sometimes they climb up his legs.

After lunch, Idris catches a taxi and asks to be taken to the hospital.

"But stop at a bazaar first," he says.

Carrying the box, he walks down the hallway, past graffiti-spangled walls, rooms with plastic sheeting for doors, a shuffling barefoot old man with an eye patch, patients lying in stifling-hot rooms with missing lightbulbs. A sour-body smell everywhere. At the end of the hallway, he pauses at the curtain before pulling it back. He feels a lurch in his heart when he sees the girl sitting on the edge of the bed. Amra is kneeling before her, brushing her small teeth.

There is a man sitting on the other side of the bed, gaunt, sunburned, with a rat's-nest beard and stubbly dark hair. When Idris enters, the man quickly gets up, flattens a hand against his chest, and bows. Idris is struck again by how easily the locals can tell he is a westernized Afghan, how the whiff of money and power affords him unwarranted privilege in this city. The man tells Idris he is Roshi's uncle, from the mother's side.

"You're back," Amra says, dipping the brush into a bowl of water.

"I hope that's okay."

"Why not," she says.

Idris clears his throat. *"Salaam, Roshi."*

The girl looks to Amra for permission. Her voice is a tentative, high-pitched whisper. *"Salaam."*

"I brought you a present." Idris lowers the box and opens it. Roshi's eyes come to life when Idris takes out the small TV and VCR. He shows her the four films he has bought. Most of the tapes at the store were Indian movies, or else action flicks, martial-arts films with Jet Li, Jean-Claude Van Damme, all of Steven Seagal's pictures. But he was able to find *E.T.*, *Babe*, *Toy Story*, and *The Iron Giant*. He has watched them all with his own boys back home.

In Farsi, Amra asks Roshi which one she wants to watch. Roshi picks *The Iron Giant*.

"You'll love that one," Idris says. He finds it difficult to look at her directly. His gaze keeps sliding toward the mess on her head, the shiny clump of brain tissue, the crisscrossing network of veins and capillaries.

There is no electric outlet at the end of this hallway, and it takes Amra some time to find an extension cord, but when Idris plugs in the cord, and the picture comes on, Roshi's mouth spreads into a smile. In her smile, Idris sees how little of the world he has known, even at thirty-five years of age, its savageness, its cruelty, the boundless brutality.

When Amra excuses herself to go see other patients, Idris takes a seat beside Roshi's bed and watches the movie with her. The uncle is a silent, inscrutable presence in the room. Halfway through the film, the power goes out. Roshi begins to cry, and the uncle leans over from his chair and roughly clutches her hand. He whispers a few quick, terse words in Pashto, which Idris does not speak. Roshi winces and tries to pull away. Idris looks at her small hand, lost in the uncle's strong, white-knuckled grasp.

Idris puts on his coat. "I'll come back tomorrow, Roshi, and we can watch another tape if you like. You want that?"

Roshi shrinks into a ball beneath the covers. Idris looks at the uncle, pictures what Timur would do to this man—Timur, who, unlike him, has no capacity to resist the easy emotion. *Give me ten minutes alone with him,* he'd say.

The uncle follows him outside. On the steps, he stuns Idris by saying, "I am the real victim here, Sahib." He must have seen the look on Idris's face because he corrects himself and says, "Of course she is the victim. But, I mean, I am a victim too. You see that, of course, you are Afghan. But these foreigners, they don't understand."

"I have to go," Idris says.

"I am a *mazdoor,* a simple laborer. I earn a dollar, maybe two, on a good day, Sahib. And I already have five children of my own. One of them blind. Now this." He sighs. "I think to myself sometimes—God forgive me—I say to myself, maybe Allah should have let Roshi . . . well, you understand. It might have been better. Because I ask you, Sahib, what boy would marry her now? She will never find a husband. And then who will take care of her? I will have to. I will have to do it forever."

Idris knows he has been cornered. He reaches for his wallet.

"Whatever you can spare, Sahib. Not for me, of course. For Roshi."

Idris hands him a pair of bills. The uncle blinks, looks

up from the money. He begins to say, "Two—" then clamps his mouth shut as though worried that he will alert Idris to a mistake.

"Buy her some decent shoes," Idris says, walking down the steps.

"Allah bless you, Sahib," the uncle calls out behind him. "You are a good man. You are a kind and good man."

Idris visits the next day, and the day after that. Soon, it becomes a routine, and he is at Roshi's side every day. He comes to know the orderlies by name, the male nurses who work the ground floor, the janitor, the underfed, tired-looking guards at the hospital gates. He keeps the visits as secret as possible. On his calls overseas, he has not told Nahil about Roshi. He does not tell Timur where he is going either, why he isn't joining him on the trip to Paghman or for a meeting with an official at the Ministry of Interior. But Timur finds out anyway.

"Good for you," he says. "It's a decent thing you're doing." He pauses before adding, "Tread carefully, though."

"You mean stop visiting."

"We leave in a week, bro. You don't want to get her too attached to you."

Idris nods. He wonders if Timur may not be slightly jealous of his relationship with Roshi, perhaps even resentful that he, Idris, may have robbed him of a spectacular opportunity to play hero. Timur, emerging in slow motion from the blazing building, holding a baby. The crowd exploding in a cheer. Idris is determined not to let Timur parade Roshi in that way.

Still, Timur is right. They are going home in a week, and Roshi has started calling him Kaka Idris. If he arrives late, he finds her agitated. She ties her arms around his waist, a tide of relief washing over her face. His visits are what she looks forward to most, she has told him. Sometimes she clutches his hand with both of hers as they watch a tape. When he is away from her, he thinks often of the faint yellow hairs on her arms, her narrow hazel eyes, her pretty feet, her rounded cheeks, the way she cups her chin in her hands as he reads her one of the children's books he has picked up from a bookstore near the French lycée. A few times, he has allowed himself to fleetingly imagine what it would be like to bring her to the U.S., how she would fit in with his boys, Zabi and Lemar, back home. This last year, he and Nahil had talked about the possibility of a third child.

"What now?" Amra says the day before he is scheduled to leave.

Earlier that day, Roshi had given Idris a picture, pencil-drawn on a sheet of hospital chart paper, of two stick figures watching a television. He'd pointed to the one with long hair. *This is you?*

And that one is you, Kaka Idris.

You had long hair, then? Before?

My sister brushed it every night. She knew how to do it so it didn't hurt.

She must have been a good sister.

When it grows back, you can brush it.

I think I'd like that.

Don't go, Kaka. Don't leave.

"She is a sweet girl," he says to Amra. And she is. Well-mannered, and humble too. With some guilt, he thinks of Zabi and Lemar back in San Jose, who have long professed their dislike of their Afghan names, who are fast turning into little tyrants, into the imperious American children he and Nahil had vowed they would never raise.

"She is survivor," Amra says.

"Yes."

Amra leans against the wall. A pair of orderlies rush past them, pushing a gurney. On it lies a young boy with blood-soaked bandaging around his head and some kind of open wound on his thigh.

"Other Afghans from America, or from Europe," Amra says, "they come and take picture of her. They take video. They make promises. Then they go home and show their families. Like she is zoo animal. I allow it because I think maybe they will help. But they forget. I never hear from them. So I ask again, what now?"

"The operation she needs?" he says. "I want to make it happen."

She looks at him hesitantly.

"We have a neurosurgery clinic in my group. I'll speak to my chief. We'll make arrangements to fly her over to California and have the surgery."

"Yes, but the money."

"We'll get the funding. Worst comes to worst, I'll pay for it."

"Out of wallet."

He laughs. "The expression is 'out of pocket,' but, yes."

"We have to get uncle's permission."

"If he ever shows up again." The uncle hasn't been seen or heard from since the day Idris gave him the two hundred dollars.

Amra smiles at him. He has never done anything like this. There is something exhilarating, intoxicating, euphoric even, in throwing himself headlong into this commitment. He feels energized. It nearly takes his breath away. To his own amazement, tears prickle his eyes.

"*Hvala,*" she says. "Thank you." She stands on tiptoes and kisses his cheek.

"Banged one of the Dutch girls," Timur says. "From the party?"

Idris lifts his head off the window. He had been marveling at the soft brown peaks of the tightly packed Hindu Kush far beneath. He turns to look at Timur in the aisle seat.

"The brunette. Popped half a Vitamin V and rode her straight to the morning call for prayer."

"Jesus. Will you ever grow up?" Idris says, irked that Timur has burdened him again with knowledge of his misconduct, his infidelity, his grotesque frat-boy antics.

Timur smirks. "Remember, cousin, what happens in Kabul . . ."

"Please don't finish that sentence."

Timur laughs.

Somewhere in the back of the plane, there is a little party going on. Someone is singing in Pashto, someone tapping on a Styrofoam plate like a *tamboura*.

"I can't believe we ran into ol' Nabi," Timur mutters. "Jesus."

Idris fishes the sleeping pill he had been saving from his breast pocket and dry-swallows it.

"So I'm coming back next month," Timur says, crossing his arms, shutting his eyes. "Probably take a couple more trips after that, but we should be good."

"You trust this guy Farooq?"

"Fuck no. It's why I'm coming back."

Farooq is the lawyer Timur has hired. His specialty is helping Afghans who have lived in exile reclaim their lost properties in Kabul. Timur goes on about the paperwork Farooq will file, the judge he is hoping will preside over the proceedings, a second cousin of Farooq's wife. Idris rests his temple once more against the window, waits for the pill to take effect.

"Idris?" Timur says quietly.

"Yeah."

"Sad shit we saw back there, huh?"

You're full of startling insight, bro. "Yup," Idris says.

"A thousand tragedies per square mile, man."

Soon, Idris's head begins to hum, and his vision blurs.

As he drifts to sleep, he thinks of his farewell with Roshi, him holding her fingers, saying they would see each other again, her sobbing softly, almost silently, into his belly.

On the ride home from SFO, Idris recalls with fondness the manic chaos of Kabul's traffic. It's strange now to guide the Lexus down the orderly, pothole-free southbound lanes of the 101, the always helpful freeway signs, everyone so polite, signaling, yielding. He smiles at the memory of all the daredevil adolescent cabbies with whom he and Timur entrusted their lives in Kabul.

In the passenger seat, Nahil is all questions. Was Kabul safe? How was the food? Did he get sick? Did he take pictures and videos of everything? He does his best. He describes for her the shell-blasted schools, the squatters living in roofless buildings, the beggars, the mud, the fickle electricity, but it's like describing music. He cannot bring it to life. Kabul's vivid, arresting details—the bodybuilding gym amid the rubble, for instance, a painting of Schwarzenegger on the window. Such details escape him now, and his descriptions sound to him generic, insipid, like those of an ordinary AP story.

In the backseat, the boys humor him and listen for a short while, or at least pretend to. Idris can sense their boredom. Then Zabi, who is eight, asks Nahil to start the movie. Lemar, who is two years older, tries to listen a little longer, but soon Idris hears the drone of a racing car from his Nintendo DS.

"What's the matter with you boys?" Nahil scolds them. "Your father's come back from Kabul. Aren't you curious? Don't you have questions for him?"

"It's all right," Idris says. "Let them." But he *is* annoyed with their lack of interest, their blithe ignorance of the arbitrary genetic lottery that has granted them their privileged lives. He feels a sudden rift between himself and his family, even Nahil, most of whose questions about his trip revolve around restaurants and the lack of indoor plumbing. He looks at them accusingly now as the locals must have looked at him when he'd first arrived in Kabul.

"I'm famished," he says.

"What do you feel like?" Nahil says. "Sushi, Italian? There's a new deli over by Oakridge."

"Let's get Afghan food," he says.

They go to Abe's Kabob House over on the east side of San Jose near the old Berryessa Flea Market. The owner, Abdullah, is a gray-haired man in his early sixties, with a handlebar mustache and strong-looking hands. He is one of Idris's patients, as is his wife. Abdullah waves from behind the register when Idris and his family enter the restaurant. Abe's Kabob House is a small family business. There are only eight tables—sheathed by often sticky vinyl covers—laminated menus, posters of Afghanistan on the walls, an old soda machine, a "merchandiser," in the corner. Abdullah greets the guests, runs the register, cleans. His wife, Sultana, is in the back; she is the one responsible for the magic. Idris can see her now in the kitchen, stooped over something, her hair stuffed up under a net cap, her eyes narrowed against the steam. She and Abdullah had married in Pakistan in the late 1970s, they have told Idris, after the communist take-over back home. They were granted asylum in the U.S. in 1982, the year their daughter, Pari, was born.

She is the one taking their orders now. Pari is friendly and courteous, has her mother's fair skin, and the same shine of emotional sturdiness in her eyes. She also has a strangely disproportionate body, slim and dainty up top but weighed below the waist by wide hips, thick thighs, and big ankles. She is wearing now one of her customary loose skirts.

Idris and Nahil order lamb with brown rice and *bolani*. The boys settle for *chapli kabobs*, the closest thing to hamburger meat they can find on the menu. As they wait for their food, Zabi tells Idris that his soccer team has made the finals. He plays right wing. The match is on Sunday. Lemar says he has a guitar recital on Saturday.

"What are you playing?" Idris asks sluggishly, feeling jet lag kicking in.

"'Paint It Black.'"

"Very cool."

"Not sure you've practiced enough," Nahil says with cautious reprimand.

Lemar drops the paper napkin he has been rolling. "Mom! Really? Do you see what I go through every day? I have so much to do!"

Midway through the meal, Abdullah comes over to them to say hello, wiping his hands on the apron tied around his waist. He asks if they like the food, whether he can get them anything.

Idris tells him that he and Timur have just returned from Kabul.

"What is Timur jan up to?" Abdullah asks.

"To no good as always."

Abdullah grins. Idris knows how fond he is of Timur.

"And how is the kabob business?"

Abdullah sighs. "Dr. Bashiri, if I ever want to put a curse on someone I say, 'May God give you a restaurant.'"

They share a brief laugh with Abdullah.

Later, as they are leaving the restaurant and climbing into the SUV, Lemar says, "Dad, does he give free food to everyone?"

"Of course not," Idris says.

"Then why wouldn't he take your money?"

"Because we're Afghans, and because I'm his doctor," Idris says, which is only partially true. The bigger reason, he suspects, is that he is Timur's cousin, and it was Timur who had years earlier lent Abdullah the money to open the restaurant.

At the house, Idris is surprised at first to find the carpets ripped from the family room and foyer, nails and wooden boards on the stairs exposed. Then he remembers that they were remodeling, replacing carpets with hardwood—wide planks of cherry in a color the flooring contractor had called *copper kettle*. The cabinet doors in the kitchen have been sanded down, and there is a gaping hole where the old microwave used to sit. Nahil tells him she is working a half day on Monday so she can meet in the morning with the flooring people and Jason.

"Jason?" Then he remembers, Jason Speer, the home-theater guy.

"He's coming in to take measurements. He's already got us the subwoofer and the projector at a discount. He's sending three guys to start work on Wednesday."

Idris nods. The home theater had been his idea, something he had always wanted. But now it embarrasses him. He feels disconnected from all of it, Jason Speer, the new cabinets and copper-kettle floors, his kids' $160 high-tops, the chenille bedspreads in his room, the energy with which he and Nahil have pursued these things. The fruits of his ambitions strike him as frivolous now. They remind him only of the brutal disparity between his life and what he'd found in Kabul.

"What's the matter, honey?"

"Jet lag," Idris says. "I need a nap."

On Saturday he makes it through the guitar recital, on Sunday through most of Zabi's soccer match. During the second half he has to steal away to the parking lot, sleep for a half hour. To his relief, Zabi doesn't notice. Sunday night, a few of the neighbors come over for dinner. They pass around pictures of Idris's trip and sit politely through the hour of video of Kabul that, against Idris's wishes, Nahil insists on playing for them. Over dinner, they ask Idris about his trip, his views on the situation in Afghanistan. He sips his mojito and gives short answers.

"I can't imagine what it's like there," Cynthia says. Cynthia is a Pilates instructor at the gym where Nahil works out.

"Kabul is . . ." Idris searches for the right words. "A thousand tragedies per square mile."

"Must have been quite the culture shock, going there."

"Yes it was." Idris doesn't say that the real culture shock has been in coming back.

Eventually, talk turns to a recent rash of mail theft that has hit the neighborhood.

Lying in bed that night, Idris says, "Do you think we have to have all this?"

"'All this'?" Nahil says. He can see her in the mirror, brushing her teeth by the sink.

"All this. This stuff."

"No we don't *need* it, if that's what you mean," she says. She spits in the sink, gargles.

"You don't think it's too much, all of it?"

"We worked hard, Idris. Remember the MCATs, the LSATs, medical school, law school, the years of residency? No one *gave* us anything. We have nothing to apologize for."

"For the price of that home theater we could have built a school in Afghanistan."

She comes into the bedroom and sits on the bed to remove her contacts. She has the most beautiful profile. He loves the way her forehead hardly dips where her nose begins, her strong cheekbones, her slim neck.

"Then do both," she says, turning to him, blinking back eyedrops. "I don't see why you can't."

A few years ago, Idris had discovered that Nahil was supporting a Colombian kid named Miguel. She'd said nothing to him about it, and since she was in charge of the mail and their finances Idris had not known about it for years until he'd seen her one day reading a letter from Miguel. The letter had been translated from Spanish by a nun. There was a picture too, of a tall, wiry boy standing outside a straw hut, cradling a soccer ball, nothing behind him but gaunt-looking cows and green hills. Nahil had started supporting Miguel when she was in law school. For eleven years now Nahil's checks had quietly crossed paths with Miguel's pictures and his thankful, nun-translated letters.

She takes off her rings. "So what is this? You caught a case of survivor's guilt over there?"

"I just see things a little differently now."

"Good. Put that to use, then. But quit the navel-gazing."

Jet lag robs him of sleep that night. He reads for a while, watches part of a *West Wing* rerun downstairs, ends up at the computer in the guest bedroom Nahil has turned into an office. He finds an e-mail from Amra. She hopes that his return home was safe and that his family is well. It has been raining "angrily" in Kabul, she writes, and the streets are packed with mud up to the ankles. The rain has caused flooding, and some two hundred families had to be evacuated by helicopter in Shomali, north of Kabul. Security has been tightening because of Kabul's support of Bush's war in Iraq and expected reprisals from al-Qaeda. Her last line reads *You have talked with your boss yet?*

Below Amra's e-mail is pasted a short paragraph from Roshi, which Amra has transcribed. It reads:

Salaam, Kaka Idris,

    *Inshallah, you have arrived safely in America. I am
sure that your family is very happy to see you. Every day
I think about you. Every day I am watching the films
you bought for me. I like them all. It makes me sad that
you are not here to watch with me. I am feeling good and
Amra jan is taking good care of me. Please say Salaam
to your family for me. Inshallah, we will see each other
soon in California.*

    With my respects,

    Roshana

He answers Amra, thanks her, writes that he is sorry to
hear about the flooding. He hopes the rains will abate. He
tells her that he will discuss Roshi with his chief this week.
Below that he writes:

Salaam, Roshi jan:

    *Thank you for your kind message. It made me very
happy to hear from you. I too think about you a lot. I
have told my family all about you and they are very
eager to meet you, especially my sons, Zabi jan and
Lemar jan, who ask a lot of questions about you. We all
look forward to your arrival. I send you my love,*

    Kaka Idris

He logs off and goes to bed.

On Monday, a pile of phone messages greets him when he enters his office. Prescription-refill requests spill from a basket, awaiting his approval. He has over one hundred and sixty e-mails to sift through, and his voice mail is full. He peruses his schedule on the computer and is dismayed to see overbooks—*squeezes*, as the doctors call them—inserted into his time slots all week. Worse, he will see the dreaded Mrs. Rasmussen that afternoon, a particularly unpleasant, confrontational woman with years of vague symptoms that respond to no treatment. The thought of facing her hostile neediness makes him break into a sweat. And last, one of the voice mails is from his chief, Joan Schaeffer, who tells him that a patient he had diagnosed with pneumonia just before his trip to Kabul turned out to have congestive heart failure instead. The case will be used next week for Peer Review, a monthly video conference watched by all the facilities during which mistakes by physicians, who remain anonymous, are used to illustrate learning points. The anonymity doesn't go very far, Idris knows. At least half the people in the room will know the culprit.

He feels the onset of a headache.

He falls woefully behind schedule that morning. An asthma patient walks in without an appointment and needs respiratory treatments and close monitoring of his peak flows and oxygen saturation. A middle-aged executive, whom Idris last saw three years before, comes in with an evolving anterior myocardial infarction. Idris cannot start lunch until halfway through the noon hour. In the conference room where the doctors eat, he takes harried bites of a dry turkey sandwich as he tries to catch up with notes. He answers the same questions from his colleagues. Was Kabul safe? What do Afghans there think of the U.S. presence? He gives economical, clipped replies, his mind on Mrs. Rasmussen, on voice mails that need answering, refills he has yet to approve, the three squeezes in his schedule that afternoon, the upcoming Peer Review, the contractors sawing and drilling and banging nails back at the house. Talking about Afghanistan—and he is astonished at how quickly and imperceptibly this has happened—suddenly feels like discussing a recently watched, emotionally drenching film whose effects are beginning to wane.

The week proves one of the hardest of his professional career. Though he had meant to, he doesn't find the time to talk to Joan Schaeffer about Roshi. A foul mood takes hold of him all week. He is short with the boys at home, annoyed with the workers streaming in and out of his house and all the noise. His sleep pattern has yet to return to normal. He receives two more e-mails from Amra, more updates on the conditions in Kabul. Rabia Balkhi, the women's hospital, has reopened. Karzai's cabinet will allow cable television networks to broadcast programs, challenging the Islamic hard-liners who had opposed it. In a postscript at the end of the second e-mail, she says that Roshi has become withdrawn since he left, and asks again whether he has spoken to his chief. He steps away from the keyboard. He returns to it later, ashamed of how Amra's note had irritated him, how tempted he had been, for just a moment, to answer her, in capital letters, *I WILL. IN DUE TIME.*

"I hope that went okay for you."

Joan Schaeffer sits behind her desk, hands laced in her lap. She is a woman of cheerful energy, with a full face and coarse white hair. She peers at him over the narrow reading glasses perched on the bridge of her nose. "You understand the point was not to impugn you."

"Yes, of course," Idris says. "I understand."

"And don't feel bad. It could happen to any of us. CHF and pneumonia on X-ray, sometimes it's hard to tell."

"Thanks, Joan." He gets up to go, pauses at the door. "Oh. Something I've been meaning to discuss with you."

"Sure. Sure. Sit."

He sits down again. He tells her about Roshi, describes the injury, the lack of resources at Wazir Akbar Khan Hospital. He confides in her the commitment he has made to Amra and Roshi. Saying it aloud, he feels weighed down by his promise in a way he had not in Kabul, standing in the hallway with Amra, when she'd kissed his cheek. He is troubled to find that it feels like buyer's remorse.

"My God, Idris," Joan says, shaking her head, "I commend you. But how dreadful. The poor child. I can't imagine."

"I know," he says. He asks if the group would be willing to cover her procedure. "Or *procedures*. My sense is, she'll need more than one."

Joan sighs. "I wish. But, frankly, I doubt the board of directors would approve it, Idris. I doubt it very much. You know we've been in the red for the last five years. And there would be legal issues as well, complicated ones."

She waits for him, maybe prepared for him, to challenge this, but he doesn't.

"I understand," he says.

"You should be able to find a humanitarian group that does this sort of thing, no? It would take some work, but . . ."

"I'll look into it. Thanks, Joan." He gets up again, surprised that he is feeling lighter, almost relieved by her response.

The home theater takes another month to be built, but it is a marvel. The picture, shot from the projector mounted on the ceiling, is sharp, the movements on the 102-inch screen strikingly fluid. The 7.1 channel surround sound, the graphic equalizers, and the bass traps they have put in the four corners, have done wonders for the acoustics. They watch *Pirates of the Caribbean*, the boys, delighted by the technology, sitting on either side of him, eating from the communal bucket of popcorn on his lap. They fall asleep before the final, drawn-out battle scene.

"I'll put them to bed," Idris says to Nahil.

He lifts one, then the other. The boys are growing, their lean bodies lengthening with alarming speed. As he tucks each into bed, an awareness sets in of the heartbreak that is in store for him with his boys. In a year, two at the outside, he will be replaced. The boys will become enamored with other things, other people, embarrassed by him and Nahil. Idris thinks longingly of when they were small and helpless, so wholly dependent on him. He remembers how terrified Zabi was of manholes when he was little, walking wide, clumsy circles around them. Once, watching an old film, Lemar had asked Idris if he had been alive back when the world was in black and white. The memory brings a smile. He kisses his sons' cheeks.

He sits back in the dark, watching Lemar sleep. He had judged his boys hastily, he sees now, and unfairly. And he had judged himself harshly too. He is not a criminal. Everything he owns he has earned. In the nineties, while half the guys he knew were out clubbing and chasing women, he had been buried in study, dragging himself through hospital corridors at two in the morning, forgoing leisure, comfort, sleep. He had given his twenties to medicine. He has paid his dues. Why should he feel badly? This is his family. This is his life.

In the last month, Roshi has become something abstract to him, like a character in a play. Their connection has frayed. The unexpected intimacy he had stumbled upon in that hospital, so urgent and acute, has eroded into something dull. The experience has lost its power. He recognizes the fierce determination that had seized him for what it really was, an illusion, a mirage. He had fallen under the influence of something like a drug. The distance between him and the girl feels vast now. It feels infinite, insurmountable, and his promise to her misguided, a reckless mistake, a terrible misreading of the measures of his own powers and will and character. Something best forgotten. He isn't capable of it. It is that simple. In the last two weeks, he has received three more e-mails from Amra. He read the first and didn't answer. He deleted the next two without reading.

The line in the bookstore is about twelve or thirteen people long. It stretches from the makeshift stage to the magazine stand. A tall, broad-faced woman passes out little yellow Post-its to those in line to write their names on and any personal message they want inscribed in the book. A saleswoman at the head of the line helps people flip to the title page.

Idris is near the head of the line, holding a copy in his hand. The woman in front of him, in her fifties and with short-clipped blond hair, turns and says to him, "Have you read it?"

"No," he says.

"We're going to read it for our book club next month. It's my turn to pick."

"Ah."

She frowns and pushes a palm against her chest. "I hope people read it. It's such a moving story. So inspiring. I bet they make it a movie."

It's true, what he told her. He has not read the book and

doubts he ever will. He does not think he has the stomach to revisit himself on its pages. But others will read it. And when they do, he will be exposed. People will know. Nahil, his sons, his colleagues. He feels sick at the thought of it.

He opens the book again, flips past the acknowledgments, past the bio of the coauthor, who has done the actual writing. He looks again at the photo on the book flap. There is no sign of the injury. If she bears a scar, which she must, the long, wavy black hair conceals it. Roshi is wearing a blouse with little gold beads, an Allah necklace, lapis ear studs. She is leaning against a tree, looking straight at the camera, smiling. He thinks of the stick figures she had drawn him. *Don't go. Don't leave, Kaka.* He does not detect in this young woman even a scrap of the tremulous little creature he had found behind a curtain six years before.

Idris glances at the dedication page.

To the two angels in my life: my mother Amra, and my Kaka Timur. You are my saviors. I owe you everything.

The line moves. The woman with the short blond hair gets her book signed. She moves aside, and Idris, heart stammering, steps forward. Roshi looks up. She is wearing an Afghan shawl over a pumpkin-colored long-sleeved blouse and little oval-shaped silver earrings. Her eyes are darker than he remembers, and her body is filling out with female curves. She looks at him without blinking, and though she gives no overt indication that she has recognized him, and though her smile is polite, there is something amused and distant about her expression, playful, sly, unintimidated. It steamrolls him, and suddenly all the words that he had composed—even written down, rehearsed in his head on the way here—dry up. He cannot bring himself to say a thing. He can only stand there, looking vaguely foolish.

The salesclerk clears her throat. "Sir, if you'll give me your book I'll flip to the title page and Roshi will autograph it for you."

The book. Idris looks down, finds it clutched tightly in his hands. He has not come here to get it signed, of course. That would be galling—grotesquely galling—after everything. Still, he sees himself handing it over, the salesclerk expertly flipping to the correct page, Roshi's hand scrawling something beneath the title. He has seconds left now to say something, not that it would mitigate the indefensible but because he thinks he owes it to her. But when the clerk hands him back his book, he cannot summon the words. He wishes now for even a scrap of Timur's courage. He looks again at Roshi. She is already gazing past him at the next person in line.

"I am—" he begins.

"We have to keep the line moving now, sir," the clerk says.

He drops his head and leaves the queue.

He has parked in the lot behind the store. The walk to the car feels like the longest of his life. He opens the car door, pauses before entering. With hands that have not stopped shaking, he flips the book open again. The scrawling is not a signature. In English, she has written him two sentences.

He closes the book, his eyes too. He supposes he should be relieved. But part of him wishes for something else.

Perhaps if she had grimaced at him, said something infantile, full of loathing and hate. An eruption of rancor. Perhaps that might have been better. Instead, a clean, diplomatic dismissal. And this note. *Don't worry. You're not in it.* An act of kindness. Perhaps, more accurately, an act of charity. He should be relieved. But it hurts. He feels the blow of it, like an ax to the head.

There is a bench nearby, beneath an elm tree. He walks over and leaves the book on it. He returns to the car and sits behind the wheel. And it is a while before he trusts himself to turn the key and drive away.

Six

February 1974

EDITOR'S NOTE,

Parallaxe 84 (Winter 1974), p. 5

Dear Readers:

Five years ago, when we began our quarterly issues featuring interviews with little-known poets, we could not have anticipated how popular they would prove. Many of you asked for more, and, indeed, your enthusiastic letters paved the way for these issues to become an annual tradition here at *Parallaxe*. The profiles have now become our staff writers' personal favorites as well. The features have led to the discovery, or rediscovery, of some valuable poets, and an overdue appreciation of their work.

Sadly, however, a shadow hovers over this present

issue. The artist featured this quarter is Nila Wahdati, an Afghan poet interviewed by Étienne Boustouler last winter in the town of Courbevoie, near Paris. Mme. Wahdati, as we are sure you will agree, gave Mr. Boustouler one of the most revealing and startlingly frank interviews we have ever published. It was with great sadness that we learned of her untimely death not long after this interview was conducted. She will be missed in the community of poets. She is survived by her daughter.

It's uncanny, the timing. The elevator door dings open at precisely—precisely—the same moment the phone begins to ring. Pari can hear the ringing because it comes from inside Julien's apartment, which is at the head of the narrow, barely lit hallway and therefore closest to the elevator. Intuitively, she knows who is calling. By the look on Julien's face, so does he.

Julien, who has already stepped into the elevator, says, "Let it ring."

Behind him is the standoffish ruddy-faced woman from upstairs. She glares impatiently at Pari. Julien calls her *La chèvre*, because of her goatlike nest of chin hairs.

He says, "Let's go, Pari. We're already late."

He has made reservations for seven o'clock at a new restaurant in the 16th arrondissement that has been making some noise for its *poulet braisé*, its *sole cardinale*, and its calf's liver with sherry vinegar. They are meeting Christian and Aurelie, old university friends of Julien's—from his student days, not his teaching. They are supposed to meet for aperitifs at six-thirty and it is already six-fifteen. They still have to walk to the Métro station, ride to Muette, then walk the six blocks to the restaurant.

The phone keeps on ringing.

The goat woman coughs.

Julien says, more firmly now, "Pari?"

"It's probably Maman," Pari says.

"Yes, I am aware of that."

Irrationally, Pari thinks Maman—with her endless flair for drama—has chosen this specific moment to call to trap her into making precisely this choice: step into the elevator with Julien or take her call.

"It could be important," she says.

Julien sighs.

As the elevator doors close behind him, he leans against the hallway wall. He digs his hands deep into the pockets of his trench coat, looking for a moment like a character from a Melville *policier*.

"I'll only be a minute," Pari says.

Julien casts a skeptical glance.

Julien's apartment is small. Six quick steps and she has crossed the foyer, passed the kitchen, and is seated on the edge of the bed, reaching for the phone on the lone nightstand for which they have room. The view, however, is spectacular. It is raining now, but on a clear day she can look out the east-facing window and see most of the 19th and 20th arrondissements.

"*Oui, allo?*" she says into the receiver.

A man's voice answers. "*Bonsoir.* Is this Mademoiselle Pari Wahdati?"

"Who is calling?"

"Are you the daughter of Madame Nila Wahdati?"

"Yes."

"My name is Dr. Delaunay. I am calling about your mother."

Pari shuts her eyes. There is a brief flash of guilt before it is overtaken by a customary dread. She has taken calls of this sort before, too many to count now, from the time that she was an adolescent, really, and even before that—once, in fifth grade, she was in the middle of a geography exam, and the teacher had to interrupt, walk her out to the hallway, and explain in a hushed voice what had happened. These calls are familiar to Pari, but repetition has not led to insouciance on her part. With each one she thinks, *This time, this is the time,* and each time she hangs up and rushes to Maman. In the parlance of economics, Julien has said to Pari that if she cut off the supply of attention, perhaps the demands for it would cease as well.

"She's had an accident," Dr. Delaunay says.

Pari stands by the window and listens as the doctor explains. She coils and uncoils the phone cord around her finger as he recounts her mother's hospital visit, the forehead laceration, the sutures, the precautionary tetanus injection, the aftercare of peroxide, topical antibiotics, dressings. Pari's mind flashes to when she was ten, when she'd come home one day from school and found twenty-five francs and a handwritten note on the kitchen table. *I've gone to Alsace with Marc. You remember him. Back in a couple of days. Be a good girl. (Don't stay up late!) Je t'aime. Maman.* Pari had stood shaking in the kitchen, eyes filling up, telling herself two days wasn't so bad, it wasn't so long.

The doctor is asking her a question.

"Pardon?"

"I was saying will you be coming to take her home, made-moiselle? The injury is not serious, you understand, but it's probably best that she not go home alone. Or else we could call her a taxi."

"No. No need. I should be there in half an hour."

She sits on the bed. Julien will be annoyed, probably embarrassed as well in front of Christian and Aurelie, whose opinions seem to matter a great deal to him. Pari doesn't want to go out in the hallway and face Julien. She doesn't want to go to Courbevoie and face her mother either. What she would rather do is lie down, listen to the wind hurl pellets of rain at the glass until she falls asleep.

She lights a cigarette, and when Julien enters the room behind her and says, "You're not coming, are you?" she doesn't answer.

EXCERPT FROM "AFGHAN SONGBIRD," AN INTERVIEW
WITH NILA WAHDATI BY ÉTIENNE BOUSTOULER,
Parallaxe 84 (WINTER 1974), P. 33

EB: So I understand you are, in fact, half Afghan, half French?

NW: My mother was French, yes. She was a Parisian.

EB: But she met your father in Kabul. You were born there.

NW: Yes. They met there in 1927. At a formal dinner in the Royal Palace. My mother had accompanied her father—my grandfather—who had been sent to Kabul to counsel King Amanullah on his reforms. Are you familiar with him, King Amanullah?

We are sitting in the living room of Nila Wahdati's small apartment on the thirtieth floor of a residential building in the town of Courbevoie, just northwest of Paris. The room is small, not well lit, and sparsely decorated: a saffron-upholstered couch, a coffee table, two tall bookshelves. She sits with her back to the window, which she has opened to air the smoke from the cigarettes she lights continually.

Nila Wahdati states her age as forty-four. She is a strikingly attractive woman, perhaps past the peak of her beauty but, as yet, not far past. High royal cheekbones, good skin, slim waist. She has intelligent, flirtatious eyes, and a penetrating gaze under which one feels simultaneously appraised, tested, charmed, toyed with. They remain, I suspect, a redoubtable seduction tool. She wears no makeup save for lipstick, a smudge of which has strayed a bit from the outline of her mouth. She wears a bandanna over her brow, a faded purple blouse over jeans, no socks, no shoes. Though it is only eleven in the morning, she pours from a bottle of Chardonnay that has not been chilled. She has genially offered me a glass and I have declined.

NW: He was the best king they ever had.

I find the remark of interest for its choice of pronoun.

EB: "They"? You don't consider yourself Afghan?

NW: Let's say I've divorced myself from my more troublesome half.

EB: I'm curious as to why that is.

NW: If he had succeeded, meaning King Amanullah, I might have answered your question differently.

I ask her to explain.

NW: You see, he woke one morning, the king, and proclaimed his plan to reshape the country—kicking and screaming, if need be—into a new and more enlightened nation. By God! he said. No more wearing of the veil, for one. Imagine, Monsieur Boustouler, a woman in Afghanistan arrested for wearing a *burqa*!

When his wife, Queen Soraya, appeared barefaced in public? *Oh là là.* The lungs of the mullahs inflated with enough gasps to fly a thousand *Hindenburg*s. And no more polygamy, he said! This, you understand, in a country where kings had legions of concubines and never set eyes on most of the children they'd so frivolously fathered. From now on, he declared, no man can force you into marriage. And no more bride price, brave women of Afghanistan, and no more child marriage. And here is more: You will all attend school.

EB: He was a visionary, then.

NW: Or a fool. I have always found the line perilously thin myself.

EB: What happened to him?

NW: The answer is as vexing as it is predictable, Monsieur Boustouler. Jihad, of course. They declared jihad on him, the mullahs, the tribal chiefs. Picture a thousand fists shot heavenward! The king had made the earth move, you see, but he was surrounded by an ocean of zealots, and you know well what happens when the ocean floor trembles, Monsieur Boustouler. A tsunami of bearded rebellion crashed down upon the poor king and carried him off, flailing helplessly, and spat him out on the shores of India, then Italy, and at last Switzerland, where he crawled from the muck and died a disillusioned old man in exile.

EB: And the country that emerged? I gather it did not suit you well.

NW: The reverse is equally true.

EB: Which was why you moved to France in 1955.

NW: I moved to France because I wished to save my daughter from a certain kind of life.

EB: What kind of life would that be?

NW: I didn't want her turned, against both her will and nature, into one of those diligent, sad women who are bent on a lifelong course of quiet servitude, forever in fear of showing, saying, or doing the wrong thing. Women who are admired by some in the West—here in France, for instance—turned into heroines for their hard lives, admired from a distance by those who couldn't bear even one day of walking in their shoes. Women who see their desires doused and their dreams renounced, and yet—and this is the worst of it, Monsieur Boustouler—if you meet them, they smile and pretend they have no misgivings at all. As though they lead enviable lives. But you look closely and you see the helpless look, the desperation, and how it belies all their show of good humor. It is quite pathetic, Monsieur Boustouler. I did not want this for my daughter.

EB: I gather she understands all this?

She lights another cigarette.

NW: Well, children are never everything you'd hoped for, Monsieur Boustouler.

In the emergency room, Pari is instructed by an ill-tempered nurse to wait by the registration desk, near a wheeled rack filled with clipboards and charts. It astonishes Pari that there are people who voluntarily spend their youths training for a profession that lands them in a place such as this. She cannot begin to understand it. She loathes hospitals. She hates seeing people at their worst, the sickly smell, the squeaky gurneys, the hallways with their drab paintings, the incessant paging overhead.

Dr. Delaunay turns out younger than Pari had expected. He has a slender nose, a narrow mouth, and tight blond curls. He guides her out of the emergency room, through the swinging double doors, into the main hallway.

"When your mother arrived," he says in a confidential tone, "she was quite inebriated . . . You don't seem surprised."

"I'm not."

"Neither were a number of the nursing staff. They say

she runs a bit of a tab here. I am new here myself, so, of course, I've never had the pleasure."

"How bad was it?"

"She was quite ornery," he says. "And, I should say, rather theatrical."

They share a brief grin.

"Will she be all right?"

"Yes, in the short term," Dr. Delaunay says. "But I must recommend, and quite emphatically, that she reduce her drinking. She was lucky this time, but who's to say next time . . ."

Pari nods. "Where is she?"

He leads her back into the emergency room and around the corner. "Bed three. I'll be by shortly with discharge instructions."

Pari thanks him and makes her way to her mother's bed.

"Salut, Maman."

Maman smiles tiredly. Her hair is disheveled, and her socks don't match. They have wrapped her forehead with bandages, and a colorless fluid drips through an intravenous linked to her left arm. She is wearing a hospital gown the wrong way and has not tied it properly. The gown has parted slightly in the front, and Pari can see a little of the thick, dark vertical line of her mother's old cesarian scar. She had asked her mother a few years earlier why she didn't bear the customary horizontal mark and Maman explained that the doctors had given her some sort of technical reason at the time that she no longer remembered. *The important thing,* she said, *was that they got you out.*

"I've ruined your evening," Maman mutters.

"Accidents happen. I've come to take you home."

"I could sleep a week."

Her eyes drift shut, though she keeps talking in a sluggish, stalling manner. "I was just sitting and watching TV. I got hungry. I went to the kitchen to get some bread and marmalade. I slipped. I'm not sure how, or on what, but my head caught the oven-door handle on the way down. I think I might have blacked out for a minute or two. Sit down, Pari. You're looming over me."

Pari sits. "The doctor said you were drinking."

Maman cracks one eye half open. Her frequenting of doctors is exceeded only by her dislike of them. "That boy? He said that? *Le petit salaud.* What does he know? His breath still smells of his mother's tit."

"You always joke. Every time I bring it up."

"I'm tired, Pari. You can scold me another time. The whipping post isn't going anywhere."

Now she does fall asleep. Snores, unattractively, as she does only after a binge.

Pari sits on the bedside stool, waiting for Dr. Delaunay, picturing Julien at a low-lit table, menu in hand, explaining the crisis to Christian and Aurelie over tall goblets of Bordeaux. He offered to accompany her to the hospital, but in a perfunctory way. It was a mere formality. Coming here would have been a bad idea anyway. If Dr. Delaunay thought he had seen theatrical earlier . . . Still, even if he couldn't come with her, Pari wishes he hadn't gone to dinner without her either. She is still a little astonished that he did. He could have explained it to Christian and Aurelie. They could have picked another night, changed the reservations. But Julien had gone. It wasn't merely thoughtless. No. There was something vicious about this move, deliberate, slashing. Pari has known for some time that he has that capacity. She has wondered of late whether he has a taste for it as well.

It was in an emergency room not unlike this one that Maman first met Julien. That was ten years ago, in 1963, when Pari was fourteen. He had driven a colleague, who had a migraine. Maman had brought Pari, who was the patient that time, having sprained her ankle badly during gymnastics in school. Pari was lying on a gurney when Julien pushed his chair into the room and struck up a conversation with Maman. Pari cannot remember now what was said between them. She does remember Julien saying, "Paris—like the city?" And from Maman the familiar reply, "No, without the s. It means 'fairy' in Farsi."

They met him for dinner on a rainy night later that week at a small bistro off Boulevard Saint-Germain. Back at the apartment, Maman had made a protracted show of indecision over what to wear, settling in the end for a pastel blue dress with a close-fitting waist, evening gloves, and sharp-pointed stiletto shoes. And even then, in the elevator, she'd said to Pari, "It's not too Jackie, is it? What do you think?"

Before the meal they smoked, all three of them, and Maman and Julien had beer in oversize frosted mugs. They finished one round, Julien ordered a second, and there was a third as well. Julien, in white shirt, tie, and a checkered evening blazer, had the controlled courteous manners of a well-bred man. He smiled with ease and laughed effortlessly. He had just a pinch of gray at the temples, which Pari hadn't noticed in the dim light of the emergency room, and she estimated his age around the same as Maman's. He was well versed in current events and spent some time talking about De Gaulle's veto of England's entry into the Common Market and, to Pari's surprise, almost succeeded in making it interesting. Only after Maman asked did he reveal that he had started teaching economics at the Sorbonne.

"A professor? Very glamorous."

"Oh, hardly," he said. "You should sit in sometime. It would cure you of that notion swiftly."

"Maybe I will."

Pari could tell Maman was already a little drunk.

"Maybe I will sneak in one day. Watch you in action."

"'Action'? You *do* recall I teach economic theory, Nila. If you do come, what you'll find is that my students think I'm a twit."

"Well, I doubt that."

Pari did too. She guessed that a good many of Julien's students wanted to sleep with him. Throughout dinner, she was careful not to get caught looking at him. He had a face right out of film noir, a face meant to be shot in black and white, parallel shadows of venetian blinds slashing across it, a plume of cigarette smoke spiraling beside it. A parenthesis-shaped piece of hair managed to fall on his brow, ever so gracefully—too gracefully, perhaps. If, in fact, it was dangling there without calculation, Pari noticed that he never bothered to fix it.

He asked Maman about the small bookshop she owned and ran. It was across the Seine, on the other side of Pont d'Arcole.

"Do you have books on jazz?"

"Bah oui," Maman said.

The rain outside rose in pitch, and the bistro grew more boisterous. As the waiter served them cheese puffs and ham brochettes, there followed between Maman and Julien a lengthy discussion of Bud Powell, Sonny Stitt, Dizzy Gillespie, and Julien's favorite, Charlie Parker. Maman told Julien she liked more the West Coast styles of Chet Baker and Miles Davis, had he listened to *Kind of Blue?* Pari was surprised to learn that Maman liked jazz *this* much and that she was so conversant about so many different musicians. She was struck, not for the first time, by both a childlike admiration for Maman and an unsettling sense that she did not really fully know her own mother. What did not surprise was Maman's effortless and thorough seduction of Julien. Maman was in her element there. She never had trouble commanding men's attention. She engulfed men.

Pari watched Maman as she murmured playfully, giggled at Julien's jokes, tilted her head and absently twirled a lock of her hair. She marveled again at how young and beautiful Maman was—Maman, who was only twenty years older than herself. Her long dark hair, her full chest, her startling eyes, and a face that glowed with the intimidating sheen of classic regal features. Pari marveled further at how little resemblance she herself bore to Maman, with her solemn pale eyes, her long nose, her gap-toothed smile, and her small breasts. If she had any beauty, it was of a more modest earth-bound sort. Being around her mother always reminded Pari that her own looks were woven of common cloth. At times, it was Maman herself who did the reminding, though it always came hidden in a Trojan horse of compliments.

She would say, *You're lucky, Pari. You won't have to work as hard for men to take you seriously. They'll pay attention to you. Too much beauty, it corrupts things.* She would laugh. *Oh, listen to me. I'm not saying I speak from experience. Of course not. It's merely an observation.*

You're saying I'm not beautiful.

I'm saying you don't want to be. Besides, you are pretty, and that is plenty good enough. Je t'assure, ma cherie. *It's better, even.*

She didn't resemble her father much either, Pari believed. He had been a tall man with a serious face, a high forehead, narrow chin, and thin lips. Pari kept a few pictures of him in her room from her childhood in the Kabul house. He had fallen ill in 1955—which was when Maman and she had moved to Paris—and had died shortly after. Sometimes Pari found herself gazing at one of his old photos, particularly a black-and-white of the two of them, she and her father, standing before an old American car. He was leaning against the fender and she was in his arms, both of them smiling. She remembered she had sat with him once as he painted giraffes and long-tailed monkeys for her on the side of an armoire. He had let her color one of the monkeys, holding her hand, patiently guiding her brushstrokes.

Seeing her father's face in those photos stirred an old sensation in Pari, a feeling that she had had for as long as she could remember. That there was in her life the absence of something, or someone, fundamental to her own existence. Sometimes it was vague, like a message sent across shadowy byways and vast distances, a weak signal on a radio dial, remote, warbled. Other times it felt so clear, this absence, so intimately close it made her heart lurch. For instance, in Provence two years earlier when Pari had seen a massive oak tree outside a farmhouse. Another time at the Jardin des Tuileries when she had watched a young mother pull her son in a little red Radio Flyer Wagon. Pari didn't understand. She read a story once about a middle-aged Turkish man who had suddenly slipped into a deep depression when the twin brother he never knew existed had suffered a fatal heart attack while on a canoe excursion in the Amazon rain forest. It was the closest anyone had ever come to articulating what she felt.

She had once spoken to Maman about it.

Well, it's hardly a mystery, mon amour, Maman had said. *You miss your father. He is gone from your life. It's natural that you should feel this way. Of course that's what it is. Come here. Give Maman a kiss.*

Her mother's answer had been perfectly reasonable but also unsatisfactory. Pari did believe that she would feel more whole if her father was still living, if he were here with her. But she also remembered feeling this way even as a child, living with both her parents at the big house in Kabul.

Shortly after they finished their meals, Maman excused herself to go to the bistro's bathroom and Pari was alone a few minutes with Julien. They talked about a film Pari had seen the week before, one with Jeanne Moreau playing a gambler, and they talked about school and music too. When she spoke, he rested his elbows on the table and leaned in a bit toward her, listening with great interest, both smiling and frowning, never lifting his eyes from her. It's a show, Pari told herself, he's only pretending. A polished act, something he trotted out for women, something he had chosen to do now on the spur of the moment, to toy with her awhile and amuse himself at her expense. And yet, under his unrelenting gaze, she could not help her pulse quickening and her belly tightening. She found herself speaking in an artificially sophisticated, ridiculous tone that was nothing like the way she spoke normally. She knew she was doing it and couldn't stop.

He told her he'd been married once, briefly.

"Really?"

"A few years back. When I was thirty. I lived in Lyon at the time."

He had married an older woman. It had not lasted because she had been very possessive of him. Julien had not disclosed this earlier when Maman was still at the table. "It was a physical relationship, really," he said. "*C'était complètement sexuelle.* She wanted to own me." He was looking at her when he said this and smiling a subversive little smile, cautiously gauging her reaction. Pari lit a cigarette and played it cool, like Bardot, like this was the sort of thing men told her all the time. But, inside, she was trembling. She knew that a small act of betrayal had been committed at the table. Something a little illicit, not entirely harmless but undeniably thrilling. When Maman returned, with her hair brushed anew and a fresh coat of lipstick, their stealthy moment broke, and Pari briefly resented Maman for intruding, for which she was immediately overcome with remorse.

She saw him again a week or so later. It was morning, and she was going to Maman's room with a bowl of coffee. She found him sitting on the side of Maman's bed, winding his wristwatch. She hadn't known he had spent the night. She spotted him from the hallway, through a crack in the door. She stood there, rooted to the ground, bowl in hand, her mouth feeling like she had sucked on a dry clump of mud, and she watched him, the spotless skin of his back, the small paunch of his belly, the darkness between his legs partly shrouded by the rumpled sheets. He clasped on his watch, reached for a cigarette off the nightstand, lit it, and then casually swung his gaze to her as if he had known she was there all along. He gave her a closemouthed smile. Then Maman said something from the shower, and Pari wheeled around. It was a marvel she didn't scald herself with the coffee.

Maman and Julien were lovers for about six months. They went to the cinema a lot, and to museums, and small art galleries featuring the works of struggling obscure painters with foreign names. One weekend they drove to the beach in Arcachon, near Bordeaux, and returned with tanned faces and a case of red wine. Julien took her to faculty events at the university, and Maman invited him to author readings at the bookstore. Pari tagged along at first—Julien asked her to, which seemed to please Maman—but soon she started making excuses to stay home. She wouldn't go, couldn't. It was unbearable. She was too tired, she said, or else she didn't feel well. She was going to her friend Collette's house to study, she said. Her friend since second grade, Collette was a wiry, brittle-looking girl with long limp hair and a nose like a crow's beak. She liked to shock people and say outrageous, scandalous things.

"I'll bet he's disappointed," Collette said. "That you don't go out with them."

"Well, if he is, he's not letting on."

"He wouldn't let on, would he? What would your mother think?"

"About what?" Pari said, though she knew, of course. She knew, and what she wanted was to hear it said.

"About what?" Collette's tone was sly, excited. "That he's with her to get to you. That it's you he wants."

"That is disgusting," Pari said with a flutter.

"Or maybe he wants you both. Maybe he likes a crowd in bed. In which case, I might ask you to put in a good word for me."

"You're repulsive, Collette."

Sometimes when Maman and Julien were out, Pari would undress in the hallway and look at herself in the long mirror. She would find faults with her body. It was too tall, she would think, too unshapely, too . . . utilitarian. She had inherited none of her mother's bewitching curves. Sometimes she walked like this, undressed, to her mother's room and lay on the bed where she knew Maman and Julien made love. Pari lay there stark-naked with her eyes closed, heart battering, basking in heedlessness, something like a hum spreading across her chest, her belly, and lower still.

It ended, of course. They ended, Maman and Julien. Pari was relieved but not surprised. Men always failed Maman in the end. They forever fell disastrously short of whatever ideal she held them up to. What began with exuberance and passion always ended with terse accusations and hateful words, with rage and weeping fits and the flinging of cooking utensils and collapse. High drama. Maman was incapable of either starting or ending a relationship without excess.

Then the predictable period when Maman would find a sudden taste for solitude. She would stay in bed, wearing an old winter coat over her pajamas, a weary, doleful, unsmiling presence in the apartment. Pari knew to leave her alone. Her attempts at consoling and companionship were not welcome. It lasted weeks, the sullen mood. With Julien, it went on considerably longer.

"Ah, merde!" Maman says now.

She is sitting up in bed, still in the hospital gown. Dr. Delaunay has given Pari the discharge papers, and the nurse is unhooking the intravenous from Maman's arm.

"What is it?"

"I just remembered. I have an interview in a couple of days."

"An interview?"

"A feature for a poetry magazine."

"That's fantastic, Maman."

"They're accompanying the piece with a photo." She points to the sutures on her forehead.

"I'm sure you'll find some elegant way to hide it," Pari says.

Maman sighs, looks away. When the nurse yanks the needle out, Maman winces and barks at the woman something unkind and undeserved.

FROM "AFGHAN SONGBIRD," AN INTERVIEW WITH
NILA WAHDATI BY ÉTIENNE BOUSTOULER,
Parallaxe 84 (WINTER 1974), P. 36

I look around the apartment again and am drawn to a framed photograph on one of the bookshelves. It is of a little girl squatting in a field of wild bushes, fully absorbed in the act of picking something, some sort of berry. She wears a bright yellow coat, buttoned to the throat, which contrasts with the dark gray overcast sky above. In the background, there is a stone farmhouse with closed shutters and battered shingles. I ask about the picture.

NW: My daughter, Pari. Like the city but no *s*. It means "fairy." That picture is from a trip to Normandy we took, the two of us. Back in 1957, I think. She must have been eight.

EB: Does she live in Paris?

NW: She studies mathematics at the Sorbonne.

EB: You must be proud.

She smiles and shrugs.

EB: I am struck a bit by her choice of career, given that you devoted yourself to the arts.

NW: I don't know where she gets the ability. All those incomprehensible formulas and theories. I guess they're not incomprehensible to her. I can hardly multiply, myself.

EB: Perhaps it's her way of rebelling. You know a thing or two about rebellion, I think.

NW: Yes, but I did it the proper way. I drank and smoked and took lovers. Who rebels with mathematics?

She laughs.

NW: Besides, she would be the proverbial rebel without a cause. I've given her every freedom imaginable. She wants for nothing, my daughter. She lacks nothing. She's living with someone. He is quite a bit older. Charming to a fault, well-read, entertaining. A raging narcissist, of course. Ego the size of Poland.

EB: You don't approve.

NW: Whether I approve or not is irrelevant. This is France, Monsieur Boustouler, not Afghanistan.

Young people don't live or die by the stamp of parental approval.

EB: Your daughter has no ties to Afghanistan, then?

NW: We left when she was six. She has limited memory of her time there.

EB: But not you, of course.

I ask her to tell me about her early life.

She excuses herself and leaves the room for a moment. When she returns, she hands me an old, wrinkled black-and-white photograph. A stern-looking man, heavyset, bespectacled, hair shiny and combed with an impeccable part. He sits behind a desk, reading a book. He wears a suit with peaked lapels, double-breasted vest, high-collared white shirt and bow tie.

NW: My father. Nineteen twenty-nine. The year I was born.

EB: He looks quite distinguished.

NW: He was part of the Pashtun aristocracy in Kabul. Highly educated, unimpeachable manners, appropriately sociable. A great raconteur too. At least in public.

EB: And in private?

NW: Venture to guess, Monsieur Boustouler?

I pick up the photo and look at it again.

EB: Distant, I would say. Grave. Inscrutable. Uncompromising.

NW: I really insist you have a glass with me. I hate— no, I loathe—drinking alone.

She pours me a glass of the Chardonnay. Out of politeness, I take a sip.

NW: He had cold hands, my father. No matter the weather. His hands were always cold. And he always wore a suit, again no matter the weather. Perfectly tailored, sharp creases. A fedora too. And wingtips, of course, two-toned. He was handsome, I suppose, though in a solemn way. Also—and I understood this only much later—in a manufactured, slightly ridicu- lous, faux-European way—complete, of course, with weekly games of lawn bowling and polo and the coveted French wife, all of it to the great approval of the young progressive king.

She picks at her nail and doesn't say anything for a while. I flip the tape in my recorder.

NW: My father slept in his own room, my mother and I in ours. Most days, he was out having lunch with ministers and advisers to the king. Or else he was out riding horses, or playing polo, or hunting. He loved to hunt.

EB: So you didn't see much of him. He was an absentee figure.

NW: Not entirely. He made it a point every couple of days to spend a few minutes with me. He would come into my room and sit on my bed, which was my signal to climb into his lap. He would bounce me on his knees for a while, neither one of us saying much, and finally he would say, "Well, what shall we do now, Nila?" Sometimes he would let me take the handkerchief from his breast pocket and let me fold it. Of course I would just ball it up and stuff it back into his pocket, and he would feign an expression of mock surprise, which I found highly comical. And we'd keep doing this until he tired of it, which was soon enough. And then he would stroke my hair with his cold hands and say, "Papa has to go now, my fawn. Run along."

She takes the photograph back to the other room and returns, fetches a new pack of cigarettes from a drawer and lights one.

NW: That was his nickname for me. I loved it. I used to hop around the garden—we had a very large garden—chanting, "I am Papa's fawn! I am Papa's fawn!" It wasn't until much later that I saw how sinister the nickname was.

EB: I'm sorry?

She smiles.

NW: My father shot deer, Monsieur Boustouler.

They could have walked the few blocks to Maman's apartment, but the rain has picked up considerably. In the taxi, Maman sits balled up in the backseat, draped by Pari's raincoat, wordlessly staring out the window. She looks old to Pari at this instant, far older than her forty-four years. Old and fragile and thin.

Pari has not been to Maman's apartment in a while. When she turns the key and lets them in, she finds the kitchen counter cluttered with dirty wineglasses, open bags of chips and uncooked pasta, plates with clumps of unrecognizable food fossilized onto them. A paper bag stuffed with empty wine bottles sits on the table, precariously close to tipping over. Pari sees newspapers on the floor, one of them soaking up the blood spill from earlier in the day, and, on it, a single pink wool sock. It frightens Pari to see Maman's living space in this state. And she feels guilt as well. Which, knowing Maman, may have been the intended effect. And then she hates that she had this last thought. It's the sort of thing Julien would think. *She wants you to feel badly.* He has said this to her several times over the last year. *She wants you to feel badly.* When he first said it, Pari felt relieved, understood. She was grateful to him for articulating what she could not, or would not. She thought she had found an ally. But, these days, she wonders. She catches in his words a glint of meanness. A troubling absence of kindness.

The bedroom floor is littered with pieces of clothing, records, books, more newspapers. On the windowsill is a glass half filled with water gone yellow from the cigarette butts floating in it. She swipes books and old magazines off the bed and helps Maman slip beneath the blankets.

Maman looks up at her, the back of one hand resting on her bandaged brow. The pose makes her look like an actress in a silent film about to faint.

"Are you going to be all right, Maman?"

"I don't think so," she says. It doesn't come out like a plea for attention. Maman says this in a flat, bored voice. It sounds tired and sincere, and final.

"You're scaring me, Maman."

"Are you leaving now?"

"Do you want me to stay?"

"Yes."

"Then I'll stay."

"Turn off the light."

"Maman?"

"Yes."

"Are you taking your pills? Have you stopped? I think you've stopped, and I worry."

"Don't start in on me. Turn off the light."

Pari does. She sits on the edge of the bed and watches her mother fall asleep. Then she heads for the kitchen to begin the formidable task of cleaning up. She finds a pair of gloves and starts with the dishes. She washes glasses reeking of long-soured milk, bowls crusted with old cereal, plates with food spotted with green fuzzy patches of fungus. She recalls the first time she had washed dishes at Julien's apartment the morning after they had slept together for the first time. Julien had made them omelets. How she'd relished this simple domestic act, washing plates at his sink, as he played a Jane Birkin song on the turntable.

She had reconnected with him the year before, in 1973, for the first time in almost a decade. She had run into him at a street march outside the Canadian Embassy, a student protest against the hunting of seals. Pari didn't want to go, and also she had a paper on meromorphic functions that needed finishing, but Collette insisted. They were living together at the time, an arrangement that was increasingly proving to their mutual displeasure. Collette smoked grass now. She wore headbands and loose magenta-colored tunics embroidered with birds and daisies. She brought home long-haired, unkempt boys who ate Pari's food and played the guitar badly. Collette was always in the streets, shouting, denouncing cruelty to animals, racism, slavery, French nuclear testing in the Pacific. There was always an urgent buzz around the apartment, people Pari didn't know milling in and out. And when they were alone, Pari sensed a new tension between the two of them, a haughtiness on the part of Collette, an unspoken disapproval of her.

"They're lying," Collette said animatedly. "They say their methods are humane. Humane! Have you seen what they use to club them over the head? Those *hakapiks*? Half the time, the poor animal hasn't even died yet, and the bastards stick their hooks in it and drag it out to the boat. They skin them alive, Pari. Alive!" The way Collette said this last thing, the way she emphasized it, made Pari want to apologize. For what, she was not quite sure, but she knew that, these days, it squeezed the breath out of her being around Collette and her reproaches and many outrages.

Only about thirty people showed up. There was a rumor that Brigitte Bardot was going to make an appearance, but it turned out to be just that, only a rumor. Collette was disappointed at the turnout. She had an agitated argument with a thin, pale bespectacled young man named Eric, who, Pari gathered, had been in charge of organizing the march. Poor Eric. Pari pitied him. Still seething, Collette took the lead. Pari shuffled along toward the back, next to a flat-chested girl who shouted slogans with a kind of nervous exhilaration. Pari kept her eyes to the pavement and tried her best to not stand out.

At a street corner, a man tapped her on the shoulder.

"You look like you're dying to be rescued."

He was wearing a tweed jacket over a sweater, jeans, a wool scarf. His hair was longer, and he had aged some, but elegantly, in a way that some women his age might find unfair and even infuriating. Still lean and fit, a couple of crow's-feet, some more graying at the temples, his face set with just a light touch of weariness.

"I am," she said.

They kissed on the cheek, and when he asked if she would have a coffee with him, she said yes.

"Your friend looks angry. Homicidally angry."

Pari glanced behind her, saw Collette standing with Eric, still chanting and pumping her fist but also, absurdly, glaring at the two of them. Pari swallowed back laughter—that would have wrought irreparable damage. She shrugged apologetically and ducked away.

They went to a small café and sat at a table by the window. He ordered them coffee and a custard *mille-feuille* each. Pari watched him speak to the waiter in the tone of genial authority that she recalled well and felt the same flutter in the gut that she had as a girl when he would come over to pick up Maman. She felt suddenly self-conscious, of her bitten fingernails, her unpowdered face, her hair hanging in limp curls—she wished now that she'd dried it after the shower, but she'd been late, and Collette had been pacing like a zoo animal.

"I hadn't pegged you as the protesting type," Julien said, lighting her cigarette for her.

"I'm not. That was more guilt than conviction."

"Guilt? Over seal hunting?"

"Over Collette."

"Ah. Yes. You know I think I may be a little frightened of her."

"We all are."

They laughed. He reached across the table and touched her scarf. He dropped his hand. "It would be trite to say that you're all grown up, so I won't. But you do look ravishing, Pari."

She pinched the lapel of her raincoat. "What, in this

Clouseau outfit?" Collette had told her it was a stupid habit, this self-deprecating clowning around with which Pari tried to mask her nervousness around men she was attracted to. Especially when they complimented her. Not for the first time, and far from the last, she envied Maman her naturally self-assured disposition.

"Next you'll say I'm living up to my name," she said.

"*Ah, non.* Please. Too obvious. There is an art to complimenting a woman, you know."

"No. But I'm certain you do."

The waiter brought the pastries and coffee. Pari focused on the waiter's hands as he arranged the cups and plates on the table, the palms of her own hands blooming with sweat. She had had only four lovers in her lifetime—a modest number, she knew, certainly compared to Maman at her age, even Collette. She was too watchful, too sensible, too compromising and adaptable, on the whole steadier and less exhausting than either Maman or Collette. But these were not qualities that drew men in droves. And she hadn't loved any of them—though she had lied to one and said she did—but pinned beneath each of them she had thoughts of Julien, of him and his beautiful face, which seemed to come with its own private lighting.

As they ate, he talked about his work. He said he had quit teaching some time ago. He had worked on debt sustainability at the IMF for a few years. The best part of that had been the traveling, he said.

"Where to?"

"Jordan, Iraq. Then I took a couple of years to write a book on informal economies."

"Were you published?"

"That is the rumor." He smiled. "I work for a private consulting firm now here in Paris."

"I want to travel too," Pari said. "Collette keeps saying we should go to Afghanistan."

"I suspect I know why *she* would want to go."

"Well, I've been thinking about it. Going back there, I mean. I don't care about the hashish, but I do want to travel the country, see where I was born. Maybe find the old house where my parents and I lived."

"I didn't realize you had this compulsion."

"I'm curious. I mean, I remember so little."

"I think one time you said something about a family cook."

Pari was inwardly flattered that he recalled something she had told him so many years before. He must have thought of her, then, in the intervening time. She must have been on his mind.

"Yes. His name was Nabi. He was the chauffeur too. He drove my father's car, a big American car, blue with a tan top. I remember it had an eagle's head on the hood."

Later, he asked, and she told him, about her studies and her focus on complex variables. He listened in a way that Maman never did—Maman, who seemed bored by the subject and mystified by Pari's passion for it. Maman couldn't even feign interest. She made lighthearted jokes that, on the surface, appeared to poke fun at her own ignorance. *Oh là là*, she would say, grinning, *my head! My head! Spinning like a totem! I'll make you a deal, Pari. I'll pour us some tea, and you return to the planet,* d'accord? She would chuckle, and Pari would humor her, but she sensed an edge to these jokes, an oblique sort of chiding, a suggestion that her knowledge had been judged esoteric and her pursuit of it frivolous. *Frivolous.* Which was rich, Pari thought, coming from a poet, though she would never say so to her mother.

Julien asked what she saw in mathematics and she said she found it comforting.

"I might have chosen 'daunting' as a more fitting adjective," he said.

"It is that too."

She said there was comfort to be found in the permanence of mathematical truths, in the lack of arbitrariness and the absence of ambiguity. In knowing that the answers may be elusive, but they could be found. They were there, waiting, chalk scribbles away.

"Nothing like life, in other words," he said. "There, it's questions with either no answers or messy ones."

"Am I that transparent?" She laughed and hid her face with a napkin. "I sound like an idiot."

"Not at all," he said. He plucked away the napkin. "Not at all."

"Like one of your students. I must remind you of your students."

He asked more questions, through which Pari saw that he had a working knowledge of analytic number theory and was, at least in passing, familiar with Carl Gauss and Bernhard Riemann. They spoke until the sky darkened. They drank coffee, and then beer, which led to wine. And then, when it could not be delayed any longer, Julien leaned in a bit and said in a polite, dutiful tone, "And, tell me, how is Nila?"

Pari puffed her cheeks and let the air out slowly.

Julien nodded knowingly.

"She may lose the bookstore," Pari said.

"I'm sorry to hear that."

"Business has been declining for years. She may have to shut it down. She wouldn't admit to it, but that would be a blow. It would hit her hard."

"Is she writing?"

"She hasn't been."

He soon changed the subject. Pari was relieved. She didn't want to talk about Maman and her drinking and the struggle to get her to keep taking her pills. Pari remembered all the awkward gazes, all the times when they were alone, she and Julien, Maman getting dressed in the next room, Julien looking at Pari and her trying to think of something to say. Maman must have sensed it. Could it be the reason she had ended it with Julien? If so, Pari had an inkling she'd done so more as a jealous lover than a protective mother.

A few weeks later, Julien asked Pari to move in with him. He lived in a small apartment on the Left Bank in the 7th arrondissement. Pari said yes. Collette's prickly hostility made for an untenable atmosphere at the apartment now.

Pari remembers her first Sunday with Julien at his place. They were reclined on his couch, pressed against each other. Pari was pleasantly half awake, and Julien was drinking tea, his long legs resting on the coffee table. He was reading an opinion piece on the back page of the newspaper. Jacques Brel played on the turntable. Every now and then, Pari would shift her head on his chest, and Julien would lean down and place a small kiss on her eyelid, or her ear, or her nose.

"We have to tell Maman."

She could feel him tightening. He folded the paper, removed his reading glasses and put them on the arm of the couch.

"She needs to know."

"I suppose," he said.

"You 'suppose'?"

"No, of course. You're right. You should call her. But be careful. Don't ask for permission or blessing, you'll get neither. Just tell her. And make sure she knows this is not a negotiation."

"That's easy for you to say."

"Well, perhaps. Still, remember that Nila is a vindictive woman. I am sorry to say this, but this is why it ended with us. She is astonishingly vindictive. So I know. It won't be easy for you."

Pari sighed and closed her eyes. The thought of it made her stomach clench.

Julien stroked her back with his palm. "Don't be squeamish."

Pari called her the next day. Maman already knew.

"Who told you?"

"Collette."

Of course, Pari thought. "I was going to tell you."

"I know you were. You are. It can't be hidden, a thing like this."

"Are you angry?"

"Does it matter?"

Pari was standing by the window. With her finger, she absently traced the blue rim of Julien's old, battered ashtray. She shut her eyes. "No, Maman. No it doesn't."

"Well, I wish I could say *that* didn't hurt."

"I didn't mean it to."

"I think that's highly debatable."

"Why would I want to hurt you, Maman?"

Maman laughed. A hollow, ugly sound.

"I look at you sometimes and I don't see me in you. Of course I don't. I suppose that isn't unexpected, after all. I don't know what sort of person you are, Pari. I don't know who you are, what you're capable of, in your blood. You're a stranger to me."

"I don't understand what that means," Pari said.

But her mother had already hung up.

From "Afghan Songbird," an interview with
Nila Wahdati by Étienne Boustouler,
Parallaxe 84 (Winter 1974), p. 38

EB: Did you learn your French here?

NW: My mother taught me in Kabul when I was little.

She spoke only French to me. We had lessons every day. It was very hard on me when she left Kabul.

EB: For France?

NW: Yes. My parents divorced in 1939 when I was ten. I was my father's only child. Letting me go with her was out of the question. So I stayed, and she left for Paris to live with her sister, Agnes. My father tried to mitigate the loss for me by occupying me with a private tutor and riding lessons and art lessons. But nothing replaces a mother.

EB: What happened to her?

NW: Oh, she died. When the Nazis came to Paris. They didn't kill her. They killed Agnes. My mother, she died of pneumonia. My father didn't tell me until the Allies had liberated Paris, but by then I already knew. I just knew.

EB: That must have been difficult.

NW: It was devastating. I loved my mother. I had planned on living with her in France after the war.

EB: I assume that means your father and you didn't get along.

NW: There were strains between us. We were quarreling. Quite a lot, which was a novelty for him. He wasn't accustomed to being talked back to, certainly not by women. We had rows over what I wore, where I went, what I said, how I said it, who I said it to. I had turned bold and adventurous, and he even more ascetic and emotionally austere. We had become natural opponents.

She chuckles, and tightens the bandanna's knot at the back of her head.

NW: And then I took to falling in love. Often, desperately, and, to my father's horror, with the wrong sort. A housekeeper's son once, another time a low-level civil servant who handled some business affairs for my father. Foolhardy, wayward passions, all of them doomed from the start. I arranged clandestine rendezvous and slipped away from home, and, of course, someone would inform my father that I'd been spotted on the streets somewhere. They would tell him that I was cavorting—they always put it like that—I was "cavorting." Or else they would say I was "parading" myself. My father would have to send a search party to bring me back. He would lock me up. For days. He would say from the other side of the door, *You humiliate me. Why do you humiliate me so? What will I do about you?* And sometimes he answered that question with his belt, or a closed fist. He'd chase me around the room. I suppose he thought he could terrorize me into submission. I wrote a great deal at that time, long, scandalous poems dripping with adolescent passion. Rather melodramatic and histrionic as well, I fear. Caged birds and shackled lovers, that sort of thing. I am not proud of them.

I sense that false modesty is not her suit and therefore can assume only that this is her honest assessment of these early writings. If so, it is a brutally unforgiving one. Her poems from this period are stunning in fact, even in translation, especially considering her young age when she wrote them. They are moving, rich with imagery, emotion, insight, and telling grace. They speak beautifully of loneliness and uncontainable sorrow. They chronicle her disappointments, the crests and troughs of young love in all its radiance and promises and trappings. And there is often a sense of transcendent claustrophobia, of a shortening horizon, and always a sense of struggle against the tyranny of circumstance—often depicted as a never named sinister male figure who looms. A not-so-opaque allusion to her father, one would gather. I tell her all this.

EB: And you break in these poems from the rhythm, rhyme, and meter that I understand to be integral to classic Farsi poetry. You make use of free-flowing imagery. You heighten random, mundane details. This was quite groundbreaking, I understand. Would it be fair to say that if you'd been born in a wealthier nation—say, Iran—that you would almost certainly be known now as a literary pioneer?

She smiles wryly.

NW: Imagine.

EB: Still, I am quite struck by what you said earlier. That you weren't proud of those poems. Are you pleased with any of your work?

NW: A thorny question, that one. I suppose I would answer in the affirmative, if only I could keep them apart from the creative process itself.

EB: You mean separate the end from the means.

NW: I see the creative process as a necessarily thievish undertaking. Dig beneath a beautiful piece of writing, Monsieur Boustouler, and you will find all manner of dishonor. Creating means vandalizing the lives of other people, turning them into unwilling and unwitting participants. You steal their desires, their dreams, pocket their flaws, their suffering. You take what does not belong to you. You do this knowingly.

EB: And you were very good at it.

NW: I did it not for the sake of some high and lofty notion about art but because I had no choice. The compulsion was far too powerful. If I did not surrender to it, I would have lost my mind. You ask if I am proud. I find it hard to flaunt something obtained through what I know to be morally questionable means. I leave the decision to tout or not to others.

She empties her glass of wine and refills it with what remains in the bottle.

NW: What I can tell you, however, is that no one was touting me in Kabul. No one in Kabul considered me a pioneer of anything but bad taste, debauchery, and immoral character. Not least of all, my father. He said my writings were the ramblings of a *whore*. He used that word precisely. He said I'd damaged his family name beyond repair. He said I had betrayed him. He kept asking why I found it so hard to be respectable.

EB: How did you respond?

NW: I told him I did not care for his notion of respectable. I told him I had no desire to slip the leash around my own neck.

EB: I suppose that only displeased him more.

NW: Naturally.

I hesitate to say this next.

EB: But I do understand his anger.

She cocks an eyebrow.

EB: He was a patriarch, was he not? And you were a direct challenge to all he knew, all that he held dear. Arguing, in a way, through both your life and your writing, for new boundaries for women, for women to have a say in their own status, to arrive at legitimate selfhood. You were defying the monopoly that men like him had held for ages. You were saying what could not be said. You were conducting a small, one-woman revolution, one could say.

NW: And all this time, I thought I was writing about sex.

EB: But that's part of it, isn't it?

I flip through my notes and mention a few of the overtly erotic poems—"Thorns," "But for the Waiting," "The Pillow." I also confess to her that they are not among my favorites. I remark that they lack nuance and ambiguity. They read as though they have been crafted with the sole aim of shocking and scandalizing. They strike me as polemical, as angry indictments of Afghan gender roles.

NW: Well, I *was* angry. I was angry about the attitude that I had to be protected from sex. That I had to be protected from my own body. Because I was a woman. And women, don't you know, are emotionally, morally, and intellectually immature. They lack self-control, you see, they're vulnerable to physical temptation. They're hypersexual beings who must be restrained lest they jump into bed with every Ahmad and Mahmood.

EB: But—forgive me for saying this—you did just that, no?

NW: Only as a protest against that very notion.

She has a delightful laugh, full of mischief and cunning intelligence. She asks if I want lunch. She says her daughter has recently restocked her refrigerator and proceeds to make what turns out to be an excellent *jambon fumé* sandwich. She makes only one. For herself, she uncorks a new bottle of wine and lights another cigarette. She sits down.

NW: Do you agree, for the sake of this chat, that we should remain on good terms, Monsieur Boustouler?

I tell her I do.

NW: Then do me two favors. Eat your sandwich and quit looking at my glass.

Needless to say, this preemptively quells any impulse I may have had to ask about the drinking.

EB: What happened next?

NW: I fell ill in 1948, when I was nearly nineteen. It was serious, and I will leave it at that. My father took me to Delhi for treatment. He stayed with me for six weeks while doctors tended to me. I was told I could have died. Perhaps I should have. Dying can be quite the career move for a young poet. When we returned, I was frail and withdrawn. I couldn't be bothered with writing. I had little interest in food or conversation or entertainment. I was averse to visitors. I just wanted to pull the curtains and sleep all day every day. Which was what I did mostly. Eventually, I got out of bed and slowly resumed my daily routines, by which I mean the stringent essentials a person must tend to in order to remain functional and nominally civil. But I felt diminished. Like I had left something vital of myself behind in India.

EB: Was your father concerned?

NW: Quite the contrary. He was encouraged. He thought that my encounter with mortality had shaken me out of my immaturity and waywardness. He didn't understand that I felt lost. I've read, Monsieur Boustouler, that if an avalanche buries you and you're lying there underneath all that snow, you can't tell which way is up or down. You want to dig yourself out but pick the wrong way, and you dig yourself to your own demise. That was how I felt, disoriented, suspended in confusion, stripped of my compass. Unspeakably depressed as well. And, in that state, you are vulnerable. Which is likely why I said yes the following year, in 1949, when Suleiman Wahdati asked my father for my hand.

EB: You were twenty.

NW: He was not.

She offers me another sandwich, which I decline, and a cup of coffee, which I accept. As she sets water on to boil, she asks if I am married. I tell her I am not and that I doubt I ever will be. She looks at me over her shoulder, her gaze lingering, and grins.

NW: Ah. I can usually tell.

EB: Surprise!

NW: Maybe it's the concussion.

She points to the bandanna.

NW: This isn't a fashion statement. I slipped and fell a couple of days ago, tore my forehead open. Still, I should have known. About you, I mean. In my experience, men who understand women as well as you seem to rarely want to have anything to do with them.

She gives me the coffee, lights a cigarette, and takes a seat.

NW: I have a theory about marriage, Monsieur Boustouler. And it's that nearly always you will know within two weeks if it's going to work. It's astonishing how many people remain shackled for years, decades even, in a protracted and mutual state of self-delusion and false hope when in fact they had their answer in those first two weeks. Me, I didn't even need that long. My husband was a decent man. But he was much too serious, aloof, and uninteresting. Also, he was in love with the chauffeur.

EB: Ah. That must have come as a shock.

NW: Well, it did thicken the proverbial plot.

She smiles a little sadly.

NW: I felt sorry for him, mostly. He could not have chosen a worse time or worse place to be born the way he was. He died of a stroke when our daughter was six. At that point, I could have stayed in Kabul. I had the house and my husband's wealth. There was a gardener and the aforementioned chauffeur. It would have been a comfortable life. But I packed our bags and moved us, Pari and me, to France.

EB: Which, as you indicated earlier, you did for her benefit.

NW: Everything I've done, Monsieur Boustouler, I've done for my daughter. Not that she understands, or appreciates, the full measure of what I've done for her. She can be breathtakingly thoughtless, my daughter. If she knew the life she would have had to endure, if not for me . . .

EB: Is your daughter a disappointment to you?

NW: Monsieur Boustouler, I've come to believe she's my punishment.

One day in 1975, Pari comes home to her new apartment and finds a small package on her bed. It is a year after she fetched her mother from the emergency room and nine months since she left Julien. Pari is living now with a nursing student named Zahia, a young Algerian woman with curly brown hair and green eyes. She is a competent girl, with a cheerful, unfrazzled disposition, and they have lived together easily, though Zahia is now engaged to her boyfriend, Sami, and moving in with him at the end of the semester.

There is a folded sheet of paper next to the package. *This came for you. I'm spending the night at Sami's. See you tomorrow. Je t'embrasse. Zahia.*

Pari rips the package open. Inside is a magazine and, clipped to it, another note, this one written in a familiar, almost femininely graceful script. *This was sent to Nila and then to the couple who live in Collette's old apartment and now it is forwarded to me. You should update your forwarding address. Read this at your own peril. Neither of us fares very well, I'm afraid. Julien.*

Pari drops the journal on the bed and makes herself a spinach salad and some couscous. She changes into pajamas and eats by the TV, a small black-and-white rental. Absently, she watches images of airlifted South Vietnamese refugees arriving in Guam. She thinks of Collette, who had protested the American war in Vietnam in the streets. Collette, who had brought a wreath of dahlias and daisies to Maman's memorial, who had held and kissed Pari, who had delivered a beautiful recitation of one of Maman's poems at the podium.

Julien had not attended the services. He'd called and said, feebly, that he disliked memorials, he found them depressing.

Who doesn't? Pari had said.

I think it's best I stay clear.

Do as you like, Pari had said into the receiver, thinking, But it won't absolve you, not coming. Any more than attending will absolve me. Of how reckless we were. How thoughtless. My God. Pari had hung up with him knowing that her fling with Julien had been the final push for Maman. She had hung up knowing that for the rest of her life it would slam into her at random moments, the guilt, the terrible remorse, catching her off guard, and that she would ache to the bones with it. She would wrestle with this, now and for all days to come. It would be the dripping faucet at the back of her mind.

She takes a bath after dinner and reviews some notes for an upcoming exam. She watches some more TV, cleans and dries the dishes, sweeps the kitchen floor. But it's no use. She can't distract herself. The journal sits on the bed, its calling to her like a low-frequency hum.

Afterward, she puts a raincoat over her pajamas and goes for a walk down Boulevard de la Chapelle, a few blocks south of the apartment. The air is chilly, and raindrops slap the pavement and shopwindows, but the apartment cannot contain her restlessness right now. She needs the cold, the moist air, the open space.

When she was young, Pari remembers, she had been all questions. *Do I have cousins in Kabul, Maman? Do I have aunts and uncles? And grandparents, do I have a* grand-pére *and a* grand-maman? *How come they never visit? Can we write them a letter? Please, can we visit them?*

Most of her questions had revolved around her father. *What was his favorite color, Maman? Tell me, Maman, was he a good swimmer? Did he know a lot of jokes?* She remembers him chasing her once through a room. Rolling her around on a carpet, tickling her soles and belly. She remembers the smell of his lavender soap and the shine of his high forehead, his long fingers. His oval-shaped lapis cuff links, the crease of his suit pants. She can see the dust motes they had kicked up together off the carpet.

What Pari had always wanted from her mother was the glue to bond together her loose, disjointed scraps of memory, to turn them into some sort of cohesive narrative. But Maman never said much. She always withheld details of her life and of their life together in Kabul. She kept Pari at a remove from their shared past, and, eventually, Pari stopped asking.

And now it turns out that Maman had told this magazine writer, this Étienne Boustouler, more about herself and her life than she ever did her own daughter.

Or had she.

Pari read the piece three times back at the apartment. And she doesn't know what to think, what to believe. So much of it rings false. Parts of it read like a parody. A lurid melodrama, of shackled beauties and doomed romances and pervasive oppression, all told in such breathless, high-spirited fashion.

Pari heads westbound, toward Pigalle, walking briskly, hands stuffed into the pockets of her raincoat. The sky is darkening rapidly, and the downpour lashing at her face is becoming heavier and more steady, rippling windows, smearing headlights. Pari has no memory of ever meeting the man, her grandfather, Maman's father, has seen only the one photograph of him reading at his desk, but she doubts that he was the mustache-twirling villain Maman has made him out to be. Pari thinks she sees through this story. She has her own ideas. In her version, he is a man rightfully worried over the well-being of a deeply unhappy and self-destructive daughter who cannot help making shambles of her own life. He is a man who suffers humiliations and repeated assaults on his dignity and still stands by his daughter, takes her to India when she's ill, stays with her for six weeks. And, on that subject, what really was wrong with Maman? What did they do to her in India? Pari wonders, thinking of the vertical pelvic scar—Pari had asked, and Zahia had told her that cesarian incisions were made horizontally.

And then what Maman told the interviewer about her husband, Pari's father. Was it slander? Was it true that he'd loved Nabi, the chauffeur? And, if it was, why reveal such a thing now after all this time if not to confuse, humiliate, and perhaps inflict pain? And, if so, on whom?

As for herself, Pari is not surprised by the unflattering treatment Maman had reserved for her—not after Julien— nor is she surprised by Maman's selective, sanitized account of her own mothering.

Lies?

And yet . . .

Maman had been a gifted writer. Pari has read every word Maman had written in French and every poem she had translated from Farsi as well. The power and beauty of her writing was undeniable. But if the account Maman had given of her life in the interview was a lie, then where did the images of her work come from? Where was the wellspring for words that were honest and lovely and brutal and sad? Was she merely a gifted trickster? A magician, with a pen for a wand, able to move an audience by conjuring emotions she had never known herself? Was that even possible?

Pari does not know—she does not know. And that, perhaps, may have been Maman's true intent, to shift the ground beneath Pari's feet. To intentionally unsteady and upend her, to turn her into a stranger to herself, to heave the weight of doubt on her mind, on all Pari thought she knew of her life, to make her feel as lost as if she were wandering through a desert at night, surrounded by darkness and the unknown, the truth elusive, like a single tiny glint of light in the distance flickering on and off, forever moving, receding.

Perhaps, Pari thinks, this is Maman's retribution. Not only for Julien but also for the disappointment that Pari has always been. Pari, who was maybe supposed to bring an end to all the drinking, the men, the years squandered making desperate lunges at happiness. All the dead ends pursued and abandoned. Each lash of disappointment leaving Maman more damaged, more derailed, and happiness more illusory. *What was I, Maman?* Pari thinks. *What was I supposed to be, growing in your womb—assuming it was even in your womb that I was conceived? A seed of hope? A ticket purchased to ferry you from the dark? A patch for that hole you carried in your heart? If so, then I wasn't enough. I wasn't nearly enough. I was no balm to your pain, only another dead end, another burden, and you must have seen that early on. You must have realized it. But what could you do? You couldn't go down to the pawnshop and sell me.*

Perhaps this interview was Maman's last laugh.

Pari steps beneath the awning of a brasserie to take refuge from the rain a few blocks west of the hospital where Zahia does part of her training. She lights a cigarette. She should call Collette, she thinks. They have spoken only once or twice since the memorial. When they were young, they used to chew mouthfuls of gum until their jaws ached, and they would sit before Maman's dresser mirror and brush each other's hair, pin it up. Pari spots an old woman across the street, wearing a plastic rain bonnet, laboring up the sidewalk trailed by a small tan terrier. Not for the first time, a little puff breaks rank from the collective fog of Pari's memories and slowly takes the shape of a dog. Not a little toy like the old woman's, but a big mean specimen, furry, dirty, with a severed tail and ears. Pari is unsure whether this, in fact, is a memory or the ghost of one or neither. She had asked Maman once if they had ever owned a dog in Kabul and Maman said, *You know I don't like dogs. They have no self-respect. You kick them and they still love you. It's depressing.*

Something else Maman said:

I don't see me in you. I don't know who you are.

Pari tosses her cigarette. She decides she will call Collette. Make plans to meet somewhere for tea. See how she is doing. Who she's seeing. Go window-shopping like they used to.

See if her old friend is still up for that trip to Afghanistan.

Pari does meet Collette. They meet at a popular bar with a Moroccan design, violet drapes and orange pillows everywhere, curly-haired oud player on a small stage. Collette has not arrived alone. She has brought a young man with her. His name is Eric Lacombe. He teaches drama to seventh and eighth graders at a lycée in the 18th. He tells Pari he has met her before, a few years earlier, at a student protest against seal hunting. At first Pari cannot recall, and then she remembers that he was the one with whom Collette had been so angry over the low turnout, the one whose chest she'd knuckled. They sit on the ground, atop fluffy mango-colored cushions, and order drinks. Initially, Pari is under the impression that Collette and Eric are a couple, but Collette keeps praising Eric, and soon Pari understands he has been brought for her benefit. The discomfort that would normally overtake her in a situation like this is mirrored in—and mitigated by—Eric's own considerable unease. Pari finds it amusing, and even endearing, the way he keeps blushing and shaking his head in apology and embarrassment. Over bread and black olive tapenades, Pari steals glances at him. He could not be called handsome. His hair is long and limp, tied with a rubber band at the base of his neck. He has small hands and pale skin. His nose is too narrow, his forehead too protruding, the chin nearly absent, but he has a bright-eyed grin and a habit of punctuating the end of each sentence with an expectant smile like a happy question mark. And though his face does not enthrall Pari as Julien's had, it is a far kinder face and, as Pari will learn before long, an external ambassador for the attentiveness, the quiet forbearance, and the enduring decency that resides within Eric.

They marry on a chilly day in the spring of 1977, a few months after Jimmy Carter is sworn into office. Against his parents' wishes, Eric insists on a small civil ceremony, no one present but the two of them and Collette as witness. He says a formal wedding is an extravagance they cannot afford. His father, who is a wealthy banker, offers to pay. Eric, after all, is their only child. He offers it as a gift, then as a loan. But Eric declines. And though he never says so, Pari knows it is to save her the awkwardness of a ceremony at which she would be alone, with no family to sit in the aisles, no one to give her away, no one to shed a happy tear on her behalf.

When she tells him of her plans to go to Afghanistan, he understands in a way that Pari believes Julien never would. And also in a way that she had never openly admitted to herself.

"You think you were adopted," he says.

"Will you go with me?"

They decide they will travel that summer, when school is out for Eric and Pari can take a brief hiatus from her Ph.D. work. Eric registers them both for Farsi classes with a tutor he has found through the mother of one of his pupils. Pari often finds him on the couch wearing headphones, cassette player on his chest, his eyes shut in concentration as he mutters heavily accented *Thank you*s and *Hello*s and *How are you?*s in Farsi.

A few weeks before summer, just as Eric is looking into airfare and accommodations, Pari discovers she is pregnant.

"We could still go," Eric says. "We should still go."

It is Pari who decides against it. "It's irresponsible," she says. They are living in a studio with faulty heating, leaky plumbing, no air-conditioning, and an assortment of scavenged furniture.

"This is no place for a baby," she says.

Eric takes on a side job teaching piano, which he had briefly entertained pursuing before he had set his sights on theater, and by the time Isabelle arrives—sweet, light-skinned Isabelle, with eyes the color of caramelized sugar—they have moved into a small two-bedroom apartment not far from Jardin du Luxembourg, this with financial assistance from Eric's father, which they accept this time on the condition that it be a loan.

Pari takes three months off. She spends her days with Isabelle. She feels weightless around Isabelle. She feels a shining around herself whenever Isabelle turns her eyes to her. When Eric comes home from the lycée in the evening, the first thing he does is shed his coat and his briefcase at the door and then he drops on the couch and extends his arms and wiggles his fingers. "Give her to me, Pari. Give her to me." As he bounces Isabelle on his chest, Pari fills him in on all the day's tidbits—how much milk Isabelle took, how many naps, what they watched together on television, the enlivening games they played, the new noises she's making. Eric never tires of hearing it.

They have postponed going to Afghanistan. The truth is, Pari no longer feels the piercing urge to search for answers and roots. Because of Eric and his steadying, comforting companionship. And because of Isabelle, who has solidified the ground beneath Pari's feet—pocked as it still may be with gaps and blind spots, all the unanswered questions, all the things Maman would not relinquish. They are still there. Pari just doesn't hunger for the answers like she used to.

And the old feeling she has always had—that there is an absence in her life of something or someone vital—has dulled. It still comes now and then, sometimes with power that catches her unawares, but less frequently than it used to. Pari has never been this content, has never felt this happily moored.

In 1981, when Isabelle is three, Pari, a few months pregnant with Alain, has to go to Munich for a conference. She will present a paper she has coauthored on the use of modular forms outside of number theory, specifically in topology and theoretical physics. The presentation is received well, and afterward Pari and a few other academics go out to a noisy bar for beer and pretzels and *Weisswurst.* She returns to the hotel room before midnight and goes to bed without changing or washing her face. The phone wakes her at 2:30 a.m. Eric, calling from Paris.

"It's Isabelle," he says. She has a fever. Her gums have suddenly swollen and turned red. They bleed profusely at the lightest touch. "I can hardly see her teeth. Pari. I don't know what to do. I read somewhere that it could be . . ."

She wants him to stop. She wants to tell him to shut up, that she cannot bear to hear it, but she's too late. She hears the words *childhood leukemia*, or maybe he says *lymphoma*, and what's the difference anyway? Pari sits on the edge of the bed, sits there like a stone, head throbbing, skin drenched with sweat. She is furious with Eric for planting a thing as horrible as this in her mind in the middle of the night when she's seven hundred kilometers away and helpless. She is furious with herself for her own stupidity. Opening herself up like this, voluntarily, to a lifetime of worry and anguish. It was madness. Sheer lunacy. A spectacularly foolish and baseless faith, against enormous odds, that a world you do not control will not take from you the one thing you cannot bear to lose. Faith that the world will not destroy you. *I don't have the heart for this.* She actually says this under her breath. *I don't have the heart for this.* At that moment, she cannot think of a more reckless, irrational thing than choosing to become a parent.

And part of her—*God help me,* she thinks, *God forgive me for it*—part of her is furious with Isabelle for doing this to her, for making her suffer like this.

"Eric. Eric! *Ecoute moi.* I'm going to call you back. I need to hang up now."

She empties her purse on the bed, finds the small maroon notebook where she keeps phone numbers. She places a call to Lyon. Collette lives in Lyon now with her husband, Didier, where she has started a small travel agency. Didier is studying to be a doctor. It's Didier who answers the phone.

"You do know I'm studying psychiatry, Pari, don't you?" he says.

"I know. I know. I just thought . . ."

He asks some questions. Has Isabelle had any weight loss? Night sweats, unusual bruises, fatigue, chronic fevers?

In the end, he says Eric should take her to a doctor in the morning. But, if he recalls correctly from his general training back in medical school, it sounds to him like acute gingivostomatitis.

Pari clutches the receiver so hard, her wrist aches. "Please," she says patiently, "Didier."

"Ah, sorry. What I mean is, it sounds like the first manifestation of a cold sore."

"A cold sore."

Then he adds the happiest words Pari has ever heard in her life. "I think she's going to be fine."

Pari has met Didier only twice, once before and once after his wedding to Collette. But at that instant, she loves him truly. She tells him so, weeping into the phone. She tells him she loves him—several times—and he laughs and wishes her a good night. Pari calls Eric, who will take Isabelle in the morning to see Dr. Perrin. Afterward, her ears ringing, Pari lies in bed, looking at the streetlight streaming in through the dull-green wooden shutters. She thinks of the time she had to be hospitalized with pneumonia, when she was eight, Maman refusing to go home, insisting on sleeping in the chair next to her bed, and she feels a new, unexpected, belated kinship with her mother. She has missed her many times over the last few years. At her wedding, of course. At Isabelle's birth. And at myriad random moments. But never more so than on this terrible and wondrous night in this hotel room in Munich.

Back in Paris the next day, she tells Eric they shouldn't have any more children after Alain is born. It only raises the odds of heartbreak.

In 1985, when Isabelle is seven, Alain four, and little Thierry two, Pari accepts an offer to teach at a prominent university in Paris. She becomes subject, for a time, to the expected academic jostling and pettiness—not surprising, given that, at thirty-six, she is the youngest professor in the department and one of only two women. She weathers it in a way that she imagines Maman never could or would have. She does not flatter or butter up. She refrains from locking horns or filing complaints. She will always have her skeptics. But by the time the Berlin Wall comes down, so have the walls in her academic life, and she has slowly won over most of her colleagues with her sensible demeanor and disarming sociability. She makes friends in her department—and in others too—attends university events, fund-raisers, the occa- sional cocktail hour and dinner party. Eric goes with her to these soirees. As an ongoing private joke, he insists on wear- ing the same wool tie and corduroy blazer with elbow patches. He wanders around the crowded room, tasting hors d'oeuvres, sipping wine, looking jovially bewildered, and occasionally Pari has to swoop in and steal him away from a group of mathematicians before he opines on 3-manifolds and Diophantine approximations.

Inevitably, someone at these parties will ask Pari her views on the developments in Afghanistan. One evening, a slightly tipsy visiting professor named Chatelard asks Pari what she thinks will happen to Afghanistan when the Soviets leave. "Will your people find peace, Madame Professeur?"

"I wouldn't know," she says. "Practically speaking, I'm Afghan only in name."

"*Non mais, quande-même,*" he says. "But, still, you must have some insight."

She smiles, trying to keep at bay the inadequacy that always creeps in with these queries. "Just what I read in *Le Monde*. Like you."

"But you grew up there, *non?*"

"I left when I was very little. Have you seen my husband? He's the one with the elbow patches."

What she says is true. She does follow the news, reads in the papers about the war, the West arming the Mujahideen, but Afghanistan has receded in her mind. She has plenty to keep her busy at home, which is now a pretty four-bedroom house in Guyancourt, about twenty kilometers from the center of Paris. They live on a small hill near a park with walking trails and ponds. Eric is writing plays now in addition to teaching. One of his plays, a lighthearted political farce, is going to be produced in the fall at a small theater near Hôtel de Ville in Paris, and he has already been commissioned to write another.

Isabelle has grown into a quiet but bright and thoughtful adolescent. She keeps a diary and reads a novel a week. She likes Sinéad O'Connor. She has long, beautiful fingers and takes cello lessons. In a few weeks, she will perform Tchaikovsky's *Chanson Triste* at a recital. She was resistant at first to taking up the cello, and Pari had taken a few lessons with her as a show of solidarity. It proved both unnecessary and unfeasible. Unnecessary because Isabelle quickly latched onto the instrument of her own accord and unfeasible because the cello made Pari's hands ache.

For a year now, Pari has been waking in the morning with stiffness in her hands and wrists that won't loosen up for half an hour, sometimes an hour. Eric has quit pressuring her to see a doctor and is now insisting. "You're only forty-three, Pari," he says. "This is not normal." Pari has set up an appointment.

Alain, their middle child, has a sly roguish charm. He is obsessed with martial arts. He was born prematurely and is still small for a boy of eleven, but what he lacks in stature he more than makes up for with desire and gumption. His opponents are always fooled by his wispy frame and slim legs. They underestimate him. Pari and Eric have often lain in bed at night and marveled at his enormous will and ferocious energy. Pari worries about neither Isabelle nor Alain.

It is Thierry who concerns her. Thierry, who perhaps on some dark primordial level, senses that he was unexpected, unintended, uninvited. Thierry is prone to wounding silences and narrow looks, to fussing and fiddling whenever Pari asks something of him. He defies her for no other reason, it seems to Pari, than defiance itself. Some days, a cloud gathers over him. Pari can tell. She can almost see it. It gathers and swells until at last it splits open, spilling a torrent of cheek-quivering, foot-stomping rage that frightens Pari and leaves Eric to blink and smile miserably. Pari knows instinctively that Thierry will be for her, like the ache in her joints, a lifelong worry.

She wonders often what sort of grandmother Maman would have made. Especially with Thierry. Intuitively, Pari thinks Maman would have proved helpful with him. She might have seen something of herself in him—though not biologically, of course, Pari has been certain of that for some time. The children know of Maman. Isabelle, in particular, is curious. She has read many of her poems.

"I wish I'd met her," she says.

"She sounds glamorous," she says.

"I think we would have made good friends, she and I. Do you think? We would have read the same books. I would have played cello for her."

"Well, she would have loved that," Pari says. "That much I am sure of."

Pari has not told the children about the suicide. They may learn one day, probably will. But they wouldn't learn it from her. She will not plant the seed in their mind, that a parent is capable of abandoning her children, of saying to them *You are not enough*. For Pari, the children and Eric have always been enough. They always will be.

In the summer of 1994, Pari and Eric take the children to Majorca. It's Collette who, through her now thriving travel agency, organizes the holiday for them. Collette and Didier meet up with them in Majorca, and they all stay together for two weeks in a beachfront rental house. Collette and Didier don't have children, not by some biological misfortune but because they don't want any. For Pari, the timing is good. Her rheumatoid is well controlled at the time. She takes a weekly dose of methotrexate, which she is tolerating well. Fortunately, she has not had to take any steroids of late and suffer the accompanying insomnia.

"Not to speak of the weight gain," she tells Collette.

"Knowing I'd have to get into a bathing suit in Spain?" She laughs. "Ah, vanity."

They spend the days touring the island, driving up the northwest coast by the Serra de Tramuntana Mountains, stopping to stroll by the olive groves and into the pine forest. They eat *porcella*, and a wonderful sea bass dish called *lubina*, and an eggplant and zucchini stew called *tumbet*. Thierry refuses to eat any of it, and at every restaurant Pari has to ask the chef to make him a plate of spaghetti with plain tomato sauce, no meat, no cheese. At Isabelle's request—she has recently discovered opera—one night they attend a production of Giacomo Puccini's *Tosca*. To survive the ordeal, Collette and Pari surreptitiously pass each other a silver flask of cheap vodka. By the middle of act two, they are sloshed, and can't help giggling like schoolgirls at the histrionics of the actor playing Scarpia.

One day, Pari, Collette, Isabelle, and Thierry pack a lunch and go to the beach; Didier, Alain, and Eric had left in the morning for a hike along Sóller Bay. On the way to the beach, they visit a shop to buy Isabelle a bathing suit that has caught her eye. As they walk into the shop, Pari catches a glimpse of her reflection in the plate glass. Normally, especially of late, when she steps in front of a mirror an automatic mental process kicks into gear that prepares her to greet her older self. It buffers her, dulls the shock. But in the shopwindow, she has caught herself off guard, vulnerable to reality undistorted by self-delusion. She sees a middle-aged woman in a drab floppy blouse and a beach skirt that doesn't conceal quite enough of the saggy folds of skin over her kneecaps. The sun picks out the gray in her hair. And despite the eyeliner, and the lipstick that defines her lips, she has a face now that a passerby's gaze will engage and then bounce from, as it would a street sign or a mailbox number. The moment is brief, barely enough for a flutter of the pulse but long enough for her illusory self to catch up with the reality of the woman gazing back from the shopwindow. It is a little devastating. This is what aging is, she thinks as she follows Isabelle into the store, these random unkind moments that catch you when you least expect them.

Later, when they return from the beach to the rental house, they find that the men have already returned.

"Papa's getting old," Alain says.

From behind the bar, Eric, who is mixing a carafe of sangria, rolls his eyes and shrugs genially.

"I thought I'd have to carry you, Papa."

"Give me one year. We'll come back next year, and I'll race you around the island, *mon pote.*"

They never do come back to Majorca. A week after they return to Paris, Eric has a heart attack. It happens while he is at work, speaking to a lighting stagehand. He survives it, but he will suffer two more over the course of the next three years, the last of which will prove fatal. And so at the age of forty-eight Pari finds herself, like Maman had, a widow.

One day, early in the spring of 2010, Pari receives a long-distance phone call. The call is not unexpected. Pari, in fact, has been preparing for it all morning.

Prior to the call, Pari makes sure she has the apartment to herself. This means asking Isabelle to leave earlier than she customarily does. Isabelle and her husband, Albert, live just north of Île Saint-Denis, only a few blocks from Pari's one-bedroom apartment. Isabelle comes to see Pari in the morning every other day, after she drops off her kids at school. She brings Pari a baguette, some fresh fruit. Pari is not yet bound to the wheelchair, an eventuality for which she has been preparing herself. Though her disease forced her into early retirement the year before, she is still fully capable of going to the market on her own, of taking a daily walk. It's the hands—the ugly, twisted hands—that fail her most, hands that on bad days feel like they have shards of crystal rattling around the joints. Pari wears gloves, whenever she is out, to keep her hands warm, but mostly because she is ashamed of them, the knobby knuckles, the unsightly fingers with what her doctor calls *swan neck deformity*, the permanently flexed left pinkie.

Ah, vanity, she tells Collette.

This morning, Isabelle has brought her some figs, a few bars of soap, toothpaste, and a Tupperware containerful of chestnut soup. Albert is thinking of suggesting it as a new menu entry to the owners of the restaurant where he is the sous-chef. As she unloads the bags, Isabelle tells Pari of the new assignment she has landed. She writes musical scores for television shows now, commercials, and is hoping to write for film one day soon. She says she will begin scoring a miniseries that is shooting at the moment in Madrid.

"Will you be going there?" Pari asks. "To Madrid?"

"*Non.* The budget is too small. They won't cover my travel cost."

"That's a pity. You could have stayed with Alain."

"Oh, can you imagine, Maman? Poor Alain. He hardly has room to stretch his legs."

Alain is a financial consultant. He lives in a tiny Madrid apartment with his wife, Ana, and their four children. He regularly e-mails Pari pictures and short video clips of the children.

Pari asks if Isabelle has heard from Thierry, and Isabelle says she has not. Thierry is in Africa, in the eastern part of Chad, where he works at a camp with refugees from Darfur. Pari knows this because Thierry is in sporadic touch with Isabelle. She is the only one he speaks to. This is how Pari knows the general outlines of her son's life—for instance, that he spent some time in Vietnam. Or that he was married to a Vietnamese woman once, briefly, when he was twenty.

Isabelle sets a pot of water on to boil and fetches two cups from the cabinet.

"Not this morning, Isabelle. Actually, I need to ask you to leave."

Isabelle gives her a wounded look, and Pari chides herself for not wording it better. Isabelle has always had a delicate nature.

"What I mean to say is, I'm expecting a call and I need some privacy."

"A call? From who?"

"I'll tell you later," Pari says.

Isabelle crosses her arms and grins. "Have you found a lover, Maman?"

"A lover. Are you blind? Have you even looked at me recently?"

"There is not a thing wrong with you."

"You need to go. I'll explain later, I promise."

"*D'accord, d'accord.*" Isabelle slings her purse over her shoulder, grabs her coat and keys. "But I'll have you know I'm duly intrigued."

The man who calls at 9:30 a.m. is named Markos Varvaris. He had contacted Pari through her Facebook account with this message, written in English: *Are you the daughter of the poet Nila Wahdati? If so, I would like very much to speak with you about something that will be of interest to you.* Pari had searched the web for his name and found that he was a plastic surgeon who worked for a nonprofit organization in Kabul. Now, on the phone, he greets her in Farsi, and continues to speak in Farsi until Pari has to interrupt him.

"Monsieur Varvaris, I'm sorry, but maybe we speak in English?"

"Ah, of course. My apologies. I assumed . . . Although, of course, it does make sense, you left when you were very young, didn't you?"

"Yes, that is true."

"I learned Farsi here myself. I would say I am more or less functional in it. I have lived here since 2002, since shortly after the Taliban left. Quite optimistic days, those. Yes, everybody ready for rebuilding and democracy and the like. Now it is a different story. Naturally, we are

267

preparing for presidential elections, but it is a different story. I'm afraid it is."

Pari listens patiently as Markos Varvaris makes protracted detours into the logistical challenge that are the elections in Afghanistan, which he says Karzai will win, and then on to the Taliban's troubling forays into the north, the increasing Islamist infringement on news media, a side note or two on the overpopulation in Kabul, then on the cost of housing, lastly, before he circles back and says, "I have lived in this house now for a number of years. I understand you lived in this house too."

"I'm sorry?"

"This was your parents' house. That is what I am led to believe, in any case."

"If I can ask, who is telling you this?"

"The landlord. His name is Nabi. It *was* Nabi, I should say. He is deceased now, sadly, as of recently. Do you remember him?"

The name conjures for Pari a handsome young face, sideburns, a wall of full dark hair combed back.

"Yes. Mostly, his name. He was a cook at our house. And a chauffeur as well."

"He was both, yes. He had lived here, in this house, since 1947. Sixty-three years. It is a little unbelievable, no? But, as I said, he passed on. Last month. I was quite fond of him. Everyone was."

"I see."

"Nabi gave me a note," Markos Varvaris says. "I was to read it only after his death. When he died, I had an Afghan colleague translate it into English. This note, it is more than a note. A letter, more accurately, and a remarkable one at that. Nabi says some things in it. I searched for you because some of it concerns you, and also because he directly asks in it that I find you and give you this letter. It took some searching, but we were able to locate you. Thanks to the web." He lets out a short laugh.

There is a part of Pari that wants to hang up. Intuitively, she does not doubt that whatever revelation this old man—this person from her distant past—has scribbled on paper, halfway across the world, is true. She has known for a long time that she was lied to by Maman about her childhood. But even if the ground of her life was broken with a lie, what Pari has since planted in that ground stands as true and sturdy and unshakable as a giant oak. Eric, her children, her grandchildren, her career, Collette. So what is the use? After all this time, what is the use? Perhaps best to hang up.

But she doesn't. Her pulse fluttering and her palms sweating, she says, "What . . . what does he say in his note, in this letter?"

"Well, for one thing, he claims he was your uncle."

"My uncle."

"Your *stepuncle*, to be precise. And there is more. He says many other things as well."

"Monsieur Varvaris, do you have it? This note, this letter, or the translation? Do you have it with you?"

"I do."

"Maybe you read it for me? Can you read it?"

"You mean now?"

"If you have the time. I can call you, to collect the charge."

"No need, no. But are you sure?"

"Oui," she says into the phone. "I'm sure, Monsieur Varvaris."

He reads it to her. He reads her the whole thing. It takes a while. When he finishes, she thanks him and tells him she will be in touch soon.

After she hangs up, she sets the coffeemaker to brew a cup and moves to her window. From it, the familiar view presents itself to her—the narrow cobblestone path below, the pharmacy up the block, the falafel joint at the corner, the brasserie run by the Basque family.

Pari's hands shake. A startling thing is happening to her. Something truly remarkable. The picture of it in her mind is of an ax striking soil and suddenly rich black oil bubbling up to the surface. This is what is happening to her, memories struck upon, rising up from the depths. She gazes out the window in the direction of the brasserie, but what she sees is not the skinny waiter beneath the awning, black apron tied at the waist and shaking a cloth over a table, but a little red wagon with a squeaky wheel bouncing along beneath a sky of unfurling clouds, rolling over ridges and down dried-up gullies, up and down ocher hills that loom and then fall away. She sees tangles of fruit trees standing in groves, the breeze catching their leaves, and rows of grapevines connecting little flat-roofed houses. She sees washing lines and women squatting by a stream, and the creaking ropes of a swing beneath a big tree, and a big dog, cowering from the taunts of village boys, and a hawk-nosed man digging a ditch, shirt plastered to his back with sweat, and a veiled woman bent over a cooking fire.

But something else too at the edge of it all, at the rim of her vision—and this is what draws her most—an elusive shadow. A figure. At once soft and hard. The softness of a hand holding hers. The hardness of knees where she'd once rested her cheek. She searches for his face, but it evades her, slips from her, each time she turns to it. Pari feels a hole opening up in her. There has been in her life, all her life, a great absence. Somehow, she has always known.

"Brother," she says, unaware she is speaking. Unaware she is weeping.

A verse from a Farsi song suddenly tumbles to her tongue:

I know a sad little fairy
Who was blown away by the wind one night.

There is another, perhaps earlier, verse, she is sure of it, but that eludes her as well.

Pari sits. She has to. She doesn't think she can stand at the moment. She waits for the coffee to brew and thinks that when it's ready she is going to have a cup, and then perhaps a cigarette, and then she is going to go to the living room to call Collette in Lyon, see if her old friend can arrange her a trip to Kabul.

But for the moment Pari sits. She shuts her eyes, as the coffeemaker begins to gurgle, and she finds behind her eyelids hills that stand soft and a sky that stands high and blue, and the sun setting behind a windmill, and always, always, hazy strings of mountains that fall and fall away on the horizon.

Seven

Summer 2009

Your father is a great man."

Adel looked up. It was the teacher Malalai who had leaned in and whispered this in his ear. A plump, middle-aged woman wearing a violet beaded shawl around her shoulders, she smiled at him now with her eyes shut.

"And you are a lucky boy."

"I know," he whispered back.

Good, she mouthed.

They were standing on the front steps of the town's new school for girls, a rectangular light green building with a flat roof and wide windows, as Adel's father, his Baba jan, delivered a brief prayer followed by an animated speech. Gathered before them in the blazing midday heat was a large crowd of squinting children, parents, and elders, roughly a hundred or so locals from the small town of Shadbagh-e-Nau, "New Shadbagh."

"Afghanistan is mother to us all," Adel's father said, one

thick index finger raised skyward. The sun caught the band of his agate ring. "But she is an ailing mother, and she has suffered for a long time. Now, it is true a mother needs her sons in order to recover. Yes, but she needs her daughters too—as much, if not more!"

This drew loud applause and several calls and hoots of approval. Adel scanned the faces in the crowd. They were rapt as they looked up at his father. Baba jan, with his black bushy eyebrows and full beard, standing tall and strong and wide above them, his shoulders nearly broad enough to fill the entryway to the school behind him.

His father continued. And Adel's eyes connected with Kabir, one of Baba jan's two bodyguards standing impassively on the other side of Baba jan, Kalashnikov in hand. Adel could see the crowd reflected in Kabir's dark-lensed aviator glasses. Kabir was short, thin, almost frail, and wore suits with flashy colors—lavender, turquoise, orange—but Baba jan said he was a hawk and that underestimating him was a mistake you made at your own peril.

"So I say this to you, young daughters of Afghanistan," Baba jan concluded, his long, thick arms outstretched in an open gesture of welcome. "You have a solemn duty now. To learn, to apply yourselves, to excel at your studies, to make proud not only your own fathers and mothers but the mother who is common to us all. Her future is in your hands, not mine. I ask that you not think of this school as a gift from me to you. It is merely a building that houses the *true* gift inside, and that is you. You are the gift, young sisters, not only to me and to the community of

Shadbagh-e-Nau but, most importantly, to Afghanistan herself! God bless you."

More applause broke out. Several people shouted, "God bless you, Commander Sahib!" Baba jan raised a fist, grinning broadly. Adel's eyes nearly watered with pride.

The teacher Malalai handed Baba jan a pair of scissors. A red ribbon had been tied across the entryway to the classroom. The crowd inched closer to get a better view, and Kabir motioned a few people back, shoved a couple of them in the chest. Hands rose from the crowd, holding cell phones to video the ribbon cutting. Baba jan took the scissors, paused, turned to Adel and said, "Here, son, you do the honors." He handed the scissors to Adel.

Adel blinked. "Me?"

"Go ahead," Baba jan said, dropping him a wink.

Adel cut the ribbon. Long applause broke out. Adel heard the clicking of a few cameras, voices crying out *"Allah-u-akbar!"*

Baba jan then stood at the doorway as the students made a queue and entered the classroom one by one. They were young girls, aged between eight and fifteen, all of them wearing white scarves and the pin-striped uniforms of black and gray that Baba jan had given them. Adel watched as each student shyly introduced herself to Baba jan on her way in. Baba jan smiled warmly, patted their heads, and offered an encouraging word or two. "I wish you success, Bibi Mariam. Study hard, Bibi Homaira. Make us proud, Bibi Ilham."

Later, by the black Land Cruiser, Adel stood by his

father, sweating now in the heat, and watched him shake hands with the locals. Baba jan fingered a prayer bead in his free hand and listened patiently, leaning in a bit, his brow furrowed, nodding, attentive to each person as he or she came to say thanks, offer prayers, pay respects, many of them taking the opportunity to ask for a favor. A mother whose sick child needed to see a surgeon in Kabul, a man in need of a loan to start a shoe-repair shop, a mechanic asking for a new set of tools.

Commander Sahib, if you could find it in your heart . . .

I have nowhere else to turn, Commander Sahib . . .

Adel had never heard anyone outside immediate family address Baba jan by anything other than "Commander Sahib," even though the Russians were long gone now and Baba jan hadn't fired a gun in a decade or more. Back at the house, there were framed pictures of Baba jan's jihadi days all around the living room. Adel had committed to memory each of the pictures: his father leaning against the fender of a dusty old jeep, squatting on the turret of a charred tank, posing proudly with his men, ammunition belt strapped across his chest, beside a helicopter they had shot down. Here was one where he was wearing a vest and a bandolier, brow pressed to the desert floor in prayer. He was much skinnier in those days, Adel's father, and always in these pictures there was nothing behind him but mountains and sand.

Baba jan had been shot twice by the Russians during battle. He had shown Adel his wounds, one just under the left rib cage—he said that one had cost him his spleen—and one about a thumb's length away from his belly button. He said he was lucky, everything considered. He had friends who had lost arms, legs, eyes; friends whose faces had burned. They had done it for their country, Baba jan said, and they had done it for God. This was what jihad was all about, he said. Sacrifice. You sacrificed your limbs, your sight—your life, even—and you did it gladly. Jihad also earned you certain rights and privileges, he said, because God sees to it that those who sacrifice the most justly reap the rewards as well.

Both in this life and the next, Baba jan said, pointing his thick finger first down, then up.

Looking at the pictures, Adel wished he had been around to fight jihad alongside his father in those more adventurous days. He liked to picture himself and Baba jan shooting at Russian helicopters together, blowing up tanks, dodging gunfire, living in mountains and sleeping in caves. Father and son, war heroes.

There was also a large framed photo of Baba jan smiling alongside President Karzai at *Arg,* the Presidential Palace in Kabul. This one was more recent, taken in the course of a small ceremony during which Baba jan had been handed an award for his humanitarian work in Shadbagh-e-Nau. It was an award that Baba jan had more than earned. The new school for girls was merely his latest project. Adel knew that women in town used to die regularly giving birth. But they didn't anymore because his father had opened a large clinic, run by two doctors and three midwives whose salaries he paid for out of his own pocket. All the townspeople received free care at the clinic; no child in Shadbagh-e-Nau went unimmunized. Baba jan had dispatched teams to locate water points all over town and dig wells. It was Baba jan who had helped finally bring full-time electricity to Shadbagh-e-Nau. At least a dozen businesses had opened thanks to his loans that, Adel had learned from Kabir, were rarely, if ever, paid back.

Adel had meant what he had said to the teacher earlier. He *knew* he was lucky to be the son of such a man.

Just as the rounds of handshaking were coming to an end, Adel spotted a slight man approaching his father. He wore round, thin-framed spectacles and a short gray beard and had little teeth like the heads of burnt matches. Trailing him was a boy roughly Adel's own age. The boy's big toes poked through matching holes in his sneakers. His hair sat on his head as a matted, unmoving mess. His jeans were stiff with dirt, and they were too short besides. By contrast, his T-shirt hung almost to his knees.

Kabir planted himself between the old man and Baba jan. "I told you already this wasn't a good time," he said.

"I just want to have a brief word with the commander," the old man said.

Baba jan took Adel by the arm and gently guided him into the backseat of the Land Cruiser. "Let's go, son. Your mother is waiting for you." He climbed in beside Adel and shut the door.

Inside, as his tinted window rolled up, Adel watched Kabir say something to the old man that Adel couldn't hear. Then Kabir made his way around the front of the SUV and let himself into the driver's seat, laying his Kalashnikov on the passenger seat before turning the ignition.

"What was that about?" Adel asked.

"Nothing important," Kabir said.

They turned onto the road. Some of the boys who had stood in the crowd gave chase for a short while before the Land Cruiser pulled away. Kabir drove through the main crowded strip that bisected the town of Shadbagh-e-Nau, honking frequently as he needled the car through traffic. Everyone yielded. Some people waved. Adel watched the crowded sidewalks on either side of him, his gaze settling on and then off familiar sights—the carcasses hanging from hooks in butcher shops; the blacksmiths working their wooden wheels, hand-pumping their bellows; the fruit merchants fanning flies off their grapes and cherries; the sidewalk barber on the wicker chair stropping his razor. They passed tea shops, kabob houses, an auto-repair shop, a mosque, before Kabir veered the car through the town's big public square, at the center of which stood a blue fountain and a nine-foot-tall black stone mujahid, looking east, turban gracefully wrapped atop his head, an RPG launcher on his shoulder. Baba jan had personally commissioned a sculptor from Kabul to build the statue.

North of the strip were a few blocks of residential area, mostly composed of narrow, unpaved streets and small, flat-roofed little houses painted white or yellow or blue. Satellite dishes sat on the roofs of a few; Afghan flags draped a number of windows. Baba jan had told Adel that most of the homes and businesses in Shadbagh-e-Nau had been built in the last fifteen years or so. He'd had a hand in the construction of many of them. Most people who lived here considered him the founder of Shadbagh-e-Nau, and Adel knew that the town elders had offered to name the town after Baba jan but he had declined the honor.

From there, the main road ran north for two miles before it connected with Shadbagh-e-Kohna, Old Shadbagh. Adel had never seen the village as it had once looked decades ago. By the time Baba jan had moved him and his mother from Kabul to Shadbagh, the village had all but vanished. All the homes were gone. The only surviving relic of the past was a decaying windmill. At Shadbagh-e-Kohna, Kabir veered left from the main road onto a wide, quarter-mile-long unpaved track that connected the main road to the thick twelve-foot-high walls of the compound where Adel lived with his parents—the only standing structure now in Shadbagh-e-Kohna, discounting the windmill. Adel could see the white walls now as the SUV jostled and bounced on the track. Coils of barbed wire ran along the top of the walls.

A uniformed guard, who always stood watch at the main gates to the compound, saluted and opened the gates. Kabir drove the SUV through the walls and up a graveled path toward the house.

The house stood three stories high and was painted bright pink and turquoise green. It had soaring columns and pointed eaves and mirrored skyscraper glass that sparkled in the sun. It had parapets, a veranda with sparkly mosaics, and wide balconies with curved wrought-iron railings. Inside, they had nine bedrooms and seven bathrooms, and sometimes when Adel and Baba jan played hide-and-seek, Adel wandered around for an hour or more before he found his father. All the counters in the bathrooms and kitchen had been made of granite and lime marble. Lately, to Adel's delight, Baba jan had been talking about building a swimming pool in the basement.

Kabir pulled into the circular driveway outside the tall front gates of the house. He killed the engine.

"Why don't you give us a minute?" Baba jan said.

Kabir nodded and exited the car. Adel watched him walk up the marble steps to the gates and ring. It was Azmaray, the other bodyguard—a short, stocky, gruff fellow—who opened the gate. The two men said a few words, then lingered on the steps, lighting a cigarette each.

"Do you really have to go?" Adel said. His father was leaving for the south in the morning to oversee his fields of cotton in Helmand and to meet with workers at the cotton factory he had built there. He would be gone for two weeks, a span of time that, to Adel, seemed interminable.

Baba jan turned his gaze to him. He dwarfed Adel, taking up more than half the backseat. "Wish I didn't, son."

Adel nodded. "I was proud today. I was proud of you."

Baba jan lowered the weight of his big hand on Adel's knee. "Thank you, Adel. I appreciate that. But I take you to these things so you learn, so you understand that it's important for the fortunate, for people like us, to live up to their responsibilities."

"I just wish you didn't have to leave all the time."

"Me too, son. Me too. But I'm not leaving until tomorrow. I'll be home later in the evening."

Adel nodded, casting his gaze down at his hands.

"Look," his father said in a soft voice, "the people in this town, they need me, Adel. They need my help to have a home and find work and make a livelihood. Kabul has its own problems. It can't help them. So if I don't, no one else will. Then these people would suffer."

"I know that," Adel muttered.

Baba jan squeezed his knee gently. "You miss Kabul, I know, and your friends. It's been a hard adjustment here, for both you and your mother. And I know that I'm always off traveling and going to meetings and that a lot of people have demands on my time. But . . . Look at me, son."

Adel raised his eyes to meet Baba jan's. They shone at him kindly from beneath the canopy of his bushy brows.

"No one on this earth matters to me more than you, Adel. You are my son. I would gladly give up all of this for you. I would give up my life for you, son."

Adel nodded, his eyes watering a little. Sometimes, when Baba jan spoke like this, Adel felt his heart swell and swell until he found it hard to draw a breath.

"Do you understand me?"

"Yes, Baba jan."

"Do you believe me?"

"I do."

"Good. Then give your father a kiss."

Adel threw his arms around Baba jan's neck and his father held him tightly and patiently. Adel remembered when he was little, when he would tap his father on the shoulder in the middle of the night still shaking from a nightmare, and his father would push back his blanket and let him climb into bed, folding him in and kissing the crown of his head until Adel stopped shivering and slipped back into sleep.

"Maybe I'll bring you a little something from Helmand," Baba jan said.

"You don't have to," Adel said, his voice muffled. He already had more toys than he knew what to do with. And there wasn't a toy on earth that could make up for his father's absence.

Late that day, Adel perched midstairway and spied on the scene unfolding below him. The doorbell had rung and Kabir had answered. Now Kabir was leaning against the doorframe with his arms crossed, blocking the entrance, as he spoke to the person on the other side. It was the old man from earlier at the school, Adel saw, the bespectacled man with the burnt-match teeth. The boy with the holes in his shoes was there too, standing beside him.

The old man said, "Where has he gone to?"

Kabir said, "Business. In the south."

"I heard he was leaving tomorrow."

Kabir shrugged.

"How long will he be gone?"

"Two, maybe three months. Who's to say."

"That's not what I heard."

"Now you're testing my patience, old man," Kabir said, uncrossing his arms.

"I'll wait for him."

"Not here, you won't."

"Over by the road, I meant."

Kabir shifted impatiently on his feet. "Suit yourself," he said. "But the commander is a busy man. No telling when he'll be back."

The old man nodded and backed away, the boy following him.

Kabir shut the door.

Adel pulled the curtain in the family room and out the window watched the old man and the boy walking up the unpaved road that connected the compound to the main road.

"You lied to him," Adel said.

"It's part of what I'm paid to do: protect your father from buzzards."

"What does he want anyway, a job?"

"Something like that."

Kabir moved to the couch and removed his shoes. He looked up at Adel and gave him a wink. Adel liked Kabir, far more than Azmaray, who was unpleasant and rarely said a word to him. Kabir played cards with Adel and invited him to watch DVDs together. Kabir loved movies. He owned a collection that he had bought on the black market and watched ten to twelve movies a week—Iranian, French, American, of course Bollywood—he didn't care.

And sometimes if Adel's mother was in another room and Adel promised not to tell his father, Kabir emptied the magazine on his Kalashnikov and let Adel hold it, like a mujahid. Now the Kalashnikov sat propped against the wall by the front door.

Kabir lay down on the couch and propped his feet up on the arm. He started flipping through a newspaper.

"They looked harmless enough," Adel said, releasing the curtain and turning to Kabir. He could see the bodyguard's forehead over the top of the newspaper.

"Maybe I should have asked them in for tea, then," Kabir murmured. "Offer them some cake too."

"Don't make fun."

"They all look harmless."

"Is Baba jan going to help them?"

"Probably," Kabir sighed. "Your father is a river to his people." He lowered the paper and grinned. "What's that from? Come on, Adel. We saw it last month."

Adel shrugged. He started heading upstairs.

"*Lawrence*," Kabir called from the couch. "*Lawrence of Arabia*. Anthony Quinn." And then, just as Adel had reached the top of the stairs: "They're buzzards, Adel. Don't fall for their act. They'd pick your father clean if they could."

One morning, a couple of days after his father had left for Helmand, Adel went up to his parents' bedroom. The music from the other side of the door was loud and thumping. He let himself in and found his mother, in shorts and a T-shirt in front of the giant flat-screen TV, mimicking the moves of a trio of sweaty blond women, a series of leaps and squats and lunges and planks. She spotted him in the big mirror of her dresser.

"Want to join me?" she panted over the loud music.

"I'll just sit here," he said. He slid down to the carpeted floor and watched his mother, whose name was Aria, leapfrog her way across the room and back.

Adel's mother had delicate hands and feet, a small upturned nose, and a pretty face like an actress from one of Kabir's Bollywood films. She was lean, agile, and young— she had been only fourteen when she'd married Baba jan. Adel had another, older mother too, and three older half brothers, but Baba jan had put them up in the east, in Jalalabad, and Adel saw them only once a month or so when Baba jan took him there to visit. Unlike his mother and stepmother, who disliked each other, Adel and his half brothers got along fine. When he visited them in Jalalabad, they took him with them to parks, to bazaars, the cinema, and Buzkashi tournaments. They played *Resident Evil* with him and shot the zombies in *Call of Duty* with him, and they always picked him on their team during neighborhood soccer matches. Adel wished so badly that they lived here, near him.

Adel watched his mother lie on her back and raise her straightened legs off the floor and lower them down again, a blue plastic ball tucked between her bare ankles.

The truth was, the boredom here in Shadbagh was

crushing Adel. He hadn't made a single friend in the two years they had lived here. He could not bike into town, certainly not on his own, not with the rash of kidnappings everywhere in the region—though he did sneak out now and then briefly, always staying within the perimeter of the compound. He had no classmates because Baba jan wouldn't let him attend the local school—for "security reasons," he said—so a tutor came to the house every morning for lessons. Mostly, Adel passed the time reading or kicking the soccer ball around on his own or watching movies with Kabir, often the same ones over and over. He wandered list-lessly around the wide, high-ceilinged hallways of their massive home, through all the big empty rooms, or else he sat looking out the window of his bedroom upstairs. He lived in a mansion, but in a shrunken world. Some days he was so bored, he wanted to chew wood.

He knew that his mother too was terribly lonely here. She tried to fill her days with routines, exercise in the morn-ing, shower, then breakfast, then reading, gardening, then Indian soaps on TV in the afternoon. When Baba jan was away, which was often, she always wore gray sweats and sneakers around the house, her face unmade, her hair pinned in a bun at the back of her neck. She rarely even opened the jewelry box where she kept all the rings and necklaces and earrings that Baba jan brought her from Dubai. She spent hours sometimes talking to her family down in Kabul. Only when her sister and parents visited for a few days, once every two or three months, did Adel see his mother come alive. She wore a long print dress and high-heeled shoes; she put on her makeup. Her eyes shone, and her laughter could be heard around the house. And it was then that Adel would catch a glimpse of the person that perhaps she had been before.

When Baba jan was away, Adel and his mother tried to be each other's reprieve. They pushed pieces of jigsaw puzzles around and played golf and tennis on Adel's Wii. But Adel's favorite pastime with his mother was building toothpick houses. His mother would draw a 3-D blueprint of the house on a sheet of paper, complete with front porch, gabled roof, and with staircases inside and walls separating the different rooms. They would build the foundation first, then the interior walls and stairs, killing hours carefully applying glue to toothpicks, setting sections to dry. Adel's mother said that when she was younger, before she had married Adel's father, she had dreamed of becoming an architect.

It was while they were building a skyscraper once that she had told Adel the story of how she and Baba jan had married.

He was actually supposed to marry my older sister, she said.

Aunt Nargis?

Yes. This was in Kabul. He saw her on the street one day and that was it. He had to marry her. He showed up at our house the next day, him and five of his men. They more or less invited themselves in. They were all wearing boots. She shook her head and laughed like it was a funny thing Baba jan had done, but she didn't laugh the way she ordinarily did when she found something funny. *You should have seen the expression on your grandparents.*

They had sat in the living room, Baba jan, his men, and her parents. She was in the kitchen making tea while they talked. There was a problem, she said, because her sister Nargis was already engaged, promised to a cousin who lived in Amsterdam and was studying engineering. How were they supposed to break off the engagement? her parents were asking.

And then I come in, carrying a platter of tea and sweets. I fill their cups and put the food on the table, and your father sees me, and, as I turn to go, your father, he says, "Maybe you're right, sir. It's not fair to break off an engagement. But if you tell me this one is taken too, then I'm afraid I may have no choice but to think you don't care for me." Then he laughs. And that was how we got married.

She lifted a tube of glue.

Did you like him?

She shrugged a little. *Truth be told, I was more frightened than anything else.*

But you like him now, right? You love him.

Of course I do, Adel's mother said. *What a question.*

You don't regret marrying him.

She put down the glue and waited a few seconds before answering. *Look at our lives, Adel,* she said slowly. *Look around you. What's to regret?* She smiled and pulled gently on the lobe of his ear. *Besides, then I wouldn't have had you.*

Adel's mother turned off the TV now and sat on the floor, panting, drying sweat off her neck with a towel.

"Why don't you do something on your own this morning," she said, stretching her back. "I'm going to shower and eat. And I was thinking of calling your grandparents. Haven't spoken to them for a couple of days."

Adel sighed and rose to his feet.

In his room, on a lower floor and in a different wing of the house, he fetched his soccer ball and put on the Zidane jersey Baba jan had given him for his last birthday, his twelfth. When he made his way downstairs, he found Kabir napping, a newspaper spread on his chest like a quilt. He grabbed a can of apple juice from the fridge and let himself out.

Adel walked on the gravel path toward the main entrance to the compound. The stall where the armed guard stood watch was empty. Adel knew the timing of the guard's rounds. He carefully opened the gate and stepped out, closed the gate behind him. Almost immediately, he had the impression that he could breathe better on this side of the wall. Some days, the compound felt far too much like a prison.

He walked in the wide shadow of the wall toward the back of the compound, away from the main road. Back there, behind the compound, were Baba jan's orchards, of which he was very proud. Several acres of long parallel rows of pear trees and apple trees, apricots, cherries, figs, and loquats too. When Adel took long walks with his father in these orchards, Baba jan would lift him high up on his shoulders and Adel would pluck them a ripe pair of apples. Between the compound and the orchards was a clearing, mostly empty save for a shed where the gardeners stored their tools. The only other thing there was the flat stump of what had once been, by the looks of it, a giant old tree. Baba jan had once counted its rings with Adel and concluded that the tree had likely seen Genghis Khan's army march past. He said, with a rueful shake of his head, that whoever had cut it down had been nothing but a fool.

It was a hot day, the sun glaring in a sky as unblemished blue as the skies in the crayon pictures Adel used to draw when he was little. He put down the can of apple juice on the tree stump and practiced juggling his ball. His personal best was sixty-eight touches without the ball hitting the ground. He had set that record in the spring, and now it was midsummer and he was still trying to best it. Adel had reached twenty-eight when he became aware that someone was watching him. It was the boy, the one with the old man who had tried to approach Baba jan at the school's open-ing ceremony. He was squatting now in the shade of the brick shed.

"What are you doing here?" Adel said, trying to bark the words like Kabir did when he spoke to strangers.

"Getting some shade," the boy said. "Don't report me."

"You're not supposed to be here."

"Neither are you."

"What?"

The boy chuckled. "Never mind." He stretched his arms wide and rose to his feet. Adel tried to see if his pockets were full. Maybe he had come to steal fruit. The boy walked over to Adel and flipped up the ball with one foot, gave it a pair of quick juggles, and kicked it with his heel to Adel. Adel caught the ball and cradled it under his arm.

"Where your goon had us wait, over by the road, me and my father? There's no shade. And not a damn cloud in the sky."

Adel felt a need to rise to Kabir's defense. "He is not a goon."

"Well, he made sure we got an eyeful of his Kalashnikov, I can tell you that." He looked at Adel, a lazy, amused grin on his lips. He dropped a wad of spit at his feet. "So I see you're a fan of the head-butter."

It took Adel a moment to realize who he was referring to. "You can't judge him by one mistake," he said. "He was the best. He was a wizard in the midfield."

"I've seen better."

"Yeah? Like who?"

"Like Maradona."

"Maradona?" Adel said, outraged. He'd had this debate before with one of his half brothers in Jalalabad. "Maradona was a cheater! 'Hand of God,' remember?"

"Everyone cheats and everyone lies."

The boy yawned and started to go. He was about the same height as Adel, maybe a hair taller, and probably just around his age too, Adel thought. But somehow he walked like he was older, without hurry and with a kind of air, as if he had seen everything there was to see and nothing surprised him.

"My name is Adel."

"Gholam." They shook hands. Gholam's grip was strong, his palm dry and callused.

"How old are you anyway?"

Gholam gave a shrug. "Thirteen, I guess. Could be fourteen by now."

"You don't know your own birthday?"

Gholam grinned. "I bet you know yours. I bet you count down."

"I do not," Adel said defensively. "I mean, I don't count down."

"I should go. My father's waiting alone."

"I thought that was your grandfather."

"You thought wrong."

"Do you want to play a shoot-out?" Adel asked.

"You mean like a penalty shoot-out?"

"Five each . . . best of."

Gholam spat again, squinted toward the road and back at Adel. Adel noticed that his chin was a bit small for his face and that he had overlapping extra canines in the front, one of them chipped badly and rotting. His left eyebrow was split in half by a short, narrow scar. Also, he smelled. But Adel hadn't had a conversation—let alone played a game—with a boy his age in nearly two years, discounting the monthly visits to Jalalabad. Adel prepared himself for disappointment, but Gholam shrugged and said, "Shit, why not? But I get first dibs on shooting."

For goalposts, they used two rocks placed eight steps apart. Gholam took his five shots. Scored one, off target twice, and Adel easily saved two. Gholam's goaltending was even worse than his shooting. Adel managed to score four, tricking him into leaning in the wrong direction each time, and the one shot he missed wasn't even on goal.

"Fucker," Gholam said, bent in half, palms on his kneecaps.

"Rematch?" Adel tried not to gloat, but it was hard. He was soaring inside.

Gholam agreed, and the result was even more lopsided. He again managed one goal, and this time Adel converted all five of his attempts.

"That's it, I'm winded," Gholam said, throwing up his hands. He trudged over to the tree stump and sat down with a tired groan. Adel cradled the ball and sat next to him.

"These probably aren't helping," Gholam said, fishing a pack of cigarettes from the front pocket of his jeans. He had one left. He lit it with a single strike of a match, inhaled contentedly, and offered it to Adel. Adel was tempted to take it, if only to impress Gholam, but he passed, worried Kabir or his mother would smell it on him.

"Wise," Gholam said, leaning his head back.

They talked idly about soccer for a while, and, to Adel's pleasant surprise, Gholam's knowledge turned out to be solid. They exchanged favorite match and favorite goal stories. They each offered a top-five-players list; mostly it was the same except Gholam's included Ronaldo the Brazilian and Adel's had Ronaldo the Portuguese. Inevitably, they got around to the 2006 Finals and the painful memory, for Adel, of the head-butting incident. Gholam said he watched the whole match standing with a crowd outside the window of a TV shop not far from the camp.

"'The camp'?"

"The one where I grew up. In Pakistan."

He told Adel that this was his first time in Afghanistan. He had lived his whole life in Pakistan in the Jalozai refugee camp where he'd been born. He said Jalozai had been like a city, a huge maze of tents and mud huts and homes built from plastic and aluminum siding in a labyrinth of narrow passageways littered with dirt and shit. It was a city in the belly of a yet greater city. He and his brothers—he was the eldest by three years—were raised in the camp. He had lived in a small mud house there with his brothers, his mother, his father, whose name was Iqbal, and his paternal grand-mother, Parwana. In its alleyways, he and his brothers had learned to walk and talk. They had gone to school there. He had played with sticks and rusty old bicycle wheels on its dirt streets, running around with other refugee kids, until the sun dipped and his grandmother called him home.

"I liked it there," he said. "I had friends. I knew every-body. We were doing all right too. I have an uncle in America, my father's half brother, Uncle Abdullah. I've never met him. But he was sending us money every few months. It helped. It helped a lot."

"Why did you leave?"

"Had to. The Pakistanis shut down the camp. They said Afghans belong in Afghanistan. And then my uncle's money stopped coming. So my father said we might as well go home and restart, now that the Taliban had run to the Pakistani side of the border anyway. He said we were guests in Pakistan who'd outstayed their welcome. I was really depressed. This place"—he waved his hand—"this is a foreign country to me. And the kids in the camp, the ones who'd actually been to Afghanistan? None of them had a good thing to say about it."

Adel wanted to say that he knew how Gholam felt. He wanted to tell him how much he missed Kabul, and his friends, and his half brothers over in Jalalabad. But he had a feeling Gholam might laugh. Instead he said, "Well, it *is* pretty boring around here."

Gholam laughed anyway. "I don't think that's quite what they meant," he said.

Adel understood vaguely that he'd been chastised.

Gholam took a drag and blew out a run of rings. Together, they watched the rings gently float away and disintegrate.

"My father said to me and my brothers, he said, 'Wait . . . wait until you breathe the air in Shadbagh, boys, and taste the water.' He was born here, my father, raised here too. He said, 'You've never had water this cool and this sweet, boys.' He was always talking to us about Shadbagh, which I guess was nothing but a small village back when he lived here. He said there was a kind of grape that you could grow only in Shadbagh and nowhere else in the world. You'd think he was describing Paradise."

Adel asked him where he was staying now. Gholam tossed the cigarette butt, looked up at the sky, squinting at the brightness. "You know the open field over by the windmill?"

"Yes."

Adel waited for more, but there was no more.

"You live in a field?"

"For the time being," Gholam mumbled. "We got a tent."

"Don't you have family here?"

"No. They're either dead or gone. Well, my father does have an uncle in Kabul. Or he did. Who knows if he's still alive. He was my grandmother's brother, worked for a rich family there. But I guess Nabi and my grandmother haven't spoken in decades—fifty years or more, I think. They're strangers practically. I guess if he really had to, my father would go to him. But he wants to make a go of it on his own here. This is his home."

They spent a few quiet moments sitting on the tree stump, watching the leaves in the orchards shiver in surges of warm wind. Adel thought of Gholam and his family sleeping nights in a tent, scorpions and snakes crawling in the field all around them.

Adel didn't quite know why he ended up telling Gholam about the reason he and his parents moved here from Kabul. Or, rather, he couldn't choose among the reasons. He wasn't sure if he did it to dispel Gholam's impression that he led a carefree existence simply because he lived in a big house. Or as a kind of school-yard one-upmanship. Maybe a plea for sympathy. Did he do it to narrow the gap between them? He didn't know. Maybe all of these things. Nor did Adel know why it seemed important that Gholam like him, only that he dimly understood the reason to be more complicated than the mere fact of his frequent loneliness and his desire for a friend.

"We moved to Shadbagh because someone tried to kill us in Kabul," he said. "A motorcycle pulled up to the house one day and its rider sprayed our house with bullets. He wasn't caught. But, thank God, none of us was hurt."

He didn't know what reaction he had expected, but it did surprise him that Gholam had none. Still squinting up at the sun, Gholam said, "Yeah, I know."

"You know?"

"Your father picks his nose and people hear about it."

Adel watched him crush the empty cigarette box into a ball and stuff it into the front pocket of his jeans.

"He *does* have his enemies, your father," Gholam sighed.

Adel knew this. Baba jan had explained to him that some of the people who had fought alongside him against the Soviets in the 1980s had become both powerful and corrupt. They had lost their way, he said. And because he wouldn't join in their criminal schemes, they always tried to undermine him, to pollute his name by spreading false, hurtful rumors about him. This was why Baba jan always tried to shield Adel— he didn't allow newspapers in the house, for instance, didn't want Adel watching the news on TV or surfing the Internet.

Gholam leaned in and said, "I also hear he's quite the farmer."

Adel shrugged. "You can see for yourself. Just a few acres of orchards. Well, and the cotton fields in Helmand too, I guess, for the factory."

Gholam searched Adel's eyes as a grin slowly spread across his face, exposing his rotting canine. "Cotton. You're a piece of work. I don't know what to say."

Adel didn't really understand this. He got up and bounced the ball. "You can say, 'Rematch!'"

"Rematch!"

"Let's go."

"Only, this time, I bet you don't score one goal."

Now Adel was the one grinning. "Name your bet."

"That's easy. The Zidane."

"And if I win, no, *when* I win?"

"I were you," Gholam said, "I wouldn't worry about that improbability."

It was a brilliant hustle. Gholam dove left and right, saved all of Adel's shots. Taking off the jersey, Adel felt stupid for getting cheated out of what was rightfully his, what was probably his most prized possession. He handed it over. With some alarm, he felt the sting of tears and fought them back.

At least Gholam had the tact not to put it on in his presence. As he was leaving, he grinned over his shoulder. "Your father, he's not really gone for three months, is he?"

"I'll play you for it tomorrow," Adel said. "The jersey."

"I may have to think about that."

Gholam headed back toward the main road. Halfway there, he paused, fished the rolled-up cigarette box from his pocket, and hurled it over the wall of Adel's house.

Every day for about a week, after his morning lessons, Adel took his ball and left the compound. He was able to time his escapades with the armed guard's schedule of rounds for the first couple of tries. But on the third try, the guard caught him and wouldn't let him leave. Adel went back to the house and returned with an iPod and a watch. From then on, the guard surreptitiously let Adel in and out provided he venture no farther than the edge of the orchards. As for Kabir and his mother, they barely noticed his one- or two-hour absences. It was one of the advantages of living in a house as big as this.

Adel played alone behind the compound, over by the old tree stump in the clearing, each day hoping to see Gholam sauntering up. He kept an eye on the unpaved path stretching to the main road as he juggled, as he sat on the stump watching a fighter jet streak across the sky, as he listlessly flicked pebbles at nothing. After a while, he picked up his ball and plodded back to the compound.

Then one day Gholam showed up, carrying a paper bag.

"Where have you been?"

"Working," Gholam said.

He told Adel that he and his father had been hired for a few days to make bricks. Gholam's job was to mix mortar. He said he lugged pails of water back and forth, dragged bags of masonry cement and builder's sand heavier than himself. He explained to Adel how he mixed mortar in the wheelbarrow, folding the mixture in the water with a hoe, folding it again and again, adding water, then sand, until the batch gained a smooth consistency that didn't crumble. He would then push the wheelbarrow to the bricklayers and trot back to start a new batch. He opened his palms and showed Adel his blisters.

"Wow," Adel said—stupidly, he knew, but he couldn't

think of another reply. The closest he had ever come to manual labor was one afternoon three years ago when he'd helped the gardener plant a few apple saplings in the backyard of their house in Kabul.

"Got you a surprise," Gholam said. He reached into the bag and tossed Adel the Zidane jersey.

"I don't understand," Adel said, surprised and cautiously thrilled.

"I see some kid in town the other day wearing it," Gholam said, asking for the ball with his fingers. Adel kicked it to him and Gholam juggled as he told the story. "Can you believe it? I go up to him and say, 'Hey that's my buddy's shirt on you.' He gives me a look. To make a long story short, we settle it in an alley. By the end, he's begging *me* to take the shirt!" He caught the ball midair, spat, and grinned at Adel. "All right, so maybe I'd sold it to him a couple of days earlier."

"That's not right. If you sold it, it was his."

"What, you don't want it now? After everything I went through to get it back for you? It wasn't all one-sided, you know. He landed a few decent punches."

"Still . . ." Adel muttered.

"Besides, I tricked you in the first place and I felt bad about it. Now you get your shirt back. And as for me . . ." He pointed to his feet, and Adel saw a new pair of blue-and-white sneakers.

"Is he all right, the other guy?" Adel asked.

"He'll live. Now, are we going to debate or are we going to play?"

"Is your father with you?"

"Not today. He's at the courthouse in Kabul. Come on, let's go."

They played for a while, kicking the ball back and forth, chasing it around. They went for a walk later, Adel breaking his promise to the guard and leading them into the orchards. They ate loquats off the trees and drank cold Fanta from cans Adel covertly fetched from the kitchen.

Soon, they began to meet this way almost daily. They played ball, chased each other through the orchards' parallel rows of trees. They chatted about sports and movies, and when they had nothing to say they looked out on the town of Shadbagh-e-Nau, the soft hillsides in the distance and the hazy chain of mountains farther yet, and that was all right too.

Every day now Adel woke up eager for the sight of Gholam sneaking up the dirt path, the sound of his loud, confident voice. He was often distracted during his morning lessons, his concentration lapsing as he thought of the games they would play later, the stories they would tell each other. He worried he would lose Gholam. He worried Gholam's father, Iqbal, wouldn't find steady work in town, or a place to live, and Gholam would move to another town, another part of the country, and Adel had tried to prepare for this possibility, steel himself against the farewell that would then follow.

One day, as they sat on the tree stump, Gholam said, "Have you ever been with a girl, Adel?"

"You mean—"

"Yeah, I mean."

Adel felt a rush of heat around his ears. He briefly contemplated lying, but he knew Gholam would see right through him. He mumbled, "You have?"

Gholam lit a cigarette and offered one to Adel. This time Adel took it, after glancing over his shoulder to make sure the guard wasn't peeking around the corner or that Kabir hadn't decided to step out. He took a drag and launched immediately into a protracted coughing fit that had Gholam smirking and pounding him on the back.

"So, have you or not?" Adel wheezed, eyes tearing.

"Friend of mine back at the camp," Gholam said in a conspiratorial tone, "he was older, he took me to a whorehouse in Peshawar."

He told the story. The small, filthy room. The orange curtains, the cracked walls, the single lightbulb hanging from the ceiling, the rat he had seen dart across the floor. The sound of rickshaws outside, sputtering up and down the street, cars rumbling. The young girl on the mattress, finishing a plate of *biryani*, chewing and looking at him without any expression. How he could tell, even in the dim light, that she had a pretty face and that she was hardly any older than he. How she had scooped up the last grains of rice with a folded piece of *naan*, pushed away the plate, lain down, and wiped her fingers on her trousers as she'd pulled them down.

Adel listened, fascinated, enraptured. He had never had a friend like this. Gholam knew more about the world than even Adel's half brothers who were several years older than him. And Adel's friends back in Kabul? They were all the sons of technocrats and officials and ministers. They all lived variations of Adel's own life. The glimpses Gholam had allowed Adel into his life suggested an existence rife with trouble, unpredictability, hardship, but also adventure, a life worlds removed from Adel's own, though it unfolded practically within spitting distance of him. Listening to Gholam's stories, Adel's own life sometimes struck him as hopelessly dull.

"So did you do it, then?" Adel said. "Did you, you know, stick it in her?"

"No. We had a cup of *chai* and discussed Rumi. What do you *think*?"

Adel blushed. "What was it like?"

But Gholam had already moved on. This was often the pattern of their conversations, Gholam choosing what they would talk about, launching into a story with gusto, roping Adel in, only to lose interest and leave both the story and Adel dangling.

Now, instead of finishing up the story he had started, Gholam said, "My grandmother says her husband, my grandfather Saboor, told her a story about this tree once. Well, that was long before he cut it down, of course. My grandfather told it to her when they were both kids. The story was that if you had a wish, you had to kneel before the tree and whisper it. And if the tree agreed to grant it, it would shed exactly ten leaves on your head."

"I never heard that," Adel says.

"Well, you wouldn't have, would you?"

It was then that Adel caught on to what Gholam had really said. "Wait. Your grandfather cut down our tree?"

Gholam turned his eyes to him. "Your tree? It's not your tree."

Adel blinked. "What does that mean?"

Gholam bore his gaze even deeper into Adel's face. For the first time, Adel could detect no trace of his friend's customary liveliness or of his trademark smirk or light-hearted mischief. His face was transformed, his expression sober, startlingly adult.

"This was my family's tree. This was my family's land. It's been ours for generations. Your father built his mansion on our land. While we were in Pakistan during the war." He pointed to the orchards. "These? They used to be people's homes. But your father had them bulldozed to the ground. Just like he brought down the house where my father was born, where he was raised."

Adel blinked.

"He claimed our land as his own and he built that"— here, he actually sneered as he threw a thumb toward the compound—"that *thing* in its stead."

Feeling a little nauseated, his heart thumping heavily, Adel said, "I thought we were friends. Why are you telling these terrible lies?"

"Remember when I tricked you and took your jersey?" Gholam said, a flush rising to his cheeks. "You almost cried. Don't deny it, I saw you. That was over a shirt. A *shirt*. Imagine how my family felt, coming all the way from Pakistan, only to get off the bus and find this *thing* on our land. And then your goon in the purple suit ordering us off our own land."

"My father is not a thief!" Adel shot back. "Ask anyone

in Shadbagh-e-Nau, ask them what he's done for this town." He thought of how Baba jan received people at the town mosque, reclined on the floor, teacup before him, prayer beads in hand. A solemn line of people, stretching from his cushion to the front entrance, men with muddy hands, toothless old women, young widows with children, every one of them in need, each waiting for his or her turn to ask for a favor, a job, a small loan to repair a roof or an irrigation ditch or buy milk formula. His father nodding, listening with infinite patience, as though each person in line mattered to him like family.

"Yeah? Then how come my father has the ownership documents?" Gholam said. "The ones he gave to the judge at the courthouse."

"I'm sure if your father talks to Baba—"

"Your Baba won't talk to him. He won't acknowledge what he's done. He drives past like we're stray dogs."

"You're not dogs," Adel said. It was a struggle to keep his voice even. "You're buzzards. Just like Kabir said. I should have known."

Gholam stood up, took a step or two, and paused. "Just so you know," he said, "I hold nothing against you. You're just an ignorant little boy. But next time Baba goes to Helmand, ask him to take you to that factory of his. See what he's got growing out there. I'll give you a hint. It's not cotton."

Later that night, before dinner, Adel lay in a bath full of warm soapy water. He could hear the TV downstairs, Kabir watching an old pirate movie. The anger, which had lingered all afternoon, had washed through Adel, and now he thought that he'd been too rough with Gholam. Baba jan had told him once that no matter how much you did, sometimes the poor spoke ill of the rich. They mainly did it out of disappointment with their own lives. It couldn't be helped. It was natural, even. *And we mustn't blame them, Adel,* he said.

Adel was not too naïve to know that the world was a fundamentally unfair place; he only had to gaze out the window of his bedroom. But he imagined that for people like Gholam, the acknowledgment of this truth brought no satisfaction. Maybe people like Gholam needed someone to stand culpable, a flesh-and-bones target, someone they could conveniently point to as the agent of their hardship, someone to condemn, blame, be angry with. And perhaps Baba jan was right when he said the proper response was to understand, to withhold judgment. To answer with kindness, even. Watching little soapy bubbles come up to the surface and pop, Adel thought of his father building schools and clinics when he knew there were people in town who spread wicked gossip about him.

As he was drying himself off, his mother poked her head through the bathroom door. "You're coming down for dinner?"

"I'm not hungry," he said.

"Oh." She came inside and grabbed a towel off the rack. "Here. Sit. Let me dry your hair."

"I can do it myself," Adel said.

She stood behind him, her eyes studying him in the mirror. "Are you all right, Adel?"

He shrugged. She rested a hand on his shoulder and looked at him as if expecting him to rub his cheek against it. He didn't.

"Mother, have you ever seen Baba jan's factory?"

He noticed the pause in his mother's movements. "Of course," she said. "So have you."

"I don't mean pictures. Have you actually seen it? Been to it?"

"How could I?" his mother said, tilting her head in the mirror. "Helmand is unsafe. Your father would never put me or you in harm's way."

Adel nodded.

Downstairs, cannons blasted and pirates hollered their war cries.

Three days later, Gholam showed up again. He walked briskly up to Adel and stopped.

"I'm glad you came," Adel said, "I have something for you." From the top of the tree stump he fetched the coat he had been bringing with him daily since their spat. It was chocolate brown leather, with a soft sheepskin lining and a hood that could be zippered on and off. He extended it to Gholam. "I've only worn it a few times. It's a little big for me. It should fit you."

Gholam didn't make a move. "We took a bus to Kabul and went to the courthouse yesterday," he said flatly. "Guess what the judge told us? He said he had bad news. He said there was an accident. A small fire. My father's ownership documents burned in it. Gone. Destroyed."

Adel slowly dropped the hand holding the jacket.

"And as he's telling us that there's nothing he can do now without the papers, do you know what he has on his wrist? A brand-new gold watch he wasn't wearing the last time my father saw him."

Adel blinked.

Gholam flicked his gaze to the coat. It was a cutting, punishing look, meant to inflict shame. It worked. Adel shrunk. In his hand, he felt the coat shifting, transforming from peace offering to bribe.

Gholam spun around and hurried back toward the road in brisk, busy steps.

The evening of the same day that he returned, Baba jan threw a party at the house. Adel was sitting now beside his father at the head of the big cloth that had been spread on the floor for the meal. Baba jan sometimes preferred to sit on the ground and to eat with his fingers, especially if he was seeing friends from his jihadi years. *Reminds me of the cave days,* he joked. The women were eating at the table in the dining room with spoons and forks, Adel's mother seated at the head. Adel could hear their chatter echoing off the marble walls. One of them, a thick-hipped woman with long hair dyed red, was engaged to be married to one of Baba jan's friends. Earlier in the evening, she had shown Adel's mother pictures on her digital camera of the bridal shop they had visited in Dubai.

Over tea after the meal, Baba jan told a story about the time his unit had ambushed a Soviet column to stop it from entering a valley up north. Everyone listened closely.

"When they entered the kill zone," Baba jan said, one hand absently stroking Adel's hair, "we opened fire. We hit the lead vehicle, then a few jeeps. I thought they would back out or try to plow through. But the sons of whores stopped, dismounted, and engaged us in gunfire. Can you believe it?"

A murmur spread around the room. Heads shook. Adel knew that at least half the men in the room were former Mujahideen.

"We outnumbered them, maybe three to one, but they had heavy weaponry and it wasn't long before *they* were attacking *us*! Attacking our positions in the orchards. Soon, everybody was scattered. We ran for it. Me and this guy, Mohammad something or other, we ran together. We're running side by side in a field of grapevines, not the kind on posts and wires but the kind that people let grow out on the ground. Bullets are flying everywhere and we're running for our lives, and suddenly we both trip and go down. In a second flat, I'm back up on my feet running, but there's no sign of this Mohammad something or other. I turn and yell, 'Get the hell up, you donkey's ass!'"

Baba jan paused for dramatic effect. He pushed a fist to his lips to fight laughter. "And then he pops up and starts running. And—would you believe it?—the crazy son of a whore is carrying two armfuls of grapes! One mound in each arm!"

Laughter erupted. Adel laughed too. His father rubbed his back and pulled him close. Someone started to tell another story, and Baba jan reached for the cigarette sitting next to his plate. But he never got the chance to light it because suddenly glass shattered somewhere in the house.

From the dining room, women screamed. Something metallic, maybe a fork or a butter knife, clanged loudly on the marble. The men bolted to their feet. Azmaray and Kabir came running into the room, handguns already drawn.

"It came from the entrance," Kabir said. And, just as he said this, glass broke again.

"Wait here, Commander Sahib, we'll have a look," Azmaray said.

"Like hell I will," Baba jan growled, already pushing forward. "I'm not cowering under my own roof."

He headed toward the foyer, trailed by Adel, Azmaray, Kabir, and all the male guests. On their way, Adel saw Kabir pick up a metal rod they used in the winter to stoke the fire in the stove. Adel saw his mother too as she ran to join them, her face pale and drawn. When they reached the foyer, a rock came flying through the window and shards of glass crashed to the floor. The woman with red hair, the bride-to-be, screamed. Outside, someone was yelling.

"How the hell did they get past the guard?" someone said behind Adel.

"Commander Sahib, no!" Kabir barked. But Adel's father had already opened the front door.

The light was dimming, but it was summer, and the sky was still awash in pale yellow. In the distance, Adel saw little clusters of light, people in Shadbagh-e-Nau settling in for dinner with their families. The hills running along the horizon had darkened and soon night would fill in all the hollows. But it wasn't dark enough, not yet, to shroud the old man Adel saw standing at the foot of the front steps, a rock in each hand.

"Take him upstairs," Baba jan said over his shoulder to Adel's mother. "Now!"

Adel's mother led him up the staircase by the shoulders, down the hallway, and into the master bedroom she shared with Baba jan. She closed the door, locked it, pulled the curtains shut, and turned on the TV. She guided Adel to the bed and together they sat. On the screen, two Arabs, dressed in long kurta shirts and knit caps, were working on a monster truck.

"What is he going to do to that old man?" Adel said. He couldn't stop from shivering. "Mother, what is he going to do to him?"

He looked up at his mother, and saw a cloud pass over her face and he suddenly knew, he knew right away, that whatever came out of her mouth next could not be trusted.

"He's going to talk to him," she said with a tremor. "He's going to reason with whoever is out there. It's what your father does. He reasons with people."

Adel shook his head. He was weeping now, sobbing. "What is he going to do, Mother? What is he going to do to that old man?"

His mother kept saying the same thing, that everything was going to be all right, that it would all turn out just fine, that no one was going to get hurt. But the more she said it, the more he sobbed, until it exhausted him and at some point he fell asleep on his mother's lap.

Former Commander Escapes Assassination Attempt.

Adel read the story in his father's study, on his father's computer. The story described the attack as "vicious" and the assailant as a former refugee with "suspected ties to the Taliban." Midway through the article, Adel's father was quoted as saying that he had feared for the safety of his family. *Especially my innocent little boy,* he'd said. The article gave no name to the assailant nor any indication of what had happened to him.

Adel shut off the computer. He wasn't supposed to be using it and he had trespassed, coming into his father's study. A month ago, he wouldn't have dared do either. He trudged back to his room, lay on his bed, and bounced an old tennis ball against the wall. *Thump! Thump! Thump!* It wasn't long before his mother poked her head in through the door and asked, then told him, to stop, but he didn't. She lingered at the door for a while before slinking away.

Thump! Thump! Thump!

On the surface, nothing had changed. A transcript of Adel's daily activities would have revealed him falling back into a normal rhythm. He still got up at the same hour, washed, had breakfast with his parents, lessons with his tutor. Afterward, he ate lunch and then spent the afternoon lying around, watching movies with Kabir or else playing video games.

But nothing was the same. Gholam may have cracked a door open to him, but it was Baba jan who had pushed him through it. Dormant gears in Adel's mind had begun to turn. Adel felt as though, overnight, he had acquired an altogether new auxiliary sense, one that empowered him to perceive things he never had before, things that had stared him in the face for years. He saw, for instance, how his mother had secrets inside of her. When he looked at her, they practically rippled over her face. He saw her struggles to keep from him all the things she knew, all the things she kept locked up, closed off, carefully guarded, like the two of them in this big house. He saw for the first time his father's house for the monstrosity, the affront, the monument to injustice, that it privately was to everyone else. He saw in people's rush to please his father the intimidation, the fear, that was the real underpinning of their respect and defer-ence. He thought Gholam would be proud of him for this insight. For the first time, Adel felt truly aware of the broader movements that had always governed his life.

And of the wildly conflicting truths that resided within a person. Not just in his father, or his mother, or Kabir.

But within himself too.

This last discovery was, in some ways, the most surpris-ing to Adel. The revelations of what he now knew his father had done—first in the name of jihad, then for what he had called *the just rewards of sacrifice*—had left Adel reeling. At least for a while. For days after that evening the rocks had come crashing through the window, Adel's stomach ached whenever his father walked into the room. He found his father barking into his mobile phone, or even heard him humming in the bath, and he felt his spine crumpling, his throat going painfully dry. His father kissed him good night, and Adel's instinct was to recoil. He had nightmares. He dreamt he was standing at the edge of the orchards, watching a thrashing about among the trees, the glint of a metal rod rising and falling, the sound of metal striking meat and bone. He woke from these dreams with a howl locked in his chest. Bouts of weeping sideswiped him at random moments.

And yet.

And yet.

Something else was happening as well. The new awareness had not faded from his mind, but slowly it had found company. Another, opposing current of consciousness coursed through him now, one that did not displace the first but claimed space beside it. Adel felt an awakening to this other, more troubling part of himself. The part of him that over time would gradually, almost imperceptibly, accept this new identity that at present prickled like a wet wool sweater. Adel saw that, in the end, he would probably accept things as his mother had. Adel had been angry with her at first; he was more forgiving now. Perhaps she had accepted out of fear of her husband. Or as a bargain for the life of luxury she led. Mostly, Adel suspected, she had accepted for the same reason he would: because she had to. What choice was there? Adel could not run from his life any more than Gholam could from his. People learned to live with the most unimaginable things. As would he. This was his life. This was his mother. This was his father. And this was him, even if he hadn't always known it.

Adel knew he would not love his father again as he had before, when he would sleep happily curled in the bay of his thick arms. That was inconceivable now. But he would learn to love him again even if now it was a different, more complicated, messier business. Adel could almost feel himself leapfrogging over childhood. Soon, he would land as an adult. And when he did, there would be no going back because adulthood was akin to what his father had once said about being a war hero: once you became one, you died one.

Lying in bed at night, Adel thought that one day—maybe the next day or the one after that, or maybe one day the following week—he would leave the house and walk over to the field by the windmill where Gholam had told him his family was squatting. He thought he would find the field empty. He would stand on the side of the road, picture Gholam and his mother and his brothers and his grandmother, the family a straggling line lugging roped-up belongings, padding along the dusty shoulders of country roads, looking for some place to land. Gholam was the head of the family now. He would have to work. He would now spend his youth clearing canals, digging ditches, making bricks, and harvesting fields. Gholam would gradually turn into one of those stooping leather-faced men Adel always saw behind plows.

Adel thought he would stand there a while in the field, watching the hills and the mountains looming over New Shadbagh. And then he thought he would reach into his pocket for what he had found one day walking through the orchards, the left half of a pair of spectacles, snapped at the bridge, the lens a spiderweb of cracks, the temple crusted with dried blood. He would toss the broken spectacles into a ditch. Adel suspected that as he turned back around and walked home, what he would feel mostly would be relief.

Eight

Fall 2010

This evening, I come home from the clinic and find a message from Thalia on the landline phone in my bedroom. I play it as I slip off my shoes and sit at my desk. She tells me she has a cold, one she is sure she picked up from Mamá, then she asks after me, asks how work is going in Kabul. At the end, just before she hangs up, she says, *Odie goes on and on about how you don't call. Of course she won't tell you. So I will. Markos. For the love of Christ. Call your mother. You ass.*

I smile.

Thalia.

I keep a picture of her on my desk, the one I took all those years ago at the beach on Tinos—Thalia sitting on a rock with her back to the camera. I have framed the photo, though if you look closely you can still see a patch of dark brown at the left lower corner courtesy of a crazed Italian girl who tried to set fire to it many years ago.

I turn on my laptop and start typing up the previous day's op notes. My room is upstairs—one of three bedrooms on the second floor of this house where I have lived since my arrival in Kabul back in 2002—and my desk sits at the window overlooking the garden below. I have a view of the loquat trees my old landlord, Nabi, and I planted a few years ago. I can see Nabi's onetime quarters along the back wall too, now repainted. After he passed away, I offered them to a young Dutch fellow who helps local high schools with their IT. And, off to the right, there is Suleiman Wahdati's 1940s Chevrolet, unmoved for decades, shrouded in rust like a rock by moss, currently covered by a light film of yesterday's surprisingly early snowfall, the first of the year thus far. After Nabi died, I thought briefly of having the car hauled to one of Kabul's junkyards, but I didn't have the heart. It seemed to me too essential a part of the house's past, its history.

I finish the notes and check my watch. It's already 9:30 p.m. Seven o'clock in the evening back in Greece.

Call your mother. You ass.

If I am going to call Mamá tonight, I can't delay it any longer. I remember Thalia wrote in one of her e-mails that Mamá was going to bed earlier and earlier. I take a breath and steel myself. I pick up the receiver and dial.

I met Thalia in the summer of 1967, when I was twelve years old. She and her mother, Madaline, came to Tinos to visit Mamá and me. Mamá, whose name is

Odelia, said it had been years—fifteen, to be exact—since she and her friend Madaline had last seen each other. Madaline had left the island at seventeen and gone off to Athens to become, for a brief time at least, an actress of some modest renown.

"I wasn't surprised," Mamá said, "when I heard of her acting. Because of her looks. Everyone was always taken with Madaline. You'll see for yourself when you meet her."

I asked Mamá why she'd never mentioned her.

"Haven't I? Are you sure?"

"I'm sure."

"I could have sworn." Then she said, "The daughter. Thalia. You must be considerate with her because she had an accident. A dog bit her. She has a scar."

Mamá wouldn't say more, and I knew better than to lean on her about it. But this revelation intrigued me far more than Madaline's past in film and stage had, my curiosity fueled by the suspicion that the scar must be both significant and visible for the girl to deserve special consideration. With morbid eagerness, I looked forward to seeing this scar for myself.

"Madaline and I met at mass, when we were little," Mamá said. Right off, she said, they had become inseparable friends. They had held hands under their desks in class, or at recess, at church, or strolling past the barley fields. They had sworn to remain sisters for life. They promised they would live close to each other, even after they'd married. They would live as neighbors, and if one or the other's husband insisted on moving away, then they would demand a divorce. I remember that Mamá grinned a little when she told me all this self-mockingly, as if to distance herself from this youthful exuberance and foolishness, all those headlong, breathless vows. But I saw on her face a tinge of unspoken hurt as well, a shade of disappointment that Mamá was far too proud to admit to.

Madaline was married now to a wealthy and much older man, a Mr. Andreas Gianakos, who years before had produced her second and, as it turned out, last film. He was in the construction business now and owned a big firm in Athens. They had had a falling-out recently, a row, Madaline and Mr. Gianakos. Mamá didn't tell me any of this information; I knew it from a clandestine, hasty, partial read of the letter Madaline had sent Mamá informing her of her intent to visit.

It grows so tiresome, I tell you, to be around Andreas and his right-wing friends and their martial music. I keep tight-lipped all the time. I say nothing when they exalt these military thugs who have made a mockery of our democracy. Should I utter so much as a word of dissent, I am confident they would label me a communist anarchist, and then even Andreas's influence would not save me from the dungeons. Perhaps he would not bother exerting it, meaning his influence. Sometimes I believe it is precisely his intent to provoke me into impugning myself. Ah, how I miss you, my dear Odie. How I miss your company . . .

The day our guests were due to arrive, Mamá awoke early to tidy up. We lived in a small house built into a hillside. Like many houses on Tinos, it was made of whitewashed stone, and the roof was flat, with diamond-shaped red tiles. The small upstairs bedroom Mamá and I shared didn't have a door—the narrow stairwell led right into it—but it did have a fanlight window and a narrow terrace with a waist-high wrought-iron balustrade from which you could look out on the roofs of other houses, on the olive trees and the goats and winding stone alleys and arches below, and, of course, the Aegean, blue and calm in the summer morning, white-capped in the afternoon when the *meltemi* winds blew in from the north.

When she was done cleaning up, Mamá put on what passed for her one fancy outfit, the one she wore every August fifteenth, the Feast of the Dormition at the Panagia Evangelistria Church, when pilgrims descended on Tinos from everywhere in the Mediterranean to pray before the church's famed icon. There is a photo of my mother in that outfit—the long, drab rusty gold dress with a rounded neckline, the shrunken white sweater, the stockings, the clunky black shoes. Mamá looking every bit the forbidding widow, with her severe face, her tufted eyebrows, and her snub nose, standing stiffly, looking sullenly pious, like she's a pilgrim herself. I'm in the picture too, standing rigidly at my mother's hip. I am wearing a white shirt, white shorts, and white kneesocks rolled up. You can tell by my scowl that I've been ordered to stand straight, to not smile, that my face has been scrubbed and my hair combed down with water, against my will and with a great deal of fuss. You can sense a current of dissatisfaction between us. You see it in how rigidly we stand, how our bodies barely make contact.

Or maybe you can't. But I do every time I see that picture,

the last time being two years ago. I can't help but see the wariness, the effort, the impatience. I can't help but see two people together out of a sense of genetic duty, doomed already to bewilder and disappoint each other, each honor-bound to defy the other.

From the bedroom window upstairs, I watched Mamá leave for the ferry port in the town of Tinos. A scarf tied under the chin, Mamá rammed into the sunny blue day headfirst. She was a slight, small-boned woman with the body of a child, but when you saw her coming you did well to let her pass. I remember her walking me to school every morning—my mother is retired now, but she was a school-teacher. As we walked, Mamá never held my hand. The other mothers did with their own kids, but not Mamá. She said she had to treat me like any other student. She marched ahead, a fist closed at the neck of her sweater, and I tried to keep up, lunch box in hand, tottering along behind in her foot-steps. In the classroom, I always sat at the back. I remember my mother at the blackboard and how she could nail a misbehaving pupil with a single, scalding glance, like a rock from a slingshot, the aim surgically true. And she could cleave you in half with nothing but a dark look or a sudden beat of silence.

Mamá believed in loyalty above all, even at the cost of self-denial. Especially at the cost of self-denial. She also believed it was always best to tell the truth, to tell it plainly, without fanfare, and the more disagreeable the truth, the sooner you had to tell it. She had no patience for soft spines. She was—*is*—a woman of enormous will, a woman without apology, and not a woman with whom you want to have a dispute—though I have never really understood, even now, whether her temperament was God-given or one she adopted out of necessity, what with her husband dying barely a year into their marriage and leaving her to raise me all on her own.

I fell asleep upstairs a short while after Mamá left. I jolted awake later to a woman's high, ringing voice. I sat up and there she was, all lipstick, powder, perfume, and slender curves, an airline ad smiling down at me through the thin veil of a pillbox hat. She stood in the middle of the room in a neon green minidress, leather valise at her feet, with her auburn hair and long limbs, grinning down at me, a shine on her face, and talking, the seams of her voice bursting with aplomb and cheer.

"So you're Odie's little Markos! She didn't tell me you were this handsome! Oh, and I see her in you, around the eyes—yes, you have the same eyes, I think, I'm sure you've been told. I've been so eager to meet you. Your mother and I—we—oh, no doubt Odie has told you, so you can imagine, you can picture, what a thrill this is for me, to see the two of you, to meet you, Markos. Markos Varvaris! Well, I am Madaline Gianakos, and, may I say, I am delighted."

She took off a cream-colored, elbow-length satin glove, the kind I'd seen worn only in magazines by elegant ladies out at a soiree, smoking on the wide steps of the opera house or being helped out of a shiny black car, their faces lit up by popping flashbulbs. She had to yank on each fingertip a bunch of times before the glove came off, and then she stooped slightly at the waist and offered me her hand.

"Charmed," she said. Her hand was soft and cool, despite the glove. "And this is my daughter, Thalia. Darling, say hello to Markos Varvaris."

She stood at the entrance of the room beside my mother, looking at me blankly, a lanky, pale-skinned girl with limp curls. Other than that, I can't tell you a single thing. I can't tell you the color of the dress she wore that day—that is, if she wore a dress—or the style of her shoes, or whether she had socks on, or whether she wore a watch, or a necklace, or a ring, or a pair of earrings. I can't tell you because if you were at a restaurant and someone suddenly stripped, hopped atop a table, and started juggling dessert spoons, you would not only look, it would be the only thing you *could* look at. The mask draped over the lower half of the girl's face was like that. It obliterated the possibility of any other observation.

"Thalia, say hello, darling. Don't be rude."

I thought I saw a faint nod of the head.

"Hello," I replied with a sandpaper tongue. There was a ripple in the air. A current. I felt charged with something that was half thrill, half dread, something that burst upward inside of me and coiled itself up. I was staring and I knew it and I couldn't stop, couldn't peel my gaze away from the sky blue cloth of the mask, the two sets of bands tying it to the back of her head, the narrow horizontal slit over the mouth. I knew right then that I couldn't bear to see it, whatever the mask was hiding. And that I couldn't wait to see it. Nothing in my life could resume its natural course and rhythm and order until I saw for myself what was so terrible, so dreadful, that I and others had to be protected from it.

The alternate possibility, that the mask was perhaps designed to shield Thalia from us, eluded me. At least it did in the dizzying throes of that first meeting.

Madaline and Thalia stayed upstairs to unpack while Mamá battered up cuts of sole for supper in the kitchen. She asked me to make Madaline a cup of *ellinikós kafés*, which I did, and she asked me to take it up to her, which I did as well, on a tray, with a little plate of *pastelli*.

All these decades later and shame still washes over me like some warm, sticky liquid at the memory of what happened next. To this day I can picture the scene like a photograph, frozen. Madaline smoking, standing at the bedroom window, looking at the sea through a set of teashade glasses with yellow lenses, one hand on her hip, ankles crossed. Her pillbox hat sits on the dresser. Above the dresser is a mirror and in the mirror is Thalia, sitting on the edge of the bed, her back to me. She is stooped down, doing something, maybe undoing her shoelaces, and I can see that she has removed her mask. It's sitting next to her on the bed. A thread of cold marches down my spine and I try to stop it, but my hands tremble, which makes the porcelain cup clink on the saucer, which makes Madaline turn her head from the window to me, which makes Thalia look up. I catch her reflection in the mirror.

The tray slipped from my hands. Porcelain shattered. Hot liquid spilled and the tray went clanking down the steps.

It was sudden mayhem, me on all fours, retching all over shards of broken porcelain, Madaline saying, "Oh dear. Oh dear," and Mamá running upstairs, yelling, "What happened? What did you do, Markos?"

A dog bit her, Mamá had told me by way of a warning. *She has a scar.* The dog hadn't bitten Thalia's face; it had *eaten* it. And perhaps there were words to describe what I saw in the mirror that day, but *scar* wasn't one of them.

I remember Mamá's hands grabbing my shoulders, her pulling me up and whirling me around, saying, "What is with you? What is wrong with you?" And I remember her gaze lifting over my head. It froze there. The words died in her mouth. She went blank in the face. Her hands dropped from my shoulders. And then I witnessed the most extraordinary thing, something I thought I'd no sooner see than King Constantine himself turning up at our door dressed in a clown suit: a single tear, swelling at the edge of my mother's right eye.

"So what was she like?" Mamá asks.

"Who?"

"Who? The French woman. Your landlord's niece, the professor from Paris."

I switch the receiver to my other ear. It surprises me that she remembers. All my life, I have had the feeling that the words I say to Mamá vanish unheard in space, as if there is static between us, a bad connection. Sometimes when I call her from Kabul, as I have now, I feel as though she has quietly lowered the receiver and stepped away, that I am speaking into a void across the continents—though I can feel my mother's presence on the line and hear her breathing in my ear. Other times, I am telling her about something I saw at the clinic—some bloodied boy carried by his father, for instance, shrapnel embedded deep in his cheeks, ear torn clean off, another victim of playing on the wrong street at the wrong time of the wrong day—and then, without warning, a loud clunk, and Mamá's voice suddenly distant and muffled, rising and falling, the echo of footsteps, of something being dragged across the floor, and I clam up, wait until she comes back on, which she does eventually, always a bit out of breath, explaining, *I told her I was fine standing up. I said it clearly. I said, "Thalia, I would like to stand at the window and look down on the water as I'm talking to Markos." But she says, "You'll tire yourself out, Odie, you need to sit." Next thing I know, she's dragging the armchair—this big leather thing she bought me last year—she's dragging it to the window. My God, she's strong. You haven't seen the armchair, of course. Well, of course.* She then sighs with mock exasperation and asks that I go on with my story, but by then I am too unbalanced to. The net effect is that she has made me feel vaguely reprimanded and, what's more, deserving of it, guilty of wrongs unspoken, offenses I've never been formally charged with. Even if I do go on with my story, it sounds diminished to my own ears. It does not measure up to Mamá's armchair drama with Thalia.

"What was her name again?" Mamá says now. "Pari something, no?"

I have told Mamá about Nabi, who was a dear friend to me. She knows the general outline of his life only. She knows that in his will he left the Kabul house to his niece, Pari, who was raised in France. But I have not told Mamá about Nila Wahdati, her escape to Paris after her husband's stroke, the decades Nabi spent caring for Suleiman. *That* history. Too many boomeranging parallels. Like reading aloud your own indictment.

"Pari. Yes. She was nice," I say. "And warm. Especially for an academic."

"What is she again, a chemist?"

"*Mathematician,*" I say, closing the lid of the laptop. It has started snowing again, lightly, tiny flakes twisting in the dark, flinging themselves at my window.

I tell Mamá about Pari Wahdati's visit late this past summer. She really was quite lovely. Gentle, slim, gray hair, long neck with a full blue vein crawling up each side, warm gap-toothed smile. She seemed a bit brittle, older than her age. Bad rheumatoid arthritis. The knobby hands, especially, still functional, but the day is coming and she knew it. It made me think of Mamá and the coming of *her* day.

Pari Wahdati stayed a week with me at the house in Kabul. I gave her a tour of it when she arrived from Paris. She had last seen the house back in 1955 and seemed quite surprised at the vividness of her own memory of the place, its general layout, the two steps between the living room and dining room, for instance, where she said she would sit in a band of sunlight midmornings and read her books. She was struck by how much smaller the house really was compared to the version of it in her memory. When I took her upstairs, she knew which had been her bedroom, though it's currently taken up by a German colleague of mine who works for the World Food Program. I remember her breath catching when she spotted the short little armoire in the corner of the bedroom—one of the few surviving relics of her childhood. I remembered it from the note that Nabi had left me prior to his death. She squatted next to it and ran her fingertips over the chipped yellow paint and over the fading giraffes and long-tailed monkeys on its doors. When she looked up at me, I saw that her eyes had teared a little, and she asked, very shyly and apologetically, if it would be possible to have it shipped to Paris. She offered to pay for a replacement. It was the only thing she wanted from the house. I told her it would be my pleasure to do it.

In the end, other than the armoire, which I had shipped a few days after her departure, Pari Wahdati returned to France with nothing but Suleiman Wahdati's sketch pads, Nabi's letter, and a few of her mother Nila's poems, which Nabi had saved. The only other thing she asked of me during her stay was to arrange a ride to take her to Shadbagh so she could see the village where she had been born and where she hoped to find her half brother, Iqbal.

"I assume she'll sell the house," Mamá says, "now that it's hers."

"She said I could stay on as long as I liked, actually," I say. "Rent-free."

I can all but see Mamá's lips tighten skeptically. She's an islander. She suspects the motives of all mainlanders, looks askance at their apparent acts of goodwill. This was one of the reasons I knew, when I was a boy, that I would leave Tinos one day when I had the chance. A kind of despair used to get hold of me whenever I heard people talking this way.

"How is the dovecote coming along?" I ask to change the subject.

"I had to give it a rest. It tired me out."

Mamá was diagnosed in Athens six months ago by a neurologist I had insisted she see after Thalia told me Mamá was twitching and dropping things all the time. It was Thalia who took her. Since the trip to the neurologist, Mamá has been on a tear. I know this through the e-mails Thalia sends me. Repainting the house, fixing water leaks, coaxing Thalia into helping her build a whole new closet upstairs, even replacing cracked shingles on the roof, though thankfully Thalia put an end to that. Now the dovecote. I picture Mamá with her sleeves rolled high, hammer in hand, sweat staining her back, pounding nails and sanding planks of wood. Racing against her own failing neurons. Wringing every last drop of use from them while there is still time.

"When are you coming home?" Mamá says.

"Soon," I say. *Soon* was what I said the year before too when she asked the same question. It has been two years since my last visit to Tinos.

A brief pause. "Don't wait too long. I want to see you before they strap me in the iron lung." She laughs. This is an old habit, this joke making and clowning in the face of bad luck, this disdain of hers for the slightest show of self-pity. It has the paradoxical—and I know calculated—effect of both shrinking and augmenting the misfortune.

"Come for Christmas if you can," she says. "Before the fourth of January, at any rate. Thalia says there is going to be a solar eclipse over Greece that day. She read it on the Internet. We could watch it together."

"I'll try, Mamá," I say.

It was like waking up one morning and finding that a wild animal has wandered into your house. No place felt safe to me. She was there at every corner and turn, prowling, stalking, forever dabbing at her cheek with a handkerchief to dry the dribble that constantly flowed from her mouth. The small dimensions of our house rendered escape from her impossible. I especially dreaded mealtime when I had to endure the spectacle of Thalia lifting the bottom of the mask to deliver spoonfuls of food to her mouth. My stomach turned at the sight and at the sound. She ate noisily, bits of half-chewed food always falling with a wet splat onto her plate, or the table, or even the floor. She was forced to take all liquids, even soup, through a straw, of which her mother kept a stash in her purse. She slurped and gurgled when she sucked broth up the straw, and it always stained the mask and dripped down the side of her jaw onto her neck. The first time, I asked to be excused from the table, and Mamá shot me a hard look. And so I trained myself to avert my gaze and not hear, but it wasn't easy. I would walk into the kitchen and there she would be, sitting still while Madaline rubbed ointment onto her cheek to prevent chafing. I began keeping a calendar, a mental countdown, of the four weeks Mamá had said Madaline and Thalia were staying.

I wished Madaline had come by herself. I liked Madaline just fine. We sat, the four of us, in the small square-shaped courtyard outside our front door, and she sipped coffee and smoked cigarettes one after the other, the angles of her face shaded by our olive tree and a gold straw cloche that should have looked absurd on her, *would* have on anyone else—like Mamá, for instance. But Madaline was one of those people to whom elegance came effortlessly as though it were a genetic skill, like the ability to curl your tongue into the shape of a tube. With Madaline, there was never a lull in the conversation; stories just trilled out of her. One morning she told us about her travels—to Ankara, for instance, where she had strolled the banks of the Enguri Su and sipped green tea laced with *raki*, or the time she and Mr. Gianakos had gone to Kenya and ridden the backs of elephants among thorny acacias and even sat down to eat cornmeal mush and coconut rice with the local villagers.

Madaline's stories stirred up an old restlessness in me, an urge I'd always had to strike out headlong into the world, to be dauntless. By comparison, my own life on Tinos seemed crushingly ordinary. I foresaw my life unfolding as an interminable stretch of nothingness and so I spent most of my childhood years on Tinos floundering, feeling like a stand-in for myself, a proxy, as though my real self resided elsewhere, waiting to unite someday with this dimmer, more hollow self. I felt marooned. An exile in my own home.

Madaline said that in Ankara she had gone to a place called Kuğulu Park and watched swans gliding in the water. She said the water was dazzling.

"I'm rhapsodizing," she said, laughing.

"You're not," Mamá said.

"It's an old habit. I talk too much. I always did. You remember how much grief I'd bring us, chattering in class? You were never at fault, Odie. You were so responsible and studious."

"They're interesting, your stories. You have an interesting life."

Madaline rolled her eyes. "Well, you know the Chinese curse."

"Did you like Africa?" Mamá asked Thalia.

Thalia pressed the handkerchief to her cheek and didn't answer. I was glad. She had the oddest speech. There was a wet quality to it, a strange mix of lisp and gargle.

"Oh, Thalia doesn't like to travel," Madaline said, crushing her cigarette. She said this like it was the unassailable truth. There was no looking to Thalia for confirmation or protest. "She hasn't got a taste for it."

"Well, neither do I," Mamá said, again to Thalia. "I like being home. I guess I've just never found a compelling reason to leave Tinos."

"And I one to stay," Madaline said. "Other than you, naturally." She touched Mamá's wrist. "You know my worst fear when I left? My biggest worry? How am I going to get on without Odie? I swear, I was petrified at the thought."

"You've managed fine, it seems," Mamá said slowly, dragging her gaze from Thalia.

"You don't understand," Madaline said, and I realized I was the one who didn't understand because she was looking directly at me. "I wouldn't have kept it together without your mother. She saved me."

"*Now* you're rhapsodizing," Mamá said.

Thalia upturned her face. She was squinting. A jet, up in the blue, silently marking its trajectory with a long, single vapor trail.

"It was my father," Madaline said, "that Odie saved me from." I wasn't sure if she was still addressing me. "He was one of those people who are born mean. He had bulging eyes, and this thick, short neck with a dark mole on the back of it. And fists. Fists like bricks. He'd come home and he didn't even have to do a thing, just the sound of his boots in the hallway, the jingle of his keys, his humming, that was enough for me. When he was mad, he always sighed through the nose and pinched his eyes shut, like he was deep in thought, and then he'd rub his face and say, *All right, girlie, all right*, and you knew it was coming—the storm, it was coming—and it could not be stopped. No one could help you. Sometimes, just him rubbing his face, or the sigh whooshing through his mustache, and I'd see gray.

"I've crossed paths since with men like him. I wish I could say differently. But I have. And what I've learned is that you dig a little and you find they're all the same, give or take. Some are more polished, granted. They may come with a bit of charm—or a lot—and that can fool you. But really they're all unhappy little boys sloshing around in their own rage. They feel wronged. They haven't been given their due. No one loved them enough. Of course they expect you to love them. They want to be held, rocked, reassured. But it's a mistake to give it to them. They can't accept it. They can't accept the very thing they're needing. They end up hating you for it. And it never ends because they can't hate you enough. It never ends—the misery, the apologies, the promises, the reneging, the wretchedness of it all. My first husband was like that."

I was stunned. No one had ever spoken this plainly in my presence before, certainly not Mamá. No one I knew laid bare their hard luck this way. I felt both embarrassed for Madaline and admiring of her candor.

When she mentioned the first husband, I noticed that, for the first time since I had met her, a shadow had settled on her face, a momentary intimation of something dark and chastening, wounding, at odds with the energetic laughs and the teasing and the loose pumpkin floral dress she was wearing. I remember thinking at the time what a good actress she must be to camouflage disappointment and hurt with a veneer of cheerfulness. Like a mask, I thought, and was privately pleased with myself for the clever connection.

Later, when I was older, it wasn't as clear to me. Thinking back on it, there was something affected about the way she paused when she mentioned the first husband, the casting down of the gaze, the catch in the throat, the slight quiver of lips, just as there was about the walloping energy and the joking, the lively, heavy-footed charm, the way even her slights landed softly, parachuted by a reassuring wink and laugh. Perhaps they were both trumped-up affectations or perhaps neither was. It became a blur for me what was performance and what real—which at least made me think of her as an infinitely more *interesting* actress.

"How many times did I come running to this house, Odie?" Madaline said. Now the smiling again, the swell of laughter. "Your poor parents. But this house was my haven. My sanctuary. It was. A little island within the greater one."

Mamá said, "You were always welcomed here."

"It was your mother who put an end to the beatings, Markos. Did she ever tell you?"

I said she hadn't.

"Hardly surprises me. That's Odelia Varvaris for you."

Mamá was unfurling the edge of the apron in her lap and flattening it again with a daydreamy look on her face.

"I came here one night, bleeding from the tongue, a patch of hair ripped from the temple, my ear still ringing from a blow. He'd really gotten his hooks into me that time. What a state I was in. What a state!" The way Madaline was telling it, you might have thought she was describing a lavish meal or a good novel. "Your mother doesn't ask because she knows. Of course she knows. She just looks at me for a long time—at me standing there, trembling—and she says, I still remember it, Odie, she said, *Well, that's about enough of this business.* She says, *We're going to pay your father a visit, Maddie.* And I start begging.

I worried he was going to kill us both. But you know how she can be, your mother."

I said I did, and Mamá tossed me a sidelong glance.

"She wouldn't listen. She had this look. I'm sure you know the look. She heads out, but not before she picks up her father's hunting rifle. The whole time we're walking to my house, I'm trying to stop her, telling her he hadn't hurt me that bad. But she won't hear it. We walk right up to the door and there's my father, in the doorway, and Odie raises the barrel and shoves it against his chin and says, *Do it again and I will come back and shoot you in the face with this rifle.*

"My father blinks, and for a moment he's tongue-tied. He can't say a word. And you want to know the best part, Markos? I look down and see a little circle, a circle of—well, I think you can guess—a little circle quietly expanding on the floor between his bare feet."

Madaline brushed back her hair and said, to another flick of the lighter, "And that, my dear, is a true story."

She didn't have to say it, I knew it was true. I recognized in it Mamá's uncomplicated, fierce loyalty, her mountainous resolve. Her impulse, her need, to be the corrector of injustices, warden of the downtrodden flock. And I could tell it was true from the closemouthed groan Mamá gave at the mention of that last detail. She disapproved. She probably found it distasteful, and not only for the obvious reason. In her view, people, even if they had behaved deplorably in life, deserved a modicum of dignity in death. Especially family.

Mamá shifted in her seat and said, "So if you don't like to travel, Thalia, what do you like to do?"

All our eyes turned to Thalia. Madaline had been speaking for a while, and I recall thinking, as we sat in the courtyard with the sunlight falling in patches all around us, that it was a measure of her capacity to absorb attention, to pull everything into her vortex so thoroughly that Thalia had gone forgotten. I also left room for the possibility that they had adapted to this dynamic out of necessity, the quiet daughter eclipsed by the attention-diverting self-absorbed mother routine, that Madaline's narcissism was perhaps an act of kindness, of maternal protectiveness.

Thalia mumbled something.

"A little louder, darling," came the suggestion from Madaline.

Thalia cleared her throat, a rumbling, phlegmy sound. "Science."

I noticed for the first time the color of her eyes, green like ungrazed pasture, the deep, coarse dark of her hair, and that she had unblemished skin like her mother. I wondered if she'd been pretty once, maybe even beautiful like Madaline.

"Tell them about the sundial, darling," Madaline said.

Thalia shrugged.

"She built a sundial," Madaline said. "Right in our backyard. Last summer. She had no help. Not from Andreas. And certainly not from me." She chortled.

"Equatorial or horizontal?" Mamá asked.

There was a flash of surprise in Thalia's eyes. A kind of double take. Like a person walking down a crowded street in a foreign city catching within earshot a snippet of her native tongue. "Horizontal," she said in that strange wet voice of hers.

"What did you use for a gnomon?"

Thalia's eyes rested on Mamá. "I cut a postcard."

That was the first time I saw how it could be between those two.

"She used to take apart her toys when she was little," Madaline said. "She liked mechanical toys, things with inner contraptions. Not that she played with them, did you, darling? No, she'd break them up, all those expensive toys, open them up as soon as we gave them to her. I used to get into such a state over it. But Andreas—I have to give him credit here—Andreas said to let her, that it was a sign of a curious mind."

"If you like, we can build one together," Mamá said. "A sundial, I mean."

"I already know how."

"Mind your manners, darling," Madaline said, extending, then bending, one leg, as though she were stretching for a dance routine. "Aunt Odie is trying to be helpful."

"Maybe something else, then," Mamá said. "We could build some other thing."

"Oh! Oh!" Madaline said, hurriedly blowing smoke, wheezing. "I can't believe I haven't told you yet, Odie. I have news. Take a guess."

Mamá shrugged.

"I'm going back to acting! In films! I've been offered a role, the lead, in a major production. Can you believe it?"

"Congratulations," Mamá said flaccidly.

"I have the script with me. I'd let you read it, Odie, but I worry you won't like it. Is that bad? I'd be crushed, I don't mind telling you. I wouldn't get over it. We start shooting in the fall."

The next morning, after breakfast, Mamá pulled me aside. "All right, what is it? What's wrong with you?"

I said I didn't know what she was talking about.

"You best drop it. The stupid act. It doesn't suit you," she said. She had a way of narrowing her eyes and tilting her head just a shade. To this day it has a grip on me.

"I can't do it, Mamá. Don't make me."

"And why not, exactly?"

It came out before I could do a thing about it. "She's a monster."

Mamá's mouth became small. She regarded me not with anger but with a disheartened look, as though I'd drawn all the sap out of her. There was a finality to this look. Resignation. Like a sculptor finally dropping mallet and chisel, giving up on a recalcitrant block that will never take the shape he'd pictured.

"She's a person who has had a terrible thing happen to her. Call her that name again, I'd like to see you. Say it and see what happens."

A little bit later there we were, Thalia and I, walking down a cobblestone path flanked by stone walls on each side. I made sure to walk a few steps ahead so passersby—or, God forbid, one of the boys from school—wouldn't think we were together, which, of course, they would anyway. Anyone could see. At the least, I hoped the distance between us would signal my displeasure and reluctance. To my relief, she didn't make an effort to keep up. We passed sunburned, weary-looking farmers coming home from the market. Their donkeys labored under wicker baskets containing unsold produce, their hooves clip-clopping on the footpath. I knew most of the farmers, but I kept my head down and averted my eyes.

I led Thalia to the beach. I chose a rocky one I sometimes went to, knowing it would not be as crowded as some of the other beaches, like Agios Romanos. I rolled up my pants and hopped from one craggy rock to the next, choosing one close to where the waves crashed and retracted. I took off my shoes and lowered my feet into a shallow little pool that had formed between a cluster of stones. A hermit crab scurried away from my toes. I saw Thalia to my right, settling atop a rock close by.

We sat for a long while without talking and watched the ocean rumbling against the rocks. A nippy gust whipped around my ears, spraying the scent of salt on my face. A pelican hovered over the blue-green water, its wings spread. Two ladies stood side by side, knee-deep in the water, their skirts held up high. To the west, I had a view of the island, the dominant white of the homes and windmills, the green of the barley fields, the dull brown of the jagged mountains from which springs flowed every year. My father died on one of those mountains. He worked for a green-marble quarry and one day, when Mamá was six months pregnant with me, he slipped off a cliff and fell a hundred feet. Mamá said he'd forgotten to secure his safety harness.

"You should stop," Thalia said.

I was tossing pebbles into an old galvanized-tin pail nearby and she startled me. I missed. "What's it to you?"

"I mean, flattering yourself. I don't want this any more than you do."

The wind was making her hair flap, and she was holding down the mask against her face. I wondered if she lived with this fear daily, that a gust of wind would rip it from her face and she would have to chase after it, exposed. I didn't say anything. I tossed another pebble and missed again.

"You're an ass," she said.

After a while she got up, and I pretended to stay. Then I looked over my shoulder and saw her heading up the beach, back toward the road, and so I put my shoes back on and followed her home.

When we returned, Mamá was mincing okra in the kitchen, and Madaline was sitting nearby, doing her nails and smoking, tapping the ash into a saucer. I cringed with some horror when I saw that the saucer belonged to the china set Mamá had inherited from her grandmother. It was the only thing of any real value that Mamá owned, the china set, and she hardly ever took it down from the shelf up near the ceiling where she kept it.

Madaline was blowing on her nails in between drags and talking about Pattakos, Papadopoulos, and Makarezos, the three colonels who had staged a military coup—the Generals' Coup, as it was known then—earlier that year in Athens. She was saying she knew a playwright—a "dear, dear man," as she described him—who had been imprisoned under the charge of being a communist subversive.

"Which is absurd, of course! Just absurd. You know what they do to people, the ESA, to make them talk?" She was saying this in a low voice as if the military police were hiding somewhere in the house. "They put a hose in your behind and turn on the water full blast. It's true, Odie. I swear to you. They soak rags in the filthiest things—human filth, you understand—and shove them in people's mouths."

"That's awful," Mamá said flatly.

I wondered if she was already tiring of Madaline. The stream of puffed-up political opinions, the tales of parties Madaline had attended with her husband, the poets and intellectuals and musicians she'd clinked champagne flutes with, the list of needless, senseless trips she had taken to foreign cities. Trotting out her views on nuclear disaster and overpopulation and pollution. Mamá indulged Madaline, smiling through her stories with a look of wry bemusement, but I knew she thought unkindly of her. She probably thought Madaline was flaunting. She probably felt embarrassed for her.

This is what rankles, what pollutes Mamá's kindness, her rescues and her acts of courage. The indebtedness that shadows them. The demands, the obligations she saddles you with. The way she uses these acts as currency, with which she barters for loyalty and allegiance. I understand now why

Madaline left all those years ago. The rope that pulls you from the flood can become a noose around your neck. People always disappoint Mamá in the end, me included. They can't make good on what they owe, not the way Mamá expects them to. Mamá's consolation prize is the grim satisfaction of holding the upper hand, free to pass verdicts from the perch of strategic advantage, since she is always the one who has been wronged.

It saddens me because of what it reveals to me about Mamá's own neediness, her own anxiety, her fear of loneliness, her dread of being stranded, abandoned. And what does it say about me that I know this about my mother, that I know precisely what she needs and yet how deliberately and unswervingly I have denied her, taking care to keep an ocean, a continent—or, preferably, both—between us for the better part of three decades?

"They have no sense of irony, the junta," Madaline was saying, "crushing people as they do. In Greece! The birthplace of democracy . . . Ah, there you are! Well, how was it? What did you two get up to?"

"We played at the beach," Thalia said.

"Was it fun? Did you have fun?"

"We had a grand time," Thalia said.

Mamá's eyes jumped skeptically from me to Thalia and back, but Madaline beamed and applauded silently. "Good! Now that I don't have to worry about you two getting along, Odie and I can spend some time of our own together. What do you say, Odie? We have so much catching up to do still!"

Mamá smiled gamely and reached for a head of cabbage.

From then on, Thalia and I were left to our own devices. We were to explore the island, play games at the beach, amuse ourselves the way children are expected to. Mamá would pack us a sandwich each, and we would set off together after breakfast.

Once out of sight, we often drifted apart. At the beach, I took a swim or lay on a rock with my shirt off while Thalia went off to collect shells or skip rocks on the water, which was no good because the waves were too big. We went walking along the footpaths that snaked through vineyards and barley fields, looking down at our own shadows, each preoccupied with our own thoughts. Mostly we wandered. There wasn't much in the way of a tourist industry on Tinos in those days. It was a farming island, really, people living off their cows and goats and olive trees and wheat. We would end up bored, eating lunch somewhere, quietly, in the shade of a tree or a windmill, looking between bites at the ravines, the fields of thorny bushes, the mountains, the sea.

One day, I wandered off toward town. We lived on the southwestern shore of the island, and Tinos town was only a few miles' walk south. There was a little knickknack shop there run by a heavy-faced widower named Mr. Roussos. On any given day, you were apt to find in the window of his shop anything from a 1940s typewriter to a pair of leather work boots, or a weathervane, an old plant stand, giant wax candles, a cross, or, of course, copies of the Panagia Evangelistria icon. Or maybe even a brass gorilla. He was also an amateur photographer and had a makeshift darkroom in the back of the shop. When the pilgrims came to

Tinos every August to visit the icon, Mr. Roussos sold rolls of film to them and developed their photos in his darkroom for a fee.

About a month back, I had spotted a camera in his display window, sitting on its worn rust-colored leather case. Every few days, I strolled over to the shop, stared at this camera, and imagined myself in India, the leather case hanging by the strap over my shoulder, taking photos of the paddies and tea estates I had seen in *National Geographic.* I would shoot the Inca Trail. On camelback, in some dust-choked old truck, or on foot, I would brave the heat until I stood gazing up at the Sphinx and the Pyramids, and I would shoot them too and see my photos published in magazines with glossy pages. This was what drew me to Mr. Roussos's window that morning—though the shop was closed for the day—to stand outside, my forehead pressed to the glass, and daydream.

"What kind is it?"

I pulled back a bit, caught Thalia's reflection in the window. She dabbed at her left cheek with the handkerchief.

"The camera."

I shrugged.

"Looks like a C3 Argus," she said.

"How would you know?"

"It's only the best-selling thirty-five millimeter in the world for the last thirty years," she said a little chidingly. "Not much to look at, though. It's ugly. It looks like a brick. So you want to be a photographer? You know, when you're all grown up? Your mother says you do."

I turned around. "Mamá told you that?"

"So?"

I shrugged. I was embarrassed that Mamá had discussed this with Thalia. I wondered how she'd said it. She could unsheathe from her arsenal a mockingly grave way of talking about things she found either portentous or frivolous. She could shrink your aspirations before your very eyes. *Markos wants to walk the earth and capture it with his lens.*

Thalia sat on the sidewalk and pulled her skirt over her knees. It was a hot day, the sun biting the skin like it had teeth. Hardly anyone was out and about except for an elderly couple trudging stiffly up the street. The husband— Demis something—wore a gray flat cap and a brown tweed jacket that looked too heavy for the season. He had a frozen, wide-eyed look to his face, I remember, the way some old people do, like they are perpetually startled by the monstrous surprise that is old age—it wasn't until years later, in medical school, that I suspected he had Parkinson's. They waved as they passed and I waved back. I saw them take notice of Thalia, a momentary pause in their stride, and then they moved on.

"Do you have a camera?" Thalia said.

"No."

"Have you ever taken a picture?"

"No."

"And you want to be a photographer?"

"You find that strange?"

"A little."

"So if I said I wanted to be a policeman, you'd think that

was strange too? Because I've never slapped handcuffs on anyone?"

I could tell from the softening in her eyes that, if she could, she would be smiling. "So you're a clever ass," she said. "Word of advice: Don't mention the camera in my mother's presence or she'll buy it for you. She's very eager to please." The handkerchief went to the cheek and back. "But I doubt that Odelia would approve. I guess you already know that."

I was both impressed and a little unsettled by how much she seemed to have grasped in so little time. Maybe it was the mask, I thought, the advantage of cover, the freedom to be watchful, to observe and scrutinize.

"She'd probably make you give it back."

I sighed. It was true. Mamá would not allow such easy amends, and most certainly not if it involved money.

Thalia rose to her feet and beat the dust from her behind. "Let me ask you, do you have a box at home?"

Madaline was sipping wine with Mamá in the kitchen, and Thalia and I were upstairs, using black markers on a shoe box. The shoe box belonged to Madaline and contained a new pair of lime green leather pumps with high heels, still wrapped in tissue paper.

"Where was she planning on wearing *those*?" I asked.

I could hear Madaline downstairs, talking about an acting class she had once taken where the instructor had asked her, as an exercise, to pretend she was a lizard sitting motionless on a rock. A swell of laughter—hers—followed.

We finished the second coat, and Thalia said we should put on a third, to make sure we hadn't missed any spots. The black had to be uniform and flawless.

"That's all a camera is," she said, "a black box with a hole to let in the light and something to absorb the light. Give me the needle."

I passed her a sewing needle of Mamá's. I was skeptical, to say the least, about the prospects of this homemade camera, of it doing anything at all—a shoe box and a needle? But Thalia had attacked the project with such faith and self-assured confidence that I had to leave room for the unlikely possibility that it just might work. She made me think she knew things I did not.

"I've made some calculations," she said, carefully piercing the box with the needle. "Without a lens, we can't set the pinhole on the small face, the box is too long. But the width is just about right. The key is to make the correct-sized pinhole. I figure point-six millimeter, roughly. There. Now we need a shutter."

Downstairs, Madaline's voice had dropped to a low, urgent murmur. I couldn't hear what she was saying but I could tell that she was speaking more slowly than before, enunciating well, and I pictured her leaning forward, elbows on knees, making eye contact, not blinking. Over the years, I have come to know this tone of voice intimately. When people speak this way, they're likely disclosing, revealing, confessing some catastrophe, beseeching the listener.

It's a staple of the military's casualty notification teams knocking on doors, lawyers touting the merits of plea deals to clients, policemen stopping cars at 3 a.m., cheating husbands. How many times have I used it myself at hospitals here in Kabul? How many times have I guided entire families into a quiet room, asked them to sit, pulled a chair up for myself, gathering the will to give them news, dreading the coming conversation?

"She's talking about Andreas," Thalia said evenly. "I bet she is. They had a big fight. Pass me the tape and those scissors."

"What is he like? Besides being rich, I mean?"

"Who, Andreas? He's all right. He travels a lot. When he's home, he always has people over. Important people— ministers, generals, that kind. They have drinks by the fireplace and they talk all night, mostly business and politics. I can hear them from my room. I'm supposed to stay upstairs when Andreas has company. I'm not supposed to come down. But he buys me things. He pays for a tutor to come to the house. And he speaks to me nicely enough."

She taped a rectangular piece of cardboard, which we'd also colored black, over the pinhole.

Things were quiet downstairs. I choreographed the scene in my head. Madaline weeping without a sound, absently fiddling with a handkerchief like it was a clump of Play-Doh, Mamá not much help, looking on stiffly with a pinch-faced little smile like she's got something sour melting under her tongue. Mamá can't stand it when people cry in her presence. She can barely look at their puffy eyes, their open, pleading faces. She sees crying as a sign of weakness, a garish appeal for attention, and she won't indulge it. She can't bring herself to console. Growing up, I learned that it was not one of her strong suits. Sorrow ought to be private, she thinks, not flaunted. Once, when I was little, I asked her if she'd cried when my father had fallen to his death.

At the funeral? I mean, the burial?

No, I did not.

Because you weren't sad?

Because it was nobody's business if I was.

Would you cry if I died, Mamá?

Let's hope we never have to find out, she said.

Thalia picked up the box of photographic paper and said, "Get the flashlight."

We moved into Mamá's closet, taking care to shut the door and snuff out daylight with towels we stuffed under it. Once we were in pitch-darkness, Thalia asked me to turn on the flashlight, which we had covered with several layers of red cellophane. All I could see of Thalia in the dim glow was her slender fingers as she cut a sheet of photographic paper and taped it to the inside of the shoe box opposite the pinhole. We had bought the paper from Mr. Roussos's shop the day before. When we walked up to the counter, Mr. Roussos peered at Thalia over his spectacles and said, *Is this a robbery?* Thalia pointed an index finger at him and cocked her thumb like pulling back the hammer.

Thalia closed the lid on the shoe box, covered the pinhole with the shutter. In the dark she said, "Tomorrow, you shoot the first photo of your career." I couldn't tell if she was making fun or not.

We chose the beach. We set the shoe box on a flat rock and secured it firmly with rope—Thalia said we couldn't have any movement at all when we opened the shutter. She moved in next to me and took a peek over the box as if through a viewfinder.

"It's a perfect shot," she said.

"Almost. We need a subject."

She looked at me, saw what I meant, and said, "No. I won't do it."

We argued back and forth and she finally agreed, but on the condition that her face didn't show. She took off her shoes, walked atop a row of rocks a few feet in front of the camera, using her arms like a tightrope walker on a cable. She lowered herself on one of the rocks facing west in the direction of Syros and Kythnos. She flipped her hair so it covered the bands at the back of her head that held the mask in place. She looked at me over her shoulder.

"Remember," she shouted, "count to one twenty."

She turned back to face the sea.

I stooped and peered over the box, looking at Thalia's back, the constellation of rocks around her, the whips of seaweed entangled between them like dead snakes, a little tugboat bobbing in the distance, the tide rising, mashing the craggy shore and withdrawing. I lifted the shutter from the pinhole and began to count.

One . . . two . . . three . . . four . . . five . . .

We're lying in bed. On the TV screen a pair of accordion players are dueling, but Gianna has turned off the sound. Midday sunlight scissors through the blinds, falling in stripes on the remains of the Margherita pizza we'd ordered for lunch from room service. It was delivered to us by a tall, slim man with impeccable slicked-back hair and a white coat with black tie. On the table he rolled into the room was a flute vase with a red rose in it. He lifted the domed plate cover off the pizza with great flourish, making a sweeping motion with his hand like a magician to his audience after the rabbit has materialized from the top hat.

Scattered around us, among the mussed sheets, are the pictures I have shown Gianna, photos of my trips over the past year and a half. Belfast, Montevideo, Tangier, Marseille, Lima, Tehran. I show her photos of the commune I had joined briefly in Copenhagen, living alongside ripped-T-shirt-and-beanie-hat-wearing Danish beatniks who had built a self-governing community on a former military base.

Where are you? Gianna asks. *You are not in the photographs.*

I like being behind the lens better, I say. It's true. I have taken hundreds of pictures, and you won't find me in any. I always order two sets of prints when I drop off the film. I keep one set, mail the other to Thalia back home.

Gianna asks how I finance my trips and I explain I pay for them with inheritance money. This is partially true, because the inheritance is Thalia's, not mine. Unlike

Madaline, who for obvious reasons was never mentioned in Andreas's will, Thalia was. She gave me half her money. I am supposed to be putting myself through university with it.

Eight . . . nine . . . ten . . .

Gianna props herself up on her elbows and leans across the bed, over me, her small breasts brushing my skin. She fetches her pack, lights a cigarette. I'd met her the day before at Piazza di Spagna. I was sitting on the stone steps that connect the square below to the church on the hill. She walked up and said something to me in Italian. She looked like so many of the pretty, seemingly aimless girls I'd seen slinking around Rome's churches and piazzas. They smoked and talked loudly and laughed a lot. I shook my head and said, *Sorry?* She smiled, went *Ah,* and then, in heavily accented English, said, *Lighter? Cigarette.* I shook my head and told her in my own heavily accented English that I didn't smoke. She grinned. Her eyes were bright and jumping. The late-morning sun made a nimbus around her diamond-shaped face.

I doze off briefly and wake up to her poking my ribs.

La tua ragazza? she says. She has found the picture of Thalia on the beach, the one I had taken years before with our homemade pinhole camera. *Your girlfriend?*

No, I say.

Your sister?

No.

La tua cugina? Your cousin, si?

I shake my head.

She studies the photo some more, taking quick drags off her cigarette. *No,* she says sharply, to my surprise, even angrily. *Questa è la tua ragazza! Your girlfriend. I think yes, you are liar!* And then, to my disbelief, she flicks her lighter and sets the picture on fire.

Fourteen . . . fifteen . . . sixteen . . . seventeen . . .

About midway through our trek back to the bus stop, I realize I've lost the photo. I tell them I need to go back. There is no choice, I have to go back. Alfonso, a wiry, tight-lipped *huaso* who is tagging along as our informal Chilean guide, looks questioningly at Gary. Gary is an American. He is the alpha male in our trio. He has dirty-blond hair and acne pits on his cheeks. It's a face that hints at habitual hard living. Gary is in a foul mood, made worse by hunger, the absence of alcohol, and the nasty rash on his right calf, which he contracted brushing up against a *litre* shrub the day before. I'd met them both at a crowded bar in Santiago, where, after half a dozen rounds of *piscolas*, Alfonso had suggested a hike to the waterfall at Salto del Apoquindo, where his father used to take him when he was a boy. We'd made the hike the next day and had camped out at the waterfall for the night. We'd smoked dope, the water roaring in our ears, a wide-open sky crammed with stars above us. We were trudging back now toward San Carlos de Apoquindo to catch the bus.

Gary pushes back the wide rim of his Cordoban hat and wipes his brow with a handkerchief. *It's a three-hour walk back, Markos,* he says.

¿Tres horas, hágale comprende? Alfonso echoes.

I know.

And you're still going?

Yes.

¿Para una foto? Alfonso says.

I nod. I keep quiet because they would not understand. I am not sure I understand it myself.

You know you're going to get lost, Gary says.

Probably.

Then good luck, amigo, Gary says, offering his hand.

Es un griego loco, Alfonso says.

I laugh. It is not the first time I have been called a crazy Greek. We shake hands. Gary adjusts the straps of his knapsack, and the two of them head back up the trail along the folds of the mountain, Gary waving once without looking as they take a hairpin turn. I walk back the way we had come. It takes me four hours, actually, because I do get lost as Gary had predicted. I am exhausted by the time I reach the campsite. I search all over, kicking bushes, looking between rocks, dread building as I rummage in vain. Then, just as I try to resign myself to the worst, I spot a flash of white in a batch of shrubs up a shallow slope. I find the photo wedged between a tangle of brambles. I pluck it free, beat dust from it, my eyes brimming with tears of relief.

Twenty-three . . . twenty-four . . . twenty-five . . .

In Caracas I sleep under a bridge. A youth hostel in Brussels. Sometimes I splurge and rent a room in a nice hotel, take long hot showers, shave, eat meals in a bathrobe. I watch color TV. The cities, the roads, the countryside, the people I meet—they all begin to blur. I tell myself I am searching for something. But more and more, it feels like I am wandering, waiting for something to happen to me, something that will change everything, something that my whole life has been leading up to.

Thirty-four . . . thirty-five . . . thirty-six . . .

My fourth day in India. I totter down a dirt road among stray cattle, the world tilting under my feet. I have been vomiting all day. My skin is the yellow of a sari, and it feels like invisible hands are peeling it raw. When I can't walk anymore, I lie down on the side of the road. An old man across the road stirs something in a big steel pot. Beside him is a cage, inside the cage a blue-and-red parrot. A dark-skinned vendor pushing a cartful of empty green bottles passes me by. That's the last thing I remember.

Forty-one . . . forty-two . . .

I wake up in a big room. The air is thick with heat and something like rotting cantaloupe. I am lying on a twin-sized steel-frame bed, cushioned from the hard, springless platform by a mattress no thicker than a paperback book. The room is filled with beds like mine. I see emaciated arms dangling over the sides, dark matchstick legs protruding from stained sheets, scant-toothed mouths open. Idle ceiling fans. Walls marked by patches of mold. The window beside me lets in hot, sticky air and sunlight that stabs the eyeballs. The nurse—a burly, glowering Muslim man named Gul—tells me I may die of hepatitis.

Fifty-five . . . fifty-six . . . fifty-seven . . .

I ask for my backpack. *What backpack?* Gul says with indifference. All my things are gone—my clothes, my cash, my books, my camera. *That's all the thief left you,* Gul says in his rolling English, pointing to the windowsill beside me. It's the picture. I pick it up. Thalia, her hair flapping in the breeze, the water bubbling with froth around her, her bare feet on the rocks, the leaping Aegean flung out before her. A lump rises to my throat. I don't want to die here, among these strangers, so far away from her. I tuck the photo in the wedge between the glass and the window frame.

Sixty-six . . . sixty-seven . . . sixty-eight . . .

The boy in the bed next to mine has an old man's face, haggard, sunken, carved. His lower belly is swollen with a tumor the size of a bowling ball. Whenever a nurse touches him there, his eyes squeeze shut and his mouth springs open in a silent, agonized wail. This morning, one of the nurses, not Gul, is trying to feed him pills, but the boy turns his head side to side, his throat making a sound like a scraping against wood. Finally, the nurse pries his mouth open, forces the pills inside. When he leaves, the boy rolls his head slowly toward me. We eye each other across the space between our beds. A small tear squeezes out and rolls down his cheek.

Seventy-five . . . seventy-six . . . seventy-seven . . .

The suffering, the despair in this place, is like a wave. It rolls out from every bed, smashes against the moldy walls, and swoops back toward you. You can drown in it. I sleep a lot. When I don't, I itch. I take the pills they give me and the pills make me sleep again. Otherwise, I look down at the bustling street outside the dormitory, at the sunlight skidding over tent bazaars and back-alley tea shops. I watch the kids shooting marbles on sidewalks that melt into muddy gutters, the old women sitting in doorways, the street vendors in *dhoti*s squatting on their mats, scraping coconuts, hawking marigold garlands. Someone lets out an earsplitting shriek from across the room. I doze off.

Eighty-three . . . eighty-four . . . eighty-five . . .

I learn that the boy's name is Manaar. It means "guiding light." His mother was a prostitute, his father a thief. He lived with his aunt and uncle, who beat him. No one knows exactly what is killing him, only that it is. No one visits him, and when he dies, a week from now—a month, two at the outside—no one will come to claim him. No one will grieve. No one will remember. He will die where he lived, in the cracks. When he sleeps, I find myself looking at him, at his cratered temples, the head that's too big for his shoulders, the pigmented scar on his lower lip where, Gul informed me, his mother's pimp had the habit of putting out his cigarette. I try speaking to him in English, then in the few Urdu words I know, but he only blinks tiredly. Sometimes I put my hands together and make shadow animals on the wall to win a smile from him.

Eighty-seven . . . eighty-eight . . . eighty-nine . . .

One day Manaar points to something outside my window. I follow his finger, raise my head, but I see nothing but the blue wisp of sky through the clouds, children below playing with water gushing from a street pump, a bus spewing exhaust. Then I realize he is pointing at the photo of Thalia. I pluck it from the window and hand it to him. He holds it close to his face, by the burnt corner, and stares at it for a long time. I wonder if it is the ocean that draws him. I wonder if he's ever tasted salt water or got dizzy watching the tide pull away from his feet. Or perhaps, though he can't see her face, he senses a kin in Thalia, someone who knows what pain feels like. He goes to hand the photo back to me. I shake my head. *Hold on to it,* I say. A shadow of mistrust crosses his face. I smile. And, I cannot be sure, but I think he smiles back.

Ninety-two . . . ninety-three . . . ninety-four . . .

I beat the hepatitis. Strange how I can't tell if Gul is pleased or disappointed at my having proved him wrong. But I know I've caught him by surprise when I ask if I can stay on as a volunteer. He cocks his head, frowns. I end up having to talk to one of the head nurses.

Ninety-seven . . . ninety-eight . . . ninety-nine . . .

The shower room smells like urine and sulfur. Every morning I carry Manaar into it, holding his naked body in my arms, careful not to bounce him—I'd watched one of the volunteers carry him before over the shoulder as if he were a bag of rice. I gently lower him onto the bench and wait for him to catch his breath. I rinse his small, frail body with warm water. Manaar always sits quietly, patiently, palms on his knees, head hung low. He is like a fearful, bony old man. I run the soapy sponge over his rib cage, the knobs of his spine, over shoulder blades that jut out like shark fins. I carry him back to his bed, feed him his pills. It soothes him to have his feet and calves massaged, so I do that for him, taking my time. When he sleeps, it is always with the picture of Thalia half tucked under his pillow.

One hundred one . . . one hundred two . . .

I go for long, aimless walks around the city, if only to get away from the hospital, the collective breaths of the sick and dying. I walk in dusty sunsets through streets lined with graffiti-stained walls, past tin-shed stalls packed tightly against one another, crossing paths with little girls carrying basketfuls of raw dung on their head, women covered in black soot boiling rags in huge aluminum vats. I think a lot about Manaar as I meander down a cat's cradle of narrow alleyways, Manaar waiting to die in that room full of broken figures like him. I think a lot about Thalia, sitting on the rock, looking out at the sea. I sense something deep inside me drawing me in, tugging at me like an undertow. I want to give in to it, be seized by it. I want to give up my bearings, slip out of who I am, shed everything, the way a snake discards old skin.

I am not saying Manaar changed everything. He didn't. I stumble around the world for still another year before I finally find myself at a corner desk in an Athens library, looking down at a medical school application. In between Manaar and the application are the two weeks I spent in Damascus, of which I have virtually no memory other than the grinning faces of two women with heavily lined eyes and a gold tooth each. Or the three months in Cairo in the basement of a ramshackle tenement run by a hashish-addicted landlord. I spend Thalia's money riding buses in Iceland, tagging along with a punk band in Munich. In 1977, I break an elbow at an antinuclear protest in Bilbao.

But in my quiet moments, in those long rides in the back of a bus or the bed of a truck, my mind always circles back to Manaar. Thinking of him, of the anguish of his final days, and my own helplessness in the face of it, makes everything

I have done, everything I want to do, seem as unsubstantial as the little vows you make yourself as you're going to sleep, the ones you've already forgotten by the time you wake up.

One hundred nineteen . . . one hundred twenty.

I drop the shutter.

One night at the end of that summer, I learned that Madaline was leaving for Athens and leaving Thalia with us, at least for a short while.

"Just for a few weeks," she said.

We were having dinner, the four of us, a dish of white bean soup that Mamá and Madaline had prepared together. I glanced across the table at Thalia to see if I was the only one on whom Madaline had sprung the news. It appeared I was. Thalia was calmly feeding spoonfuls into her mouth, lifting her mask just a bit with each trip of the spoon. By then, her speech and eating didn't bother me anymore, or at least no more than watching an old person eat through ill-fitting dentures, like Mamá would years later.

Madaline said she would send for Thalia after she had shot her film, which she said should wrap well before Christmas.

"Actually, I will bring you all to Athens," she said, her face rinsed with the customary cheer. "And we will go to the opening together! Wouldn't that be marvelous, Markos? The four of us, dressed up, waltzing into the theater in style?"

I said it would be, though I had trouble picturing Mamá in a fancy gown or waltzing into anything.

Madaline explained how it would work out just fine, how Thalia could resume her studies when school opened in a couple of weeks—at home, of course—with Mamá. She said she would send us postcards and letters, and pictures of the film set. She said more, but I didn't hear much of it. What I was feeling was enormous relief and outright giddiness. My dread of the coming end of summer was like a knot in my belly, winding tighter with each passing day as I steeled myself against the approaching farewell. I woke every morning now eager to see Thalia at the breakfast table, to hear the bizarre sound of her voice. We barely ate before we were out climbing trees, chasing each other through the barley fields, plowing through the stalks and letting out war cries, lizards scattering away from our feet. We stashed make-believe treasures in caves, found spots on the island with the best and loudest echoes. We shot photos of windmills and dovecotes with our pinhole camera and took them to Mr. Roussos, who developed them for us. He even let us into his darkroom and taught us about different developers, fixers, and stop baths.

The night of Madaline's announcement, she and Mamá shared a bottle of wine in the kitchen, Madaline doing most of the drinking, while Thalia and I were upstairs, playing a game of *tavli*. Thalia had the *mana* position and had already moved half her checkers onto her home board.

"She has a lover," Thalia said, rolling the dice.

I jumped. "Who?"

"'Who?' he says. Who do you think?"

I had learned, over the course of the summer, to read Thalia's expressions through her eyes, and she was looking at me now like I was standing on the beach asking where the water was. I tried to recover quickly. "I know who," I said, my cheeks burning. "I mean, who's the . . . you know . . ." I was a twelve-year-old boy. My vocabulary didn't include words like *lover.*

"Can't you guess? The director."

"I was going to say that."

"Elias. He's something. He plasters his hair down like it's the 1920s. He has a thin little mustache too. I guess he thinks it makes him look rakish. He's ridiculous. He thinks he's a great artist, of course. Mother does too. You should see her with him, all timid and submissive, like she needs to bow to him and pamper him because of his genius. I can't understand how she doesn't see it."

"Is Aunt Madaline going to marry him?"

Thalia shrugged. "She has the worst taste in men. The *worst.*" She shook the dice in her hands, seemed to reconsider. "Except for Andreas, I suppose. He's nice. Nice enough. But, of course, she's leaving him. It's always the bastards she falls for."

"You mean, like your father?"

She frowned a little. "My father was a stranger she met on her way to Amsterdam. At a train station during a rainstorm. They spent one afternoon together. I have no idea who he is. And neither does she."

"Oh. I remember she said something about her first husband. She said he drank. I just assumed . . ."

"Well, that would be Dorian," Thalia said. "He was something too." She moved another checker onto her home board. "He used to beat her. He could go from nice and pleasant to furious in a blink. Like the weather, how it can change suddenly? He was like that. He drank most of the day, didn't do much but lie around the house. He got real forgetful when he drank. He'd leave the water running, for instance, and flood the house. I remember he forgot to turn off the stove once and almost burned everything down."

She made a little tower with a stack of chips. Worked quietly for a while straightening it.

"The only thing Dorian really loved was Apollo. All the neighborhood kids were scared of him—of Apollo, I mean. And hardly any of them had even seen him; they'd only heard his bark. That was enough for them. Dorian kept him chained in the back of the yard. Fed him big slabs of lamb."

Thalia didn't tell me any more. I pictured it easily enough, though. Dorian passed out, the dog forgotten, roaming the yard unchained. An open screen door.

"How old were you?" I asked in a low voice.

"Five."

Then I asked the question that had been on my mind since the beginning of summer. "Isn't there something that . . . I mean, can't they do—"

Thalia snagged her gaze away. "Please don't ask," she said heavily with what I sensed to be a deep ache. "It tires me out."

"I'm sorry," I said.

"I'll tell you someday."

And she did tell me, later. The botched surgery, the cata-
strophic post-op wound infection that turned septic, shut
down her kidneys, threw her into liver failure, ate through
the new surgical flap and forced the surgeons to slice off not
only the flap but yet more of what remained of her left cheek
and part of her jawbone as well. The complications had kept
her in the hospital for nearly three months. She'd almost
died, should have died. After that, she wouldn't let them
touch her again.

"Thalia," I said, "I'm sorry too for what happened when
we met."

She tipped her eyes up at me. The old playful shine was
back. "You should be sorry. But I knew even before you
hurled all over the floor."

"Knew what?"

"That you were an ass."

Madaline left two days before school started. She
wore a tight butter yellow sleeveless dress that clung
to her slim frame, horn-rimmed sunglasses, and a firmly
knotted white silk scarf to hold down her hair. She was
dressed as though she worried parts of her might come
loose—like she was, literally, holding herself together. At
the ferry port in Tinos town, she embraced us all. She held
Thalia the tightest, and the longest, her lips on the crown of
Thalia's head in an extended, unbroken kiss. She didn't take
off her sunglasses.

"Hug me back," I heard her whisper.

Rigidly, Thalia obliged.

When the ferry groaned and lurched away, leaving behind a trail of churned-up water, I thought Madaline would stand at the stern and wave and blow us kisses. But she quickly moved toward the bow and took a seat. She didn't look our way.

When we got home, Mamá told us to sit down. She stood before us and said, "Thalia, I want you to know that you don't have to wear that thing in this house anymore. Not on my account. Nor his. Do it only if it suits you. I have no more to say about this business."

It was then that, with sudden clarity, I understood what Mamá already had seen. That the mask had been for Madaline's benefit. To save *her* embarrassment and shame.

For a long time Thalia didn't make a move or say a word. Then, slowly, her hands rose, and she untied the bands at the back of her head. She lowered the mask. I looked at her directly in the face. I felt an involuntary urge to recoil, the way you would at a sudden loud noise. But I didn't. I held my gaze. And I made it a point to not blink.

Mamá said she would homeschool me until Madaline came back so Thalia wouldn't have to stay home by herself. She gave us our lessons in the evening, after dinner, and assigned us homework to do in the morning while she went off to school. It sounded workable, at least in theory.

But doing our studies, especially with Mamá away, proved nearly impossible. News of Thalia's disfigurement had spread all over the island, and people kept knocking on the door, fueled by curiosity. You would have thought the island was suddenly running out of flour, garlic, even salt, and our house was the only place you could find it. They barely made an effort to disguise their intent. At the door, their eyes always flew over my shoulder. They craned their necks, stood on tiptoes. Most of them weren't even neighbors. They'd walked miles for a cup of sugar. Of course I never let them in. It gave me some satisfaction to close the door on their faces. But I also felt gloomy, dispirited, aware that if I stayed my life would be too deeply touched by these people. I would, in the end, become one of them.

The kids were worse and far bolder. Every day I caught one prowling outside, climbing our wall. We would be working, and Thalia would tap my shoulder with her pencil, tip her chin, and I would turn to find a face, sometimes more than one, pressed to the window. It got so bad, we had to go upstairs and pull all the curtains. One day I opened the door to a boy I knew from school, Petros, and three of his friends. He offered me a handful of coins for a peek. I said no, where did he think he was, a circus?

In the end, I had to tell Mamá. A deep red flush marched up her face when she heard. She clenched her teeth.

The next morning she had our books and two sandwiches ready on the table. Thalia understood before I did and she curled up like a leaf. Her protests started when it came time to leave.

"Aunt Odie, no."

"Give me your hand."

"No. Please."

"Go on. Give it to me."

"I don't want to go."

"We're going to be late."

"Don't make me, Aunt Odie."

Mamá pulled Thalia up from the seat by the hands, leaned in, and fixed her with a gaze I knew well. Not a thing on this earth could deter her now. "Thalia," she said, managing to sound both soft and firm, "I am not ashamed of you."

We set out, the three of us—Mamá, with her lips pursed, pushing forth like she was plowing against a fierce wind, her feet working quick, mincing little steps. I imagined Mamá walking in this same determined manner to Madaline's father's house all those years ago, rifle in hand.

People gawked and gasped as we blew past them along the winding footpaths. They stopped to stare. Some of them pointed. I tried not to look. They were a blur of pale faces and open mouths in the corners of my vision.

In the school yard, children parted to let us pass. I heard some girl scream. Mamá rolled through them like a bowling ball through pins, all but dragging Thalia behind her. She shoved and pushed her way to the corner of the yard, where there was a bench. She climbed the bench, helped Thalia up, and then blew her whistle three times. A hush fell over the yard.

"This is Thalia Gianakos," Mamá cried. "As of today . . ." She paused. "Whoever is crying, shut your mouth before I give you reason to. Now, as of today, Thalia is a student at this school. I expect all of you to treat her with decency and good manners. If I hear rumors of taunting, I will find you and I will make you sorry. You know I will. I have no more to say about this business."

She climbed down from the bench and, holding Thalia's hand, headed toward the classroom.

From that day forth, Thalia never again wore the mask, either in public or at home.

A couple of weeks before Christmas that year, we received a letter from Madaline. The shoot had run into unexpected delays. First, the director of photography—Madaline wrote *DOP* and Thalia had to explain it to me and Mamá—had fallen off a scaffold on the set and broken his arm in three places. Then the weather had complicated all the location shoots.

So we are in a bit of a "holding pattern," as they say. It would not be an entirely bad thing, since it gives us time to work out some wrinkles in the script, if it did not also mean that we won't be reunited as I had hoped. I am crushed, my darlings. I miss you all so dearly, especially you, Thalia, my love. I can only count the days until later this spring when this shoot has wrapped and we can be together again. I carry all three of you in my heart every minute of every day.

"She's not coming back," Thalia said flatly, handing the letter back to Mamá.

"Of course she is!" I said, dumbfounded. I turned to Mamá, waiting for her to say something, at least pipe a word of encouragement. But Mamá folded the letter, put it on the table, and quietly went to boil water for coffee. And I remember thinking how thoughtless it was of her to not comfort Thalia even if she agreed that Madaline wasn't coming back. But I didn't know—not yet—that they already understood each other, perhaps better than I did either of them. Mamá respected Thalia too much to coddle her. She would not insult Thalia with false assurances.

Spring came, in all of its flush green glory, and went. We received from Madaline one postcard and what felt like a hastily written letter, in which she informed us of more troubles on the set, this time having to do with financiers who were threatening to balk because of all the delays. In this letter, unlike the last, she did not set a time line as to when she would come back.

One warm afternoon early in the summer—that would be 1968—Thalia and I went to the beach with a girl named Dori. By then, Thalia had lived with us on Tinos for a year and her disfigurement no longer drew whispers and lingering stares. She was still, and always would be, girded by an orb of curiosity, but even that was waning. She had friends of her own now—Dori among them—who were no longer spooked by her appearance, friends with whom she ate lunch, gossiped, played after school, did her studies. She had become, improbably enough, almost ordinary, and I had to admit to a degree of admiration for the way the islanders had accepted her as one of their own.

That afternoon, the three of us had planned to swim, but the water was still too cold and we had ended up lying on the rocks, dozing off. When Thalia and I came home, we found Mamá in the kitchen, peeling carrots. Another letter sat unopened on the table.

"It's from your stepfather," Mamá said.

Thalia picked up the letter and went upstairs. It was a long time before she came down. She dropped the sheet of paper on the table, sat down, picked up a knife and a carrot.

"He wants me to come home."

"I see," Mamá said. I thought I heard the faintest flutter in her voice.

"Not home, exactly. He says he has contacted a private school in England. I could enroll in the fall. He'd pay for it, he said."

"What about Aunt Madaline?" I asked.

"She's gone. With Elias. They've eloped."

"What about the film?"

Mamá and Thalia exchanged a glance and simultaneously tipped their gaze up toward me, and I saw what they knew all along.

One morning in 2002, more than thirty years later, around the time I am preparing to move from Athens to Kabul, I stumble upon Madaline's obituary in the newspaper. Her last name is listed now as Kouris, but I recognize in the old woman's face a familiar bright-eyed grin, and more than detritus of her youthful beauty. The small paragraph below says that she had briefly been an actress in her youth prior to founding her own theater company in the early 1980s. Her company had received critical praise for several productions, most notably for extended runs of Eugene O'Neill's *Long Day's Journey into Night* in the mid-1990s, Chekhov's *The Seagull,* and Dimitrios Mpogris's *Engagements.* The obituary says she was well known among Athens's artistic community for her charity work, her wit, her sense of style, her lavish parties, and her willingness to take chances on unheralded playwrights. The piece says she died after a lengthy battle with emphysema but makes no mention of a surviving spouse or children. I am further stunned to learn that she lived in Athens for more than two decades, at a house barely six blocks from my own place on Kolonaki.

I put down the paper. To my surprise, I feel a tinge of impatience with this dead woman I have not seen for over thirty years. A surge of resistance to this story of how she had turned out. I had always pictured her living a tumultuous, wayward life, hard years of bad luck—fits and starts, collapse, regret—and ill-advised, desperate love affairs. I had always imagined that she'd self-destructed, likely drank herself to the kind of early death that people always call *tragic.* Part of me had even credited her with the possibility that she had known this, that she had brought Thalia to Tinos to spare her, rescue her from the disasters Madaline knew she was helpless from visiting upon her daughter. But now I picture Madaline the way Mamá always must have: Madaline, the cartographer, sitting down, calmly drawing the map of her future and neatly excluding her burdensome daughter from its borders. And she'd succeeded spectacularly, at least according to this obituary and its clipped account of a mannered life, a life rich with achievement, grace, respect.

I find I cannot accept it. The success, the getting away with it. It is preposterous. Where was the toll, the exacting comeuppance?

And yet, as I fold the newspaper, a nagging doubt begins to set in. A faint intimation that I have judged Madaline harshly, that we weren't even that different, she and I. Hadn't we both yearned for escape, reinvention, new identities? Hadn't we each, in the end, unmoored ourselves by cutting loose the anchors that weighed us down? I scoff at this, tell myself we are nothing alike, even as I sense that the anger I feel toward her may really be a mask for my envy over her succeeding at it all better than I had.

I toss the newspaper. If Thalia is going to find out, it won't be from me.

Mamá pushed the carrot shavings off the table with a knife and collected them in a bowl. She loathed it when people wasted food. She would make a jar of marmalade with the shavings.

"Well, you have a big decision to make, Thalia," she said.

Thalia surprised me by turning to me and saying, "What would you do, Markos?"

"Oh, I know what *he* would do," Mamá said quickly.

"I would go," I said, answering Thalia, looking at Mamá,

taking satisfaction in playing the insurrectionist that Mamá thought I was. Of course I meant it too. I couldn't believe Thalia would even hesitate. I would have leapt at the chance. A private education. In London.

"You should think about it," Mamá said.

"I already have," Thalia said hesitantly. Then, even more hesitant, as she raised her eyes to meet Mamá's, "But I don't want to assume."

Mamá put down the knife. I heard a faint expulsion of breath. Had she been holding it? If so, her stoic face betrayed no sign of relief. "The answer is yes. Of course it's yes."

Thalia reached across the table and touched Mamá's wrist. "Thank you, Aunt Odie."

"I'll only say this once," I said. "I think this is a mistake. You're both making a mistake."

They turned to look at me.

"Do you want me to go, Markos?" Thalia said.

"Yes," I said. "I'd miss you, a lot, and you know that. But you can't pass up a private school education. You'd go to university afterward. You could become a researcher, a scientist, a professor, an inventor. Isn't that what you want? You're the smartest person I know. You could be anything you want."

I broke off.

"No, Markos," Thalia said heavily. "No I couldn't."

She said this with a thudding finality that sealed off all channels of rebuttal.

Many years later, when I began training as a plastic surgeon, I understood something that I had not that day in the kitchen arguing for Thalia to leave Tinos for the boarding school. I learned that the world didn't see the inside of you, that it didn't care a whit about the hopes and dreams, and sorrows, that lay masked by skin and bone. It was as simple, as absurd, and as cruel as that. My patients knew this. They saw that much of what they were, would be, or could be hinged on the symmetry of their bone structure, the space between their eyes, their chin length, the tip projection of their nose, whether they had an ideal nasofrontal angle or not.

Beauty is an enormous, unmerited gift given randomly, stupidly.

And so I chose my specialty to even out the odds for people like Thalia, to rectify, with each slice of my scalpel, an arbitrary injustice, to make a small stand against a world order I found disgraceful, one in which a dog bite could rob a little girl of her future, make her an outcast, an object of scorn.

At least this is what I tell myself. I suppose there were other reasons I chose plastic surgery. Money, for instance, prestige, social standing. To say I chose it solely because of Thalia is too simple—lovely as the idea may be—a bit too orderly and balanced. If I've learned anything in Kabul, it is that human behavior is messy and unpredictable and unconcerned with convenient symmetries. But I find comfort in it, in the idea of a pattern, of a narrative of my life taking shape, like a photograph in a darkroom, a story that slowly emerges and affirms the good I have always wanted to see in myself. It sustains me, this story.

I spent half of my practice in Athens, erasing wrinkles, lifting eyebrows, stretching jowls, reshaping misbegotten noses. I spent the other half doing what I *really* wanted to, which was to fly around the world—to Central America, to sub-Saharan Africa, to South Asia, and to the Far East—and work on children, repairing cleft lips and palates, removing facial tumors, repairing injuries to their faces. The work in Athens was not nearly as gratifying, but the pay was good, and it afforded me the luxury of taking weeks and months off at a time for my volunteer work.

Then, early in 2002, I took a phone call in my office from a woman I knew. Her name was Amra Ademovic. She was a nurse from Bosnia. She and I had met at a conference in London a few years back and had had a pleasant, week-end-long thing that we'd mutually kept inconsequential, though we had remained in touch and seen each other socially on occasion. She said she was working for a nonprofit in Kabul now and that they were searching for a plastic surgeon to work on children—cleft lips, facial injuries inflicted by shrapnel and bullets, that sort of thing. I agreed on the spot. I intended to stay for three months. I went late in the spring of 2002. I never came back.

Thalia picks me up from the ferry port. She has on a green wool scarf and a thick dull-rose-colored coat over a cardigan sweater and jeans. She wears her hair long these days, loose over the shoulders and parted in the center. Her hair is white, and it is this feature—not the muti-lated lower face—that jars me and takes me aback when I see her. Not that it surprises me; Thalia started going gray in her mid-thirties and had cotton-white hair by the end of the following decade. I know I have changed too, the stubbornly growing paunch, the just-as-determined retreat of the hair-line, but the decline of one's own body is incremental, as nearly imperceptible as it is insidious. Seeing Thalia white-haired presents jolting evidence of her steady, inevitable march toward old age—and, by association, my own.

"You're going to be cold," she says, tightening the scarf around her neck. It's January, late morning, the sky overcast and gray. A cool breeze makes the shriveled-up leaves clatter in the trees.

"You want cold, come to Kabul," I say. I pick up my suitcase.

"Suit yourself, Doctor. Bus or walk? Your choice."

"Let's walk," I say.

We head north. We pass through Tinos town. The sail-boats and yachts moored in the inner harbor. The kiosks selling postcards and T-shirts. People sipping coffee at little round tables outside cafés, reading newspapers, playing chess. Waiters setting out silverware for lunch. Another hour or two and the smell of cooking fish will waft from kitchens.

Thalia launches energetically into a story about a new set of whitewashed bungalows that developers are building south of Tinos town, with views of Mykonos and the Aegean. Primarily, they will be filled by either tourists or the wealthy summer residents who have been coming to Tinos since the 1990s. She says the bungalows will have an outdoor pool and a fitness center.

She has been e-mailing me for years, chronicling for me these changes that are reshaping Tinos. The beachside hotels with the satellite dishes and dial-up access, the night-clubs and bars and taverns, the restaurants and shops that cater to tourists, the cabs, the buses, the crowds, the foreign women who lie topless at the beaches. The farmers ride pickup trucks now instead of donkeys—at least the farmers who stayed. Most of them left long ago, though some are coming back now to live out their retirement on the island.

"Odie is none too pleased," Thalia says, meaning with the transformation. She has written me about this too—the older islanders' suspicion of the newcomers and the changes they are importing.

"You don't seem to mind the change," I say.

"No point in griping about the inevitable," she says. Then adds, "Odie says, 'Well, it figures *you'd* say that, Thalia. You weren't born here.'" She lets out a loud, hearty laugh. "You'd think after forty-four years on Tinos I would have earned the right. But there you have it."

Thalia has changed too. Even with the winter coat on, I can tell she has thickened in the hips, become plumper—not soft plump, sturdy plump. There is a cordial defiance to her now, a slyly teasing way she has of commenting on things I do that I suspect she finds slightly foolish. The brightness in her eyes, this new hearty laugh, the perpetual flush of the cheeks—the overall impression is, a farmer's wife. A salt-of-the-earth kind of woman whose robust friendliness hints at a bracing authority and hardness you might be unwise to question.

"How is business?" I ask. "Are you still working?"

"Here and there," Thalia says. "You know the times." We both shake our heads. In Kabul, I had followed news about the rounds of austerity measures. I had watched on CNN masked young Greeks stoning police outside the parliament, cops in riot gear firing tear gas, swinging their batons.

Thalia doesn't run a business in the real sense. Before the digital age, she was essentially a handywoman. She went to people's homes and soldered power transistors in their TVs, replaced signal capacitors in old tube-model radios. She was called in to fix faulty refrigerator thermostats, seal leaky plumbing. People paid her what they could. And if they couldn't afford to pay, she did the work anyway. *I don't really need the money,* she told me. *I do it for the game of it. There's still a thrill for me in opening things up and seeing how they work inside.* These days, she is like a freelance one-woman IT department. Everything she knows is self-taught. She charges nominal fees to troubleshoot people's PCs, change IP settings, fix their application-file freeze-ups, their slow-downs, their upgrade and boot-up failures. More than once I have called her from Kabul, desperate for help with my frozen IBM.

When we arrive at my mother's house, we stand outside for a moment in the courtyard beside the old olive tree. I see evidence of Mamá's recent frenzy of work—the repainted walls, the half-finished dovecote, a hammer and an open box of nails resting on a slab of wood.

"How is she?" I ask.

"Oh, thorny as ever. That's why I had that thing installed." She points to a satellite dish perched on the roof. "We watch foreign soaps. The Arabic ones are the best, or the worst, which comes down to the same thing. We try to figure out the plots. It keeps her claws off me." She charges through the front door. "Welcome home. I'll fix you something to eat."

It's strange being back in this house. I see a few unfamiliar things, like the gray leather armchair in the living room and a white wicker end table beside the TV. But everything else is more or less where it used to be. The kitchen table, now covered by a vinyl top with an alternating pattern of eggplants and pears; the straight-backed bamboo chairs; the old oil lamp with the wicker holder, the scalloped chimney stained black with smoke; the picture of me and Mamá—me in the white shirt, Mamá in her good dress—still hanging above the mantel in the living room; Mamá's set of china still on the high shelf.

And yet, as I drop my suitcase, it feels as though there is a gaping hole in the middle of everything. The decades of my mother's life here with Thalia, they are dark, vast spaces to me. I have been absent. Absent for all the meals Thalia and Mamá have shared at this table, the laughs, the quarrels, the stretches of boredom, the illnesses, the long string of simple rituals that make up a lifetime. Entering my childhood home is a little disorienting, like reading the end of a novel that I'd started, then abandoned, long ago.

"How about some eggs?" Thalia says, already donning a print bib apron, pouring oil in a skillet. She moves about the kitchen with command, in a proprietary way.

"Sure. Where is Mamá?"

"Asleep. She had a rough night."

"I'll take a quick look."

Thalia fishes a whisk from the drawer. "You wake her up, you'll answer to me, Doctor."

I tiptoe up the steps to the bedroom. The room is dark. A single long narrow slab of light shoots through the pulled curtains, slashes across Mamá's bed. The air is heavy with sickness. It's not quite a smell; rather, it's like a physical presence. Every doctor knows this. Sickness permeates a room like steam. I stand at the entrance for a moment and allow my eyes to adjust. The darkness is broken by a rectangle of shifting colored light on the dresser on what I take to be Thalia's side of the bed, my old side. It's one of those digital picture frames. A field of rice paddies and wooden houses with gray-tiled roofs fade to a crowded bazaar with skinned goats hanging from hooks, then to a dark-skinned man squatting by a muddy river, finger-brushing his teeth.

I pull up a chair and sit at Mamá's bedside. Looking at her now that my eyes have adjusted, I feel something in me drop. I am startled by how much my mother has shrunk. Already. The floral-print pajamas appear loose around her small shoulders, over the flattened chest. I don't care for the way she is sleeping, with her mouth open and turned down, as though she is having a sour dream. I don't like seeing that her dentures have slid out of place in her sleep. Her eyelids flutter slightly. I sit there awhile. I ask myself, What did you expect? and I listen to the clock ticking on the wall, the clanging of Thalia's spatula against the frying pan from downstairs. I take inventory of the banal details of Mamá's life in this room. The flat-screen TV fastened to the wall; the PC in the corner; the unfinished game of Sudoku on the nightstand, the page marked by a pair of reading glasses; the TV remote; the vial of artificial tears; a tube of steroid cream; a tube of denture glue; a small bottle of pills; and, on the floor, an oyster-colored pair of fuzzy slippers. She would have never worn those before. Beside the slippers, an open bag of pull-on diapers. I cannot reconcile these things with my mother. I resist them. They look to me like the belongings of a stranger. Someone indolent, harmless. Someone with whom you could never be angry.

Across the bed, the image on the digital picture frame shifts again. I track a few. Then it comes to me. I know these photos. I shot them. Back when I was . . . What? Walking the earth, I suppose. I'd always made sure to get double prints and mail one set to Thalia. And she'd kept them. All these years. Thalia. Affection seeps through me sweet as honey. She has been my true sister, my true Manaar, all along.

She calls my name from downstairs.

I get up quietly. As I leave the room, something catches my eye. Something framed, mounted on the wall beneath the clock. I can't quite make it out in the dark. I open my cell phone and take a look in its silver glow. It's an AP story about the nonprofit I work with in Kabul. I remember the interview. The journalist was a pleasant Korean-American fellow with a mild stutter. We had shared a plate of *qabuli*— Afghan pilaf, with brown rice, raisins, lamb. There is in the center of the story a group photo. Me, some of the children, Nabi in the back, standing rigidly, hands behind his back, looking simultaneously foreboding, shy, and dignified, as Afghans often manage to in pictures. Amra is there too with her adopted daughter, Roshi. All the children are smiling.

"Markos."

I flip the mobile closed and make my way downstairs.

Thalia puts before me a glass of milk and a steaming plate of eggs on a bed of tomatoes. "Don't worry, I already sugared the milk."

"You remember."

She takes a seat, not bothering to remove the apron. She rests her elbows on the table and watches me eat, dabbing now and then at her left cheek with a handkerchief.

I remember all the times I tried to convince her to let me work on her face. I told her that surgical techniques had come a long way since the 1960s, and that I was certain I could, if not fix, then at least significantly improve her disfigurement. Thalia refused, to enormous bewilderment on my part. *This is who I am,* she said to me. An insipid, unsatisfactory answer, I thought at the time. What did that even mean? I didn't understand it. I had uncharitable thoughts of prison inmates, lifers, afraid to get out, terrified of being paroled, terrified of change, terrified of facing a new life outside barbed wire and guard towers.

My offer to Thalia still stands to this day. I know she won't take it. But I understand now. Because she was right—this *is* who she is. I cannot pretend to know what it must have been like to gaze at that face in the mirror each day, to take stock of its ghastly ruin, and to summon the will to accept it. The mountainous strain of it, the effort, the patience. Her acceptance taking shape slowly, over years, like rocks of a beachside cliff sculpted by the pounding tides. It took the dog minutes to give Thalia her face, and a lifetime for her to mold it into an identity. She would not let me undo it all with my scalpel. It would be like inflicting a fresh wound over the old one.

I dig into the eggs, knowing it will please her, even though I am not really hungry. "This is good, Thalia."

"So, are you excited?"

"What do you mean?"

She reaches behind her and pulls open a kitchen-counter drawer. She retrieves a pair of sunglasses with rectangular lenses. It takes me a moment. Then I remember. The eclipse.

"Ah, of course."

"At first," she says, "I thought we'd just watch it through a pinhole. But then Odie said you were coming. And I said, 'Well, then, let's do it in style.'"

We talk a bit about the eclipse that is supposed to happen the next day. Thalia says it will start in the morning and be complete by noon or so. She has been checking the weather updates and is relieved that the island is not due for a cloudy day. She asks if I want more eggs and I say yes, and she tells me about a new Internet café that has gone up where Mr. Roussos's old pawnshop used to sit.

"I saw the pictures," I say. "Upstairs. The article too."

She wipes my bread crumbs off the table with her palm, tosses them over her shoulder into the kitchen sink without looking. "Ah, that was easy. Well, scanning and uploading them was. The hard part was organizing them into countries. I had to sit and figure it out because you never sent notes, just the pictures. She was very specific about that, the having it organized into countries. She had to have it that way. She insisted on it."

"Who?"

She issues a sigh. "'Who?' he says. Odie. Who else?"

"That was her idea?"

"The article too. She was the one who found it on the web."

"Mamá looked me up?" I say.

"I should have never taught her. Now she won't stop." She gives a chuckle. "She checks on you every day. It's true. You have yourself a cyberspace stalker, Markos Varvaris."

Mamá comes downstairs early in the afternoon. She is wearing a dark blue bathrobe and the fuzzy slippers that I have already come to loathe. It looks like she has brushed her hair. I am relieved to see that she appears to be moving normally as she walks down the steps, as she opens her arms to me, smiling sleepily.

We sit at the table for coffee.

"Where is Thalia?" she asks, blowing into her cup.

"Out to get some treats. For tomorrow. Is that yours, Mamá?" I point to a cane leaning against the wall behind the new armchair. I hadn't noticed it when I had first come in.

"Oh, I hardly use it. Just on bad days. And for long walks. Even then, mostly for peace of mind," she says too dismissively, which is how I know she relies on it far more than she lets on. "It's you I worry for. The news from that awful country. Thalia doesn't want me listening to it. She says it will agitate me."

"We do have our incidents," I say, "but mostly it's just people going about their lives. And I'm always careful, Mamá." Of course I neglect to tell her about the shooting at the guesthouse across the street or the recent surge in attacks on foreign-aid workers, or that by *careful* I mean I have taken to carrying a 9mm when I am out driving around the city, which I probably shouldn't be doing in the first place.

Mamá takes a sip of coffee, winces a bit. She doesn't push me. I am not sure whether this is a good thing. Not sure whether she has drifted off, descended into herself as old people do, or whether it is a tactic to not corner me into lying or disclosing things that would only upset her.

"We missed you at Christmas," she says.

"I couldn't get away, Mamá."

She nods. "You're here now. That's what matters."

I take a sip of my coffee. I remember when I was little Mamá and me eating breakfast at this table every morning, quietly, almost solemnly, before we walked to school together. We said so little to each other.

"You know, Mamá, I worry for you too."

"No need to. I take care of myself all right." A flash of the old defiant pride, like a dim glint in the fog.

"But for how long?"

"As long as I can."

"And when you can't, then what?" I am not challenging her. I ask because I don't know. I don't know what my own role will be or whether I will even play one.

She levels her gaze at me evenly. Then she adds a teaspoon of sugar to her cup, slowly stirs it in. "It's a funny thing, Markos, but people mostly have it backward. They think they live by what they want. But really what guides them is what they're afraid of. What they *don't* want."

"I don't follow, Mamá."

"Well, take you, for instance. Leaving here. The life you've made for yourself. You were afraid of being confined here. With me. You were afraid I would hold you back. Or, take Thalia. She stayed because she didn't want to be stared at anymore."

I watch her taste her coffee, pour in another spoonful of sugar. I remember how out of my depth I'd always felt as a boy trying to argue with her. She spoke in a way that left no room for retort, steamrolling over me with the truth, told right at the outset, plainly, directly. I was always defeated before I'd so much as said a word. It always seemed unfair.

"What about you, Mamá?" I ask. "What are you scared of? What don't you want?"

"To be a burden."

"You won't be."

"Oh, you're right about that, Markos."

Disquiet spreads through me at this cryptic remark. My mind flashes to the letter Nabi had given me in Kabul, his posthumous confession. The pact Suleiman Wahdati had made with him. I can't help but wonder if Mamá has forged a similar pact with Thalia, if she has chosen Thalia to rescue her when the time comes. I know Thalia could do it. She is strong now. She would save Mamá.

Mamá is studying my face. "You have your life and your work, Markos," she says, more softly now, redirecting the course of the conversation, as if she has peeked into my mind, spotted my worry. The dentures, the diapers, the fuzzy slippers—they have made me underestimate her. She still has the upper hand. She always will. "I don't want to weigh you down."

At last, a lie—this last thing she says—but it's a kind lie. It isn't me she would weigh down. She knows this as well as I do. I am absent, thousands of miles away. The unpleasantness, the work, the drudgery, it would fall on Thalia. But Mamá is including me, granting me something I have not earned, nor tried to.

"It wouldn't be like that," I say weakly.

Mamá smiles. "Speaking of your work, I guess you know that I didn't exactly approve when you decided to go to that country."

"I had my suspicions, yes."

"I didn't understand why you would go. Why would

you give everything up—the practice, the money, the house in Athens—all you'd worked for—and hole up in that violent place?"

"I had my reasons."

"I know." She raises the cup to her lips, lowers it without sipping. "I'm no damn good at this," she says slowly, almost shyly, "but what I'm getting around to telling you is, you've turned out good. You've made me proud, Markos."

I look down at my hands. I feel her words landing deep within me. She has startled me. Caught me unprepared. For what she said. Or for the soft light in her eyes when she said it. I am at a loss as to what I am expected to say in response.

"Thank you, Mamá," I manage to mutter.

I can't say any more, and we sit quietly for a while, the air between us thick with awkwardness and our awareness of all the time lost, the opportunities frittered away.

"I've been meaning to ask you something," Mamá says.

"What is it?"

"James Parkinson. George Huntington. Robert Graves. John Down. Now this Lou Gehrig fellow of mine. How did men come to monopolize disease names too?"

I blink and my mother blinks back, and then she is laughing and so am I. Even as I crumple inside.

The next morning, we lie outside on lounge chairs. Mamá wears a thick scarf and a gray parka, her legs warmed against the sharp chill by a fleece blanket.

We sip coffee and nibble on bits of the cinnamon-flavored baked quince Thalia has bought for the occasion. We are wearing our eclipse glasses, looking up at the sky. The sun has a small bite taken from its northern rim, looking somewhat like the logo on the Apple laptop Thalia periodically opens to post remarks on an online forum. Up and down the street, people have settled on the sidewalks and rooftops to watch the spectacle. Some have taken their families to the other end of the island, where the Hellenic Astronomical Society has set up telescopes.

"What time is it supposed to peak?" I ask.

"Close to ten-thirty," Thalia says. She lifts her glasses, checks her watch. "Another hour or so." She rubs her hands with excitement, taps something on the keyboard.

I watch the two of them, Mamá with her dark glasses, blue-veined hands laced on her chest, Thalia furiously pounding the keys, white hair spilling from under her beanie cap.

You've turned out good.

I lay on the couch the night before, thinking about what Mamá had said, and my thoughts had wandered to Madaline. I remembered how, as a boy, I would stew over all the things Mamá wouldn't do, things other mothers did. Hold my hand when we walked. Sit me up on her lap, read bedtime stories, kiss my face good night. Those things were true enough. But, all those years, I'd been blind to a greater truth, which lay unacknowledged and unappreciated, buried deep beneath my grievances. It was this: that my mother would never leave me. This was her gift to me, the ironclad knowledge that she would never do to me what Madaline had done to Thalia. She was my mother and she would not leave me. This I had simply accepted and expected. I had no more thanked her for it than I did the sun for shining on me.

"Look!" Thalia exclaims.

Suddenly, all around us—on the ground, on the walls, on our clothing—little shining sickles of light have materialized, the crescent-shaped sun beaming through the leaves of our olive tree. I find a crescent shimmering on the coffee inside my mug, another dancing on my shoelaces.

"Show me your hands, Odie," Thalia says. "Quick!"

Mamá opens her hands, palms up. Thalia fetches from her pocket a square of cut glass. She holds it over Mamá's hands. Suddenly, little crescent rainbows quiver on the wrinkled skin of my mother's hands. She gasps.

"Look at that, Markos!" Mamá says, grinning unabashedly with delight like a schoolgirl. I have never before seen her smile this purely, this guilelessly.

We sit, the three of us, watching the trembling little rainbows on my mother's hands, and I feel sadness and an old ache, each like a claw at my throat.

You've turned out good.

You've made me proud, Markos.

I am fifty-five years old. I have waited all my life to hear those words. Is it too late now for this? For us? Have we squandered too much for too long, Mamá and I? Part of me thinks it is better to go on as we have, to act as though we don't know how ill suited we have been for each other. Less painful that way. Perhaps better than this belated offering. This fragile, trembling little glimpse of how it could have been between us. All it will beget is regret, I tell myself, and what good is regret? It brings back nothing. What we have lost is irretrievable.

And yet when my mother says, "Isn't it beautiful, Markos?" I say to her, "It is, Mamá. It is beautiful," and as something begins to break wide open inside me I reach over and take my mother's hand in mine.

Nine

Winter 2010

When I was a little girl, my father and I had a nightly ritual. After I'd said my twenty-one *Bismillah*s and he had tucked me into bed, he would sit at my side and pluck bad dreams from my head with his thumb and forefinger. His fingers would hop from my forehead to my temples, patiently searching behind my ears, at the back of my head, and he'd make a *pop* sound— like a bottle being uncorked—with each nightmare he purged from my brain. He stashed the dreams, one by one, into an invisible sack in his lap and pulled the drawstring tightly. He would then scour the air, looking for happy dreams to replace the ones he had sequestered away. I watched as he cocked his head slightly and frowned, his eyes roaming side to side, like he was straining to hear distant music. I held my breath, waiting for the moment when my father's face unfurled into a smile, when he sang, *Ah, here is one,* when he cupped his hands, let the dream land in his palms like a petal slowly twirling down from a tree. Gently, then, so very gently—my father said all good things in life were fragile and easily lost—he would raise his hands to my face, rub his palms against my brow and happiness into my head.

What am I going to dream about tonight, Baba? I asked.

Ah, tonight. Well, tonight is a special one, he always said before going on to tell me about it. He would make up a story on the spot. In one of the dreams he gave me, I had become the world's most famous painter. In another, I was the queen of an enchanted island, and I had a flying throne. He even gave me one about my favorite dessert, Jell-O. I had the power to, with a wave of my wand, turn anything into Jell-O—a school bus, the Empire State Building, the entire Pacific Ocean, if I liked. More than once, I saved the planet from destruction by waving my wand at a crashing meteor. My father, who never spoke much about his own father, said it was from him that he had inherited his storytelling ability. He said that when he was a boy, his father would sometimes sit him down—if he was in the mood, which was not often— and tell stories populated with *jinn*s and fairies and *div*s.

Some nights, I turned the tables on Baba. He shut his eyes and I slid my palms down his face, starting at his brow, over the prickly stubble of his cheeks, the coarse hairs of his mustache.

And so, what is my dream tonight? he would whisper, taking my hands. And his smile would open. Because he knew already what dream I was giving him. It was always the same. The one of him and his little sister lying beneath a blossoming apple tree, drifting toward an afternoon nap. The sun warm against their cheeks, its light picking out the grass and the leaves and clutter of blossoms above.

I was an only, and often lonely, child. After they'd had me, my parents, who'd met back in Pakistan when they were both around forty, had decided against tempting fate a second time. I remember how I would eye with envy all the kids in our neighborhood, in my school, who had a little brother or sister. How bewildered I was by the way some of them treated each other, oblivious to their own good luck. They acted like wild dogs. Pinching, hitting, pushing, betraying one another any way they could think of. Laughing about it too. They wouldn't speak to one another. I didn't understand. Me, I spent most of my early years craving a sibling. What I *really* wished I had was a twin, someone who'd cried next to me in the crib, slept beside me, fed from Mother's breast with me. Someone to love helplessly and totally, and in whose face I could always find myself.

And so Baba's little sister, Pari, was my secret companion, invisible to everyone but me. She was *my* sister, the one I'd always wished my parents had given me. I saw her in the bathroom mirror when we brushed our teeth side by side in the morning. We dressed together. She followed me to school and sat close to me in class—looking straight ahead at the board, I could always spot the black of her hair and the white of her profile out of the corner of my eye. I took her with me to the playground at recess, feeling her presence behind me when I whooshed down a slide, when I swung from one monkey bar to the next. After school, when I sat at the kitchen table sketching, she doodled patiently nearby or stood looking out the window until I finished and we ran outside to jump rope, our twin shadows bopping up and down on the concrete.

No one knew about my games with Pari. Not even my father. She was my secret.

Sometimes, when no one was around, we ate grapes and talked and talked—about toys, which cereals were tastiest, cartoons we liked, schoolkids we didn't, which teachers were mean. We shared the same favorite color (yellow), favorite ice cream (dark cherry), TV show (*Alf*), and we both wanted to be artists when we grew up. Naturally, I imagined we looked exactly the same because, after all, we were twins. Sometimes I could almost see her—really *see* her, I mean— just at the periphery of my eyesight. I tried drawing her, and, each time, I gave her the same slightly uneven light green eyes as mine, the same dark curly hair, the same long, slashing eyebrows that almost touched. If anyone asked, I told them I had drawn myself.

The tale of how my father had lost his sister was as familiar to me as the stories my mother had told me of the Prophet, tales I would learn again later when my parents would enroll me in Sunday school at a mosque in Hayward. Still, despite the familiarity, each night I asked to hear Pari's story again, caught in the pull of its gravity. Maybe it was simply because we shared a name. Maybe that was why I sensed a connection between us, dim, enfolded in mystery, real nonetheless. But it was more than that. I felt *touched* by her, like I too had been marked by what had happened to her. We were interlocked, I sensed, through some unseen order in ways I couldn't wholly understand, linked beyond our names, beyond familial ties, as if, together, we completed a puzzle.

I felt certain that if I listened closely enough to her story, I would discover something revealed about myself.

Do you think your father was sad? That he sold her?

Some people hide their sadness very well, Pari. He was like that. You couldn't tell looking at him. He was a hard man. But I think, yes, I think he was sad inside.

Are you?

My father would smile and say, *Why should I be when I have you?* but, even at that age, I could tell. It was like a birthmark on his face.

The whole time we talked like this, a fantasy played out in my head. In it, I would save all my money, not spend a dollar on candy or stickers, and when my piggy bank was full—though it wasn't a pig at all but a mermaid sitting on a rock—I would break it open and pocket all the money and set out to find my father's little sister, wherever she was, and, when I did, I would buy her back and bring her home to Baba. I would make my father happy. There was nothing in the world I desired more than to be the one to take away his sadness.

So what's my dream tonight? Baba would ask.

You know already.

Another smile. *Yes, I know.*

Baba?

Mmm?

Was she a good sister?

She was perfect.

He would kiss my cheek and tuck the blanket around my neck. At the door, just after he'd turned off the light, he would pause.

She was perfect, he would say. *Like you are.*

I always waited until he'd shut the door before I slid out of bed, fetched an extra pillow, and placed it next to my own. I went to sleep each night feeling twin hearts beating in my chest.

I check my watch as I veer onto the freeway from the Old Oakland Road entrance. It's already half past noon. It will take me forty minutes at least to reach SFO, barring any accidents or roadwork on the 101. On the plus side, it *is* an international flight, so she will still have to clear customs, and perhaps that will buy me a little time. I slide over to the left lane and push the Lexus up close to eighty.

I remember a minor miracle of a conversation I had had with Baba, about a month back. The exchange was a fleeting bubble of normalcy, like a tiny pocket of air down in the deep, dark, cold bottom of the ocean. I was late bringing him lunch, and he turned his head to me from his recliner and remarked, with the gentlest critical tone, that I was genetically programmed to not be punctual. *Like your mother, God rest her soul.*

But then, he went on, smiling, as if to reassure me, *a person has to have a flaw somewhere.*

So this is the one token flaw God tossed my way, then? I said, lowering the plate of rice and beans on his lap. *Habitual tardiness?*

And He did so with great reluctance, I might add. Baba reached for my hands. *So close, so very close He had you to perfection.*

Well, if you like, I'll happily let you in on a few more.

You have them hidden away, do you?

Oh, heaps. Ready to be unleashed. For when you're old and helpless.

I am *old and helpless.*

Now you want me to feel sorry for you.

I play with the radio, flipping from talk to country to jazz to more talk. I turn it off. I'm restless and nervous. I reach for my cell phone on the passenger seat. I call the house and leave the phone flipped open on my lap.

"Hello?"

"*Salaam, Baba.* It's me."

"Pari?"

"Yes, Baba. Is everything okay at the house with you and Hector?"

"Yes. He's a wonderful young man. He made us eggs. We had them with toast. Where are you?"

"I'm driving," I say.

"To the restaurant? You don't have a shift today, do you?"

"No, I'm on my way to the airport, Baba. I'm picking someone up."

"Okay. I'll ask your mother to make us lunch," he says. "She could bring something from the restaurant."

"All right, Baba."

To my relief, he doesn't mention her again. But, some days, he won't stop. *Why won't you tell me where she is, Pari? Is she having an operation? Don't lie to me! Why is everyone lying to me? Has she gone away? Is she in Afghanistan? Then I'm going too! I'm going to Kabul, and you can't stop me.* We go back and forth like this, Baba pacing, distraught; me feeding him lies, then trying to distract him with his collection of home-improvement catalogs or something on television. Sometimes it works, but other times he is impervious to my tricks. He worries until he is in tears, in hysterics. He slaps at his head and rocks back and forth in the chair, sobbing, his legs quivering, and then I have to feed him an Ativan. I wait for his eyes to cloud over, and, when they do, I drop on the couch, exhausted, out of breath, near tears myself. Longingly, I look at the front door and the openness beyond and I want to walk through it and just keep walking. And then Baba moans in his sleep, and I snap back, simmering with guilt.

"Can I talk to Hector, Baba?"

I hear the receiver transferring hands. In the background, the sound of a game-show crowd groaning, then applause.

"Hey, girl."

Hector Juarez lives across the street. We've been neighbors for many years and have become friends in the last few. He comes over a couple of times a week and he and I eat junk food and watch trash TV late into the night, mostly reality shows. We chew on cold pizza and shake our heads with morbid fascination at the antics and tantrums on the screen. Hector was a marine, stationed in the south of Afghanistan. A couple of years back, he got himself badly hurt in an IED attack. Everyone from the block showed up when he finally came home from the VA. His parents had hung a *Welcome Home, Hector* sign out in their front yard, with balloons and a lot of flowers. Everyone clapped when his parents pulled up to the house. Several of the neighbors had baked pies. People thanked him for his service. They said, *Be strong, now. God bless.* Hector's father, Cesar, came over to our house a few days later and he and I installed the same wheelchair ramp Cesar had built outside his own house leading up to the front door, the American flag draped above it. I remember, as the two of us worked on the ramp, I felt a need to apologize to Cesar for what had happened to Hector in my father's homeland.

"Hi," I say. "I thought I'd check in."

"It's all good here," Hector says. "We ate. We did *Price Is Right.* We're chillin' now with *Wheel.* Next up is *Feud.*"

"Ouch. Sorry."

"What for, *mija*? We're having a good time. Aren't we, Abe?"

"Thanks for making him eggs," I say.

Hector lowers his voice a notch. "Pancakes, actually. And guess what? He loved them. Ate up a four-stack."

"I really owe you."

"Hey, I really like the new painting, girl. The one with the kid in the funny hat? Abe here showed it to me. He was all proud too. I was, like, damn! You *should* be proud, man."

I smile as I shift lanes to let a tailgater pass. "Maybe I know what to give you for Christmas now."

"Remind me again why we *can't* get married?" Hector says. I hear Baba protesting in the background and Hector's laugh, away from the receiver. "I'm joking, Abe. Go easy on me. I'm a cripple." Then, to me, "I think your father just flashed me his inner Pashtun."

I remind him to give Baba his late-morning pills and hang up.

It's like seeing the photo of a radio personality, how they never turn out to look the way you had pictured them in your mind, listening to their voice in your car. She is old, for one thing. Or oldish. Of course I knew this. I had done the math and estimated she had to be around her early sixties. Except it is hard to reconcile this slim gray-haired woman with the little girl I've always envisioned, a three-year-old with dark curly hair and long eyebrows that almost meet, like mine. And she is taller than I imagined. I can tell, even though she is sitting, on a bench near a sandwich kiosk, looking around timidly like she's lost. She has narrow shoulders and a delicate build, a pleasant face, her hair pulled back taut and held with a crocheted headband. She wears jade earrings, faded jeans, a long salmon tunic sweater, and a yellow scarf wrapped around her neck with casual European elegance. She had told me in her last e-mail that she would wear the scarf so I could spot her quickly.

She has not seen me yet, and I linger for a moment among the travelers pushing luggage carts through the terminal, the town-car chauffeurs holding signs with clients' names. My heart clamoring inside my rib cage, I think to myself, *This is her. This is her. This is really her.* Then our eyes connect, and recognition ripples across her face. She waves.

We meet at the bench. She grins and my knees wobble. She has Baba's grin exactly—except for a rice grain's gap between her upper front teeth—crooked on the left, the way it scrunches up her face and nearly squeezes shut her eyes, how she tilts her head just a tad. She stands up, and I notice the hands, the knobby joints, the fingers bent away from the thumb at the first knuckle, the chickpea-sized lumps at the wrist. I feel a twist in my stomach, it looks so painful.

We hug, and she kisses me on the cheeks. Her skin is soft like felt. When we pull back, she holds me at a distance, hands cupping my shoulders, and looks into my face as if she were appraising a painting. There is a film of moisture over her eyes. They're alive with happiness.

"I apologize for being late."

"It's nothing," she says. "At last, to be with you! I am just so glad"—*Is nussing. At lass, too be weez yoo!* The French accent sounds even thicker in person than it did on the phone.

"I'm glad too," I say. "How was your flight?"

"I took a pill, otherwise I know I cannot sleep. I will stay awake the whole time. Because I am too happy and too excited." She holds me with her gaze, beaming at me—as if she is afraid the spell will break if she looks away—until the

PA overhead advises passengers to report any unsupervised luggage, and then her face slackens a bit.

"Does Abdullah know yet that I am coming here?"

"I told him I was bringing home a guest," I say.

Later, as we settle into the car, I steal quick looks at her. It's the strangest thing. There is something oddly illusory about Pari Wahdati, sitting in my car, mere inches from me. One moment, I see her with perfect clarity—the yellow scarf around her neck, the short, flimsy hairs at the hairline, the coffee-colored mole beneath the left ear—and, the next, her features are enfolded in a kind of haze, as if I am peering at her through bleary glasses. I feel, in passing, a kind of vertigo.

"You are okay?" she says, eyeing me as she snaps the seat-belt buckle.

"I keep thinking you'll disappear."

"I'm sorry?"

"It's just . . . a little unbelievable," I say, laughing nervously. "That you really exist. That you're actually here."

She nods, smiling. "Ah, for me too. For me too it is strange. You know, my whole life I never meet anyone with the same name as me."

"Neither have I." I turn the ignition key. "So tell me about your children."

As I pull out of the parking lot, she tells me all about them, using their names as though I had known them all my life, as though her children and I had grown up together, gone on family picnics and to camp and taken summer vacations to seaside resorts where we had made seashell necklaces and buried one another under sand.

I do wish we had.

She tells me her son Alain—"and your cousin," she adds—and his wife, Ana, have had a fifth baby, a little girl, and they have moved to Valencia, where they have bought a house. "*Finalement*, they leave that detestable apartment in Madrid!" Her firstborn, Isabelle, who writes musical scores for television, has been commissioned to compose her first major film score. And Isabelle's husband, Albert, is now head chef at a well-regarded restaurant in Paris.

"You owned a restaurant, no?" she asks. "I think you told me this in your e-mail."

"Well, my parents did. It was always my father's dream to own a restaurant. I helped them run it. But I had to sell it a few years back. After my mother died and Baba became . . . incapable."

"Ah, I am sorry."

"Oh, don't be. I wasn't cut out for restaurant work."

"I should think not. You are an artist."

I had told her, in passing the first time we spoke and she asked me what I did, that I had dreams of going to art school one day.

"Actually, I am what you call a *transcriptionist*."

She listens intently as I explain to her that I work for a firm that processes data for big Fortune 500 companies. "I write up forms for them. Brochures, receipts, customer lists, e-mail lists, that sort of thing. The main thing you need to know is how to type. And the pay is decent."

"I see," she says. She considers, then says, "Is it interesting for you, doing this work?"

We are passing by Redwood City on our way south. I reach across her lap and point out the passenger window. "Do you see that building? The tall one with the blue sign?"

"Yes?"

"I was born there."

"Ah, bon?" She turns her neck to keep looking as I drive us past. "You are lucky."

"How so?"

"To know where you came from."

"I guess I never gave it much thought."

"Bah, of course not. But it is important to know this, to know your roots. To know where you started as a person. If not, your own life seems unreal to you. Like a puzzle. *Vous comprenez?* Like you have missed the beginning of a story and now you are in the middle of it, trying to understand."

I imagine this is how Baba feels these days. His life, riddled with gaps. Every day a mystifying story, a puzzle to struggle through.

We drive in silence for a couple of miles.

"Do I find my work interesting?" I say. "I came home one day and found the water running in the kitchen sink. There was broken glass on the floor, and the gas burner had been left on. That was when I knew that I couldn't leave him alone anymore. And because I couldn't afford a live-in caretaker, I looked for work I could do from home. 'Interesting' didn't figure much into the equation."

"And art school can wait."

"It has to."

I worry she will say next how lucky Baba is to have me

for a daughter, but, to my relief and gratitude, she only nods, her eyes swimming past the freeway signs. Other people, though—especially Afghans—are always pointing out how fortunate Baba is, what a blessing I am. They speak of me admiringly. They make me out to be a saint, the daughter who has heroically forgone some glittering life of ease and privilege to stay home and look after her father. *But, first, the mother,* they say, their voices ringing, I imagine, with a glistening kind of sympathy. *All those years of nursing her. What a mess that was. Now the father. She was never a looker, sure, but she had a suitor. An American, he was, the solar fellow. She could have married him. But she didn't. Because of them. The things she sacrificed. Ah, every parent should have a daughter like this.* They compliment me on my good humor. They marvel at my courage and nobility the way people do those who have overcome a physical deformity or maybe a crippling speech impediment.

But I don't recognize myself in this version of the story. For instance, some mornings I spot Baba sitting on the edge of his bed, eyeing me with his rheumy gaze, impatient for me to slip socks onto his dry, mottled feet, and he growls my name and makes an infantile face. He wrinkles his nose in a way that makes him look like a wet, fearful rodent, and I resent him when he makes this face. I resent him for being the way he is. I resent him for the narrowed borders of my existence, for being the reason my best years are draining away from me. There are days when all I want is to be free of him and his petulance and neediness. I am nothing like a saint.

I take the exit at Thirteenth Street. A handful of miles later, I pull into our driveway, on Beaver Creek Court, and turn off the engine.

Pari looks out the window at our one-story house, the garage door with the peeling paint job, the olive window trim, the tacky pair of stone lions on guard on either side of the front door—I haven't had the heart to get rid of them because Baba loves them, though I doubt he would notice. We have lived in this house since 1989, when I was seven, renting it first, before Baba bought it from the owner back in '93. Mother died in this house, on a sunny Christmas Eve morning, in a hospital bed I set up for her in the guest bedroom and where she spent the last three months of her life. She asked me to move her to that room because of the view. She said it raised up her spirits. She lay in the bed, her legs swollen and gray, and spent her days looking out the window at the cul-de-sac, the front yard with its rim of Japanese maples she had planted years before, the star-shaped flower bed, the swath of lawn split by a narrow path of pebbles, the foothills in the distance and the deep, rich gold they turned midday when sunlight shone full tilt on them.

"I am very nervous," Pari says quietly.

"It's understandable," I say. "It's been fifty-eight years."

She looks down at her hands folded in her lap. "I remember almost nothing about him. What I remember, it is not his face or his voice. Only that in my life something has been missing always. Something good. Something . . . Ah, I don't know what to say. That is all."

I nod. I think better of telling her just how well I understand. I come close to asking whether she had ever had any intimations of my existence.

She toys with the frayed ends of her scarf. "Do you think it is possible that he will remember me?"

"Do you want the truth?"

She searches my face. "Of course, yes."

"It's probably best he doesn't." I think of what Dr. Bashiri had said, my parents' longtime physician. He said Baba needed regimen, order. A minimum of surprise. *A sense of predictability.*

I open my door. "Would you mind staying in the car a minute? I'll send my friend home, and then you can meet Baba."

She puts a hand over her eyes, and I don't wait to see if she is going to cry.

When I was eleven, all the sixth-grade classes in my elementary school went for an overnight field trip to the Monterey Bay Aquarium. The whole week leading up to that Friday, it was all my classmates talked about, in the library or playing four square at recess, how much fun they would have, once the aquarium closed for the day, free to run around the exhibits, in their pajamas, among the hammerheads, the bat rays, the sea dragons, and the squid. Our teacher, Mrs. Gillespie, told us dinner stations would be set up around the aquarium, and students would have their choice of PB&J or mac and cheese. *You can have brownies for dessert or vanilla ice cream,* she said. Students would crawl into their sleeping bags that night and listen to teachers read them bedtime stories, and they would drift off to sleep among the sea horses and sardines and the leopard sharks gliding through tall fronds of swaying kelp. By Thursday, the anticipation in the classroom was electric. Even the usual troublemakers made sure to be on their best for fear that mischief would cost them the trip to the aquarium.

For me, it was a bit like watching an exciting movie with the sound turned off. I felt removed from all the cheerfulness, cut off from the celebratory mood—the way I did every December when my classmates went home to Douglas firs and stockings dangling over fireplaces and pyramids of presents. I told Mrs. Gillespie I wouldn't be going along. When she asked why, I said the field trip fell on a Muslim holiday. I wasn't sure she believed me.

The night of the trip, I stayed home with my parents, and we watched *Murder, She Wrote*. I tried to focus on the show and not think about the field trip, but my mind insisted on wandering off. I imagined my classmates, at that same moment, in their pajamas, flashlights in hand, their foreheads pressed against the glass of a giant tank of eel. I felt something clenching in my chest, and I shifted my weight on the couch. Baba, slung back on the other couch, tossed a roasted peanut into his mouth and chuckled at something Angela Lansbury said. Next to him, I caught Mother watching me pensively, her face clouded over, but when our eyes met her features cleared quickly and she smiled—a stealthy, private smile—and I dug inward and willed myself to smile back. That night, I dreamt I was at a beach, standing waist-deep in the ocean, water that was myriad shades of green and blue, jade, sapphire, emerald, turquoise, gently rocking at my hips. At my feet glided legions of fish, as if the ocean were my own private aquarium. They brushed against my toes and tickled my calves, a thousand darting, glistening flashes of color against the white sand.

That Sunday, Baba had a surprise for me. He shut down the restaurant for the day—something he almost never did—and drove the two of us to the aquarium in Monterey. Baba talked excitedly the whole way. How much fun we were going to have. How he looked forward to seeing all the sharks especially. What should we eat for lunch? As he spoke, I remembered when I was little and he would take me to the petting zoo at Kelley Park and the Japanese gardens next door to see the koi, and how we would give names to all the fish and how I would cling to his hand and think to myself that I would never need anyone else as long as I lived.

At the aquarium, I wandered gamely through the exhib-its and did my best to answer Baba's questions about different types of fish I recognized. But the place was too bright and noisy, the good exhibits too crowded. It was nothing like the way I imagined it had been the night of the field trip. It was a struggle. It wore me out, trying to make like I was having a good time. I felt a stomachache coming on, and we left after an hour or so of shuffling about. On the drive home, Baba kept glancing my way with a bruised look like he was on the verge of saying something. I felt his eyes pressing in on me. I pretended to sleep.

The next year, in junior high, girls my age were wearing eye shadow and lip gloss. They went to Boyz II Men concerts, school dances, and on group dates to Great America, where they screeched through the dips and corkscrews of the Demon. Classmates tried out for basketball and cheerleading. The girl who sat behind me in Spanish, pale-skinned with freckles, was going out for the swim team, and she casually suggested one day, as we were clearing our desks just after the bell, that I give it a shot too. She didn't understand. My parents would have been mortified if I wore a bathing suit in public. Not that I wanted to. I was terribly self-conscious about my body. I was slim above the waist but disproportionately and strikingly thick below, as if gravity had pulled all the weight down to my lower half. I looked like I had been put together by a child playing one of those board games where you mix and match body parts or, better yet, mismatch them so everyone has a good laugh. Mother said what I had was "strong bones." She said her own mother had had the same build. Eventually, she stopped, having figured, I guess, that big-boned was not something a girl wanted to be called.

I did lobby Baba to let me try out for the volleyball team, but he took me in his arms and gently cupped his hands around my head. Who would take me to practice? he reasoned. Who would drive me to games? *Oh, I wish we had the luxury, Pari, like your friends' parents, but we have a living to make, your mother and I. I won't have us back on welfare. You understand, my love. I know you do.*

Despite the need to make a living, Baba found the time to drive me to Farsi lessons down in Campbell. Every Tuesday afternoon, after regular school, I sat in Farsi class and, like a fish made to swim upstream, tried to guide the pen, against my hand's own nature, from right to left. I begged Baba to end the Farsi classes, but he refused. He said I would appreciate later the gift he was giving me. He said that if culture was a house, then language was the key to the front door, to all the rooms inside. Without it, he said, you ended up wayward, without a proper home or a legitimate identity.

Then there was Sundays, when I put on a white cotton scarf, and he dropped me off at the mosque in Hayward for Koran lessons. The room where we studied—a dozen other Afghan girls and I—was tiny, had no air-conditioning, and smelled of unwashed linen. The windows were narrow and set high, the way prison-cell windows always are in the movies. The lady who taught us was the wife of a grocer in Fremont. I liked her best when she told us stories about the Prophet's life, which I found interesting—how he had lived his childhood in the desert, how the angel Gabriel had appeared to him in a cave and commanded him to recite verses, how everyone who met him was struck by his kind and luminous face. But she spent the bulk of the time running down a long list, warning us against all the things we had to avoid at all cost as virtuous young Muslim girls lest we be corrupted by Western culture: boys—first and foremost, naturally—but also rap music, Madonna, *Melrose Place*, shorts, dancing, swimming in public, cheerleading, alcohol, bacon, pepperoni, non-halal burgers, and a slew of other things. I sat on the floor, sweating in the heat, my feet falling asleep, wishing I could lift the scarf from my hair, but, of course, you couldn't do that in a mosque. I looked up at the windows, but they allowed only narrow slits of sky. I longed for the moment when I exited the mosque, when fresh air first struck my face and I always felt a loosening inside my chest, the relief of an uncomfortable knot coming undone.

But until then, the only escape was to slacken the reins on my mind. From time to time, I would find myself thinking of Jeremy Warwick, from math. Jeremy had laconic blue eyes and a white-boy Afro. He was secretive and brooding. He played guitar in a garage band—at the school's annual talent show, they played a raucous take on "House of the Rising Sun." In class, I sat four seats behind and to the left of Jeremy. Sometimes I pictured us kissing, his hand cupped around the back of my neck, his face so close to mine it eclipsed the whole world. A sensation would spread through me like a warm feather gently shivering across my belly, my limbs. Of course it could never happen. *We* could never happen, Jeremy and I. If he had even the dimmest inkling of my existence, he had never given a clue. Which was just as well, really. This way, I could pretend the only reason we couldn't be together was that he didn't like me.

I worked summers at my parents' restaurant. When I was younger, I had loved to wipe the tables, help arrange plates and silverware, fold paper napkins, drop a red gerbera into the little round vase at the center of each table. I pretended I was indispensable to the family business, that the restaurant would fall apart without me to make sure all the salt and pepper shakers were full.

By the time I was in high school, days at Abe's Kabob House dragged long and hot. Much of the luster that the things inside the restaurant had held for me in childhood had faded. The old humming soda merchandiser in the corner, the vinyl table covers, the stained plastic cups, the tacky item names on the laminated menus—*Caravan Kabob, Khyber Pass Pilaf, Silk Route Chicken*—the badly framed poster of the Afghan girl from *National Geographic*, the one with the eyes—like they had passed an ordinance that every single Afghan restaurant had to have her eyes staring back from the wall. Next to it, Baba had hung an oil painting I had done in seventh grade of the big minarets in Herat. I remember the charge of pride and glamour I had felt when he had first put it up, when I watched customers eating their lamb kabobs beneath my artwork.

At lunch hour, while Mother and I ping-ponged back and forth from the spicy smoke in the kitchen to the tables where we served office workers and city employees and cops, Baba worked the register—Baba and his grease-stained white shirt, the bushel of gray chest hair spilling over the open top button, his thick, hairy forearms. Baba beaming, waving cheerfully to each entering customer. *Hello, sir! Hello, madam! Welcome to Abe's Kabob House. I'm Abe. Can I take your order please?* It made me cringe how he didn't realize that he sounded like the goofy Middle Eastern sidekick in a bad sitcom. Then, with each meal I served, there was the sideshow of Baba ringing the old copper bell. It had started as a kind of joke, I suppose,

the bell, which Baba had hooked to the wall behind the register counter. Now each table served was greeted by a hearty
clang of the copper bell. The regulars were used to it—they
barely heard it anymore—and new customers mostly chalked
it up to the eccentric charm of the place, though there were
complaints from time to time.

You don't want to ring the bell anymore, Baba said one
night. It was in the spring quarter of my senior year in high
school. We were in the car outside the restaurant, after we
had closed, waiting for Mother, who had forgotten her
antacid pills inside and had run back in to fetch them.
Baba wore a leaden expression. He had been in a dark
mood all day. A light drizzle fell on the strip mall. It was
late, and the lot was empty, save for a couple of cars at the
KFC drive-thru and a pickup parked outside the dry-clean-
ing shop, two guys inside the truck, smoke corkscrewing
up from the windows.

It was more fun when I wasn't supposed to, I said.

Everything is, I guess. He sighed heavily.

I remembered how it used to thrill me, when I was little,
when Baba lifted me up by the underarms and let me ring
the bell. When he put me down again, my face would shine
happy and proud.

Baba turned on the car heater, crossed his arms.

Long way to Baltimore.

I said brightly, *You can fly out to visit anytime.*

Fly out anytime, he repeated with a touch of derision. *I
cook kabob for a living, Pari.*

Then I'll come visit.

Baba rolled his eyes toward me and gave me a drawn look. His melancholy was like the darkness outside pushing against the car windows.

Every day for a month I had been checking our mailbox, my heart riding a swell of hope each time the delivery truck pulled up to the curb. I would bring the mail inside, close my eyes, think, *This could be it.* I would open my eyes and sift through the bills and the coupons and the sweepstakes. Then, on Tuesday of the week before, I had ripped open an envelope and found the words I had been waiting for: *We are pleased to inform you . . .*

I leapt to my feet. I screamed—an actual throat-ripping yowl that made my eyes water. Almost instantaneously, an image streaked through my head: opening night at a gallery, me dressed in something simple, black, and elegant, encircled by patrons and crinkle-browed critics, smiling and answering their questions, as clusters of admirers linger before my canvases and servers in white gloves float around the gallery pouring wine, offering little square bites of salmon with dill or asparagus spears wrapped in puff pastry. I experienced one of those sudden bursts of euphoria, the kind where you want to wrap strangers in a hug and dance with them in great big swoops.

It's your mother I worry for, Baba said.

I'll call every night. I promise. You know I will.

Baba nodded. The leaves of the maples near the entrance to the parking lot tossed about in a sudden gust of wind.

Have you thought some more, he said, *about what we discussed?*

You mean, junior college?

Only for a year, maybe two. Just to give her time to get accustomed to the idea. Then you could reapply.

I shuddered with a sudden jolt of anger. *Baba, these people reviewed my test scores and transcripts, and they went through my portfolio, and they thought enough of my artwork not only to accept me but to offer me a scholarship. This is one of the best institutes of art in the country. It's not a school you say no to. You don't get a second chance like this.*

That's true, he said, straightening up in his seat. He cupped his hands and blew warm air into them. *Of course I understand. Of course I'm happy for you.* I could see the struggle in his face. And the fear too. Not just fear *for* me and what might happen to me three thousand miles from home. But fear *of* me, of losing me. Of the power I wielded, through my absence, to make him unhappy, to maul his open, vulnerable heart, if I chose to, like a Doberman going to work on a kitten.

I found myself thinking of his sister. By then, my connection with Pari—whose presence had once been like a pounding deep within me—had long waned. I thought of her infrequently. As the years had swept past, I had outgrown her, the way I had outgrown favorite pajamas and stuffed animals I had once clung to. But now I thought of her once more and of the ties that bound us. If what had been done to her was like a wave that had crashed far from shore, then it was the backwash of that wave now pooling around my ankles, then receding from my feet.

Baba cleared his throat and looked out the window at the dark sky and the clouded-over moon, his eyes liquid with emotion.

Everything will remind me of you.

It was in the tender, slightly panicky way he spoke these words that I knew my father was a wounded person, that his love for me was as true, vast, and permanent as the sky, and that it would always bear down upon me. It was the kind of love that, sooner or later, cornered you into a choice: either you tore free or you stayed and withstood its rigor even as it squeezed you into something smaller than yourself.

I reached over from the darkened backseat and touched his face. He leaned his cheek onto my palm.

What's taking so long? he murmured.

She's locking up, I said. I felt exhausted. I watched Mother hurry to the car. The drizzle had turned into a downpour.

A month later, a couple of weeks before I was due to fly east for a campus visit, Mother went to Dr. Bashiri to tell him the antacid pills had done nothing to help her stomach pain. He sent her for an ultrasound. They found a tumor the size of a walnut in her left ovary.

"Baba?"

He is on the recliner, sitting motionless, slumped forward. He has his sweatpants on, his lower legs covered by a checkered wool shawl. He is wearing the brown cardigan sweater I bought him the year before over a flannel shirt he has buttoned all the way. This is the way he insists on wearing his shirts now, with the collar buttoned, which makes him look both boyish and frail, resigned to old age.

He looks a little puffy in the face today, and strands of his white hair spill uncombed over his brow. He is watching *Who Wants to Be a Millionaire?* with a somber, perplexed expression. When I call his name, his gaze lingers on the screen like he hasn't heard me before he drags it away and looks up with displeasure. He has a small sty growing on the lower lid of his left eye. He needs a shave.

"Baba, can I mute the TV for a second?"

"I'm watching," he says.

"I know. But you have a visitor." I had already told him about Pari Wahdati's visit the day before and again this morning. But I don't ask him if he remembers. It is something that I learned early on, to not put him on the spot, because it embarrasses him and makes him defensive, sometimes abusive.

I pluck the remote from the arm of the recliner and turn off the sound, bracing myself for a tantrum. The first time he threw one, I was convinced it was a charade, an act he was putting on. To my relief, Baba doesn't protest beyond a long sigh through the nose.

I motion to Pari, who is lingering in the hallway at the entrance to the living room. Slowly, she walks over to us, and I pull her up a chair close to Baba's recliner. She is a bundle of nervous excitement, I can tell. She sits erect, pale, leaning forward from the edge of the chair, knees pressed together, her hands clamped, and her smile so tight her lips are turning white. Her eyes are glued on Baba, as if she has only moments with him and is trying to memorize his face.

"Baba, this is the friend I told you about."

He eyes the gray-haired woman across from him. He has an unnerving way of looking at people these days, even when he is staring directly at them, that gives nothing away. He looks disengaged, closed off, like he meant to look elsewhere and his eyes happened upon them by accident.

Pari clears her throat. Even so, her voice shakes when she speaks. "Hello, Abdullah. My name is Pari. It's so wonderful to see you."

He nods slowly. I can practically *see* the uncertainty and confusion rippling across his face like waves of muscle spasm. His eyes shift from my face to Pari's. He opens his mouth in a strained half smile the way he does when he thinks a prank is being played on him.

"You have an accent," he finally says.

"She lives in France," I said. "And, Baba, you have to speak English. She doesn't understand Farsi."

Baba nods. "So you live in London?" he says to Pari.

"Baba!"

"What?" He turns sharply to me. Then he understands and gives an embarrassed little laugh before switching from Farsi. "Do you live in London?"

"Paris, actually," Pari says. "I live in a small apartment in Paris." She doesn't lift her eyes from him.

"I always planned to take my wife to Paris. Sultana—that was her name, God rest her soul. She was always saying, *Abdullah, take me to Paris. When will you take me to Paris?*"

Actually, Mother didn't much like to travel. She never saw why she would forgo the comfort and familiarity of her own home for the ordeal of flying and suitcase lugging. She had no sense of culinary adventure—her idea of exotic food was the *Orange Chicken* at the Chinese take-out place on Taylor Street. It is a bit of a marvel how Baba, at times, summons her with such uncanny precision—remembering, for instance, that she salted her food by bouncing the salt grains off the palm of her hand or her habit of interrupting people on the phone when she never did it in person—and how, other times, he can be so wildly inaccurate. I imagine Mother is fading for him, her face receding into shadows, her memory diminishing with each passing day, leaking like sand from a fist. She is becoming a ghostly outline, a hollow shell, that he feels compelled to fill with bogus details and fabricated character traits, as though false memories are better than none at all.

"Well, it is a lovely city," Pari says.

"Maybe I'll take her still. But she has the cancer at the moment. It's the female kind—what do you call it?—the . . ."

"Ovarian," I say.

Pari nods, her gaze flicking to me and back to Baba.

"What she wants most is to climb the Eiffel Tower. Have you seen it?" Baba says.

"The Eiffel Tower?" Pari Wahdati laughs. "Oh yes. Every day. I cannot avoid it, in fact."

"Have you climbed it? All the way to the top?"

"I have, yes. It is beautiful up there. But I am scared of high places, so it is not always comfortable for me. But at the top, on a good sunny day, you can see for more than sixty kilometers. Of course a lot of days in Paris it is not so good and not so sunny."

Baba grunts. Pari, encouraged, continues talking about the tower, how many years it took to build it, how it was never meant to stay in Paris past the 1889 World's Fair, but she can't read Baba's eyes like I can. His expression has flattened. She doesn't realize that she has lost him, that his thoughts have already shifted course like windblown leaves. Pari nudges closer on the seat. "Did you know, Abdullah," she says, "that they have to paint the tower every seven years?"

"What did you say your name was?" Baba says.

"Pari."

"That's my daughter's name."

"Yes, I know."

"You have the same name," Baba says. "The two of you, you have the same name. So there you have it." He coughs, absently picks at a small tear in the leather of the recliner's arm.

"Abdullah, can I ask you a question?"

Baba shrugs.

Pari looks up at me like she is asking for permission. I give her the go-ahead with a nod. She leans forward in the chair. "How did you decide to choose this name for your daughter?"

Baba shifts his gaze to the window, his fingernail still scraping the tear in the recliner's arm.

"Do you remember, Abdullah? Why this name?"

He shakes his head. With a fist, he yanks at his cardigan and clutches it shut at his throat. His lips barely move as he begins to hum under his breath, a rhythmic muttering he always resorts to when he is marauded by anxiety and at a loss for an answer, when everything has blurred to vagueness and he is bowled over by a gush of disconnected thoughts, waiting desperately for the murkiness to clear.

"Abdullah? What is that?" Pari says.

"Nothing," he mutters.

"No, that song you are singing—what is it?"

He turns to me, helpless. He doesn't know.

"It's like a nursery rhyme," I say. "Remember, Baba? You said you learned it when you were a boy. You said you learned it from your mother."

"Okay."

"Can you sing it for me?" Pari says urgently, a catch in her voice. "Please, Abdullah, will you sing it?"

He lowers his head and shakes it slowly.

"Go ahead, Baba," I say softly. I rest my hand on his bony shoulder. "It's okay."

Hesitantly, in a high, trembling voice and without looking up, Baba sings the same two lines several times:

I found a sad little fairy
Beneath the shade of a paper tree.

"He used to say there was a second verse," I say to Pari, "but that he'd forgotten it."

Pari Wahdati lets out a sudden laugh that sounds like a deep, guttural cry, and she covers her mouth. *"Ah, mon Dieu,"* she whispers. She lifts her hand. In Farsi, she sings:

I know a sad little fairy
Who was blown away by the wind one night.

Folds appear on Baba's forehead. For a transitory moment, I think I detect a tiny crack of light in his eyes. But then it winks out, and his face is placid once more. He shakes his head. "No. No, I don't think that's how it goes at all."

"Oh, Abdullah . . ." Pari says.

Smiling, her eyes teared over, Pari reaches for Baba's hands and takes them into her own. She kisses the back of each and presses his palms to her cheeks. Baba grins, moisture now pooling in his eyes as well. Pari looks up at me, blinking back happy tears, and I see she thinks she has broken through, that she has summoned her lost brother with this magic chant like a genie in a fairy tale. She thinks he sees her clearly now. She will understand momentarily that he is merely reacting, responding to her warm touch and show of affection. It's just animal instinct, nothing more. This I know with painful clarity.

A few months before Dr. Bashiri passed me the phone number to a hospice, Mother and I took a trip to the Santa Cruz Mountains and stayed in a hotel for the weekend. Mother didn't like long trips, but we did go off on short ones now and then, she and I, back before she was really sick. Baba would man the restaurant, and I would drive Mother and me to Bodega Bay, or Sausalito, or San

429

Francisco, where we would always stay in a hotel near Union Square. We would settle down in our room and order room service, watch on-demand movies. Later, we would go down to the Wharf—Mother was a sucker for all the tourist traps—and buy gelato, watch the sea lions bobbing up and down on the water over by the pier. We would drop coins into the open cases of the street guitarists and the back-packs of the mime artists, the spray-painted robot men. We always made a visit to the Museum of Modern Art, and, my arm coiled around hers, I would show her the works of Rivera, Kahlo, Matisse, Pollock. Or else we would go to a matinee, which Mother loved, and we would see two, three films, come out in the dark, our eyes bleary, ears ringing, fingers smelling of popcorn.

It was easier with Mother—always had been—less complicated, less treacherous. I didn't have to be on my guard so much. I didn't have to watch what I said all the time for fear of inflicting a wound. Being alone with her on those weekend getaways was like curling up into a soft cloud, and, for a couple of days, everything that had ever troubled me fell away, inconsequentially, a thousand miles below.

We were celebrating the end of yet another round of chemo—which also turned out to be her last. The hotel was a beautiful, secluded place. They had a spa, a fitness center, a game room with a big-screen TV, and a billiards table. Our room was a cabin with a wooden porch, from which we had a view of the swimming pool, the restaurant, and entire groves of redwood that soared straight up into the clouds. Some of the trees were so close, you could tell the subtle shades of color on a squirrel's fur as it dashed up the trunk. Our first morning there, Mother woke me up, said, *Quick, Pari, you have to see this.* There was a deer nibbling on shrubs outside the window.

I pushed her wheelchair around the gardens. *I'm such a spectacle,* Mother said. I parked her by the fountain and I would sit on a bench close to her, the sun warming our faces, and we would watch the hummingbirds darting between flowers until she fell asleep, and then I wheeled her back to our cabin.

On Sunday afternoon, we had tea and croissants on the balcony outside the restaurant, which was a big cathedral-ceilinged room with bookshelves, a dreamcatcher on one wall, and an honest-to-God stone hearth. On a lower deck, a man with the face of a dervish and a girl with limp blond hair were playing a lethargic game of Ping-Pong.

We have to do something about these eyebrows, Mother said. She was wearing a winter coat over a sweater and the maroon wool beanie hat she had knitted herself a year and a half earlier when, as she put it, all the festivities had begun.

I'll paint them back on for you, I said.

Make them dramatic, then.

Elizabeth Taylor in Cleopatra *dramatic?*

She grinned weakly. *Why not?* She took a shallow sip of tea. Grinning accentuated all the new lines in her face. *When I met Abdullah, I was selling clothes on the side of the street in Peshawar. He said I had beautiful eyebrows.*

The Ping-Pong pair ditched the paddles. They were leaning now against the wooden railing, sharing a cigarette, looking up at the sky, which was luminous and clear but for a few frayed clouds. The girl had long, bony arms.

I read in the paper there's an arts-and-crafts fair up in Capitola today, I said. *If you're up to it, maybe I'll drive us, we'll have a look. We could even have dinner there, if you like.*

Pari?

Yeah.

I want to tell you something.

Okay.

Abdullah has a brother in Pakistan, Mother said. *A half brother.*

I turned to her sharply.

His name is Iqbal. He has sons. He lives in a refugee camp near Peshawar.

I put down my cup, began to speak, but she cut me off.

I'm telling you now, aren't I? That's all that matters. Your father has his reasons. I'm sure you can figure them out, you give it some time. Important thing is, he has a half brother and he's been sending him money to help out.

She told me how, for years now, Baba had been sending this Iqbal—my half uncle, I thought with an inner lurch—a thousand dollars every three months, going down to Western Union, wiring the money to a bank in Peshawar.

Why are you telling me now? I asked.

Because I think you should know even if he doesn't. Also, you will have to take over the finances soon and then you would find out anyway.

I turned away, watched a cat, its tail erect, sidle up to the Ping-Pong couple. The girl reached to pet it and the cat tensed up at first. But then it curled up on the railing, let the girl run her hands over its ears, down its back. My mind was reeling. I had family outside of the U.S.

You'll be doing the books for a long time yet, Mother, I said. I did my best to disguise the wobble in my voice.

There was a dense pause. When she spoke again, it was in a lower tone, slower, like when I was little and we would go to the mosque for a funeral and she would hunker down next to me beforehand and patiently explain how I had to remove my shoes at the entrance, how I had to keep quiet during prayers and not fidget, not complain, and how I should use the bathroom now so I wouldn't have to later.

I won't, she said. *And don't you go thinking I will. The time has come, you have to be ready for it.*

I blew out a gush of air; a hardness lodged in my throat. Somewhere, a chain saw buzzed to life, the crescendo of its whine at violent odds with the stillness of the woods.

Your father is like a child. Terrified of being abandoned. He would lose his way without you, Pari, and never find his way back.

I made myself look at the trees, the wash of sunlight falling on the feathery leaves, the rough bark of the trunks. I slid my tongue between the incisors and bit down hard. My eyes watered, and the coppery taste of blood flooded my mouth.

A brother, I said.

Yes.

I have a lot of questions.

Ask me tonight. When I'm not as tired. I'll tell you everything I know.

I nodded. I gulped the rest of my tea, which had gone cold. At a nearby table, a middle-aged couple traded pages of the newspaper. The woman, red-haired and open-faced, was quietly watching us over the top of her broadsheet, her eyes switching from me to my gray-faced mother, her beanie hat, her hands mapped with bruises, her sunken eyes and skeletal grin. When I met her gaze, the woman smiled just a tad like there was a secret knowledge between us, and I knew that she had done this too.

So what do you think, Mother? The fair, are you up for it?

Mother's gaze lingered on me. Her eyes looked too big for her head and her head too big for her shoulders.

I could use a new hat, she said.

I tossed the napkin on the table and pushed back my chair, walked around to the other side. I released the brake on the wheelchair and pulled the chair away from the table.

Pari? Mother said.

Yes?

She rolled her head all the way back to look up at me. Sunlight pushed through the leaves of the trees and pinpricked her face. *Do you even know how strong God has made you?* she said. *How strong and good He has made you?*

There is no accounting for how the mind works. This moment, for instance. Of the thousands and thousands of moments my mother and I shared together through all the years, this is the one that shines the brightest, the one that vibrates with the loudest hum at the back of my mind: my mother looking up at me over her shoulder, her face upside down, all those dazzling points of light shimmering on her

434

skin, her asking did I know how good and strong God had made me.

After Baba falls asleep on the recliner, Pari gently zips up his cardigan and pulls up the shawl to cover his torso. She tucks a loose strand of hair behind his ear and stands over him, watching him sleep for a while. I like watching him sleep too because then you can't tell something is wrong. With his eyes closed, the blankness is lifted, and the lackluster, absent gaze too, and Baba looks more familiar. Asleep, he looks more alert and present, as if something of his old self has seeped back into him. I wonder if Pari can picture it, looking at his face resting on the pillow, how he used to be, how he used to laugh.

We move from the living room to the kitchen. I fetch a pot from the cabinet and fill it at the sink.

"I want to show you some of these," Pari says, a charge of excitement in her voice. She's sitting at the table, busily flipping through a photo album that she fished from her suitcase earlier.

"I'm afraid the coffee won't be up to Parisian standards," I say over my shoulder, pouring water from the pot into the coffeemaker.

"I promise you I am not a coffee snob." She has taken off the yellow scarf and put on reading glasses, through which she is peering at pictures.

When the coffeemaker begins to gurgle, I take my seat

at the kitchen table beside Pari. "*Ah oui. Voilà.* Here it is," she says. She flips the album around and pushes it over to me. She taps on a picture. "This is the place. Where your father and I were born. And our brother Iqbal too."

When she first called me from Paris, she mentioned Iqbal's name—as proof, perhaps, to convince me she was not lying about who she said she was. But I already knew she was telling the truth. I knew it the moment I picked up the receiver and she spoke my father's name into my ear and asked whether it was his residence she had reached. And I said, *Yes, who is this?* and she said, *I am his sister.* My heart kicked violently. I fumbled for a chair to drop into, everything around me suddenly pin-drop quiet. It was a shock, yes, the sort of third-act theatrical thing that rarely happens to people in real life. But on another plane—a plane that defies rationalizing, a more fragile plane, one whose essence would fracture and splinter if I even vocalized it—I wasn't surprised that she was calling. As if I had expected it, even, my whole life, that through some dizzying fit of design, or circumstance, or chance, or fate, or whatever name you want to slap on it, we would find each other, she and I.

I carried the receiver with me to the backyard then and sat on a chair by the vegetable patch, where I have kept growing the bell peppers and giant squash my mother had planted. The sun warmed my neck as I lit a cigarette with quivering hands.

I know who you are, I said. *I've known all my life.*

There was silence at the other end, but I had the

impression she was weeping soundlessly, that she had rolled her head away from the phone to do it.

We spoke for almost an hour. I told her I knew what had happened to her, how I used to make my father recount the story for me at bedtime. Pari said she had been unaware of her own history herself and would have probably died without knowing it if not for a letter left behind by her stepuncle, Nabi, before his own death in Kabul, in which he had detailed the events of her childhood among other things. The letter had been left in the care of someone named Markos Varvaris, a surgeon working in Kabul, who had then searched for and found Pari in France. Over the summer, Pari had flown to Kabul, met with Markos Varvaris, who had arranged for her to visit Shadbagh.

Near the end of the conversation, I sensed her gathering herself before she finally said, *Well, I think I am ready. Can I speak with him now?*

That was when I had to tell her.

I slide the photo album closer now and inspect the picture that Pari is pointing to. I see a mansion nestled behind high shiny-white walls topped with barbed wire. Or, rather, someone's tragically misguided idea of a mansion, three stories high, pink, green, yellow, white, with parapets and turrets and pointed eaves and mosaics and mirrored skyscraper glass. A monument to kitsch gone woefully awry.

"My God!" I breathe.

"C'est affreux, non?" Pari says. "It is horrible. The Afghans, they call these *Narco Palaces*. This one is the house of a well-known criminal of war."

"So this is all that's left of Shadbagh?"

"Of the old village, yes. This, and many acres of fruit trees of—what do you call it?—*des vergers.*"

"Orchards."

"Yes." She runs her fingers over the photo of the mansion. "I wish I know where our old house was exactly, I mean in relation to this Narco Palace. I would be happy to know the precise spot."

She tells me about the new Shadbagh—an actual town, with schools, a clinic, a shopping district, even a small hotel—which has been built about two miles away from the site of the old village. The town was where she and her translator had looked for her half brother. I had learned all of this over the course of that first, long phone conversation with Pari, how no one in town seemed to know Iqbal until Pari had run into an old man who did, an old childhood friend of Iqbal's, who had spotted him and his family staying on a barren field near the old windmill. Iqbal had told this old friend that when he was in Pakistan, he had been receiving money from his older brother who lived in northern California. *I asked,* Pari said on the phone, *I asked, Did Iqbal tell you the name of this brother? and the old man said, Yes, Abdullah. And then,* alors, *after that the rest was not so difficult. Finding you and your father, I mean.*

I asked Iqbal's friend where Iqbal was now, Pari said. *I asked what happened to him, and the old man said he did not know. But he seemed very nervous, and he did not look at me when he said this. And I think, Pari, I worry that something bad happened to Iqbal.*

She flips through more pages now and shows me photographs of her children—Alain, Isabelle, and Thierry—and snapshots of her grandchildren—at birthday parties, posing in swimming trunks at the edge of a pool. Her apartment in Paris, the pastel blue walls and white blinds pulled down to the sills, the shelves of books. Her cluttered office at the university, where she had taught mathematics before the rheumatoid had forced her into retirement.

I keep turning the pages of the album as she provides captions to the snapshots—her old friend Collette, Isabelle's husband Albert, Pari's own husband Eric, who had been a playwright and had died of a heart attack back in 1997. I pause at a photo of the two of them, impossibly young, sitting side by side on orange-colored cushions in some kind of restaurant, her in a white blouse, him in a T-shirt, his hair, long and limp, tied in a ponytail.

"That was the night that we met," Pari says. "It was a setup."

"He had a kind face."

Pari nods. "Yes. When we get married, I thought, Oh, we will have a long time together. I thought to myself, Thirty years at least, maybe forty. Fifty, if we are lucky. Why not?" She stares at the picture, lost for a moment, then smiles lightly. "But time, it is like charm. You never have as much as you think." She pushes the album away and sips her coffee. "And you? You never get married?"

I shrug and flip another page. "There was one close call."

"I am sorry, 'close call'?"

"It means I almost did. But we never made it to the ring stage."

This is not true. It was painful and messy. Even now, the memory of it is like a soft ache behind my breastbone.

She ducks her head. "I am sorry. I am very rude."

"No. It's fine. He found someone both more beautiful and less . . . encumbered, I guess. Speaking of beautiful, who is this?"

I point to a striking-looking woman with long dark hair and big eyes. In the picture, she is holding a cigarette like she is bored—elbow tucked into her side, head tilted up insouciantly—but her gaze is penetrating, defiant.

"This is Maman. My mother, Nila Wahdati. Or, I thought she was my mother. You understand."

"She's gorgeous," I say.

"She was. She committed suicide. Nineteen seventy-four."

"I'm sorry."

"*Non, non*. It's all right." She brushes the picture absently with the side of her thumb. "Maman was elegant and talented. She read books and had many strong opinions and always she was telling them to people. But she had also very deep sadness. All my life, she gave to me a shovel and said, *Fill these holes inside of me, Pari*."

I nod. I think I understand something of that.

"But I could not. And later, I did not want to. I did care-less things. Reckless things." She sits back in the chair, her shoulders slumping, puts her thin white hands in her lap. She considers for a minute before saying, "*J'aurais dû être plus gentille*—I should have been more kind. That is something a person will never regret. You will never say to yourself when you are old, *Ah, I wish I was not good to that person*. You will never think that." For a moment, her face looks stricken. She is like a helpless schoolgirl. "It would not have been so difficult," she says tiredly. "I should have been more kind. I should have been more like you."

She lets out a heavy breath and folds the photo album shut. After a pause, she says brightly, "*Ah, bon.* Now I wish to ask something of you."

"Of course."

"Will you show me some of your paintings?"

We smile at each other.

Pari stays a month with Baba and me. In the mornings, we take breakfast together in the kitchen. Black coffee and toast for Pari, yogurt for me, and fried eggs with bread for Baba, something he has found a taste for in the last year. I worried it was going to raise his cholesterol, eating all those eggs, and I asked Dr. Bashiri during one of Baba's appointments. Dr. Bashiri gave me one of his tight-lipped smiles and said, *Oh, I wouldn't worry about it.* And that reassured me—at least until a bit later when I was helping Baba buckle his seat belt and it occurred to me that maybe what Dr. Bashiri had really meant was, *We're past all that now.*

After breakfast, I retreat into my office—otherwise known as my bedroom—and Pari keeps Baba company while I work. At her request, I have written down for her the schedule of the TV shows he likes to watch, what time to give him his midmorning pills, which snacks he likes and when he's apt to ask for them. It was her idea I write it all down.

You could just pop in and ask, I said.

I don't want to disturb you, she said. *And I want to know. I want to know him.*

I don't tell her that she will never know him the way she longs to. Still, I share with her a few tricks of the trade. For instance, how if Baba starts to get agitated I can usually, though not always, calm him down—for reasons that baffle me still—by quickly handing him a free home-shopping catalog or a furniture-sale flyer. I keep a steady supply of both.

If you want him to nap, flip on the Weather Channel or anything to do with golf. And never let him watch cooking shows.

Why not?

They agitate him for some reason.

After lunch, the three of us go out for a stroll. We keep it short for both their sakes—what with Baba tiring quickly and Pari's arthritis. Baba has a wariness in his eyes, tottering anxiously along the sidewalk between Pari and me, wearing an old newsboy cap, his cardigan sweater, and wool-lined moccasins. There is a middle school around the block with an ill-manicured soccer field and, across that, a small playground where I often take Baba. We always find a young mother or two, strollers parked near them, a toddler stumbling around in the sandbox, now and then a teenage couple cutting school, swinging lazily and smoking. They rarely look at Baba—the teenagers—and then only with cold indifference, or even subtle disdain, as if my father should have known better than to allow old age and decay to happen to him.

One day, I pause during dictation and go to the kitchen to refresh my coffee and I find the two of them watching a movie together. Baba on the recliner, his moccasins sticking out from under the shawl, his head bent forward, mouth gaping slightly, eyebrows drawn together in either concentration or confusion. And Pari sitting beside him, hands folded in her lap, feet crossed at the ankles.

"Who's this one?" Baba says.

"That is Latika."

"Who?"

"Latika, the little girl from the slums. The one who could not jump on the train."

"She doesn't look little."

"Yes, but a lot of years have passed," Pari says. "She is older now, you see."

One day the week before, at the playground, we were sitting on a park bench, the three of us, and Pari said, *Abdullah, do you remember that when you were a boy you had a little sister?*

She'd barely finished her sentence when Baba began to weep. Pari pressed his head into her chest, saying, *I am sorry, I am so sorry*, over and over in a panicky way, wiping his cheeks with her hands, but Baba kept seizing with sobs, so violently he started to choke.

"And do you know who this is, Abdullah?"

Baba grunts.

"He is Jamal. The boy from the game show."

"He is not," Baba says roughly.

"You don't think?"

"He's serving tea!"

"Yes, but that was—what do you call it?—it was from the past. From before. It was a . . ."

Flashback, I mouth into my coffee cup.

"The game show is now, Abdullah. And when he was serving tea, that was before."

Baba blinks vacantly. On the screen, Jamal and Salim are sitting atop a Mumbai high-rise, their feet dangling over the side.

Pari watches him as though waiting for a moment when something will open in his eyes. "Let me ask you something, Abdullah," she says. "If one day you win a million dollars, what would you do?"

Baba grimaces, shifting his weight, then stretches out farther in the recliner.

"I know what *I* would do," Pari says.

Baba looks at her blankly.

"If I win a million dollars, I buy a house on this street. That way, we can be neighbors, you and me, and every day I come here and we watch TV together."

Baba grins.

But it's only minutes later, when I am back in my room wearing earphones and typing, that I hear a loud shattering sound and Baba screaming something in Farsi. I rip the earphones off and rush to the kitchen. I see Pari backed up against the wall where the microwave is, hands bunched protectively under her chin, and Baba, wild-eyed, jabbing her in the shoulder with his cane. Broken shards of a drinking glass glitter at their feet.

"Get her out of here!" Baba cries when he sees me. "I want this woman out of my house!"

"Baba!"

Pari's cheeks have gone pale. Tears spring from her eyes.

"Put down the cane, Baba, for God's sake! And don't take a step. You'll cut your feet."

I wrestle the cane from his hand but not before he gives me a good fight for it.

"I want this woman gone! She's a thief!"

"What is he saying?" Pari says miserably.

"She stole my pills!"

"Those are hers, Baba," I say. I put a hand on his shoulder and guide him out of the kitchen. He shivers under my palm. As we pass by Pari, he almost lunges at her again, and I have to restrain him. "All right, that's enough of that, Baba. And those are her pills, not yours. She takes them for her hands." I grab a shopping catalog from the coffee table on the way to the recliner.

"I don't trust that woman," Baba says, flopping into the recliner. "You don't know. But I know. I know a thief when I see one!" He pants as he grabs the catalog from my hand and starts violently flipping the pages. Then he slams it in his lap and looks up at me, his eyebrows shot high. "And a damn liar too. You know what she said to me, this woman? You know what she said? That she was my sister! *My sister!* Wait 'til Sultana hears about this one."

"All right, Baba. We'll tell her together."

"Crazy woman."

"We'll tell Mother, and then us three will laugh the crazy woman right out the door. Now, you go on and relax, Baba. Everything is all right. There."

I flip on the Weather Channel and sit beside him, stroking his shoulder, until his shaking ceases and his breathing slows. Less than five minutes pass before he dozes off.

Back in the kitchen, Pari sits slumped on the floor, back against the dishwasher. She looks shaken. She dabs at her eyes with a paper napkin.

"I am very sorry," she says. "That was not prudent of me."

"It's all right," I say, reaching under the sink for the dustpan and brush. I find little pink-and-orange pills scattered on the floor among the broken glass. I pick them up one by one and sweep the glass off the linoleum.

"*Je suis une imbécile.* I wanted to tell him so much. I thought maybe if I tell him the truth . . . I don't know what I was thinking."

I empty the broken glass into the trash bin. I kneel down, pull back the collar of Pari's shirt, and check her shoulder where Baba had jabbed her. "That's going to bruise. And I speak with authority on the matter." I sit on the floor beside her.

She opens her palm, and I pour the pills into it. "He is like this often?"

"He has his spit-and-vinegar days."

"Maybe you think about finding professional help, no?"

I sigh, nodding. I have thought a lot lately of the inevitable morning when I will wake up to an empty house while

Baba lies curled up on an unfamiliar bed, eyeing a breakfast tray brought to him by a stranger. Baba slumped behind a table in some activity room, nodding off.

"I know," I say, "but not yet. I want to take care of him as long as I can."

Pari smiles and blows her nose. "I understand that."

I am not sure she does. I don't tell her the other reason. I can barely admit it to myself. Namely, how afraid I am to be free despite my frequent desire for it. Afraid of what will happen to me, what I will do with myself, when Baba is gone. All my life, I have lived like an aquarium fish in the safety of a glass tank, behind a barrier as impenetrable as it has been transparent. I have been free to observe the glimmering world on the other side, to picture myself in it, if I like. But I have always been contained, hemmed in, by the hard, unyielding confines of the existence that Baba has constructed for me, at first knowingly, when I was young, and now guilelessly, now that he is fading day by day. I think I have grown accustomed to the glass and am terrified that when it breaks, when I am alone, I will spill out into the wide open unknown and flop around, helpless, lost, gasping for breath.

The truth I rarely admit to is, I have always needed the weight of Baba on my back.

Why else had I so readily surrendered my dreams of art school, hardly mounting a resistance when Baba asked me not to go to Baltimore? Why else had I left Neal, the man I was engaged to a few years ago? He owned a small solar-panel-installation company. He had a square-shaped, creased face I liked the moment I met him at Abe's Kabob House, when I asked for his order and he looked up from the menu and grinned. He was patient and friendly and even-tempered. It isn't true what I told Pari about him. Neal didn't leave me for someone more beautiful. I sabotaged things with him. Even when he promised to convert to Islam, to take Farsi classes, I found other faults, other excuses. I panicked, in the end, and ran back to all the familiar nooks and crannies, and crevasses, of my life at home.

Next to me, Pari begins to get up. I watch her flatten the wrinkles of her dress, and I am struck anew by what a miracle it is that she is here, standing inches from me.

"I want to show you something," I say.

I get up and go to my room. One of the quirks of never leaving home is that no one cleans out your old room and sells your toys at a garage sale, no one gives away the clothes you have outgrown. I know that for a woman who is nearly thirty, I have too many relics of my childhood sitting around, most of them stuffed in a large chest at the foot of my bed whose lid I now lift. Inside are old dolls, the pink pony that came with a mane I could brush, the picture books, all the Happy Birthday and Valentine's cards I had made my parents in elementary school with kidney beans and glitter and little sparkling stars. The last time we spoke, Neal and I, when I broke things off, he said, *I can't wait for you, Pari. I won't wait around for you to grow up.*

I shut the lid and go back to the living room, where Pari has settled into the couch across from Baba. I take a seat next to her.

"Here," I say, handing her the stack of postcards.

She reaches for her reading glasses sitting on the side table and yanks off the rubber band holding the postcards together. Looking at the first one, she frowns. It is a picture of Las Vegas, of Caesars Palace at night, all glitter and lights. She flips it over and reads the note aloud.

July 21, 1992

Dear Pari,

You wouldn't believe how hot this place gets. Today Baba got a blister when he put his palm down on the hood of our rental car! Mother had to put toothpaste on it. In Caesars Palace, they have Roman soldiers with swords and helmets and red capes. Baba kept trying to get Mother to take a picture with them but she wouldn't. But I did! I'll show you when I get home. That's it for now. I miss you. Wish you were here.

Pari

P.S. I'm having the most awesome ice cream sundae as I write this.

She flips to the next postcard. Hearst Castle. She reads the note under her breath now. *Had his own zoo! How cool is that? Kangaroos, zebras, antelopes, Bactrian camels—they're the ones with two humps!* One of Disneyland, Mickey in the wizard's hat, waving a wand. *Mother screamed when the hanged guy fell from the ceiling! You should have heard her!* La Jolla Cove.

Big Sur. 17 Mile Drive. Muir Woods. Lake Tahoe. *Miss you. You would have loved it for sure. Wish you were here.*

I wish you were here.

I wish you were here.

Pari takes off her glasses. "You wrote postcards to yourself?"

I shake my head. "To you." I laugh. "This is embarrassing."

Pari puts the postcards down on the coffee table and nudges closer to me. "Tell me."

I look down at my hands and rotate my watch around on my wrist. "I used to pretend we were twin sisters, you and I. No one could see you but me. I told you everything. All my secrets. You were real to me, always so near. I felt less alone because of you. Like we were *Doppelgänger*s. Do you know that word?"

A smile comes to her eyes. "Yes."

I used to picture us as two leaves, blowing miles apart in the wind yet bound by the deep tangled roots of the tree from which we had both fallen.

"For me, it was the contrary," Pari says. "You say you felt a presence, but I sensed only an absence. A vague pain without a source. I was like the patient who cannot explain to the doctor where it hurts, only that it does." She puts her hand on mine, and neither of us says anything for a minute.

From the recliner, Baba groans and shifts.

"I'm really sorry," I say.

"Why are you sorry?"

"That you found each other too late."

"But we *have* found each other, no?" she says, her voice

cracking with emotion. "And this is who he is now. It's all right. I feel happy. I have found a part of myself that was lost." She squeezes my hand. "And I found you, Pari."

Her words tug at my childhood longings. I remember how when I felt lonely, I would whisper her name—*our* name—and hold my breath, waiting for an echo, certain that it would come someday. Hearing her speak my name now, in this living room, it is as though all the years that divided us are rapidly folding over one another again and again, time accordioning itself down to nothing but the width of a photograph, a postcard, ferrying the most shining relic of my childhood to sit beside me, to hold my hand, and say my name. Our name. I feel a tilting, something clicking into place. Something ripped apart long ago being sealed again. And I feel a soft lurch in my chest, the muffled thump of another heart kick-starting anew next to my own.

In the recliner, Baba props himself up on his elbows. He rubs his eyes, looks over to us. "What are you girls plotting?"

He grins.

Another nursery rhyme. This one about the bridge in Avignon.

Pari hums the tune for me, then recites the lyrics:

Sur le pont d'Avignon
L'on y danse, l'on y danse

451

Sur le pont d'Avignon
L'on y danse tous en rond.

"Maman taught it to me when I was little," she says, tightening the knot of her scarf against a sweeping gust of cold wind. The day is chilly but the sky blue and the sun strong. It strikes the gray-metal-colored Rhône broadside and breaks on its surface into little shards of brightness. "Every French child knows this song."

We are sitting on a wooden park bench facing the water. As she translates the words, I marvel at the city across the river. Having recently discovered my own history, I am awestruck to find myself in a place so chockful of it, all of it documented, preserved. It's miraculous. Everything about this city is. I feel wonder at the clarity of the air, at the wind swooping down on the river, making the water slap against the stony banks, at how full and rich the light is and how it seems to shine from every direction. From the park bench, I can see the old ramparts ringing the ancient town center and its tangle of narrow, crooked streets; the west tower of the Avignon Cathedral, the gilded statue of the Virgin Mary gleaming atop it.

Pari tells me the history of the bridge—the young shepherd who, in the twelfth century, claimed that angels told him to build a bridge across the river and who demonstrated the validity of his claim by lifting up a massive rock and hurling it in the water. She tells me about the boatmen on the Rhône who climbed the bridge to honor their patron, Saint Nicholas. And about all the floods over the centuries that ate away at the bridge's arches and caused them to collapse. She says these words with the same rapid, nervous energy she had earlier in the day when she led me through the Gothic Palais des Papes. Lifting the audio-guide head-phones to point to a fresco, tapping my elbow to draw my attention to an interesting carving, stained glass, the inter-secting ribs overhead.

Outside the Papal Palace, she spoke nearly without pause, the names of all the saints and popes and cardinals spilling from her as we strolled through the cathedral square amid the flocks of doves, the tourists, the African merchants in bright tunics selling bracelets and imitation watches, the young, bespectacled musician, sitting on an apple crate, playing "Bohemian Rhapsody" on his acoustic guitar. I don't recall this loquaciousness from her visit in the U.S., and it feels to me like a delaying tactic, like we are circling around the thing she really wants to do—what we will do—and all these words are like a bridge.

"But you will see a real bridge soon," she says. "When everybody arrives. We will go together to the Pont du Gard. Do you know it? No? *Oh là là. C'est vraiment merveilleux.* The Romans built it in the first century for transporting water from Eure to Nîmes. Fifty kilometers! It is a masterpiece of engineering, Pari."

I have been in France for four days, in Avignon for two. Pari and I took the TGV here from an overcast, chilly Paris, stepped off it to clear skies, a warm wind, and a chorus of cicadas chirping from every tree. At the station, a mad rush to haul my luggage out ensued, and I nearly didn't make it, hopping off the train just as the doors whooshed shut behind me. I make a mental note now to tell Baba how three seconds more and I would have ended up in Marseille.

How is he? Pari asked in Paris during the taxi ride from Charles de Gaulle to her apartment.

Further along the path, I said.

Baba lives in a nursing home now. When I first went to scout the facility, when the director, Penny—a tall, frail woman with curly strawberry hair—showed me around, I thought, This isn't so bad.

And then I said it. *This isn't so bad.*

The place was clean, with windows that looked out on a garden, where, Penny said, they held a tea party every Wednesday at four-thirty. The lobby smelled faintly of cinnamon and pine. The staff, most of whom I have now come to know by first name, seemed courteous, patient, competent. I had pictured old women, with ruined faces and whiskers on their chins, dribbling, chattering to themselves, glued to television screens. But most of the residents I saw were not that old. A lot of them were not even in wheelchairs.

I guess I expected worse, I said.

Did you? Penny said, emitting a pleasant, professional laugh.

That was offensive. I'm sorry.

Not at all. We're fully conscious of the image most people have of places like this. Of course, she added over her shoulder with a sober note of caution, *this is the facility's assisted-living area. Judging by what you've told me of your father, I'm not sure he would function well here. I suspect the Memory Care Unit would be more suitable for him. Here we are.*

She used a card key to let us in. The locked unit didn't smell like cinnamon or pine. My insides shriveled up, and my first instinct was to turn around and walk back out. Penny put her hand around my arm and squeezed. She looked at me with great tenderness. I fought through the rest of the tour, bowled over by a massive wave of guilt.

The morning before I left for Europe, I went to see Baba. I passed through the lobby in the assisted-living area and waved at Carmen, who is from Guatemala and answers the phones. I walked past the community hall, where a roomful of seniors were listening to a string quartet of high school students in formal attire; past the multipurpose room with its computers and bookshelves and domino sets, past the bulletin board and its array of tips and announcements—*Did you know that soy can reduce your bad cholesterol? Don't forget Puzzles and Reflection Hour this Tuesday at 11 a.m.!*

I let myself into the locked unit. They don't have tea parties on this side of the door, no bingo. No one here starts their morning with tai chi. I went to Baba's room, but he wasn't there. His bed had been made, his TV was dark, and there was a half-full glass of water on the bedside table. I was a little relieved. I hate finding Baba in the hospital bed, lying on his side, hand tucked under the pillow, his recessed eyes looking out at me blankly.

I found Baba in the rec room, sunk into a wheelchair, by the window that opens into the garden. He was wearing flannel pajamas and his newsboy cap. His lap was covered with what Penny called a *fidget apron*. It has strings he can braid and buttons he likes to open and close. Penny says it keeps his fingers nimble.

I kissed his cheek and pulled up a seat. Someone had given him a shave, and wetted and combed his hair too. His face smelled like soap.

So tomorrow is the big day, I said. *I'm flying out to visit Pari in France. You remember I told you I would?*

Baba blinked. Even before the stroke, he had already started withdrawing, falling into long, silent lapses, looking disconsolate. Since the stroke, his face has become a mask, his mouth frozen perpetually in a lopsided, polite little smile that never climbs to his eyes. He hasn't said a word since the stroke. Sometimes, his lips part, and he makes a husky, exhaling sound—*Aaaah!*—with enough of an upturn at the tail end to make it sound like surprise, or like what I said has triggered a minor epiphany in him.

We're meeting up in Paris, and then we'll take the train down to Avignon. That's a town near the South of France. It's where the popes lived in the fourteenth century. So we'll do some sightseeing there. But the great part is, Pari has told all her children about my visit and they're going to join us.

Baba smiled on, the way he did when Hector came by the week before to see him, the way he did when I showed him my application to the College of Arts and Humanities at San Francisco State.

Your niece, Isabelle, and her husband, Albert, have a vaca-tion home in Provence, near a town called Les Baux. I looked it up online, Baba. It's an amazing-looking town. It's built on these limestone peaks up in the Alpilles Mountains. You can visit the ruins of an old medieval castle up there and look out on the plains and the orchards. I'll take lots of pictures and show you when I get back.

Nearby, an old woman in a bathrobe complacently slid around the pieces of a jigsaw puzzle. At the next table, another woman with fluffy white hair was trying to arrange forks and spoons and butter knives in a silverware drawer. On the big-screen TV over in the corner, Ricky and Lucy were arguing, their wrists locked together by a pair of handcuffs.

Baba said, *Aaaah!*

Alain, that's your nephew, and his wife, Ana, are coming over from Spain with all five of their kids. I don't know all their names, but I'm sure I'll learn them. And then—and this is the part that makes Pari really happy—your other nephew—her youngest, Thierry—is coming too. She hasn't seen him in years. They haven't spoken. But he's taking his R & R from his job in Africa and he's flying over. So it's going to be a big family reunion.

I kissed his cheek again later when I rose to leave. I lingered with my face against his, remembering how he used to pick me up from kindergarten and drive us to Denny's to pick up Mother from work. We would sit at a booth, waiting for Mother to sign out, and I would eat the scoop of ice cream the manager always gave me and I would show Baba the drawings I had made that day. How patiently he gazed at each of them, glowering in careful study, nodding.

Baba smiled his smile.

Ah. I almost forgot.

I stooped down and performed our customary farewell ritual, running my fingertips from his cheeks up to his creased forehead and his temples, over his gray, thinning hair and the scabs of his roughened scalp to behind the ears, plucking along the way all the bad dreams from his head. I opened the invisible sack for him, dropped the nightmares into it, and pulled the drawstrings tight.

There.

Baba made a guttural sound.

Happy dreams, Baba. I'll see you in two weeks. It occurred to me that we had never been apart for this long before.

As I was walking away, I had the distinct feeling that Baba was watching me. But when I turned to see, his head was down and he was toying with a button on his fidget apron.

Pari is talking about Isabelle and Albert's house now. She has shown me pictures of it. It is a beautiful, restored Provençal farmhouse made of stone, set up on the Luberon hills, fruit trees and an arbor at the front door outside, terracotta tiles and exposed beams inside.

"You could not see in the picture that I showed to you, but it has fantastic view of the Vaucluse Mountains."

"Are we all going to fit? It's a lot of people for a farmhouse."

"*Plus on est de fous, plus on rit,*" she says. "What is the English? The more the happier?"

"Merrier."

"*Ah voilà. C'est ça.*"

"How about the children? Where are they—"

"Pari?"

I look over to her. "Yes?"

She empties her chest of a long breath. "You can give it to me now."

I nod. I reach into the handbag sitting between my feet.

I suppose I should have found it months ago when I moved Baba to the nursing home. But when I was packing for Baba, I reached in the hallway closet for the top suitcase, from the stack of three, and was able to fit all of Baba's clothes in it. Then I finally worked up the nerve to clear my parents' bedroom. I ripped off the old wallpaper, repainted the walls. I moved out their queen-size bed, my mother's dresser with the oval vanity mirror, cleared the closets of my father's suits, my mother's blouses and dresses sheathed in plastic. I made a pile in the garage for a trip or two to Goodwill. I moved my desk to their bedroom, which I use now as my office and as my study when classes begin in the fall. I emptied the chest at the foot of my bed too. In a trash bag, I tossed all my old toys, my childhood dresses, all the sandals and tennis shoes I had outworn. I couldn't bear to look any longer at the Happy Birthday and Father's Day and Mother's Day cards I had made my parents. I couldn't sleep at night knowing they were there at my feet. It was too painful.

It was when I was clearing the hallway closet, when I pulled out the two remaining suitcases to store them in the garage, that I felt a thump inside one of them. I unzipped the suitcase and found a package inside wrapped with thick brown paper. An envelope had been taped to the package.

On it were written, in English, the words *For my sister, Pari.* Immediately, I recognized Baba's handwriting from my days working at Abe's Kabob House when I picked up the food orders he would jot down at the cash register.

I hand the package now to Pari, unopened.

She looks down at it in her lap, running her hands over the words scribbled on the envelope. From across the river, church bells begin to ring. On a rock jutting from the edge of the water, a bird tears at the entrails of a dead fish.

Pari rummages in her purse, digging through its contents. *"J'ai oublié mes lunettes,"* she says. "I forgot my reading glasses."

"Do you want me to read it for you?"

She tries to tear the envelope from the package, but today is not a good day for her hands, and, after some struggle, she ends up handing me the package. I free the envelope and open it. I unfold the note tucked inside.

"He wrote it in Farsi."

"But you can read it, no?" Pari says, her eyebrows knotted with worry. "You can translate."

"Yes," I say, feeling a tiny smile inside, grateful—if belatedly—for all the Tuesday afternoons Baba had driven me to Campbell for Farsi classes. I think of him now, ragged and lost, staggering across a desert, the path behind him littered with all the shiny little pieces that life has ripped from him.

I hold the note tightly against the blustering wind. I read for Pari the three scribbled sentences.

They tell me I must wade into waters, where I will soon drown.

Before I march in, I leave this on the shore for you. I pray you find it, sister, so you will know what was in my heart as I went under.

There is a date too. August 2007. "August of 2007," I say. "That's when he was first diagnosed." Three years before I had even heard from Pari.

Pari nods, wiping her eyes with the heel of her hand. A young couple rolls by on a tandem bicycle, the girl in the lead—blond, pink-faced, and slim—the boy behind, with dreadlocks and coffee-colored skin. On the grass a few feet away, a teenage girl in a short black leather skirt sits, talking into a cell phone, holding the leash to a tiny charcoal-colored terrier.

Pari hands me the package. I tear it open for her. Inside is an old tin tea box, on its lid a faded picture of a bearded Indian man wearing a long red tunic. He is holding up a steaming cup of tea like an offering. The steam from the teacup has all but faded and the red of the tunic has mostly bleached to pink. I undo the latch and lift the lid. I find the interior stuffed with feathers of all colors, all shapes. Short, dense green feathers; long black-stemmed ones the color of ginger; a peach-colored feather, possibly from a mallard, with a light purple cast; brown feathers with dark blotches along the inner vanes; a green peacock feather with a large eye at the tip of it.

I turn to Pari. "Do you know what this means?"

Chin quivering, Pari slowly shakes her head. She takes the box from me and peers inside it. "No," she says. "Only that when we lost each other, Abdullah and I, it hurt him much more than me. I was the lucky one because I was protected by my youth. *Je pouvais oublier.* I still had the luxury of forgetting. He did not." She lifts a feather, brushes it against her wrist, eyeing it as though hoping it might spring to life and take flight. "I don't know what this feather means, the story of it, but I know it means he was thinking of me. For all these years. He remembered me."

I put an arm around her shoulder as she weeps quietly. I watch the sun-washed trees, the river flowing past us and beneath the bridge—the Pont Saint-Bénezet—the bridge the children's song is about. It's a half bridge, really, as only four of its original arches remain. It ends midway across the river. Like it reached, tried to reunite with, the other side and fell short.

That night at the hotel, I lie awake in bed and watch the clouds nudging against the big swollen moon hanging in our window. Down below, heels click on the cobblestones. Laughter and chatter. Mopeds rattling past. From the restaurant across the street, the clinking of glasses on trays. The tinkling of a piano meanders up through the window and to my ears.

I turn over and watch Pari sleeping soundlessly beside me. Her face is pale in the light. I see Baba in her face—youthful, hopeful Baba, happy, how he used to be—and I know I will always find him whenever I look at Pari. She is my flesh and blood. And soon I will meet her children, and her children's children, and my blood courses through them too. I am not alone. A sudden happiness catches me unawares. I feel it trickling into me, and my eyes go liquid with gratitude and hope.

As I watch Pari sleep, I think of the bedtime game Baba and I used to play. The purging of bad dreams, the gift of happy ones. I remember the dream I used to give him. Careful not to wake Pari, I reach across now and gently rest my palm on her brow. I close my own eyes.

It is a sunlit afternoon. They are children once more, brother and sister, young and clear-eyed and sturdy. They are lying in a patch of tall grass in the shade of an apple tree ablaze with flowers. The grass is warm against their backs and the sun on their faces, flickering through the riot of blossoms above. They rest sleepily, contentedly, side by side, his head resting on the ridge of a thick root, hers cushioned by the coat he has folded for her. Through half-lidded eyes, she watches a blackbird perched on a branch. Streams of cool air blow through the leaves and downward.

She turns her face to look at him, her big brother, her ally in all things, but his face is too close and she can't see the whole of it. Only the dip of his brow, the rise of his nose, the curve of his eyelashes. But she doesn't mind. She is happy enough to be near him, with him—her brother—and as a nap slowly steals her away, she feels herself engulfed in a wave of absolute calm. She shuts her eyes. Drifts off, untroubled, everything clear, and radiant, and all at once.

Acknowledgments

A couple of logistical matters before I give thanks. The village of Shadbagh is fictional, though it is possible that one by that name exists somewhere in Afghanistan. If so, I have never been to it. Abdullah and Pari's nursery rhyme, specifically the reference to a "sad little fairy," was inspired by a poem by the late, great Persian poet Forough Farrokhzad. Finally, the title of this book was inspired in part by William Blake's lovely poem, "Nurse's Song."

I would like to extend my thanks to Bob Barnett and Deneen Howell for being such wonderful guides and advocates for this book. Thank you Helen Heller, David Grossman, Jody Hotchkiss. Thanks to Chandler Crawford, for her enthusiasm, patience, and advice. Many thanks to a host of friends at Riverhead Books: Jynne Martin, Kate Stark, Sarah Stein, Leslie Schwartz, Craig D. Burke, Helen Yentus, and many more I have left unnamed but to whom I am deeply grateful for helping bring this book to readers.

I thank my wonderful copy editor, Tony Davis, who ventures way beyond the call of duty.

Very special gratitude goes out to my editor, the hugely talented Sarah McGrath, for her insight and vision, her gentle guidance, and for helping me shape this book in more ways than I can recall. I've never enjoyed the editing process more, Sarah.

Lastly, I thank Susan Petersen Kennedy and Geoffrey Kloske, for their trust and unwavering faith in me and my writing.

Thank you and *Tashakor* to all my friends and all the people in my family for always being in my corner, and for patiently, gamely, and kindly putting up with me. As ever, I thank my beautiful wife, Roya, not only for reading and editing many incarnations of this book but also for running our day-to-day life, without a whisper of protest, so I could write. Without you, Roya, this book would have died somewhere in the first paragraph of page one. I love you.